TRUTH . . . OR JUSTICE?

Burnside leaned forward until his face was in the light. There was a scar of recent origin on his cheek. "Is this your first trip to death row, Miss Hays?"

"I've seen an execution downtown at the Walls, when I was a prosecutor. But, yes, my first time to this unit."

"Most of us here," Burnside said, "have accepted the fact that we're going to die. We live with it. Some of the newer men have hope, but you learn that hope is a cancer eating away at your insides. A death penalty eliminates all carrots, Miss Hays. There's nothing anyone can dangle in front of me to induce me to do anything I don't want to do. You ask why it doesn't bother me to upset the warden. If I don't please him, what's he going to do? Kill me twice?"

Sharon hoisted up her briefcase and produced her notes. "I have a client who claims to know something about your wife's murder. If what my client says is true, then you're not guilty."

PUBLIC TRUST

Sarah Gregory

A SIGNET BOOK

SIGNET
Published by the Penguin Group
Penguin Books USA Inc., 375 Hudson Street,
New York, New York 10014, U.S.A.
Penguin Books Ltd, 27 Wrights Lane,
London W8 5TZ, England
Penguin Books Australia Ltd, Ringwood,
Victoria, Australia
Penguin Books Canada Ltd, 10 Alcorn Avenue,
Toronto, Ontario, Canada M4V 3B2
Penguin Books (N.Z.) Ltd, 182–190 Wairau Road,
Auckland 10, New Zealand

Penguin Books Ltd, Registered Offices:
Harmondsworth, Middlesex, England

First published by Signet, an imprint of Dutton Signet,
a division of Penguin Books USA Inc.

First Printing, March, 1997
10 9 8 7 6 5 4 3 2

 REGISTERED TRADEMARK—MARCA REGISTRADA

Printed in Canada

"This administration will bear in mind that the trust of the public is sacred, hard-earned, and never to be taken lightly."

———from the January 1973
     inaugural address of
     Richard Nixon

"You have all seen the public man. We intend to show you the private man."

———Assistant Los Angeles
     County District Attorney
     Christopher Darden,
     his opening statement
     in the murder trial
     of Orenthal James Simpson

1

Sharon Hays' client made his appearance around mid-morning on an August day. She thought immediately, Oh, God.

He plodded along in shackle-restricted baby steps, Dycus Wilt by name, his manner menacing, his chest broad, his forearms burly. His wrists were cuffed to a chain wrapped around his waist. His jailer/escort moved in a half crouch, ready to spring into action at the prisoner's first false move. Wilt's skin was the color of bittersweet chocolate. His hair was greased into pointed dreadlocks, just the style to make prosecutors drool and jurors shorten their deliberation time, and he wore a scraggly beard. He clanked to a halt beside the defense table, and surveyed the courtroom with dead-coal eyes.

Assistant District Attorney Milton Breyer leaned over and whispered to Sharon, "I think that's your boy, cutes," and then smirked in the direction of the prisoner.

Sharon permitted herself one angry blink, letting Breyer know that she didn't like him calling her "cutes," tucked her file under her arm, and walked over to the defense side. As she passed in front of the bench, Judge Arnold Shiver coughed into his hand. In the spectator section, papers rattled as lawyers put motions and briefs away. Seated on the front row, two *Dallas Morning News* reporters opened spiral notebooks and scribbled like mad.

Sharon approached her client and showed him her

best encouraging smile. The morning Metro page had displayed Wilt's mug shot over the headline "PAROLEE CHARGED IN RAPE-MURDER," but Sharon thought he resembled his photo more from a distance than he did close-up. She'd snatched the article away from her twelve-year-old at the breakfast table, trading Melanie the movie section, and then had devoured the murder story word for word. "Mr. Wilt?" she said. "I'm Sharon Hays, appointed by the court to represent you."

Wilt looked her over head to toe, stared incredulously at the uniformed guard, then glared at Sharon once more. "Don't want no lady attunney," Wilt said.

The guard stepped forward. "I told you, watch your mouth in court." He was a thickset sheriff's deputy in his twenties.

Wilt vigorously shook his head and raised his voice. "Ain't watchin' no mouth. I don't want no fuckin' lady attunney, an' I ain't havin' none. You told me my lawyuh name Russell Black."

In the spectator section, someone laughed. Sharon's ears were suddenly warm.

"Listen, meathead," the deputy said.

"No fuckin' lady lawyuh," Wilt said.

Sharon stood her ground. "Mr. Wilt?"

"I don't want no—"

"Can I ask you something?"

"—Lady lawyuh. Whazzat?"

"The court's appointed Russell Black to represent you, right?"

The deputy folded his arms and moved closer to Wilt, the prisoner now challenging Sharon, her forehead on a level with his nose. Wilt wore a light tan jumpsuit with COUNTY JAIL stenciled between his shoulder blades. Sharon's hair was dark, with slightly flippant bangs fluffed out over her forehead. She was dressed in a white cotton blouse and charcoal-gray summer-weight vest and skirt, with black medium-heeled pumps.

Wilt seemed deep in thought. "I don't want no woman representin' me. I wants a *may*-un." He sucked in air for emphasis.

Sharon shifted her file from one arm to the other. "Well, so you'll understand, I'm Russell Black's co-counsel. So me being your lawyer is just like him being your lawyer." Which wasn't quite true, but close enough. As Russ Black's associate, Sharon handled all court appointments so that Russ could devote his time to fee-paid matters. She didn't think Dycus Wilt gave a hoot about the conditions of her employment, so she fudged just a bit to get her point across.

"Ain't *just* like," Wilt said, " 'cause you a woman."

"All this is," Sharon said, "is an arraignment. They're going to read you the charges and tell you your rights. According to the file they've given me, you've done time before. So this shouldn't be anything new."

Wilt watched her, his dull gray eyes not quite seeming to focus.

"So all we've got to do," Sharon said, smiling, "is stand up before the judge for about fifteen minutes. And then if you want another lawyer, I'm sure the court will appoint you one. How does that sound?"

"Sound like shit," Wilt said. "Don't want no damn woman tellin' me nothin' about no law."

Sharon decided that she wasn't communicating.

Judge Shiver said angrily from the bench, "Young man, come up here." His bony finger was pointed at Wilt, his eyes owlish behind thick bifocals. "You, too, Miss Hays. And the prosecution." Arnold Shiver had heavy bags under his eyes and thick snow-white disheveled hair. S.M.U. Law School, Sharon thought, class of ought-something-or-other, been on the bench since the time of Christ.

Wilt hobbled up to face the judge with the deputy trailing close behind. Sharon stood alongside Wilt, and Milton Breyer came over from near the jury box. The judge said, "What's the problem here?"

Sharon turned her hand palm up and indicated her client. "Mr. Wilt isn't happy with the court's choice of lawyers, judge."

Shiver scowled at Wilt. "That true?"

Wilt folded cuffed hands and watched the floor. "Don't want no lady attunney."

"Let's cut this silliness short," Shiver said. "The court's appointed Miss Hays as your lawyer. She was a prosecutor for several years, and she's got experience. You're creatin' a disturbance in my courtroom."

"Do more'n that," Wilt said, "if'n I don't get no man for a lawyuh."

Shiver's complexion turned dark red. "You've *got* a lawyer, and if I hear one more word outta you, I'll have you gagged. You got that, bud? Now, let's get this hearin' on the road."

"It's an arraignment, judge," Milton Breyer offered. He stood at attention with his fingers touching his navy blue coattails.

"Arraignment or whatever," Shiver said. "You, Mr. Wilt, and your lawyer Miss Hays are gonna stand here, and she's gonna protect your rights. You got that?"

Sharon thought, Now wait a minute. She squared her posture. "I'd have to object to that, Your Honor."

Judge Shiver took off his glasses and dropped them on the bench. "Nobody's even offered any evidence, Miss Hays. What are you objectin' about?"

"I'm objecting because my client . . . excuse me, I mean Mr. Wilt. I'm not sure if he's my client or not at this point. But I'm objecting because he's got a right to choose counsel."

Shiver picked up his glasses and sucked on an earpiece. "You don't *want* to represent this defendant?" He gave Wilt a look that was practically an open sneer. "Can't say as I'd blame you."

"I'm willing to represent anyone the court appoints me to," Sharon said. "But that's not the issue. Mr. Wilt's facing a possible death penalty."

Shiver testily waved his glasses around. "I've resolved the issue. Miss Hays, meet Mr. Wilt. You got you a client. Mr. Wilt, meet Miss Hays. You got you a lawyer. Now, let's get on with it."

Sharon looked at Wilt, who watched her with a curious cant to his mouth. She faced the bench and tilted her chin. "I'm filing a formal objection, then. Are we on the record?" She leaned back to look around Milton Breyer toward the court reporter. The court reporter, a pleasant Hispanic woman in her forties, sat with her fingers poised over her machine. Sharon stood erect, in announcement posture. "Please let the record reflect that Mr. Wilt objects to the court's forced appointment of counsel, and cites as authority the Fourth and Fifth Amendments to the Constitution of the United States, along with *Faretta* v. *California,* Fed Second . . ." She turned to the court reporter once more. "I'll supply chapter and verse later, Betty, okay? Just leave that part open." The court reporter nodded. Sharon faced the bench. "Our objection stands, Your Honor."

Milton Breyer had the look of a man who'd just swallowed a raw tobasco pepper. Dycus Wilt seemed confused. Judge Shiver was livid, chewing so hard on his earpiece that Sharon wondered if the plastic would break.

Finally Shiver said, "Miss Hays, you're cloggin' up my docket with all this legal baloney." He looked to the court reporter. "Strike that, Betty, we're off the record here. I ain't complainin' about anybody usin' law in court, that understood?" The court reporter stuck her tongue in her cheek as she penciled through what she'd just typed into her machine. Shiver said, "Miss Hays, you stickin' to your guns?"

Sharon suspected that in her next appearance in Shiver's court, she was in for it. "I am, Your Honor," she said.

"On the record, Betty," Shiver said. "Mr. Wilt, Miss Hays has a good point. So I'm askin' you. Who you want for a lawyer? F. Lee Bailey ain't available, he's

not licensed in Texas. Strike the last sentence, Betty."
Shiver raised white eyebrows.

Wilt continued to stare at Sharon.

Judge Shiver said, "I'm talkin' to you, Mr. Wilt."

Wilt looked to the bench. "Huh?"

"I just ast you who you wanted for a lawyer. Your
call, son. That's what we're here for, to serve you
people."

Wilt raised manacled hands as far as the waist chain
would permit, and pointed sideways at Sharon. The
defendant grinned. "I wants her, judge. I ain't never
heard nothin' like that from no lawyuh befo'."

Having gotten the judge in an uproar, Sharon
poured more coals on the fire. SOP in arraignments
was to waive the reading of the indictment. But since
the court had only appointed Sharon five minutes before Wilt came in from the holding cell—as she took
a shortcut through the 386th, in fact, on her way to
file some motions with the clerk of the court next
door—she needed some idea of what the case was
all about and asserted her client's right to have the
indictment read. Milton Breyer gave the formal charge
in his best We-the-People tenor while Judge Shiver
simmered at the bench, drumming his fingers. The indictment contained even less information than that
morning's newspaper story; Dycus Wilt, the People
charged, had caused the death of one Mary Ann
Blakely, a white female, aged twenty-two, during the
commission of another felony, to wit rape, all in viola-
tion of the Texas capital murder statute. A couple of
ten-year-olds, Sharon knew, had found Miss Blakely's
remains in a culvert while they were playing hooky
from school. The manhunt—which consisted, Sharon
also knew, of the sheriff's department opening a file
and waiting for a snitch to come forward—had received a lot of ink. The sheriff's men had leaked the
following information to the newspapers: testing of
hair and semen matched samples from Dycus Wilt,

and Wilt's alibi that he was "over at his cousin's" at the time of the murder didn't hold a drop of water. The fact that her client was fresh from the Texas Department of Corrections—on a rape charge—didn't help his defense one iota. Been there, done that, Sharon thought. When Breyer was finished reading, Sharon smiled her sweetest thank-you to the bench. Shiver rolled his eyes, gave Wilt his Miranda warning, and terminated the hearing with a bang of his gavel.

Sharon leaned over the defense table and said to the deputy, "I want to confer with my client. The jury box okay?" She pointed to the box, where two prisoners sat handcuffed to theater seats. The guard nodded and led Wilt in that direction. Sharon gathered up her file and briefcase, and fell in step behind the two.

An alto male voice in the spectator section said, "Miss Hays? Miss Hays."

Sharon stopped and turned. Andy Wade of the *News* leaned over the rail. Wade was the regular court beat man, a couple of years out of college, a round-faced youngster with black plastic-framed glasses. He had an absolutely teeth-grinding habit of blowing his nose during closing arguments, so that lawyers often had to repeat some of their statements in order for the jury to hear. Wade waved his steno pad. Sharon went over and said hello.

"Just wanted to know," Wade said, "exactly what case you were citing." He wore Docker slacks, a pale blue shirt, and a navy blue tie. A hint of gut hung out over his belt.

Sharon frowned, not getting it for an instant, then snapped to. "You mean, when I objected to the judge's forced court appointment?"

"That's it." Wade shook his head in admiration. "Feisty, Miss Hays. Feisty."

Sharon glanced at the bench. Judge Shiver had held up the next proceeding to watch the exchange between reporter and lawyer. Shiver watched *any* discussion involving the newspaper in his courtroom like a

zealous hawk. It occurred to Sharon that this was an
election year, that Shiver normally ran unopposed, but
that grumblings from the bar association over the
judge's heavy-handedness had increased in volume
over the years. Rumors had developed that Milton
Breyer might challenge Shiver in the upcoming primary. If Breyer were to win, Sharon thought, then all
the female court clerks had best weight down the
hems of their skirts and wear armored panties. Sharon
returned her attention to Andy Wade, and flashed the
reporter with her humblest, help-me smile. "Hey,
Andy, give me a break. Don't report it, huh?"

Wade rubbed his notebook cover with the eraser
end of his pencil. "It's news. You did go on record."

"Yeah, but . . . criminy, I'm in enough hot water
with the judge as it is. If he reads it in the paper, the
next thing will be my disbarment proceedings, with
Shiver as the complainant."

Wade raised an eyebrow like a man in heavy negoti-
ation. "Make a trade?"

Sharon turned up one corner of her mouth in a
crooked grin. "How dare you, sir."

Wade squinched his eye up in a wink. "I won't compromise your virtue, Miss Hays. Just a little inside
stuff as the case moves on."

Sharon's forehead tightened. "Not if it hurts my
client."

"I wouldn't ask you to. For starters, is Russell Black
going to join you in defending this guy?"

"Russ doesn't even know I've got the case, Andy.
Plus, you know how he feels about rapos."

Wade steadied his pencil over his pad. "Is that a
'no'?"

"It's an 'I don't have the slightest idea.' Tell you
what. You don't print the scene at the bench, as soon
as I talk to Russ I'll give you a call."

Wade stood back and folded his arms. "The presses
are on hold, Miss Hays."

Sharon smiled her thanks, turned from the rail, took

two steps in the direction of the jury box, and froze in her tracks. Dycus Wilt was cuffed to a chair two rows up, his dull-normal gaze on her, his loose lips in a surly pout. All levity rushed out of Sharon like a whoosh of air. God save the Queen, Sharon Hays thought, then continued on to confer with her client. She'd as soon be on an ocean raft, alone with Milton Breyer.

Dycus Wilt had been in jail four days, as a result of a tip to the sheriff from one of his drinking buddies. During his time in lockup he'd developed a hint of body odor, which was likely to worsen as time progressed. Sharon got a whiff that almost knocked her over, so left a vacant chair in between her and her client in the jury box. If Wilt resented her lack of chumminess, he didn't let on.

Sharon spoke softly so as not to disturb the proceedings now before the bench, which consisted of a chubby lawyer arguing that the state had violated his client's right to a speedy trial. Sharon said to Wilt, "First off. You're not to discuss anything with anyone but me. If the jail deputies bring you dinner, say thank you. That's it with those guys."

"I been down befo'," Wilt said. "I don't say shit to no laws." He had one gold inlay, between the right front tooth and its neighboring bicuspid. Likely prison dentistry, Sharon thought.

"Without talking it over with the prosecution," Sharon said, "I'll have to warn you there may not be any plea-bargain offer. There's been a lot in the papers about your case, and that's the kind they like to try. If they do make an offer, it won't be less than for a life sentence." She snapped open her briefcase, produced a legal pad, and prepared to take notes.

Wilt's upper lip curled. "Shee-it, I never took no pussy from that woman. I 'as over to my cousin's." He pronounced it "*cuz*-in."

Sharon decided that Wilt wouldn't make the best

witness in his own behalf. *Are you guilty, Mr. Wilt? Shee-it, no.* "Who's your cousin, Mr. Wilt?" she said. "Maybe the cousin will testify."

"She stays over on Pennsylvania Street."

"Yes? What's her name?"

Wilt fiddled with the bracelet around his wrist. "Ain't too sho."

"You don't know your cousin's name?"

"She done moved."

"She moved." Sharon crossed her legs and laid her forearms on top of her legal pad, holding her ballpoint loosely between her thumb and forefinger. "I've got to tell you, that doesn't look good. According to a witness, a Mr. . . ." Sharon quickly checked the file. "A Mr. Woodrow Lee, you told him that you did assault Mary Ann Blakely, that you forced your way into her car at knifepoint, and when you finished raping her you stabbed her. County forensics says your semen matches that found in the victim, and your pubic hair matches a sample taken from the scene. The car was found a half mile from your apartment. Your thumbprint was on the steering wheel. Now, if there is a cousin . . ."

"Shee-it." Wilt testily shifted his position. "Shee-it. Woody-man, bastard drop a dime on me."

Sharon's features tightened. "Drop a dime" was an expression going all the way back to ten-cent telephone calls, where the snitch sneaks to a booth and rings up the law. They should update it, Sharon thought, call it dropping a quarter. "That's right, Mr. Wilt," she said. "He dropped a dime. And I'll clue you in on something else: You need to tell me the truth. I'm your lawyer, and anything you tell me's privileged."

Wilt wore a hospital-type wristband, bearing his name and prisoner ID number. The face of the band was orange, the color code for a maximum security risk. "I don't got no privilege," he said. "Shee-it, Deppity don't lemme use the phone when he s'posed to."

Sharon was stumped for an instant, then got it. "I'm not talking about privileges while you're in jail. Privileged, that means whatever you tell me, I can't tell anybody else. Is that clearer?" She wondered if the state would pay for having Sheila Winston examine her client, Sheila's fees being more reasonable than the psychiatrists whom the county generally employed. Sharon suspected that Dycus Wilt was crazy, all right, just not crazy enough to get himself off on a capital murder charge. She pictured him forcing his way into her own car wielding a switchblade. A quiver ran the length of Sharon's backbone.

Wilt snickered. "You don't tell nobody? Shee-it, that what Woody Lee tell me. Dude drop a dime on me, woman."

Sharon allowed air to escape from between her lips. "You know, you may have been right to begin with. You might need a different attorney."

Wilt showed a dull-normal expression that somehow managed to appear crafty as well. "You my lawyuh. Judge say so."

"I can withdraw. Come on, Dycus, help me in this. If you did it, you did it. Let's try to keep your punishment down as much as we can." Such as having the executioner tell you a joke before he sticks the needle in your arm, Sharon thought.

Wilt raised his hands as far as his manacles would permit, and bent his neck to yank on a dreadlock. "Shee-it. Dude drop a dime on me, maybe I drop a dime on him."

Sharon surveyed the courtroom. The pudgy lawyer continued to argue before the bench while a couple of attorneys in the spectator section waited their turns. The uniformed jailer lounged in a chair at the defense table. Milton Breyer was still present on the prosecution side, shooting the breeze with the assistant D.A. assigned to the court. Wonder why Milt's sticking around, Sharon thought. Usually after his court show's over, he goes back to his office and worships himself

in the mirror. She leaned nearer to her client, closing
her nasal passages against the odor, and whispered,
"If you know something derogatory about the state's
witness, maybe we can use that to try and discredit
him."

"Drop a dime on that mothafuckah," Wilt mumbled, nodding.

Sharon turned her ear in a listening attitude. "Speak
softly. I can hear you, but we don't want anyone
else to . . ."

"Sump'n we done one time. 'Bout six years ago."

"You did together. I'll warn you, for the state to
consider reducing a capital murder charge, it'd have
to be something important."

"Out in North Dallas. We went in one of them
big houses."

"A simple burglary's not going to help you,"
Sharon said.

"White man's lookin' at execution over what we
done."

Sharon closed her mouth.

"Was Woody's idea, wadn none o' mine. Said he
done some work for them people before this lady an'
her old man split. Said she was by herself in that big
old house, and I thought we wadn doin' nothin' 'cept
robbin' the bitch. Ooo, lady, it was rainin' like hell."
Wilt looked at the ceiling. "I drop a dime on that
bastard, serve him right."

Sharon steadied her pen over her pad. "Where was
this house?"

"Ain't never forgot it. Woody pick me up in his
Chevrolet. Big house on Crooked Lane, 'bout four
doors down offa Walnut Hill. House got a gate. Big
fountain in front, buncha them angels jumpin'
around."

"You mean cherubs," Sharon said.

"Yeah. Lady's daddy's a senator up in Washington."

Sharon's eyes widened as realization dawned.

"You're talking about Joseph Bright, his daughter. Come on. I used to work for the D.A. My first year on the staff, that was our biggest case."

"That be the dude, Joseph Bright."

Sharon studied Wilt, his expression bland, as if breaking into someone's home and murdering the lady of the house was akin to a trip to the supermarket. Or in Wilt's case, the cocaine store. She tried reminding herself that he was her client, but the thought of representing Dycus Wilt lowered her own self-esteem. She tried to remember Joseph Bright's daughter's married name, but drew a blank. She said, "I don't believe you."

"Woody done some yard work for them people. Knew just how to get in over the fence. We went in there up a trellis, one of them things with vines growin' on it, climbed in through a second-story window Woody knew had the latch broke."

"That case has been litigated," Sharon said. "Her estranged husband."

Wilt went on as if he hadn't heard. "Come into a big bedroom. Had one of them beds with a roof."

"A four-poster with a canopy," Sharon said.

"Crep' through real quiet, I had water squishin' in my shoes 'cause o' the rain. Had on a stockin' cap so wet I had water runnin' in my ears. Woody, too, that was one wet dude. He went down these big wide stairs, an' I was right behind him. I remember his feets left these big wet spots on the rug.

"The lady," Wilt said, "she 'as downstairs watchin' television, pretty little paleface thing. Had these big dark eyes with all that black shit around 'em."

"Black . . . ?" Sharon's jaw slacked in confusion.

"Ladies brush that shit on."

"You mean eye shadow."

"She went to beggin' not to hurt her," Wilt said. "Fucked up she did, callin' Woody by name, 'cause that's when I think the dude decided to do her. He had me tie her up, he'd brought some twine in wid

him, an' I put her right in that chair in front o' the
television." He brightened. "You sayin' you don't believe me, how 'bout this? What she was watchin' was
the last night *Hill Street Blues* was ever on. Man, I
liked that, Captain Furillo and shit."

Sweet God, Sharon thought, he noticed what was
on television. "You could know the dates coincide,"
she said. "The murder and the last episode. What we'd
need would be something only the murderer could
know."

"Woody, he gets this garbage sack and goes to
throwin' in shit. Silverware, he got this one little clock
I remember, had these little puppets, a man and a
lady, come out of this house every time the hour
come by."

"An animated clock," Sharon said. "And one of the
big things that convicted the guy was, there was no
evidence of a robbery. Nothing missing." She smiled,
hoping that she didn't look overly triumphant but feeling that way. "No robbery. You'll have to try again,
Mr. Wilt."

Wilt lifted his hand. His handcuff clinked. "I'm
sayin' what we done, I don't know nothin' about no
other shit. I seen that clock, not a mont' ago, over
to Woody's."

Sharon didn't believe a word of it, but did write
down, "Missing animated clock—*check out.*"

"Woody went off to some other part o' the house,"
Wilt said, "an' left me alone with the lady. She tried
to hit on me to turn her loose, but I just went on
watchin' television. Woody come back in. He was
drinkin' this glass o' green, Kool-Aid, I think, Ga-
torade, maybe, but he was drinkin' it. Had this bonin'
knife he got from the kitchen. That's when the lady
started to yell, only nobody could hear her for the
rain outside, an' the nearest house was a half mile,
maybe more."

Sharon pictured the neighborhood, seven-figure
homes where Sharon sometimes took Melanie on

drives while mother and daughter dreamed their dreams. A long stretch between houses—though not near a half mile—acre tracts and some even larger lots; moats, lakes, big groves of trees, just the landscape for shielding two cretin murderers from view.

"Ol' Woody, he cuts her loose and strips her, an' he gets me to hold her down while he goes to fuckin' her. All the time she's lookin' at me an' screamin' for me to make him stop, but he's doin' it anyhow."

"Didn't that bother you?"

"Sho' did," Wilt said. "Bitch was makin' so much noise I told Woody to lemme stick a rag or somethin' in her mouth, I couldn' hear no television. But he said, shee-it, can't nobody hear this woman. After he got done I fucked her, too, figured, shee-it, I might as well."

Sharon watched her client with the same fascination she would show for the biggest, ugliest cockroach alive. She gripped her ballpoint so tightly that her fingers were white. Her forehead was suddenly damp. "How do you," she began, then cleared her throat. "He stabbed her then?"

"Sho', wid dat bone knife. Whole buncha times." Wilt rolled his eyes upward. "Drop a dime on 'at mothafuckah."

Law, Sharon thought. Law, law, law, legal issues. Unemotional, detached reasoning. Precise logic. *God, I want to throw up.* "Mr. Wilt," she finally managed, "if we were to, say, go to the district attorney with this, we're going to have to know things you couldn't have learned from the newspaper. That trial was in the headlines every day, some of the testimony on television. See if you can remember some details, maybe that the papers wouldn't have had."

Wilt seemed thoughtful, like a man going over his shopping list. From seemingly miles away, Milton Breyer said, "Sharon? Sharon, got a minute?"

She turned. Breyer had come over from the prosecution table, and now fidgeted near the witness box.

Judge Shiver had left the bench. The spectator section was empty, the deputy/jailer seated near the rail behind the defense table, pointedly checking his watch. Sharon looked at her own timepiece. Eleven-fifty-six. Lunchtime. She wondered if she could possibly eat anything after hearing what her client had to say.

"Sharon?" Breyer said more urgently.

She said vacantly, "Yes?"

"Listen, I need a minute."

"We're . . . finishing up, okay?"

Breyer nodded impatiently, and stalked over to the prosecution table. Sharon turned to her client. "Mr. Wilt, if you need more time to think . . ."

"Bitch had a scar on her ass," Wilt said.

Six years ago, Sharon thought, how could he remember? Or, God, how could he ever forget? She said, "Surgical, or . . . ?"

Wilt slowly nodded and smacked his lips. "Like a operation, yeah. Run up between her cheeks, I seen it good when I was spreadin' her ass out to—"

"I think," Sharon said quickly, writing it down, "that's something we might use. Anything else? Quickly now, we've got to go." Parting company with a jailed client was an art that Sharon had never mastered; incarcerated felons loved to go on and on about anything and everything, to anyone who would listen to them.

"That glass Woody was drinkin' out of," Wilt said. "He left it on the flo' between her legs."

"That would show in the crime scene photos," Sharon said. "Probably not much use to us, but I'll see." She closed her legal pad. "It's late, Mr. Wilt. Here's my card. I'll be over to the jail to see you in a couple of days, but if you think of anything else, call me."

"Deputy don't gimme the phone when he s'posed to."

Sharon snapped her briefcase to, and stood. "I'll see what I can do, Mr. Wilt." She nodded to the deputy, who came over to lead the prisoner away. Wilt frowned as his keeper undid the cuff from the chair arm and remanacled the prisoner's wrist. Sharon did her best to smile encouragingly at her client, but her lips were stiff. Milton Breyer waited at the prosecution table. Sharon walked over to him and stood gripping her forearm, the briefcase resting on her thigh. "You wanted to see me?" she said.

"I've been hearing some rumors," Breyer said, checking cautiously around for eavesdroppers.

Sharon put Dycus Wilt temporarily in the back of her mind. "Lots of rumors float around, Milt."

"It's about . . . Listen, Sharon, you might've heard I'm running for judge."

"Seems like I might've." She kept her tone steady and did her best to hide her contempt. It was a real struggle.

"It's because of that, I need to squelch any rumors before they get out of hand."

Sharon watched him.

"I'll be direct with you," Breyer said, folding his hands on the table. "Have the EEOC people contacted you?"

Sharon stuck out her lower lip and puffed air upward, her bangs rustling, and didn't say anything.

"You know these Equal Employment Opportunity guys," Breyer said. "Federal jerks, interfering in everything. They've called our office a couple of times."

Sharon shifted her briefcase from one hand to the other. "I don't think we have anything to discuss, unless you want to talk about Dycus Wilt's case. Are you going to prosecute it personally, or one of your assistants?"

Breyer showed anguish, dyed black hair dropping over his forehead. "Christ, Sharon, one of them's been talking to all the girls in the office, trying to build a case. It's got me on pins and needles, what with the election . . ."

"I think my client may have the makings of a deal," Sharon said.

"Ever since Cissy filed for divorce, my life has been hell," Breyer said.

"Milton . . ." Sharon breathed an exasperated sigh. "Okay, you want to know. What I hope is, I hope you get your fanny in a crack you can't get out of. Divorce is hell, but I think Cissy made the right choice. If it had been me instead of her, we might have another Lorena Bobbit case on the news." She smiled sweetly. "Anything else I can help you with?"

"You know there's other opportunity, besides the judgeship. Ralph Toner's thrown his hat in the gubernatorial ring, and some people have mentioned my name in connection with the D.A. vacancy. This could ruin me, Sharon."

"My God, Milt, aren't you listening?" Sharon slowly shook her head. "I'll tell you what I think. Mr. Toner was okay as district attorney, I suppose, though I'm not really sure because the only thing he ever said to me while I was on his staff was, 'Could you put some more cream in this?' He makes a good speech, so he'd probably be okay as a governor, but I don't think he could beat the Republicans if they spotted him two knights and a rook. As far as you, maybe district attorney is the route you should take. Then the upper-echelon female lawyers would have to put up with the same bullshit as the low girls on the totem pole, you pinching their butts all the time. I can't even believe you're talking to me about this."

"We've had our differences, Sharon."

"That's the understatement of the freaking century."

"I just . . . well, I'd hoped you had more sense than to be talking to the EEO, that's all."

"I'll talk to whoever I want. Now, unless we've got something to discuss on the Dycus Wilt case . . ." Sharon went through the railing and toward the exit at the back of the courtroom.

Breyer stood and called out, "Sharon?"

She turned in the aisle.

Breyer seemed to have his confidence back, the prosecutorial arrogance returning, something Milt could turn on and off at will. "We're going to burn your boy, Sharon," he said.

"He wasn't my boy until an hour ago," Sharon said. "But maybe you won't. I think he may have some plea-bargain ammo."

"If you're talking about the Delores Burnside murder," Breyer said, "then forget it. He's already told the jail guards all those lies."

Burnside, Sharon thought, that was the Bright woman's married name. How could she forget? The convicted guy, her ex-husband . . . Raymond, sure. Raymond Burnside. Sharon said to Breyer, "Dycus sounds pretty convincing to me."

"We're not kicking that dead horse. The guy that did it's got an execution date in November, for God's sake, suddenly there's this big revelation."

Sharon arched an eyebrow. "You won't discuss a deal?"

Breyer shook his head. "Not if he's going to solve a case that's been history for over five years. No way."

Sharon lifted, and then dropped her shoulders. "See you in court then, old man." She turned and walked out the exit into the corridor, and punched the DOWN button on the elevator. She shifted her briefcase from one hand to the other, watching a slim black jail trustee sweep the corridor with a push broom. The elevator light came on with a high-pitched *ding,* and then the twin doors rumbled open. Surgical scar on the woman's fanny, Sharon thought as she entered the car. Probably not much, but worth looking into.

2

Matthew Bark had said adios to the U.S. Forest Service because of a GS-9 salary cap in his position as an insect research assistant. His next job had been an improvement, contracting for government leases on behalf of the General Services Administration; in fact, after only three years in GSA, he'd battled all the way up to GS-12. There the promotions had ended, however, so Bark had looked around once more, and a flier distributed from the Civil Service Commission had tipped him off to an opening in Equal Employment Opportunity. Being Caucasian had been a problem for Bark, because his rival for the job was an African-American and a female to boot, but the young black woman had found a better deal at IRS. Thank the Lord for small favors. So here Bark was at age thirty-nine, a GS-13 with a month under his belt at EEOC, investigating sexual harassment cases. Long live grab-and-grope management, Bark thought

And not only was he a GS-13, his expense account was nothing to sneeze about, either. As Bark sat by himself at a table in Ninfa's Mexican Restaurant, waiting to conduct an interview, he popped his Amex down. He inhaled the aroma of fresh flour tortillas. Hispanic waiters hustled here and there toting platters of enchiladas, *tacos al carbon,* and *pechugas* rubbed with lemon butter. Plates clanked, silverware rattled, and ice tinkled in glasses accompanied by a hubbub of conversation. Bark wore a hairpiece that had set him back thirteen hundred bucks—plus a trip a week

to the stylist in order to keep the rug undetectable—
but he thought that anything which improved his appearance was well worth the money. His waistline had
expanded, that was a problem, but a month of sit-ups
would cure all ills. The waiter came over and stood
by, a pleasant Hispanic guy in his twenties wearing a
white shirt, black pants, and black string tie. In the
far corner of the restaurant, a mariachi band played
beneath hanging baskets of ferns.

"Un té, por favor, con hielo," Bark said, closing his
menu and laying it aside. The tabletop was tiled, blue-
and-white floral designs.

The waiter let his order book dangle at his hip.
"You want a glass of tea? Nothing to eat?" He had
an olive complexion and a dark mustache. The rest of
his face was hairless.

Bark lifted a finger. *"Quiero comer en . . .* uh, *un
momento. Una señorita . . ."* He gestured helplessly
toward the lobby.

The waiter's gaze followed Bark's direction. In the
waiting area, men and women sat on cushioned benches.
A smiling Hispanic girl in an off-the-shoulder Mexican
blouse stood at a podium, taking names. Celophane-
wrapped pralines lay in a basket near the cash register.
The waiter said, "What, you've got a lady coming?"

"Una señorita," Bark said. *"Sí, sí, una señorita."*

The waiter opened the menu and laid it back in
front of Bark, then opened a second menu and placed
it before an empty chair. "Yeah, okay, one iced tea
coming up. When you're ready to order, I'm Butch.
Or you can call me Pedro if you like that better."

"Gracias," Bark said.

"No sweat," the waiter said, then moved over to a
nearby table and began taking orders from four
women.

Bark patted the top of his hairpiece and pretended
to study the menu as a young lady came in from outside and stood in the archway to look around. She's
really pretty, Bark thought, a shade short of beautiful,

dark hair fluffed out in flippant bangs and razored close around the back of her head. Her gaze was calm and steady, no hesitation in her look as she surveyed nearby tables and the waiting area, obviously looking for someone. She wore a white blouse, charcoal-gray vest and skirt, and medium-heeled black pumps. Perfect if it's her, Bark thought, no suggestiveness to her bearing, the conservative businessperson female. Perhaps a bit too saucy with the cant of her mouth, but nothing that some coaching wouldn't fix should she have to testify. Bark dug in the inside breast pocket of his suit and checked his referral card. Then he got up and approached the lady, catching a faint scent of lilac as he said, "Miss Hays? Sharon Hays?"

Her look was friendly, direct brown eyes. "Yes?"

He extended his hand. "Matt Bark. Glad you could come. We're right over here." He pointed in the direction of his table.

Her grip was firm. "Sorry to be late," she said. "Got hung up with a client. And I'm afraid I'm still running, I have a two o'clock."

"They give fast service," he said. "Helps to know a little of the lingo." He extended his arm and followed her over to the table. She sat and folded slim hands.

The waiter appeared as if he'd materialized, set iced tea in front of Bark, and then readied himself, pencil and pad in hand. "You folks ready to order?"

Sharon quickly glanced at the menu. "Look, can I get just a scoop of guacamole, maybe with a little lettuce and tomato?"

"Sure thing," the waiter said. "Anything to drink?"

Sharon touched her stemmed goblet of water. "This'll be fine."

"Gotcha," the waiter said.

"It's on me," Bark said, fingering his American Express. "Order up."

Sharon folded her menu. "I eat light lunches. Chow down at dinner."

"How about you, sir?" the waiter said.

Bark leaned back and held his menu open in both hands. *"Sí, Pedro, yo quiero dos enchiladas con queso, con arroz, y . . ."*

The waiter winked at Sharon, who smirked and looked away.

". . . Y . . . Y . . . uh, *pechuga . . ."*

The waiter let his arms dangle by his sides. "You want a chicken breast with enchiladas?"

Bark frowned. *"No, un . . . un . . ."*

"Maybe you mean a taco," the waiter said.

"It's the same in Spanish?" Bark looked dubious.

Sharon covered her mouth, her shoulders heaving.

"Taco *is* Spanish, sir. That's a Number Five. Be out in a jiffy." The waiter picked up the menus and hurried off. As he passed underneath the hanging baskets on his way to the kitchen, he nodded to the guy playing guitar with the mariachi band.

Sharon had a sip of water. "I'll get to the point, Mr. Bark."

Bark took three sugar packets from the container, tore them open, and poured white crystals into his tea. "I believe in that. Our preliminary reports indicate you've got an excellent case."

"I've got a problem with people doing investigations I haven't authorized, frankly."

Bark stirred his tea with a loud clanking sound. "The women in the district attorney's office say you're not the only one he's been after. Seems this guy's a real wolf in sheep's clothing."

"I don't know about the sheep's clothing," Sharon said. "But he just stopped me in court and asked if I'd been talking to you. Caught me off guard."

"The calls make 'em sweat. They always do. This could be a real high-profile case, with the people involved. Send a message to these predators."

"I'm just living my life," Sharon said. "I don't like sending messages. And I don't really want my daughter reading that her mother's involved in anything like that."

Bark's wide forehead wrinkled in a scowl. He laid his spoon down. "My file says you contacted EEOC. Not the other way around."

"I've been gone from the D.A.'s staff and in private practice for nearly a year and a half, Mr. Bark. My call to your office was on the day I quit, and I confess, I was a bit pissed off at the time. My answering machine was loaded down with calls from Equal Employment for a couple of months, none of which I returned. Finally the calls quit coming, and I thought the matter was finished. Now a lifetime later, suddenly your office is making noises again."

"There's a five-year statute of limitations."

"I just want it all to go away," Sharon said. "And that's the reason I'm here, to put a stop to it."

Bark put his elbows on the table and touched his fingertips together. Her gaze was directed slightly upward, and he wondered with a flash of panic if she was looking at his hairpiece. He resisted the urge to pat the top of his head. "The person originally handling it was Mrs. Williams. She retired nine months ago. I've just filled her vacant position, and that's the reason you haven't heard from us until now."

The waiter came over and set a plate down in front of Sharon. The plate contained pulped avocado mixed with lemon juice and spices, a slice of tomato and two lettuce leaves. In front of Bark he put a saucer that held one crispy taco. "The enchiladas will be ready in a minute," he said, and retreated from the table.

"I told you they were fast," Bark said.

"I hope they're fast enough," Sharon said, checking her watch. "I'm really running today." Two men in suits finished their meal at the next table, and left. A busboy dragged a cart over and loaded dirty dishes into a tub.

Bark studied his prospect card. "Didn't you and Mr. Breyer have a physical confrontation?"

"Your office didn't get that from me. Whoall have you been talking to?"

"A number of women that've fallen victim to this guy."

Sharon used her fork to mix her guacamole. "If you've got a number of women to file complaints, why do you need me?"

"These other women still work there. With your leadership and direction, they'll hop on the bandwagon." Bark bit into his taco, chomping down on crispy tortilla, lettuce, spicy meat, and shredded cheese, laid the taco down, and wiped his fingers on his napkin.

"Well, the bandwagon's going to have to leave without me," Sharon said. "I've got too many other things to do."

"That's a major problem, I'm afraid. No one wants to follow through. After what he did to you . . ."

Sharon swallowed and laid down her fork. "I'm a big girl, and I can handle myself. I went through law school waiting tables, and Milt Breyer's certainly not the only one that's ever tried pinching my bottom. I got mad and I quit the D.A., and I've certainly got no regrets about that. I've got another job now, which I like a whole lot more. I'm not filing a formal complaint, Mr. Bark."

"I've got to say," Bark said, "that your refusal to act is a setback to womanhood. Something we run into all the time, women afraid to come forth."

Sharon arched an eyebrow. "You think I'm afraid?"

Bark picked up his taco. "It would appear so."

Sharon looked away, toward the corner where the band now played "Cuando Caliente del Sol." She looked at her lap. She raised her gaze. "Once and for all, sir, and I know you've got a job to do. Milton Breyer grabbed my breast one day after we'd won a big trial. I reacted by kneeing him a good one in the crotch, and I wish I'd done more damage than that. My boobs are tender, but they heal quickly. I don't have any lasting psychological problems, nightmares, or anything. Since then, his wife has left him over his screwing around and the calls from your office to his staff have made a basket case out of him. So he's being punished. Guys like him always are, one way or the other."

Bark swallowed more of his taco, feeling the crispy tortilla stick momentarily in his throat, then slide on into his gullet. He washed down the bite with a swig of tea. "No one's an island in this, Miss Hays. Public example is what sends out the message."

"Oh? What message is that?"

"To these men that think, when they have a woman in a tight spot they can take advantage."

"I don't go along with all that. It so happens that I like men. Guys have been trying things with women since before Noah and the Ark. Often you don't want them to, but there are other times that you do. It's only been recently everybody's tried to make a federal case out of it, and I think all this publicity has caused a big problem in the world. A man's afraid to ask a woman for a date anymore, for God's sake."

Bark's eyebrows lifted. "You like men?"

Sharon shrugged. "Not all men. But there are some I wish would get friendly with me, that I think won't because they're afraid of all this sexual harassment business."

"It's in the workplace we're interested in. All these women being asked to lie down for their promotions."

"Sure, that happens. It's a fact of life that's unfortunate, but not worth destroying the entire male/female relationship over." Sharon lifted her napkin from her lap and dropped it on the table. "I'm afraid we're wasting time. I've got a daughter to raise, and to be blunt, I'm not interested in making a spectacle out of myself so a bunch of federal people can make speeches to the newspapers. Not my cup of tea, Mr. Bark." She pushed her plate away.

"There are worse things than publicity," Bark said. "Haven't you ever considered taking up where you left off with your acting career? This could be a shot in the arm for you." She wishes someone would ask her for a date, he thought. He wondered if she was coming on to him. Must be the hairpiece, Bark thought.

Sharon's posture relaxed. Her lips parted. "My acting career? How did you know . . . ?"

"And I doubt it would hurt you," Bark said, "that your daughter's father is already a star."

Sharon closed, then opened her eyes. "I've got to confess, that just takes the cake. I'd like to know where you get off digging in my private life."

"We don't take on just any case. Just those we feel have the potential."

"My acting *career,* if you want to call it that, consisted of fifteen months of starving to death in New York, riding the subway with a bologna sandwich in a sack, and managing to get myself pregnant. Why would I want to return to that, Mr. Bark?"

"Call me Matt. Please."

"And as for Rob being a star, well, the proof is in the pudding. This is his first season on, and his ratings are somewhere above *Saturday Night Live,* and somewhere below *NYPD Blue.* I'll grudgingly admit his show's pretty good, which is more due to the writers than to him. He's a whole lot better actor than he is a father. My daughter's twelve, and last year was the first time he's been interested enough to inquire about her, and that was on the advice of his agent. He pays sporadic child support when it improves his public image, and Melanie and I see him as seldom as possible. And the next time you want to know something about my personal life, just ask me."

"You're upset," Bark said.

"You betcha," Sharon said.

"I think," Bark said, picking up his Amex, turning it over to be certain he'd signed on the back, "that you should relax. Take a few days to think it over."

"I think," Sharon said, "that messages directed from the EEOC to me should cease. And if they don't,

I'm going to investigate marching straight to federal court to get a restraining order."

"Your feelings on the subject seem pretty firm."

Sharon rolled her eyes. "Look, I need to go." She pushed her chair back and stood.

Bark rested his chin on his intertwined fingers. "Well, if you're that certain . . ."

"I sure am." Sharon picked up her purse by its strap.

"Listen, if we can't get together in a business sense, maybe we could have dinner some evening." Bark looked her up and down.

Sharon gasped. "You're asking me for a date? Jesus Christ, I don't believe this."

"Well, you said you like men." Bark grinned.

"I do. *Some* men, not anything in pants. No more messages from EEOC, Mr. Bark. And for God's sake, no messages from you." Sharon hooked the purse strap over her shoulder and left the restaurant at a fast clip.

The waiter appeared and set down a plate of steaming enchiladas, chili topped with melted, runny cheese. "What happened to the lady?"

Bark slipped his Amex into his breast pocket, looking dreamily toward the exit. "She had an appointment. Look, do I get soft tortillas with this, or is that an additional charge?"

3

The air conditioner in Sharon's ancient blue Volvo reminded her of the way she'd handled the guy from EEOC. A bit short of cool, old girl, she thought, her sentiments directed as much at herself as toward the Volvo. According to the deejay on Country 96.3, the mercury was to hit a hundred this afternoon for the eleventh consecutive day. Hotter than hell, Sharon thought, but hardly a record for Texas. She rolled her window down a couple of turns; the blast-furnace wind was hotter than her car's interior, by a total of perhaps five degrees. She closed the window and jammed the AC control lever as far to the left as it would go. The old heap uttered a series of squeals from under the hood, but the air inside did seem a shade less torrid. She gave a sigh of resignation as she made the figure-eight curve off of Stemmons Freeway onto Commerce Street and headed into the center of downtown. Men strolled down the sidewalks with their collars undone and their coats slung over their shoulders. The pavement in front of her shimmered like a mirage.

She'd stopped off at her personal shade tree mechanic's place that morning, on her way to court, to learn that the charge for pumping Freon into the Volvo's system had gone all the way up to sixty-five dollars. Long live the Environmental Protection Agency. Freon in air-conditioning systems was soon to be a thing of the past, the mechanic had explained, and beginning in a couple of years everyone would have to have their AC overhauled to accommodate

the new ozone-free stuff. Sharon had held her breath
and asked what the overhaul was going to cost, and
the mechanic had done his best to hide his glee in
telling her, Somewhere in the vicinity of a thousand
bucks. The EPA is determined to protect the citizenry
out of its very last nickel, Sharon thought. No matter,
Melanie's private school tuition was due this week—
school openings in the middle of August were something that Sharon would never get used to—and until
the eagle flew again, she'd have to simmer in her
juices. Literally.

She circled around to the back of the George Allen
Courts Building, and hesitated at the corner to fight
an inner battle. To her right was the converted gas
station that offered covered parking, taking advantage
of its across-from-the-courthouse location to the tune
of six dollars a day with no in-and-out privileges. Four
blocks straight ahead were open lots at half the price,
but taking the cheapo route required a quarter mile
of hoofing it in weather that could give Lawrence of
freaking Arabia a stroke. Finally Sharon allowed com-
fort to win out over frugality; she gunned the Volvo
underneath the awning and located a spot four spaces
from the entrance. With a final wry glance at the dent
in the Volvo's fender, she lugged her purse and briefcase across the street to the office.

As she ascended the steps and pushed open the
glass-paneled door, a rivulet of perspiration ran down
her cheek. The door displayed a sign reading, "RUS-
SELL BLACK, LAWYER," with "SHARON J. HAYS, ATTOR-
NEY," in smaller letters underneath. Sharon let the
entry hiss close on its own and hurried on through the
reception area.

The reception area contained a waiting couch along
with a secretarial desk and chair, but no receptionist;
Russ Black wanted as few employees as possible, and
let his answering machine handle the calls. Years
ago—long before Sharon had so much as graduated

law school, in fact—Black's wife had acted as his assistant, but Mrs. Black had long since died. Russ's daughter Virginia, a senior at S.M.U., did the office typing during the summer months. Ginny's tour of duty had ended last week, however, as—tuition check from Daddy in hand—she'd gone off to battle the college wars. For the next eight months Sharon would have to tote her motions, letters, and briefs to the secretarial pool down the street. She sighed, went to her left past the law library, entered her own office, and set her briefcase on the floor. Then she sank into her padded chair, fluffed her bangs with her fingertips, and enjoyed the refrigerated air for a moment.

The building was over forty years old, though refurbished to a certain extent, and still had transoms over the doors. Russ Black had employed a number of associates over the years, all males who'd eventually moved into practice for themselves, and when Sharon had first occupied the office the decorum had been early man ad nauseam. There'd been a tasteless Naugahyde couch, slat-backed chairs, and an imitation rubber plant, all of which had made Sharon absolutely want to barf. She'd redecorated her cubbyhole piece by piece over the past year and a half, and thought with a touch of smugness that the place was all but shipshape.

The desk, surprisingly enough, had been serviceable, old but nicely refinished a conservative brown, and other than repairing some of the more prominent scars with putty and paint, Sharon had left the desk alone. She'd dug into her own meager funds for the chair in which she sat, a high-backed leather job which didn't squeak, and had pressured Russ into a new sofa which came within a hairbreadth of matching her chair. The imitation rubber plant had long since gone to the garbage collector, and in its place sat a flower box of potting soil in which impatiens grew. Russ grumbled some about the red and blue flowers, especially on the

days when Sharon rolled the box out on the sidewalk
so the impatiens could catch some sun, but Sharon
generally responded to her boss's gripes with a series
of oh-poohs. It hadn't taken her long as his associate
to learn that Russell Black's bark was a whole lot
worse than his bite.

Sharon had dutifully hung her framed degrees—
bachelor's from the University of Texas at Dallas with
a major in drama; L.L.B. from U.T. down in Austin
after completion of her short-lived thespian career—
on the wall behind her desk, then had placed desert
scenes in bright warm colors around the rest of the
office. She'd spent an entire Saturday and Sunday in
jean cutoffs and sandals painting the walls light beige,
and had bought an assemble-it-yourself end table on
which to set her radio. Sharon was a C & W nut. She
considered the radio as much of a tool in preparing
motions and briefs as her lawbooks, and had scripted
many a legal argument while jiggling her foot in
rhythm to Garth Brooks or Jerry Jeff Walker. Earphones with a twenty-foot cord lay on one corner of
her desk. The only eyesores left in the office were her
two file cabinets, both ugly gray metal, but she had
plans to replace the cabinets when first she could afford it.
Which, with private-school tuition, air-conditioner Freon,
and whatnot, might be a thousand years.

She went out in the reception area, dug a call slip
pad out of a drawer, sat down, and pressed the message retrieval button on the answering machine. Light
shone underneath Russ's door, a dead-certain sign that
he was in. It bugged Sharon somewhat that in spite
of the presence of the machine, he insisted that his
messages be copied and impaled on a metal spike on
his desk. A glorified secretary she wasn't—and, God,
never intended to be, not for anyone—but she'd swallowed her pride on learning that his male associates
had been stuck with the same chore in the past. Her
own calls were mixed in with Russ's anyway, and it

took only a few minutes to write both down. Sharon cocked an ear to the answering machine, ballpoint in hand.

The first message was from a woman wanting to talk divorce—likely someone who'd randomly picked Black's name from the yellow pages—and Sharon didn't bother notating the call. Russ handled nothing but criminal matters, and those only one at a time, and his reputation as one of the two or three best trial lawyers in the county gave him the luxury to pick and choose. Sharon acted as Russ's cocounsel on all of his major cases, doing all of the research and some of the witness questioning at trial. While any income from court appointments or paying clients whom she could dredge up on her own was Sharon's to keep, divorces simply weren't down her alley. The salary Russ had offered was less than half what she'd made as A.D.A., and she depended on the extras to keep beans on the table and Melanie in private school. Her own criminal practice was building, slowly but surely. Next year she might even shop for a car. She loved being in practice with Russell Black, and felt that the temporary decrease in income had been well worth her while.

The next message was from Billy Delt, a cute little guy in the county jail on a burglary rap, and Billy merely wanted to complain about the jailhouse food. Sharon jotted the message down and mentally filed it under "Matters to be Handled When There's Nothing Else to Do." She personally thought that Billy Delt was lucky to have anything at all to eat. She clicked the button on the machine and waited for the next lucky caller.

A slightly cracking male baritone voice said on the tape, "Russ? Russ, you there? Pick up if you are." Sharon smiled; Russ's old buddies knew that he was often in but not of a mind to answer. In a few seconds the voice went on. "This is Arnie Shiver, Russ, returnin' your call. If you're wantin' to talk about me appointin' your little girl on the Dycus Wilt case, you're wastin' your time. What's done is done. If you want to talk about anything else, give me a ring." There was a click, and the message tape halted in place.

Sharon froze, pen in hand. Her eyes widened. She backed the tape up and replayed the message up to, "This is Arnie Shiver, Russ," then stopped the machine and copied down the name, pressing so hard on the page that she nearly snapped her ballpoint in two. She then switched the recorder into its answering mode, tore the slip from the pad, marched over to Russ's door, and entered without knocking.

He was leaned back with his feet up on the corner of his desk, reading the newspaper. As Sharon entered he looked up, rattled and straightened the pages, and returned his attention to the sports section. "You make it to court?"

Sharon sat across from him. "You know I did."

"Anything goin' on over there?" He had the rugged square-jawed face of an old-time western lawman. He wore a blue suit, pale blue shirt and red tie, and gray lizard boots. His coat hung on a hall tree by the window. "Hot outside, girl," he said.

"What's between you and Judge Shiver, boss?"

Black continued to scan the sports page. Shaggy graying eyebrows lifted. "Oh? Arnie call?" His law degree from the University of Houston, Class of '69, hung behind him along with a photo of Black, in jeans and western shirt, beside a steaming pot at the Terlingua Chili Cook-off.

"Quite a coincidence." Sharon testily held up the call message. "He said he's returning *your* call."

"Must want somethin' about the bar association. We're on some committee or other."

"Nice try. He says he thinks you're calling about a case he appointed me on."

Black swiveled his head to look at her. "He appoint you on a case?"

Sharon folded her arms. "Why, no. Whatever gave you that idea?"

Black frowned. "He didn't?"

"I'm a member of the bar, boss, right along with all the other lawyers. One of my duties as such is to accept court appointments. If I'm appointed, I'm appointed, so why the secret conversations?"

Black folded the paper and put his feet on the floor. "I don't like the idea of Arnie Shiver appointin' you to represent a guy like that."

"Well, actually he appointed you. Since I'm your associate, it becomes my case. Unless you'd like to go over there and represent Mr. Wilt yourself, for what the county pays on court appointments. It's not enough to make major home renovations, boss."

"Hadn' been a year since you went through all that stalkin' business. Hadn'a been for somebody shootin' the guy, you might not be sittin' here now."

Sharon had a quick cold chill, picturing Bradford Brie rushing her inside his grungy rented house, her finger pressing the trigger, the boom of the .45 in her grasp as she shot him in the head. Something that no one knew, and that no one would ever know. She swallowed.

"Now Shiver's wantin' you to represent a lunatic," Black said. "Just somethin' I don't want happenin' to my associate."

Sharon's tone lost some of its force. "How did you know? I only found out myself around ten o'clock, when I took a shortcut through Shiver's courtroom on my way to file some papers."

"Arnie's secretary called over here, to make sure you were gonna be in court today. That's when I left the message for him to get me on the honk. I don't want you foolin' around with people like this Dycus Wilt, Sharon, an' if I have to take his case myself, I will."

"If I don't," she began, then licked her lips and said, "if I don't take every case I'm appointed on, the appointments will cease. Besides, the guy's got a right to a lawyer like anyone else."

"He's got a right to *some* lawyer," Black said, "as long as it idn you."

She was touched at his concern, but pushed ahead anyway. "Dycus Wilt's my client, Russ, for better or worse. I'll need your help."

"Huh? I thought I hired you 'cause I needed *your* help."

"That you did. And taking on all court appointments is part of my job."

"Now you're gettin' technical."

Sharon couldn't resist a little laugh. "You hired me to handle the technical stuff, remember? You remember the Delores Burnside murder case?"

"Joe Bright's daughter? Who dudn? Now, that'd be all right, you representin' the boy that got convicted of that. This Dycus Wilt, that could be dangerous."

"According to what Dycus Wilt told me this morning, he did it."

"Did what?"

"Raped Delores Burnside. He says his sidekick killed her, and he wants to cut a deal."

Black reached into a clear glass jar for a peppermint. "That's what happens when you're dealin' with scum. These people get in a bind . . . some of 'em try to say they know who did Kennedy."

"He described it all. Gave me goose bumps."

"That case was all in the papers. I doubt anybody livin' in Dallas coudn' tell you about everything that happened." Black held the peppermint in his cheek and crunched with his jaw teeth. "You're not tellin' me you believe this guy."

"I don't know if I do or not, Russ. As his lawyer, I think I've got a duty to check out his story. He told me a thing or two that I don't remember being in the papers or on TV."

"Such as what?"

"Such as a scar in a delicate place on the victim."
Sharon leaned back and scooted her rump forward in
the chair. "We're not talking a trial here. Dycus Wilt's
guilty as sin of Mary Ann Blakely's murder, and as a
citizen I'd like to see him get the death penalty. As a
lawyer the best I can do for him is try to work out a
plea bargain where he gets a life sentence. Lets him
out in thirty-five years, though I don't like the idea of
having his release on my conscience. Being a lawyer's
not real fun sometimes."

"Idn supposed to be." Black studied her, his blue-
eyed gaze missing nothing. At times like this Sharon
felt that the older lawyer was looking right through
her. Finally he said, "You made your decision on
this?"

"I don't see that I've got a decision to make,"
Sharon said. "Dycus Wilt's my man, like it or not. I'm
going through the motions of investigating his story
on Delores Burnside. If I can do something with that,
I will. Otherwise, it's going to be a case of representing him in court where I'm shooting blanks. Milt Breyer's already told me they're not interested in any plea
bargains. Something on Delores Burnside might change
their minds, but . . ."

"That's another thing I don't like, you goin' up
against Milton Breyer." Black rummaged in his top
desk drawer and came up with an envelope with some
writing on the back. "Who in blazes is Matthew
Bark?"

Sharon sat up straighter. "God, he's called here?"

"Wants an appointment with me," Black said. Visible through the window a street sweeper rolled down
Jackson Street, spraying the gutter, its brush whisking
along behind.

"Don't give him one," Sharon said. "I hope I put
that matter to rest at lunch today."

"These EEOC folks don't give up easy."

"Don't I know it," Sharon said.

"Point is," Black said, "Milt Breyer's got it in for you enough as it is, over us whippin' his tail in the Midge Rathermore case. Now, if the EEOC's snoopin' around, old Milt's really going to try and put it to you."

"He tried that," Sharon said. "I kneed him, remember?"

Black looked away, obviously embarrassed. "That idn what I'm talkin' about. I mean, in the courtroom."

"I know what you mean. Look, Russ, I can take care of myself. I've been doing it for years."

Black eyed the ceiling. "I don't guess it's my place to stand in your way, if you're goin' to do this. You just be careful, you hear?"

Sharon stood. "Girl Scout's honor."

Black snapped his fingers. "Oh. Speakin' of Midge Rathermore, I got a postcard. She'll graduate from high school this year, and says she's down to a hundred and twenty pounds. Sends you her love."

"Makes me proud of her," Sharon said. "Cases like that one make it almost worth it to represent all these bad people."

"Dycus Wilt ain't no Midge Rathermore, Sharon."

Sharon walked over to the door. "I'm on my guard, boss. I'll check out Wilt's story, and then that'll be that. I'm sure there's nothing to it."

"Well, if there *is* somethin' to it," Black said, "keep quiet about it. Anything about the Burnside killin's not likely to make you popular at this thing we're goin' to tonight."

Sharon frowned. "What thing?"

"A political thing. I hate 'em. Joe Bright's throwin' an unofficial comin' out party, for Ralph Toner. I don't personally think Ralph Toner's been a very good D.A., much less toutin' him for governor. But me an' Joe Bright go way back; I don't see how I can turn him down."

"Those people don't know me from Eve," Sharon said.

"The invitation's for me an' a companion," Black said. "In case you don't remember, I got no wife no more."

"A lot of people come alone to those things."

Black pointed a finger. "I don't. Not when I got my associate to run interference for me with everybody wantin' a donation."

Sharon sighed. "Anything but a political bash, Russ."

"If I can't get out of it, you can't get out of it. Here's one o' the invitations. You be there by eight, you hear?" He held out a stiff folded card, printed in script.

Sharon leaned her shoulder against the doorjamb. "I've been asked for dates before, boss. But you take the cake. Don't give a girl much of a choice, you know?"

Sharon left for the day around three o'clock, and detoured by the Frank Crowley Criminal Courts Building on her way home. She drove into the six-story garage, parked her Volvo on the second level, and took the crosswalk, *click-clicking* in businesslike rhythm over to the courthouse, the hem of her skirt rustling around her calves. The mammoth bulk of the Lew Sterrett Justice Center—an uptown name for the main branch of the Dallas County Jail—loomed on Sharon's right, all but obliterating the horizon.

She rolled through the revolving entry to the Crowley Building, craning her neck to gaze at the ceiling five stories overhead, at escalators extending upward like Jacob's ladders. She offered a timid smile to the security guard as she dropped her purse and briefcase onto the conveyor, and passed muster through the metal detectors. Then she took the escalator to the basement, entered the records clerk's office, and used one of the computer keyboards to call up *State* v. *Raymond Burnside* on the monitor screen. Doin' my duty for Dycus Wilt, she thought, though she didn't really expect to discover a thing.

According to the computer, the Burnside Capital Murder case had gone to trial in the 427th, Judge Sandy Griffin's court, in April of 1988. God, Sharon thought, has it really been six whole years? Sandy Griffin presided over the same courtroom where Sharon and Russ Black had won an acquittal for Midge Rathermore, only last summer. Sharon searched her memory bank. Sandy had quit the D.A.'s staff to run for the bench about six months after Sharon had hired on as a prosecutor, which meant that the Burnside trial had gone on during Griffin's first year in office. Unusual as all get-out, Sharon thought, for a rookie judge to try a case in the media spotlight. Normally, with all the political posturing and competition among the older jurists, one of the old-guard judges would have simply bumped Sandy Griffin out of the way. Unusual, but nothing that would help Sharon's client. She rattled the keys and brought up the records-history screen.

Just like every death-penalty case in Sharon's memory, the case-file jackets had bounced back and forth between the appellate and trial courts like Ping-Pong balls. There'd been the usual new-trial motions and constitutional issues raised before the Texas Court of Criminal Appeals and the federal Fifth Circuit in New Orleans, all appeals denied. Currently—according to the monitor, which wasn't always up to snuff—the records lay upstairs with Sandy Griffin's clerk, where they would remain until the eleventh-hour motions that were sure to come as Raymond Burnside's execution date approached. As Sharon zeroed in on the name of Burnside's current appeals attorney, her forehead wrinkled. Hagood T. Malone.

God, Sharon thought, Motions Malone, once considered Mr. Pain-in-the-P'toot by the D.A.'s office, his constant raising of inconsequential issues stringing two-day trials out into weeks and weeks and . . .

Sharon recalled a great celebration among A.D.A.s
when Malone had announced his retirement five years
earlier. Old Motions now supplemented his Social Security, IRAs, and whatnot by handling a series of
state-paid indigent appeals cases, none of which were
ever reversed, all quietly confirmed. That Raymond
Burnside was now dependent on charity in the battle
for his life struck a chord in Sharon; she recalled hearing back when the murder had been front-page material, that Raymond was from a family of modest
means. Rumor had it that his marriage to Delores
Bright had come about only after maximum resistance
from his future in-laws. Sharon switched off the computer, hustled down the hall to the elevator, rode up
to the seventh floor, and went into Judge Griffin's
court via the side entry.

The court clerk's office was an open-bay counter
arrangement. Sharon patted the dinger to call for service. The clerk came over. She was a fortyish black
woman with permed graying hair and thick glasses.
When Sharon took a pad of request forms from the
counter and wrote down the number of the Burnside
matter, the clerk grinned. "I know that one by heart,"
she said. "*Hard Copy*, *Inside Edition*, all the tabloids
have asked for that file at one time or another. I've
been expecting more requests ever since they set the
execution date." She disappeared through a door to
the rear and returned in a few minutes, lugging four
files the thickness of New York telephone directories.
She thudded the records up on the counter, said to
Sharon, "I hope you've got a couple of weeks to kill,"
and then went on about her business.

The indictment was front and center, in the first
folder right behind the title page. Sharon read over
the grand jury finding and ruefully shook her head.
How'd they qualify this guy for capital punishment to
begin with? she thought. Texas law provided the death
penalty in specific instances: murder for hire, murder
of a law enforcement officer, murder during the com-

mission of another felony such as a rape or robbery. After hearing Dycus Wilt's story, Sharon had assumed that the rape had been the deciding factor in asking for lethal injection. The indictment, however, made no mention of any assault on Delores Burnside. Instead the prosecution had asked for and received a capital indictment based on murder committed during a burglary, to wit the residence in which Delores Burnside lived. Weak, Sharon thought. Weak, weak, weak. The couple had been separated, not divorced. Sharon would bet that the title to the house had been in Delores and Raymond's names jointly, and would further bet that Raymond had a key to the front door. How can a man burglarize his own house? she thought.

She thumbed through two more of the folders before she located the arrest warrant. Local cops had taken Raymond Burnside into custody at his rented condo at two in the morning, after the warrant had been signed at one-thirty. They had had to wake the judge up in the middle of the night to handle that one. The probable cause—a requirement in any arrest where the police haven't witnessed the felony in progress—was based on the coroner's report along with statements from two of Delores Burnside's family—one, Sharon noted, was Joseph Bright himself—that Raymond Burnside had threatened his wife, over and over, ever since the couple had separated. Sharon thought the grounds for the warrant a bit on the shaky side, but that wasn't unusual where the police wanted to pick someone up for a grilling session. In fact, Sandy Griffin, the trial judge, hadn't signed the warrant at all. The document bore the signature of Judge Malcolm Edge, who Sharon knew to be one of Joseph Bright's political cronies. Sandy Griffin was a bang-up lawyer as well as a fair jurist, and Sharon doubted that Sandy would have issued the warrant to begin with due to lack of probable cause. Sharon lifted the four-page warrant out of the folder and turned her attention to the attachments, barely glancing at the witness statements and moving on to the medical examiner's report.

Dr. Willem Foster had done the autopsy in person. Big Potatoes with a capital *P*, Sharon thought, the duly elected chief medical examiner of Dallas County, also another political-hack buddy of Joseph Bright's. Foster hadn't had much trouble in coming to the conclusion that someone had murdered Delores. One of the stab wounds had penetrated her voice box from the front and nicked her spinal column. Her left breast had been hanging from a shred of skin. The knife had penetrated her brain through her right eye socket. Fourteen wounds in all, each laid out in grisly detail. Sharon swallowed hard, skipped the rest of the carnage, and went on to the balance of the text.

The M.E. had noted vaginal bruising. Sharon wondered again why the prosecutors hadn't hung their hats on the rape instead of the shaky burglary charge when asking for the death penalty, especially when they'd had the medical honcho's report to back them up. Didn't make any sense at all. She read the doctor's description of the corpse's lower body area. Delores Burnside had had a butterfly tattooed on her fanny. Shades of Cher, Sharon thought. Come to think about it, why hadn't Dycus Wilt noticed that? If he'd noticed a scar, he should have . . . Sharon's throat tightened as she read on.

"Lumbar region. Vertical scar noted, consistent with pilonidal cyst surgery, extending downward from 3 cm to the right of the spinal column."

Sharon blinked.

She read over the passage again, her lips moving silently.

Vertical scar, consistent with pilonidal cyst surgery.

Bitch had a scar on her ass. Sharon pictured Dycus Wilt, and gently closed her eyes.

She used her finger to mark her place and closed the file. She patted the dinger. When the clerk came over, Sharon said, "I need to make copies. Can I . . ."

"Dollar a page if I do it, Miss Hays. Do it yourself for a quarter a throw."

Sharon reached for her purse. "I'll need change. Listen, how late are you guys open? This may take awhile."

4

———✦———

Sharon stood in pantyhose and bra in front of her closet, and jammed the tip of her tongue into one corner of her mouth. Political bash, huh? She stuck out her lower lip and blew upward through her bangs. To hell with it. If she was going to have a miserable time, at least she was going to look good. She plowed into the closet, rasped the hangers containing the conservative courtroom suits to the front, and reached in back for something a tad on the slinky side.

She'd bought the black sequined strapless cocktail number the previous spring, with the idea of seducing a lawyer named Jason Ray. Ray was a litigation specialist with a white-collar firm, and spent more time in the weight room than in the courtroom. He had the shoulders and pecs of a muscle mag ad, but, it had turned out, drank with even more enthusiasm than he practiced law or pumped iron. Sharon had ended the total dud of an evening sitting on the curb as she cradled the poster boy's head in her lap, and he'd shown his appreciation by puking on her. All she'd seduced was one monster of a cleaning bill, and ever since then had stuck out her tongue every time the Lord & Taylor statement arrived in the mail. By the time the revolving charge was less than the national debt, Melanie would be ready for college. Sharon wiggled into the dress, stepped into black spike heels, and surveyed herself in the mirror. Not half bad. Russ would be aghast. Serve him right for forcing her to come to the damned thing. She draped the matching waist-length jacket over her arm as she sashayed down the steps into the breakfast room.

Melanie sat at the table finishing off her supper. Her eyes grew big and round. "Wow, Mom," she said. "Who are you trying to catch?"

Warmth flooded Sharon's cheeks. She shrugged quickly into her jacket. "Are you about ready to go?"

Melanie forked a bite of steamed broccoli into her mouth. "I'll need my shoes." She wore knee-length white shorts and a Collective Soul T-shirt. Sharon monitored Melanie's music-listening habits with a vengeance, and thought Collective Soul's "Shine" one of the better jumpin' numbers she'd heard in many moons. Any T-shirts bearing images of Ozzy Osborne, musicians of that stripe, went quickly into the garbage.

Sharon checked the clock in the living room, on the VCR. "Mrs. Winston's expecting you at seven."

"Sheila won't care if we're late."

Sharon felt a surge of irritation. Melanie would be thirteen in a couple of months, and the teenage years which Sharon had dreaded ever since giving birth were fast upon her. "Mrs. Winston," Sharon said firmly.

"Sheila doesn't care if I call her that."

Sharon smoothed her dress. "She's too polite to complain, is what you mean. She's Mrs. Winston, Melanie. And I'd better not hear you addressing her as anything else."

Melanie had a bite of green beans and a sip of water. A year ago Sharon would have had to tie Melanie in a chair and force-feed the vegetable diet, but now Melanie was so figure-conscious that she wrinkled her nose at Big Mac TV ads. Her long supple legs and budding small breasts were inherited from her mother. If the heredity extended to the menstrual cycle, her periods would begin in less than a year, and Melanie would have painful cramps. Sharon dreaded the prospect of the trashed-out room, the wastebaskets filled to overflowing with used Tampax, but was determined to love her daughter through adolescence just as she had through the cute-cuddly years. Give me strength, Sharon thought. "Oh, be cool, Mom," Melanie said.

Sharon inhaled through her nose. "I *am* cool. And she's Mrs. Winston. Now, go get your shoes and let's go."

As Melanie flounced insolently to her room, Sharon sat down on her old Spanish-style sofa. She picked up the phone and punched the dial buttons to reverse the call forwarding. Melanie would have already set the system to send her calls on over to Sheila Winston's number. Sheila had plenty to do, thank you, without fielding an endless stream of giggly little boys on the phone, asking for Melanie, and Sharon simply wasn't in any mood to argue with her daughter about the matter. Sharon had given up confronting Melanie over certain issues, and Melanie could jolly well spend the evening at Sheila's wondering if her boyfriends had all deserted her.

Melanie came back in wearing canvas Keds. "Can me and Trish watch *Minions of Justice* tonight?" she said.

"Trish and I. And you know you can't," Sharon said. "So why ask?"

"You just don't want me to get to watch my dad."

Sharon's jaws clenched. "Of course you can watch your father, dear. In fact, I've already got the VCR programmed to record his show. And after I've edited all the nudity out, you can watch him to your heart's content as long as he's got his clothes on."

"You can't really see anything," Melanie said.

"You can see enough. Now, get in the car."

Melanie's bottom gave one final haughty twitch as she went out the front. Down with puberty, Sharon thought. She retreated to her bedroom for her black sequined handbag, carefully turned off all the lights, then went to the back door and let Commander inside. The shepherd ran in pell-mell, raised up on hindquarters, and tried to lick Sharon's face. She battled his paws to keep them off of her dress, and scratched

Commander behind the ears. The scar from Bradford Brie's bullet, which had nearly killed him, was a knot of gristle on his chest, and Sharon suspected that the slug rubbing his hipbone caused the shepherd's occasional unprovoked whimper. Even though the danger was only a memory, Sharon couldn't bring herself to leave the dog alone in the yard. As she went out the front door, Commander lay contentedly in front of the fireplace with his tail beating a tattoo on the carpet.

Sharon turned on the ignition, then jumped and practically banged her head on the ceiling as hard-rock guitars blared from the speakers. "Cow, Melanie," Sharon said, then turned the volume down and adjusted the dial to Country 96.3. Merle Haggard's twangy baritone cut in instantly. "Twinkle, Twinkle, Lucky Star."

"*Mah*-um," Melanie squealied. "Not that country stuff. The Edge is rad."

"Well, it can be rad someplace else. I like the old country standards, Melanie. Because I'm old, okay? Now, humor me."

Sharon backed out of her drive, and had a twinge of conscience as she glanced at the Breedloves' house across the street. The Breedloves had lived over there since Sharon had been seven years old, and since she'd inherited her own parents' house when her dad had passed away, Sharon had done her best to be a good and interested neighbor. Mr. Breedlove had gone in for gall bladder surgery two days ago, and Sharon had been so busy she hadn't had time to inquire about his condition. She made a firm resolve to remedy her neglect the first thing in the morning, and if visiting with Mrs. Breedlove made her late to the office, well, that was just tough.

Sharon dropped the lever into DRIVE, and steered the Volvo down the street toward Sheila Winston's. Sheila lived in a sixty-year-old redbrick with a porch swing and freshly painted eaves, just a block and a half away. Merle Haggard crooned on.

Melanie stiffened and stared out the window. "Nerd-oh, bore-oh."

Sharon increased the volume, and raised her voice to sing along with Merle.

Trish Winston peered around her mother to say, "Come on, Melanie, I've got some new tapes. Hi, Sharon."

As Melanie tried to bolt around Sheila for the inner reaches of the Winston house, Sheila said sternly, "She's Miss Hays, Trish, and I'm tired of telling you that."

Sharon stood on the front porch with her feet together, and didn't say anything.

"Oh, be cool, Mom," Trish said. "Sharon doesn't mind." She had her mother's flawless milk-chocolate complexion and cute button nose. In the past year she'd matured from a spindly colt into a young lady with wide shoulders like Sheila's. At going on thirteen, Trish could now pass for sixteen or seventeen and had far outstripped Melanie in the maturity department. Of late Sheila had begun to complain about the older boys coming around.

"Well, *I* mind," Sheila said. "And she's just too polite to say anything."

Melanie paused in the entry. Trish looked to Sharon as if for confirmation. Sharon finally said, "I think Miss Hays would be better, Trish."

Trish's face screwed up in disappointment. As she and Melanie took off for the back of the house, Sheila said to Sharon, "Jesus Christ, I can't wait for school to start."

"One more week," Sharon said. "Look, I'll pick her up by eight in the morning."

"Don't bother. Let them sleep in. With Melanie around tomorrow to occupy Trish's time, I might get some peace around here." Sheila was dressed in jeans and a man's white shirt with the tail out. She had direct, dark eyes and wore pale pink lipstick. Sharon barely noticed that Sheila was black; as mid-thirties single moms, the two women shared a bond that went far beyond race.

"I might not be home from the office until around six," Sharon said.

"No sweat. She'll be fine."

Sharon hesitated, then said, "Melanie will try to watch *Minions of Justice* if you aren't careful."

"I've got the TV isolated so they can't get to it without going through me," Sheila said, "and I'll defend my station to the death. What do you hear from old Rob?"

"No messages. No checks, either. I suspect around Christmas he'll try to catch up on the payments, so he can try and get Melanie some for the holidays. I'd as soon he'd keep his money."

"Just thank the stars you never married the man. This way he doesn't have the legal rights that Trish's father does." Sheila let it go at that. In spite of what her inner feelings might be, Sheila never bad-mouthed her ex to anyone.

"Rob and I never marrying saved a lot in attorney fees," Sharon said.

"Amen. You go on and have yourself a bully old time." Sheila started to close the door.

"How's your practice, Sheila?" Sharon said.

Sheila stood with the door ajar a crack. "I've got enough patients to keep me busy. No severe nutcases at present. Why?"

"I've got a client I may want you to take a look at. It's a court appointment, so I'll have to get the psychiatrist fee approved by the county."

"I probably wouldn't be much help with Dycus Wilt, Sharon."

Sharon's eyebrows lifted. "How did you know?"

"You made the six o'clock news. They say you got into it with the judge over whether the guy had a right to pick his lawyer. Tried to fire yourself and wound up getting hired." Sheila's gaze flicked down. "Without seeing your man, I can tell you that guys like that are emotionally disturbed. Crazy as loons, but they do know right from wrong. I'd be stealing the expert witness fee. My testimony would do you more harm than good."

"I'm more interested in whether he's telling the truth about another matter," Sharon said. "Something we may use for plea-bargain ammo."

"Why don't you try the lie detector route?"

"Because it's inadmissible, and the county's already let me know they don't want to make a deal with the guy. A psychiatrist's report might change their minds."

Sheila seemed deep in thought. Finally she said, "I'm available. It's what I do."

"Thanks, Sheila. As soon as I get the expenditure approved, I'll be back to you on it."

"Great," Sheila said. She looked Sharon over head to toe. "Some glad rags, kid. If you're trolling for men, you've sure got it in gear."

5

Sharon found Senator Joseph Bright's giant, far–North Dallas Tudor-style home, and then considered hiding her Volvo behind a bush. BMWs, Bentleys, and Jags lined the curbs and the wide circular drive in front, and made even Russ Black's Buick Park Avenue look shabby and secondhand. Russ had parked a quarter block from the house, and Sharon hesitated for a moment to eye-measure the distance between the Buick's bumper and the Mark VII behind. She decided there wasn't room to squeeze the Volvo in, so continued up the street to wedge in between a green Porsche and a white Mercedes. As she got out, locked the car, and stepped onto the sidewalk, a couple passed by. Both were in their sixties, the man wearing a tux and the woman dressed in a floor-length evening gown, and both threw sidelong glances at the Volvo. Sharon smiled hello, looked down her nose at the Volvo as if she'd never seen the car before, and followed the couple to the corner and up the drive.

The hundred feet or so from the street to the house was quite a climb, past a swatch of perfectly mowed and clipped lawn and a fountain complete with sculptured cherubs. The cherubs held seashells from which water spewed. By the time she reached the marble-tiled porch, Sharon's leg muscles were crampy and the older couple wheezed like cardiac patients. The woman said breathlessly to her companion, "My goodness." Sharon pressed a button. From inside the house, chimes *bong-bong*-ed. Sharon stood first on one foot and then the other. By the time the massive oak door swung open, the couple's breathing had returned practically to normal.

A butler complete with tie and tails stood aside, and Sharon followed the couple into an entry parlor the size of Sharon's living room. A woman wearing necklaces like Tiffany's commercials greeted the couple with separate hugs. "Daphne. Herb. So glad you could . . ." She paused and looked at Sharon. "And this is . . . ?" The couple regarded Sharon with open curiosity.

"Sharon Hays," Sharon said quickly. "I'm to meet Russell Black here." She started to dig in her handbag for her invitation, then changed her mind.

The hostess played with a diamond on her wrist the size of a marble. She had snow-white coiffured hair and wore a yellow evening gown with folds below her breastbone. She extended her hand. "Dorothy Bright. And Russ is your . . . ?"

This woman has a question for every occasion, Sharon thought. "Boss," she said. "I'm his associate."

"I . . . see." Dorothy Bright looked down, then back up. "You'll find Russ in back with the other guests. Briggs will take your jacket." She turned her back on Sharon and spoke to the couple. "Come on, I'll show you to the bar." She clasped the man's arm in her right hand and the woman's arm in her left, and escorted them away.

Is that rude, or what? Sharon thought. She watched Mrs. Bright's ample retreating backside, and mentally wrinkled her nose. Sharon felt like turning on her heel and going home. The butler stood expectantly by. She shrugged out of her jacket and gave the wrap to the butler, and headed for the rear of the house on her own. On the way she passed an oil painting of Joseph Bright himself, behind his table on the Senate floor with Ted Kennedy and Phil Gramm in the background. Bright was a square-faced, jut-jawed man with dark curly receding hair. In the painting he was eyes-front, wearing his best We-the-People expression. A rough oak frame surrounded the picture. Sharon wondered if she should bow to the east as she entered a den that was seventy feet long, minimum.

The den was two stories high, surrounded by upper-level balconies. A parlor combo consisting of a violin, a viola, a bass, and an incredibly skinny man on a grand piano played the theme from *Picnic* at one end of the room. On the opposite end from the music, two red-jacketed Hispanics free-poured, mixed martinis in chrome shakers, and whipped pink something-or-others in electric blenders. The den was wall-to-wall tuxes and evening gowns, men and women chatting in groups, pairs and threesomes, sipping from goblets, swirling ice around in stubby rock glasses. The state rep from the Oak Cliff district, a light-complexioned black man with thick glasses, talked animatedly to a woman with blued-white hair. Sharon did a double take as her gaze rested on the woman. Why, it's old Congresswoman What's-Her-Name, Sharon thought, currently under indictment in her own home district but still the odds-on favorite to sweep the primary. Sharon's nerves fluttered slightly as she crossed the room in the direction of the bar. A dishwater-blond man eyed her openly as she passed. The man's female companion looked at Sharon as well, and yanked testily on her escort's arm. Sharon reached the bar, ordered a Tanqueray on the rocks, and sipped her drink as she looked around. All at once she spotted Russ.

Black wasn't happy. He looked as if his tux was strangling him, and his forehead bunched as he argued with Senator Joseph Bright and another man. As Sharon watched, Bright said something nasty and punctuated the remark by punching Russ's breastbone with a stiffened forefinger. Russ brushed the finger aside and said something back. Now the other man butted in, moving in close to say something to Russ as well. The third guy was tall and slim, with dark razored hair and the bearing of a talk-show host. Sharon's jaw slacked.

Criminy, the third man had lost so much weight she hadn't recognized him. Ralph Toner, her ex-guru at the D.A.'s office and currently bucking for governor. Toner, in fact, was what this gathering was all about. Sharon weaved her way through the crowd and yanked on Russ's sleeve. "Hi, boss," she said. "Fancy meeting you here."

Black's scowl relaxed as he turned to her. He started as he looked her cocktail dress over, then said to the other men, "Here she is, Ralph, in case you'd like to repeat that. Sharon Hays, my associate, meet two scamps. That's Joe Bright and that's Ralph Toner. Look close and see if you remember the young lady, Ralph. Sharon used to work for you."

Toner didn't show a hint of recognition, but said tersely, "Miss Hays." He'd shaved his pencil mustache since resigning as D.A., which didn't surprise Sharon at all. His consultants would know that a clean-shaven man makes a better impression with the voters, even if Toner didn't get the picture. That he didn't remember her wasn't surprising, either; when she'd been on his staff, Sharon had always suspected that Toner thought she was one of the secretaries. He'd kept his distance from the day-to-day activities in the office, and before conducting an interview over one of his high-profile cases had depended on his assistants to fill him in.

Sharon smiled. "Glad to see you again, Mr. Toner." Then she nodded to the senator. "Senator Bright. I'm awed by your presence, sir."

Bright said tersely, "I feel like I'm seeing a rerun of the six o'clock news." Then he looked away from her and said to Toner, "Come on, Ralph, let's have a refresher." He and Tone turned their backs and moved away toward the bar.

A smoldering anger built in Sharon as she watched the two politicos leave. She said to Black, "The dress might not be especially modest, Russ, but it's appropriate attire. Did I forget to use deodorant or something?"

Black was watching the politicians' retreat as well. "I want to sleep on this, girl," he said. "I don't believe in makin' decisions when somebody's got me in an uproar."

Sharon would have resented most men calling her "girl." Black was from the old school, however, and she took most of what he said with a grain of salt, anyway. She said, "Do I get a clue what that was all about?"

Black held a tall glass of what Sharon thought was plain soda. Russ wasn't a whiskey drinker. He sipped. "They both jumped right in the middle of me about you representin' Dycus Wilt. Seems Milt Breyer's already been on the hotline to 'em about your wantin' to use the Delores Burnside murder as plea-bargain material. I'm tryin' not to be mad at Joe Bright. The man lost his daughter, but still . . ."

Speak of the devil, Sharon thought, as she caught sight of Milton Breyer on the far side of the room. The prosecutor was all smiles, talking to a group of women, likely tooting his horn for the upcoming judge's race. She said to Russ Black, "I'm confused, boss. It looks to me like Mr. Bright would want the right man convicted."

Black shook his head. "It's a can o' worms, Sharon. He wants it all over. Anybody tryin' to reopen that case, that'd bring it all back to haunt the man."

Sharon recalled Mrs. Bright's icy reception, and began to understand. "Okay for Senator Bright," Sharon said. "But what's Mr. Toner's interest?"

Black's eyebrows moved closer together. "You don't remember that case?"

"It happened my first year with the D.A.," Sharon said. "I was prosecuting misdemeanors then, and what I knew about the Delores Burnside case was strictly from the newspapers and television."

"It's what launched Ralph Toner's political career," Black said. "He was first assistant then, an' prosecutin' that case put him in the spotlight. He ran for D.A. the next term, and Joe Bright's backin' was the main thing that got him elected. Now Bright's the main man pushin' Ralph for governor. Anything openin' that case, showin' maybe that he prosecuted the wrong man, that could hurt him. Especially if his opponent gets wind of it."

"I don't think that's a good reason to execute a man who didn't do it, Russ."

"You're talkin' what's right, Sharon. Those guys're talkin' politics. It's two different things."

Sharon bit her lower lip, then had a sip of gin. The alcohol burned going down. "Maybe you'd enjoy the party more if I just went home."

"Not on your life," Black said. "No way am I givin' them the satisfaction of thinkin' they made me send you off. You just mingle and keep on grinnin'. Anybody asks you anything about Dycus Wilt, you start talkin' about the baseball scores. Now I see a guy over there I need a set-to with."

Sharon nodded, and Black started to move away through the crowd. He halted and returned to her. "An' you be real careful in dealin' with Dycus Wilt. Likely he's lyin', tryin' to get himself off the hook. Chances are you won't find a thing to back your man up."

Sharon pictured the copies she'd made of the Burnside case file, and particularly the M.E.'s report on the victim. She hesitated, licked her lips, then said, "I've already found something to back him up, Russ. I'll show you tomorrow. I don't want to do anything more to mess up your evening right now, okay?"

The heavy woman told Sharon, "Everybody that's anybody will be there. Lauren Hutton's coming." She sipped a martini from a stemmed glass.

Sharon wondered if three Tanquerays on the rocks

had gotten her just a bit snockered. Her expression of interest felt frozen on her face. She opened her mouth to say something, hoping she wouldn't come across as the ultimate dumb bunny—Sharon wasn't sure at this point whether Lauren Hutton was the "Poor Little Rich Girl," or the actress who'd married Bogart—when the emaciated woman on her left came to the rescue, saying, "Are you sure of that, Dottie?"

"Of course, I'm sure," the heavy woman said. "I'm the chair." Sharon thought the woman looked more like an ottoman than a chair. She wore a lavender gown, tented over enormous breasts and hanging straight down to the floor. Sharon sipped more Tanqueray and repressed a giggle.

The emaciated woman's gown was pink. "Every year it's someone. Last year it was Donald Sutherland, and I wore my feet out parading around looking for him, but no Donald. My point is, I give to the Crystal Charity Ball regardless, and I think all the rumors of celebrities attending are unnecessary. Gets everyone in an uproar, usually over nothing."

Sharon downed the last of her Tanqueray and looked toward the bar. Midway through the crowd, Russ Black was jaw to jaw with Judge Arnold Shiver, likely giving Shiver what-for over appointing Sharon on the Dycus Wilt case. One conversation, Sharon thought, that I'd just as soon not hear.

The heavy woman looked down her nose. "Lauren Hutton, I say. I have confirmation from her press agent."

"I'll believe it when I see it," the emaciated woman said. "Next they'll be saying Kirk Douglas."

"Can you ladies excuse me," Sharon said. "I have to—"

"No, Lauren Hutton." The heavy woman breathed through her nose. "Kirk wasn't available."

The emaciated woman drew herself up to full indignant height. "I'll just bet he wasn't. And neither was his son Michael, since you're not acquainted with either."

"I'll have you know—" the heavy woman said.

"Excuse me," Sharon said, and made tracks. She wormed her way in between a man with a cigarette holder and a woman with permed curls, sidestepped a waiter carrying a tray of champagne glasses, circled around Russ and Judge Shiver with her head down, and spotted a corridor in between a black man and a Hispanic guy. She'd made it halfway to the bar when a strong male hand reached out and plucked her glass away. Sharon halted and turned, and looked into deep-set brown eyes.

The eyes held a mildly inquisitive expression. The brows were full and smooth. The face had prominent cheekbones with a nice set of dimples. The chin was square, the neck muscles firm, the shoulders broad. The mouth was curved slightly in an expression of open appraisal.

"Let me get that for you," he said. He sniffed her drink. "Gin, right?"

But, wow, Sharon thought.

His chin tilted. "Is it gin, or . . . ?"

Sharon blinked. "Tanqueray."

"Perfect. I didn't take you for the Beefeater type."

He laughed, and she laughed with him. Little tremors ran up the insides of her legs.

He took her arm. "You look like a lady in need of having some interference run. Come on." He led her toward the bar, his grip firm without being harsh, his bearing easy. She risked a glance downward at his third finger, left hand. No ring, though that didn't mean a helluva lot. No telltale mark around the finger, either, which was even better.

They arrived at the bar. He ordered for her, and chipped in a request for Chivas and water. The bartender uncapped a bottle and got busy. The brown-eyed stranger said to Sharon, "You also look like a lady in need of some boredom relief. I thought for a minute that the old girls were going to hold you captive."

Sharon peered through the crowd to where the emaciated woman now looked down her nose at the heavy woman, a pretty good trick since the heavy woman was half-a-head the taller of the two. Sharon smiled and looked back at the man.

"If you're wondering whether I've been watching you," he said, "I'll plead guilty. I hope you don't mind."

She continued to grin, hoping that she didn't look like a moron, and tried to think of something really in and with-it to say. She finally managed, "No, I don't mind." And accompanied the statement with a lowering of her lashes, praying that her expression was demure instead of looking as if there was something in her eye. Ingrid Bergman you ain't, kid, Sharon thought.

The bartender set their drinks on the counter, and the man dropped a couple of dollars into the tip jar. He handed hers over, then raised his glass in a toast. "Richard Branson," he said.

She touched his glass with her own. "Sharon Hays," she said, and thought, Now that's a zippy comeback. Her cheeks flushed a bit. Richard Branson oozed sophistication. Sharon wondered if a couple of more drinks might untie the knots in her tongue.

"Are you here with someone?" he said. His expression was as direct and to the point as was his question.

"My . . . boss," Sharon said.

One brown eye widened slightly. "He's just your boss?"

"Just. He's the guy over there who looks like the Sheriff of Last Ditch Gulch, arguing with the white-haired guy."

Branson's gaze followed her direction. He said, "Oh, Judge Shiver? You work for Russell Black, then."

She felt surprise. "You're a lawyer?"

"Of sorts. I'm with Stratford, Field."

Oh, classy, Sharon thought. As in Stratford, Field, Ruston, Howard, and Long, offices in Dallas, Washington, and points wherever, the biggest and oldest firm in town, so well-known that mention of the first two partners' names was sufficient everywhere but in a gathering of ninnies. "I'm impressed," Sharon said.

"Don't be. I'm so far down on the totem pole I can't see the head Indian's nose. I'm the one impressed. Russell Black's a living legend." He sipped, and regarded her over the rim of his glass.

"You know Russ?"

"Only from afar. I've got a confession to make. Wills and title searches bore me to death. Criminal law's my passion, but I didn't have the nerve to go it on my own straight out of law school. Russ Black have other people besides you?"

Sharon felt a slight edge of resentment. She'd never considered herself to be anyone's "person," not even when she'd been an assistant D.A., and Russ had always made her feel more like a cog in the machinery than someone's flunky. Richard Branson smelled of Bay Rum. Sharon's resentment passed in a hurry. "Just him and yours truly," she said.

"He a hard guy to work for? In the courtroom he's so laid-back, but I've always figured he kept his secretaries running their legs off."

The edge of resentment returned and smoldered into anger. "I wouldn't know about that," Sharon said. "I'm a lawyer, too."

He looked at her with respect. "Oops. Hey, I didn't mean to put you off."

"You didn't. And don't worry about it." Sharon liked it that his apology seemed genuine. And that his look was that of a man gazing on a woman. The attention was something she'd missed terribly, no Milton Breyer wolfishness in the grin, just appreciation and more than a little interest. "You do campaigning for Joseph Bright?" she said.

"Well, not personally. I'm here under sort of a summons."

"Me, too. What, one of your honcho partners sent you?" Sharon was suddenly relaxed, partly from the Tanquerays, more because of this hunk of a man. She wondered if her skin was glowing.

He grinned. "Well, now that you mention it . . ."

Sharon gave a throaty laugh. "My boss's orders were, 'If I can't get out of it, my associate *damn* sure can't.' "

"Ellis Ruston gives a lot to the Bright campaigns," Branson said. "Russell Black's a donator, too, I guess."

Ellis Ruston, though his name was third down the list at Stratford, Field, was the Number One Honcho of the bunch. Sharon said, "Oh, Russ doesn't donate to anybody. Most of the big shots around town are old buddyroos of his, and they cater to him a lot more than he does to them. Russ is that kind of guy. What you see is what you get, and if you don't like it you can take a hike."

"I've heard that," Branson said. He didn't try to hide his appraisal of her, his expression saying that he liked what he say. Sharon blushed. He said, "How about you? What's your political leaning?"

Sharon shrugged bare shoulders. "I defend bad guys, but I don't necessarily root for them. I feel the same way about politicians. They're okay, as long as they don't try to drag me in on their rat-killing."

He toasted her again. "Well said. Which makes us in sync. Functions like this one bore you, right?"

"To tears," Sharon said.

His dimples deepened as he smiled, his eyes narrowing slightly in merriment. "So we're just a couple of boreds."

Sharon felt warm inside. "So it would seem."

"And when people are bored," he said, sipping and winking, "is when they need a change in scenery."

It seemed to Sharon that the party guests were suddenly in background shadow, with a spotlight trained on this broad-shouldered guy whose upper arm was now firmly against her own. "I've heard that helps sometimes," she said.

"Such as maybe a piano bar I know," Branson said. "Not too many of those around anymore. This place has a view that's, hey, something else."

Sharon had a twinge of uncertainty, swept aside immediately by pure excitement. God, she thought, how long has it been? She looked over to where Russ continued to stand nose to nose with Judge Shiver. Your cocounsel's about to become indisposed, old boss, Sharon thought. She looked up at Branson and wrinkled her nose. "We'd need to go in separate cars," Sharon said. "And leave a few minutes apart, to keep some tongues I know of from wagging. But I think we could work something out, don't you?"

Sharon toyed with her glass, and hummed along with the pianist's rendition of "Moonlight in Vermont." She sat close to Richard Branson in a booth, their arms intertwined, his left, her right, his solid body towering over her and making her feel very small. God, she thought, I'm five foot nine. He had big hands with prominent knuckles.

"Here's a 'small world' story for you," Branson said. "You wouldn't believe where I saw this guy the first time." His voice was deep, an educated manner of speaking blended with the faintest of Texas twangs.

Sharon's gaze was out the window, at rows of lights twinkling thirty stories below, the parade of nighttime traffic on LBJ Freeway, the glistening outlines of skyline buildings. Two more Tanquerays had warmed her insides and given her an eerie feeling, as if she were floating on a cloud above the city. "Hmm?" she said.

"This pianist," Branson said, gesturing toward the dais where a thin man in tie and tails tickled the ivories. "You don't notice his accent when he's singing, do you?"

"I'm not good on accents," Sharon said. "I guess New York sometimes, when it's really Chicago."

"You'd catch his accent," Branson said, "within a few miles anyway. The first time I heard him was in London."

Sharon looked over at Branson, the strong jaw and sculptured chin in profile angle against a backdrop of pinpoint freeway lights.

"We used to go in weekends when I was at Oxford, and he was playing a hotel in the northeast quad. Then one night shortly after I returned to Texas, some people I know . . . we came in here strictly by accident and there the guy was. I waited around after his performance to verify that he and the guy I'd seen in London were one and the same. And he was." Branson lifted his glass toward the pianist, who smiled acknowledgment without missing a beat, ending "Moonlight in Vermont" and going directly into "I Left My Heart in San Francisco."

One of Sharon's cheeks tightened. "Oxford? Don't tell me you were a Rhodes."

"It's not near as big a deal as they make it sound. I made good undergraduate grades, mainly because I was scared to death of flunking out. Then I got lucky."

"God, a Rhodes. I'm in awe."

He moved a bit in the booth, his ribs nestling close to her. "That makes two of us."

"I was a roads, r-o-a-d-s," Sharon said. "Dallas to New York to Austin and then to Dallas again."

"You went to school in Manhattan?" He bent his head in interest.

"School of hard knocks," Sharon said. "I did undergrad at grand old University of Texas at Dallas, majored in drama. Tried acting school and off-Broadway for a little over a year. When my daughter was born up there, I decided I had to do something other than be a starving artist, so I went to Austin to law school. Many bumps and grinds later, here I am."

"You have a daughter? You were married, then."

She hesitated. It was a task for Sharon and always had been, explaining Melanie to people without sounding dramatic and just a bit whiny. Finally she said simply, "No."

He showed surprise for an instant, then shrugged matter-of-factly. "Sounds like a good time to change the subject."

"Up to you. There are things about me, hey, if I'm going to get to know somebody, they're going to find out sooner or later. I'll tell you up front, I don't make apologies. So if you want to know . . ." Sharon had made a long-ago pact with herself not to hide the truth, thus preventing any shock scenes later on. She hoped that Branson would want to know. If he didn't, the beginnings of a neat relationship might drift out of the window.

"I'm mesmerized," he said. "And I'm flattered you'd share it."

Sharon smiled at her glass. She looked up at him. "I lived with a guy, an actor. We parted company, and a short time after that I found out I was pregnant. Right in the middle of a performance, in fact, the doctor called me backstage. I did a lot of soul-searching over abortion, but no way could I go through with that. Best choice I ever made. My little girl's my life." She jiggled her foot under the table.

"As she should be," Branson said. "Hey, you want to dance?"

Sharon was thrilled. A gushing of sympathy would have been a total turnoff to her, a soul-searching even worse. *Yeah, okay, you've told me, so do you want to dance?* Sharon looked out at the empty floor. "You think we can find room?"

He slid out of the booth and extended his hand. "Not one scream if I step on your toes. Not even a whimper, understand?"

She gripped his hand and slid over. "It's been awhile. I don't know how many left feet I've got." And felt instantly uncool, saying that instead of flow-

ing confidently into his arms. God, she thought, talking
like one of the ladies from the retirement home.

He pulled her up and led her out, paused and nodded to the pianist, then drew her smoothly to him.
Her cheek touched his shoulder, muscle over solid
bone, the smell of Bay Rum mixed with the man scent
of him. The pianist rolled smoothly into "People."
Sharon moved in response to the pressure of his hand
in the small of her back. More quivers and shivers
paraded up and down her body. I wish he'd squeeze
my bottom, she thought, then felt instantly wicked;
then the wicked feeling went away as she wished
even harder.

He said into her ear, "I think something's happening here."

She didn't answer, but snuggled closer.

"Hey, if I have a feeling," he said, "I think I should
say so."

She backed off and looked up at him, then moved
in close, released his hand, and put both arms around
him. He kissed her softly on the cheek, then her lips
were to his, their mouths moving sensuously, their
tongues meeting and probing. Sharon ached for him,
standing here in public, making a spectacle of herself
and not giving a damn what anyone might think of
it. Very unprofessional and unreserved, old girl, she
allowed herself to think as she pressed against him
even harder.

He placed his cheek next to hers and said huskily,
"My apartment's not far."

She softly closed her eyes. Nothing corny, nothing
about coming by to hear his latest tapes or to see his
new furniture, just an open invitation with nothing left
to the imagination.

She looked up at him. "I don't think that's a good
idea," she said.

She bit her lower lip as he entered her, and tasted
salty blood. His first thrust was deep, hurting her,

making her cry out, making her think, oh, God it . . .
make it hurt, oh God, please, harder, harder . . . A
whimper escaped her throat as she clung to him with
her legs, squeezing with her thighs, her bottom pumping on satin sheets, her mouth now against his bare
chest and making animal sounds. He pinned her hands
with his and rose up, towering over her, his lower
torso working, his pelvis pushing forward, his member
throbbing inside of her. *More,* Sharon thought, oh,
more, more, more, please don't ever . . .

"Christ," he whimpered.

"Oh, God," she screamed.

6

Sharon didn't get home until seven-thirty in the morning. She let Commander out into the yard—after first apologizing to the dog for neglecting him all night, then checking her carpets for any telltale wet spots—hustled through her shower, blew her hair dry with one hand while brushing her teeth with the other, literally dived into a pale green business dress, and was in the Volvo backing out of the drive by a quarter past eight. As she dropped the shift lever into the DRIVE position, she glanced across the street at the Breedlove home. God, she thought, I could kick myself. She whipped into the Breedlove driveway, cut the engine, and walked at a fast clip up the sidewalk toward the front door. A sprinkler threw glistening droplets among Mrs. Breedlove's rosebushes. Though Sharon doubted if she'd had a total of three hours' sleep, she was fresh as new kitty litter and there was a spring in her step. Amazing what multiple orgasms will do for a girl, Sharon thought.

Mrs. Breedlove answered her doorbell in less than a minute, frowning at Sharon through a crack the width of her chain lock, then closed her door, slid the latch, and opened up wide. Mrs. Breedlove was wearing a quilted flowered housecoat and her snow-white hair was hidden under a bandanna.

"I feel about an inch high," Sharon said, "because I haven't been by since Mr. Breedlove's operation. How is he?"

Mrs. Breedlove eyed Sharon as if wondering whatever happened to the little girl who used to come by selling fund-raiser cookies. I'll always be a child to her, Sharon thought. Mrs. Breedlove said, "He's fine. I don't know about the nurses, though, havin' to put up with his complainin' and yellin' to come home. I think he'll be out tomorrow."

"I'll send over a pot of chicken stew," Sharon said, then said more hesitantly, "Mother's old recipe. I suppose he can eat that, can't he?"

"Chicken's on the diet, just nothing fatty. No ice cream or pies, which is likely to cause an argument between us." Mrs. Breedlove peered around Sharon, across the street. "You an' your caller make connections?"

Sharon turned and followed the older woman's gaze, toward her own front porch. "My . . . ?"

"A young man drove up right around eight o'clock. Spent a lot of time on your porch, ringin' the bell."

Sharon frowned, then shrugged. "I wasn't home at eight. Must have been a salesman."

Mrs. Breedlove shook her head. "Dressed up too much for that. Nice suit, drivin' a Cadillac. Went around to the side of your house when no one answered, but I guess your dog scared him away. I almost wrote the license number down. Might should've."

"No matter. If it's anything important he'll come back." Sharon looked at her watch. "I've got to run to the office, Mrs. Breedlove. Chicken stew. Tomorrow. And tell Mr. Breedlove I'm thinking about him." She turned and started away down the sidewalk.

Mrs. Breedlove called out after her, "You sure you and that young man didn't make connections?"

Sharon paused and looked over her shoulder. "Of course we didn't. Why?"

The elderly face crinkled in a smile. " 'Cause you got a glow about you, girl. My experience is, only one thing can make a woman as peppy as you are."

Sharon blushed. She gave Mrs. Breedlove a smile and a wink, then continued on her way.

* * *

Sharon came into the office just before nine, and checked the calls on the machine. Four clients had left messages for Russ, one for Sharon. Nothing from Richard Branson. Well, what did I expect? Sharon thought. It's been less than three hours since I left the guy. She went in and dropped her lone call slip on her desk, put her purse away, and carried the rest of the messages over to Russ's office. Black was in. The morning paper was folded on one corner of his desk as he pored over a stack of Xeroxes. He pointed to one of his visitor's chairs and said, "Sit." Sharon sat.

"You disappeared in a hurry last night," Black said. "I was lookin' for you."

Sharon's gaze flickered. "I didn't feel welcome. First opportunity . . ."

"I wadn too welcome myself, but I kept my ears open." Black turned one of the Xeroxes around so that Sharon could see. It was a copy of a newspaper article, complete with the headline, "BURNSIDE MURDER GOES TO TRIAL." "This dudn say anything about any rape," Black said. "I thought I was rememberin' the case the way it happened, and I was."

"Where did you get those?" Sharon said. She squinted to read the date on the copy, but only caught the year. 1988.

"Library archives. I think I got every old newspaper story about the case, but I got the library people doin' a search in case I missed any."

"The coroner's report noted vaginal bruising," Sharon said. "I saw it yesterday in the case file." A pulse jumped in her neck. When something pricked Black's interest, he wouldn't let go.

"I don't want you in an uproar, thinkin' some miracle's about to happen," Black said, tossing the Xerox back on the stack. "But I heard enough last night so I think it's worthwhile to follow up. You told me you had some things to show me." He folded his arms expectantly.

"My client Dycus Wilt. Really a grisly character, Russ. He gave me a pretty vivid description of the Burnside property, the house . . . a blow-by-blow of the rape and murder itself that you wouldn't want to hear. I'd as soon not have listened.

"I told him I needed something that he couldn't have learned from the newspapers," Sharon said, "something to prove he was really there. He described a scar on the victim's heinie that duplicates a pilonidal cyst surgery scar in the coroner's report."

Black lifted, then dropped the pile of Xeroxes. "Nothin' about that in here, either. You say he knew the grounds?"

"I've never been there myself," Sharon said. "But it'd be interesting to get a map of the Burnside place, as it was back then."

Black grabbed a pad and wrote something down. "It's on my list."

Sharon couldn't resist a smile. "What is it, boss? Yesterday you didn't even want to hear abut this, but now . . ."

"Joe Bright an' Ralph Toner did everything short of punchin' me in the nose, to try an' talk me into pullin' you off that Wilt case. Then they lit into the judge. Arnie Shiver told me they wanted him to take the case away from you and appoint some other lawyer. I don't know where the fire is, but there's sure a lotta smoke.

"Now, today," Black said, "I want you to go over to the D.A.'s, actin' innocent, and try and talk about a plea bargain for Dycus Wilt based on information he's goin' to give about the Burnside murder. Milt Breyer stonewalled you in court yesterday, but the Burnside deal wadn Breyer's case. It was Ralph Toner's, an' that case is what got him where he is today.

"If the stonewallin' was just Milt Breyer actin' on his own, that's one thing. Milt follows Ralph Toner around like a puppy dog, and Toner not wantin' any skeletons fallin' outta the closet on the Burnside case, that's understandable. But if it's departmental, if everybody at the D.A.'s says there's no chance for a deal with Dycus Wilt based on a case of Burnside magnitude . . . then that's skulduggery, Sharon, pure an' simple. If it's skulduggery, then you an' I are jumpin' into it with both feet. I got to live in this fair county, girl. There's plenty o' crooks out there already, without the district attorney gettin' in on the act.''

7

Sharon came in out of mid-nineties heat with perspiration dampening her underwear. The sudden cool inside the Frank Crowley Courts Building made her sneeze. She passed through the metal detectors and rode the escalator upward amid peak morning courthouse activity, lawyers toting briefcases, clerks and sheriff's deputies crowding both the up and down moving staircases. Sharon drummed her fingers on the handrail, remembering the Burnside case file. Something about a tattoo. Another question that needed answering before Sharon bearded the prosecution in its den. She reached the second level, crossed over to the other side, and rode back down to the lobby. There she boarded still another moving staircase, continued on to the basement, exited the back of the Crowley Building, and entered the jail. The thought of visiting Dycus Wilt raised goose bumps on her arms the size of spider eggs.

Wilt came from the innards of the jail into the attorneys' visiting booth with his dreadlocks braided, sat in a chair, and peered at Sharon through the bars. His jumpsuit was freshly ironed. His lips were slack. A ray of light glinted from his one gold inlay.

Sharon stopped doodling on her legal pad and smiled. "You look much better today."

Muscle rippled in Wilt's forearm as he yanked on a dreadlock. "Gots a good punk. Dude does my hair an' keeps my clothes nice. Got a ass jus' like a woman." He yawned. "Keep me up all night, fuckin' that dude."

Sharon's smile froze in place. "Now that you've had time to think it over, do you still want to pursue a plea bargain based on what you know about the Burnside murder?"

Wilt's features creased in a frown. "Don't know no Burnside."

"The thing we talked about yesterday, with the woman in the big house."

"Oh. The one me an' Woody done."

"That's it. Do you want to?"

Wilt nodded emphatically. "Sho. Dude drop a dime on me, I drop a dime on 'at mothafuckah. What they gonna gimme if I tell about that?"

"I've got to be upfront with you," Sharon said. "I don't know that they'll offer you anything. The prosecutor told me yesterday that you've already told this story to the guards, but that the state's not inclined to believe you."

"Deppities don't believe nothin' a dude say in here."

"Often they don't, Dycus. You told me that you and your partner had sex with her, is that right?"

Wilt curled his lip in a half snarl. "Woody's idea, none o' mine. I jus' go along wid de dude."

Sharon ducked her head to write down "Burnside" in order to hide the fact that her lips were trembling. "That you just went along with it wouldn't be a defense, Dycus. I did some checking on your story yesterday, and I found that some things you said were true."

"Now, hold on, lawyuh lady. You don't say shit to nobody about what I'm tellin' you. You run yu' mouth you can get me in trouble in here."

"All I did was look in the case file," Sharon said. "The coroner's report backs up your description of the scar."

Wilt's body relaxed. "Sho. On her ass. Run down—"

Sharon nodded. "That's right."

"—between her cheeks. Seen it when I was spreadin' 'em out to—"

"There were other things about the body," Sharon said quickly. "Can you recall anything else?"

Wilt seemed thoughtful. "Seem like she had big tits."

"Something more specific. A lot of women have large breasts."

Wilt grinned. "Yeah? You got some?"

A shudder ran through her, head to toe. "Something you'd have had to notice."

Wilt chewed his lower lip. "I told you, Woody lef' that glass on de flo'."

Sharon vigorously shook her head. "The glass was in the crime scene photos and placed in evidence. You could have seen those pictures. I'm talking about something intimate. Something secret."

Wilt's brows moved closer together. "Sump'n what?"

"Something unusual that you would have had to see the woman naked to know about."

"Neckid women's neckid women, lawyuh lady. All of 'em got that thing between they legs."

Sharon watched him. He remembered the scar but couldn't recall the butterfly, simple as that. Which would give the D.A. plenty of ammunition in shooting down a plea agreement. Sharon closed her legal pad. "If you don't remember anything else, you don't. I'm going to the D.A. now, and I'll be back later to let you know what they have to say." She rose and took a step toward the exit. God, she wanted out of there.

Dycus Wilt said, "Say."

Sharon turned. Wilt's face was lit up as if a lightbulb had exploded in his head.

"You ain't talkin' about no tattoo?"

Sharon's face softened. "Why, what else would I be talking about?"

"Don't know. Hey, lotsa broads got tattoos. This one had a butterfly on her ass, wings out, the head pointin' right at her crack. Ain't nothin' unusual about that, lawyuh lady. Shee-it, I seen that tattoo on a lotta women."

Sharon's meeting with her client left her feeling as if she needed a bath. She exited the elevator on the eleventh floor of the Crowley Building, walked quickly down the corridor, and entered the D.A.'s chamber through transparent double doors. She'd visited the district attorney's catacombs several times since she'd been in private practice, and never did she go inside the place without feeling as though every frigging assistant she passed was staring at her. Her kneeing of Milton Breyer on her final day as a prosecutor was one of the juiciest tidbits in the D.A.'s gossip mill. Two male A.D.A.'s came from the back and goose-stepped by on their way to court. One nodded at Sharon and said curtly, "Miss Hays." Sharon couldn't remember the guy's name. She smiled impersonally, returned the nod, and approached the receptionist's counter. As the men exited into the corridor, they spoke in whispers and glanced at Sharon over their shoulders.

Molly Teague sat behind the counter, pressing flashing buttons and routing calls. She was mid-twenties, with big breasts and chubby cheeks, and she and Sharon had hit it off at one time. She smiled and said, "Hi."

Sharon set her briefcase down and crossed her forearms on the counter. "I think I need to see two people. One is Mr. Breyer, about my client Dycus Wilt."

Molly arched an eyebrow. The news that Sharon Hays had come in asking for Breyer would be all over the office by lunchtime.

"Then I also need to speak with," Sharon said, "whoever in the appellate section is handling the Raymond Burnside matter. He's got a November execution date."

Molly played the switchboard like a concert pianist, never missing a beat in answering calls as she punched "Burnside, Raymond" into her computer keyboard and depressed the ENTER button. Then she put the calling party on hold and shifted the suspended phone mike away from her mouth. "Both the same people. Milton Breyer."

Sharon frowned and hunched farther over the counter. "Check that again, will you? The Burnside case is on appeal."

"That's what the screen tells me," Molly said. "But for some reason the appellate section doesn't have that file. Milt Breyer does. Or more particularly, Kathleen Fraterno has it. There's a cross-reference in the computer, and anyone wanting to talk about Dycus Wilt or Raymond Burnside needs to see her. You want to talk to Kathleen?"

Sharon breathed in through her nose. Kathleen Fraterno was Breyer's number-one backup, and had also been the other woman in Breyer's nasty divorce proceeding. She was slim, trim, efficient, and, Sharon thought, awfully hard up if she was sleeping with Milt. Sharon and Kathleen had been pub-crawling buds when Sharon was a prosecutor. The acquittal that she and Russ had won for Midge Rathermore had ended her friendship with Kathleen; when they passed in courthouse hallways now, Kathleen barely spoke to her. This is going to be more fun than a root canal, Sharon thought. "Sure, I'll talk to her," she said. She had a seat on the waiting couch and picked up a *People* magazine. Prince Charles and Lady Di graced the cover, wearing uncomfortable frowns. Sharon opened the magazine, crossed her legs, and began to read.

Kathleen Fraterno was in, but let Sharon cool her heels for twenty minutes before giving Molly the green light. The snub was intentional, Sharon knew it, and

Molly *knew* that Sharon knew it, and slightly averted
her gaze in telling Sharon that the prosecutor would
see her now. Molly said, "You know the way back,"
and Sharon nodded that she did. One of the D.A.'s
rules was that no one was to let a guest find their way
in on their own; the prosecutor receiving a visitor was
to hustle into the reception area with a smile of welcome. More downright rudeness from Kathleen.
Sharon did a slow burn as she passed the counter and
headed for the back.

Kathleen's office was two right turns down the corridor, directly across from the cubbyhole that Sharon
herself had once occupied. She glanced into her old
office as she went by; a clean-cut youngster of about
twenty-two was behind her old desk, reading a file.
He didn't glance up. Sharon did a column right and
entered Kathleen Fraterno's.

Kathleen remained seated. Her hair was in shoul-
der-length ringlets, seventies style, and she wore a
man's white shirt with the sleeves rolled up a couple
of turns. On the days she went to court, Kathleen was
into stylish form-fitting suits. She had a traffic-stopping
figure that Sharon secretly envied, but Sharon thought
her old friend's dress tended on the sloppy side ever
since she'd become an item with Milton Breyer. The
shirt that Kathleen wore was on the D.A.'s no-no list
for office attire. That she thumbed her nose at the
rules because she was sleeping with her boss wouldn't
make Kathleen popular with the troops. All of which,
Sharon thought, is none of my business. She sat down
without being invited and put her briefcase on the
floor. Her shoulder bag she balanced on her lap.

"Have you been waiting long?" Fraterno said.

"Just a couple of minutes," Sharon lied. "How are
you, Kathleen?"

"I'm fine, thanks." Cold, impersonal. "You're here
about the Dycus Wilt matter?" Fraterno reached for a
bulging file. "We want to try this within ninety days."

Sixty days between indictment and trial was the

minimum under the law. Continuances agreed on between the defense and prosecution were, in most cases, automatic, and Sharon had had in mind to ask for an additional ninety days. Fraterno's expression said that to request more time in the Wilt case would be a waste of breath, so Sharon didn't bother. She could ask the court for a delay. With Judge Shiver presiding, the granting of a continuance was a toss-up. "My client wants a deal," Sharon said.

"I should think you'd know better than to ask." Fraterno opened the file. "Rape and murder. We owe it to the victims not to bargain on this."

Sharon blinked. Blaming decisions on victim concern was a favorite prosecutor's ploy; the fact was that the district attorney of Dallas County didn't give a flip about the victims and never had. Sharon said, "He knows who killed Delores Burnside in '88, Kathleen."

Fraterno smirked. "So do we. *Raymond* Burnside, haven't you heard?"

"My client's buddy did that one."

"Hasn't Milton Breyer already discussed this with you?"

Sharon undid her shoulder strap and placed her bag alongside her briefcase on the floor. "If you want to call it a discussion. I was hoping to get more sensible answers from you."

Fraterno folded her hands. "What's unsensible about not believing a liar who's trying to get out of jail?"

"He's telling the truth."

"*You* say."

Sharon sighed. She hated getting nasty with a passion, but Kathleen wasn't leaving her much choice. "That's right, Kathleen. I say. He knows things that no one could know unless they were there. Do you want a list?"

"Not particularly. The Burnside case is closed."

"Well, you need to open it, then."

"Not in this lifetime, Sharon. We're going to execute the guy."

"Regardless of whether he did it or not, huh?"

Fraterno's gaze wavered. She folded her arms and didn't say anything.

Christ, Sharon thought, give me strength. She tried the sympathetic approach. "Look, Kathleen, I know with the election and all, it's not going to look good for Mr. Toner if it turns out his biggest case, he convicted the wrong guy. You and I have had this discussion before. We're lawyers. We're on different sides, but we're not politicians. We're supposed to be concerned with doing the right thing."

Fraterno's eyes narrowed into slits. "We've *done* the right thing."

"Look. My client Dycus Wilt and his buddy Woodrow Lee—the same Woody Lee, I might add, who snitched on my client in the Mary Ann Blakely murder. Six years ago these two guys broke into a big house in North Dallas, and both of them raped Delores Burnside. Then your informant Mr. Lee stabbed her to death."

For the first time, Fraterno's look showed uncertainty. "There wasn't any rape charge in the . . ."

Sharon mentally snapped her fingers. Sure. Kathleen had no personal knowledge of the Burnside case at all. She merely had instructions to stonewall all inquiries until Raymond Burnside was safely off to meet his maker. Sharon said quietly, "They raped her, Kathleen. Then Woodrow Lee killed her. My client has knowledge of some identifying marks on her body, things he couldn't possibly know unless he was there."

Fraterno firmed up her mouth. "You're not drawing me into a discussion, Sharon. Our policy is stated."

Sharon was as mad as she'd ever been in her life. "Oh, God, up your policy."

Fraterno closed her file. "Look, I've got some other people waiting."

Sharon reached for her purse. "Don't think I'll stop with this, Kathleen."

One corner of Fraterno's mouth turned up. "Oh? Are you going over my head, Sharon? Why don't you talk to Mr. Toner about it? I'm sure he'll be receptive."

Sharon looped her purse strap over her shoulder. "I wouldn't do that, since your orders come from Toner to begin with. You might talk to Mr. Toner about amicus curiae, though. You know, friend of the court?"

"I know what it means, Sharon, I went to law school. So, someone files a friend of the court brief in every death penalty case I ever heard of. That's not going to scare anybody in _this_ department."

Sharon paused halfway to her feet, with her hand on her briefcase handle. "Oh, yeah?"

Fraterno nodded. "Oh, yeah."

Sharon stood. "Okay, you can relay to Mr. Toner that we were willing to talk about this, to do it with minimum publicity. If I don't hear from you by five o'clock this afternoon, I'm calling a press conference and sending a copy of what I've got to Toner's opponent in the election. I'll give you till five, Kathleen." Sharon exited into the hall.

"May as well do it now, dear," Fraterno called out. "If you're waiting on a call from this office, you'll get awfully old."

Sharon pulled into a parking place across from the office, pressing the pedal so hard that her breaks squealed. A stylish-looking woman in a Buick, two spaces away, stared at her. Sharon got out, yanked her purse and briefcase from the front seat, and stalked out of the converted gas station. Halfway across the street, she paused.

A midnight blue El Dorado sat at the curb in front of the office entry, in a no-parking zone. Someone begging for a ticket, Sharon thought. She circled the

Caddy's nose, went up the steps, and barged in through the reception area. So intent was she on fixing Kathleen Fraterno's little red wagon, she nearly missed the note taped on her door.

The note was in Russ's familiar scrawl: "Get in here, quick." She looked across the way; light streamed from under his door. She put her things away, hurried over to Russ's, and entered without knocking. "I read your . . ."

Russ sat behind his desk with his arms folded. The man seated in the visitor's chair wasn't bad-looking. In fact, he was handsome as hell. He had a ruddy complexion, a thick muscular neck, and the broad, sometime-broken nose of a football jock who hadn't been out of action very long. Center-parted, razored and blow-dried hair fluffed up over a wide forehead. Thick lips, nice smile, straight teeth. Sharon decided that the overall creepy effect was because of his eyes.

The color was all right, clear gray. But his eyes didn't crinkle when the corners of his mouth turned up, the result being that the grin he showed her resembled the painted-on smile of a mannequin. He stood and extended his hand. "Hi. Jack Torturro."

His paw was huge, and Sharon had the feeling that he could have crushed her hand into pulp without breaking a sweat. He released her. She dropped her hand quickly to her side.

Black got up. "This here's Miss Hays. Sit down, Sharon, Mr. Torturro was just talkin' about you."

"Hey, now . . ." Torturro spread his hands, palms out. "Not just about you. About this . . ."

Black handed Sharon a business card. She looked at it. Morgan Hill Corp., Morgan Hill, California. Torturro held the title of vice president, which could mean about anything. Sharon sat on Russ's couch and dropped the card in her lap. "Nice to meet you, Mr. Torturro."

Torturro spun his chair around so that he was partially facing her, and had a seat. He looked at Russ and waited expectantly.

"Mr. Torturro wants to hire us," Black said.

Torturro raised a hand. "Hey, not me. The company."

"Brought his check." Black waved a slip of paper with a bank imprint. "Already made out. Fifty thousand dollars. Which ain't hay."

Sharon tilted her head. "I guess that makes it even nicer to meet you, Mr. Torturro. What is it we're supposed to do?"

"That's the best part," Black said. "Nothin'."

"Now, wait a minute." Torturro showed a nasty scowl, which dissolved immediately into his same mirthless smile, eyes dead. "She'd be doing some contracts. Closing a few land deals. Not just sitting around."

Sharon batted her eyes in confusion. "Are you sure you've got the right Hays, Mr. Torturro?"

Both men looked at her. Black's eyes twinkled as if he were about to burst out laughing.

"I've never drawn up a contract in my life," Sharon said. "The only piece of land I've got experience with is my house, and I inherited that. I'd be about as much use at a land closing as a chimney sweep."

Torturro leaned back and crossed his legs in boardroom posture. "It's not like you'd be doing it on your own. We got this local law firm under a retainer, Bowles and Hackney. And if *they* run up against it they can call our L.A. lawyers. Biggest outfit on Wilshire Boulevard, anybody asks. You know Bowles and Hackney, dontcha?"

Sharon listened to the guy, and wondered briefly if Morgan Hill Corp. held its board meetings in an alley, seated on garbage can lids. "Know of," Sharon said. "In fact, Russ, wasn't one of them at that thing last night?"

Black dug a mint out of a bowl and pulled off the cellophane. "Simon Hackney. He was the fat one that stayed in the corner all night with Milt Breyer. I never liked that SOB to begin with."

"Hey, this is strictly business," Torturro said. "So if you don't like the guy, personal don't enter into it."

Black popped the mint in his mouth and folded his hands over his chest. "That's why I'm not in business, Mr. Torturro. Personal *does* enter into it. Somebody I don't like, I'd as soon not fool with."

Sharon's gaze flicked back and forth between the two like a tennis fan's. "Will someone please tell me what's going on here? Mr. Torturro, if you're into real estate, you've got the biggest firm in town for that. What on earth would you need me for?"

"Just what I said," Black said. "Nothing."

"Contracts and stuff," Torturro said.

Sharon put her elbow on the armrest and let her wrist hang limp off the end. "Excuse me while I go out and come back in. I think I must have wandered into Disneyland. What business is this"—she glanced down at the business card in her lap—"Morgan Hill Corp. in?"

Torturro touched thick fingers together. "We do amusements."

Sharon smiled sweetly. "Oh. You're building a midway, isn't that nice."

Torturro laughed without sounding as if he thought anything was funny.

Black scooped up the check and read it over. "Okay, Sharon, here's the deal. Mr Torturro comes in here a few minutes ago and asks for you. I tell him you're out, but you're my associate. He gives me this check and tells me he wants to put you on full-time retainer to help with buyin' up some land around here."

"How strange," Sharon said. "I wonder if he found me in the yellow pages."

"I've heard about Mr. Torturro's outfit," Black said. "What they do is, they're a dummy corporation set up by people that own casinos."

"We're a wholly owned subsidiary." Torturro sounded as if he'd memorized the term out of a manual, and had had a hard time learning the words.

Black snorted. "Like I said, a dummy corporation. If I remember right from Ralph Toner's donation list, they're the main guys backin' his gubernatorial campaign. Give a tad to Joseph Bright, too, don't you?"

Torturro shrugged and looked slightly uncomfortable. "We help out a lot of people. It's what we do, you know?"

"So what they want you for," Black said to Sharon, "is to pretend to do all this real estate stuff for 'em, while Bowles and Hackney do the work. I bet she'd have a cushy expense account, wouldn' she?" He looked at Torturro.

"Strictly first class," Torturro said.

"Excuse me for looking a gift horse in the mouth," Sharon said, "but why buy land at this point? The gambling referendum isn't even up for a vote until next legislative session. If Texas doesn't legalize casinos, you'd be wasting a lot of time and money."

"Let's say we got confidence," Torturro said.

"Meaning that if Toner's elected, gamblin's in," Black said.

Torturro looked at the floor.

"An' this full-time job Miss Hays is supposed to have," Black said. "That'd mean she wouldn' have time for anything else, right?"

"Sure, that's part of it," Torturro said. "We wouldn't want our lawyer messing around in any two-bit criminal stuff."

"An' the cases she's got now," Black said. "She'd have to get rid o' those."

"Hey, that's part of the deal," Torturro said.

Sharon got it. She arched an eyebrow at the California guy.

"Including defendin' Dycus Wilt," Black said. "The guy over in the jail that's so full of it, nobody wants to believe his story about the Burnside killin'. Which if he's right, could spoil old Ralph Toner's election results."

Torturro spread his hands. "Well, let's just say, we couldn't have our lawyer representin' no nigger rapos. Make the company look bad."

"So what you think, Sharon?" Black held up the check. "You ready to be Mr. Torturro's full-time lawyer?"

Sharon looked at the ceiling. She demurely folded her hands in her lap. "As soon as pigs fly, Russ," she finally said. She recalled her talk that morning with Mrs. Breedlove, and said to Torturro, "Did you stop by my house last night?"

Torturro averted his gaze.

"You're double-parked outside," Sharon said. "If you hurry and move your car, you might get it in gear before I can find a cop to give you a ticket. You think?"

Andy Wade had protruding front teeth with a gap in between. He peered around the door to Russ's office, his eyes magnified by thick lenses, and looked as if he was ready to bolt and run. "Come on in, Andy," Sharon said. "We won't bite. Honest."

Wade relaxed and came the rest of the way in. He expelled breath. "When I first got the call, I thought somebody was playing a joke."

Black had his feet on the corner of his desk with his ankles crossed. "No joke. Grab a chair."

Wade scooted a chair over beside the sofa and sat. "I've got to tell you, I'm suspicious. Every time I try to interview either one of you at the courthouse, I get the runaround. Now suddenly you're calling me." A spiral steno pad dangled from his fingers. He turned over a page.

Sharon rocked a foot up and down, below crossed knees. "We're about to give you your big break, Andy. Put you right up there with Woodward and Bernstein. Aren't you excited?"

Wade looked at Black, who stared back at the reporter. "Aw, come on, Miss Hays," Wade said.

"There's ground rules," Black said, pointing.

Wade rubbed the eraser end of a pencil on the edge of his pad, and didn't say anything.

"Rule the First and Rule the Only," Sharon said. "If we're going to be Deep Throat, you're going to keep us out of it. This is going to be a big deal, Andy. All we're interested in is what's best for our client. In this case, what's best for our client also happens to be best for the public, the whole state of Texas. But if we read one word about Russ and me, then I'll haunt you in your dreams. Is that clear?"

Wade managed a crooked grin. "You're in my dreams already."

Sharon grinned as well. As much as she steered clear of the press, and as little as she trusted Andy Wade or any other reporter, she couldn't help but like him. "I'm not talking about your wet dreams," she said. "I'm talking about your nightmares."

Black gave a *harrumph* of embarrassment. Wade fiddled with his pants leg.

"Are we clear on that?" Sharon said.

Wade put on his best honest look. "I protect my sources."

"Well, see that you do," Black said gruffly.

"I think he will, boss," Sharon said. "Andy, you know who Raymond Burnside is, don't you?"

Wade snugged his glasses up with his middle finger. "Who doesn't? Guy they're about to execute. That case happened long before I went with the *News,* but we're keeping up with it."

"Burnside didn't do it," Sharon said. "My client Dycus Wilt and one of his buddies did."

"Jesus," Wade said, then said, "Jesus," again, this time more softly. "I thought you were trying to *help* your client. What, you're going to turn him in for another killing?"

"Some things we'll tell you, some things we won't,"

Sharon said. "Our motives aren't important right now. Go to Judge Griffin's court and look at the record in the Burnside killing. There's plenty in there to get you started. Once you're hot on the trail, come back to see me."

Wade wrote something down. "What is it I'm looking for?"

"You know that was Ralph Toner's landmark case, don't you?" Sharon looked to Black, who nodded.

"Sure," the reporter said. "Senator Bright's daughter. Raymond Burnside's the son-in-law."

"They prosecuted the case as spouse-in-a-rage," Sharon said. "Got the death sentence by saying Burnside committed burglary, breaking into the house. His *own* house, though he and his wife were separated. The burglary theory was weak, but so far it's stood up on appeal. Look at the coroner's report, Andy. There was vaginal bruising. The woman was raped. Not a word about the rape in the entire prosecution."

"Hell, if he raped her," Wade said, "why wouldn't they bring that out?"

Sharon exchanged a look with Black. Rus remained stone-faced. It had taken all of Sharon's diplomacy to talk Russ into letting her call the reporter to begin with, and she couldn't tell from Black's expression whether he was happy with the results thus far. Proof will be in the pudding and all that, Sharon thought.

"They didn't bring out the rape," Sharon said, "because Raymond Burnside didn't rape her. My client did, along with another animal named Woodrow Lee. If they'd made the assault public, then hair samples and semen would have had to match Burnside. Which they didn't."

Wade took some notes, and looked up with his mouth canted curiously. "That's pretty strong stuff, Miss Hays. For all that to be true, Toner would have had to have known . . ."

"Don't be puttin' any words in her mouth," Black cut in. "She's not sayin' what Toner knew an' didn' know. You're supposed to be the investigative reporter; any surmisin's up to you."

Wade raised his eyebrows. "Well, as long as I'm investigating, what about the senator? There's all kinds of possibilities here. Could Joseph Bright have known his son-in-law's not the guy?"

"Makes me sick to think about it, because me an' Joe Bright go way back. But he's a politician, pure and simple, an' I'm not too keen on him gettin' in bed with these gambling people. I won't buy that Joe knows his son-in-law didn't do it. If Raymond Burnside got prosecuted, that's because the D.A. convinced Joe Bright that Raymond Burnside was their man. But he didn't like his son-in-law and wanted him to be guilty. So as to whether Joe knew they'd used some suspect evidence to get a conviction . . ." Black sadly looked down.

Wade's eyes widened as if a lightbulb had exploded in his head. "What's this about gambling people?"

Black tucked his chin and fell silent. Sharon nearly laughed out loud. For all his courtroom guile, Russ Black had a tendency to put his foot in his mouth when one least expected.

Sharon said quickly, "Any information on gambling will come later. Hold your horses, Andy. For now, if I was a reporter, I'd be concentrating on the rape in the Burnside case."

Wade leaned thoughtfully back. "You're telling me I'll hear about the gambling later."

"That's what I said. Russ didn't mean to let that cat out of the bag."

"Okay, I accept that," Wade said, "but there's something else. What's supposed to trigger all this? You want to keep it a secret that you're furnishing this information, so what do I tell my editor? That six years after the fact, suddenly I decided to go look at the coroner's report in the Burnside killing, and that suddenly I decided maybe there was a rape involved?

That won't hold much water with my boss, Miss Hays."

Sharon glanced at Black, then back at the reporter. Her eyes twinkled mischievously. "Well, if I was a reporter, and if *I* wanted a lead," Sharon said, "then I'd park myself in Judge Arnold Shiver's court about two hours from now. That's when I'm filing my writ of habeas corpus, to have Raymond Burnside transferred up to Dallas from Huntsville as a material witness in Dycus Wilt's defense. If I was a reporter and wanted a scoop, that's just where I'd be. That would give me all the incentive I'd need to start poking into the Burnside matter."

"You're going to have Burnside brought up here?"

"Yep. Miles to go before I sleep, Andy. You'll excuse us if we cut this short for now, won't you? Us Deep Throats have other things to do."

The artificial light inside the courtroom made Kathleen Fraterno look as if she'd aged ten years or so. Definite creases around the nose and mouth that Sharon hadn't noticed earlier, upstairs in Kathleen's office. Fraterno bent from the waist, her chin near the bench, and said to Judge Arnold Shiver, "This is ridiculous, Your Honor. There's no basis for this writ whatsoever."

Shiver took his glasses off and pinched the bridge of his nose. The bags under his eyes were inflamed. "I'll go along it's highly unusual. You got a man on death row, Miss Hays, that's been in prison six years. Your client Wilt's accused of a murder less than a month ago. I don't see what knowledge this Burnside could have that's gonna help your man."

Sharon tightened her jaw muscles to prevent a yawn. She briefly pictured Richard Branson, his naked torso squirming on top of her at three in the morning. Her thighs tensed involuntarily. She felt as if she could sleep for a week, and then some. "Our habeas writ speaks for itself, Judge," she said. "All that's necessary is a statement that the prospective witness has knowledge pertinent to our client's defense."

"I know what the law is, young lady." Shiver set his features in a no-nonsense attitude. "The law's the law, but usin' it to waste a lot of the court's time, there's no excuse for that."

"We're not wasting time, Your Honor," Sharon said. She glanced over her shoulder to where Andy Wade sat in the spectators' section, taking notes. Shiver had done a double take on seeing the reporter in his courtroom at midafternoon; by this time the press had usually retired for the day to bang out tomorrow's editions. Minus an audience, Shiver might have denied Sharon's writ and let her take him on appeal if she felt like it. But with the election brewing, the judge wouldn't dare risk his denial making the papers. Milton Breyer sat at the prosecution table and was the picture of befuddlement. Milt had had the good sense to let Fraterno do the state's arguing; Breyer knew when he was out of his element, that much Sharon would have to say for the guy. Sharon directed her gaze back to the judge.

Fraterno said stiffly, "To get things out in the open, Your Honor, Miss Hays' client claims to have information relating to the Burnside killing six years ago. Our office has investigated his claim and found it without a shred of merit. Now Miss Hays is trying to backdoor us with legal broken-field running, which we resent. We move to have her writ denied."

Sharon stood mute. As Shiver had noted, the law was the law. I don't have to say a word, Sharon thought, and if the judge denies me, I'll head straight for the appellate courts. I can habeas anybody I want to, and with Andy Wade hanging around to report this hearing, I'll win my point.

As if reading Sharon's thoughts, Shiver bent over the writ and picked up a pen. "I got no choice but to approve it, Miss Fraterno." He paused. "This Raymond Burnside's got an execution date, doesn't he? He represented by counsel?"

"Yes, sir," Sharon said. "His appellate lawyer is Hagood T. Malone."

Shiver's chin lifted. "What's Motions Malone have to say about all this?"

"I tried to call him as a courtesy, but I had to leave a message on his machine. The information we want from Raymond Burnside isn't related to his appeal of his death penalty. I don't think the law requires us to go through his counsel on this."

Shiver expelled air through his nose. "You figured it all out in advance, huh? Well, all right, Miss Hays. But if you an' Russ Black are jerking the court around on this, you won't like the result of doin' that. I'll have the writ delivered by the next busload of prisoners headed down for the pen, and Mr. Burnside should be in our custody up here in Dallas in a week or so."

Sharon took a shallow breath and stepped forward. "If the court please, that's not soon enough. Dycus Wilt's got a hearing day after tomorrow on our search and seizure motion, and I have to talk to Raymond Burnside before then." Which was a little white lie. On second thought, it was a *big fat* lie. She wanted Raymond Burnside in the Dallas County Jail as leverage, to force the state's hand on Dycus Wilt's plea bargain, and doubted if Raymond Burnside had ever heard of Dycus Wilt. If I'm not careful, Sharon thought, my nose is going to grow.

Shiver's mouth firmed into a pugnacious scowl. "I'm goin' by the law in approvin' this writ, Miss Hays. But I don't have to send a jet plane after this man."

"I wouldn't expect you to, Your Honor. If you'll just deliver the writ to me, here and now, I'll carry it to Huntsville and serve it on the warden myself. Then we can have Mr. Burnside brought to Dallas tomorrow by a couple of prison guards."

Fraterno looked helplessly over her shoulder at Milton Breyer, who gave a hands-up gesture.

Shiver toyed with his pen. "That's extra expense, Miss Hays. And bein' as how you're court-appointed on the Dycus Wilt case, the court would have to approve of paying for all that. Which I won't do, because it's not necessary."

Sharon smiled. "We've considered that. Mr. Black and I have agreed that we'll foot the bill. I'm prepared to deliver a check to the prison warden to cover the travel expenses for Mr. Burnside and two Department of Justice people."

Shiver lifted his eyebrows and scratched his head through snow-white hair. He looked pointedly at Andy Wade, then applied pen to paper. The scratching was loud in the silent courtroom. Shiver pushed the writ across his desk. "Have at it, Miss Hays," Shiver said. "All my years on the bench, this Dycus Wilt's causing more of a commotion than any indigent defendant I've ever seen."

Sheila Winston regarded Sharon over the rim of a coffee cup, sipped, then set the cup down with a soft glassy clink. "You've got dark circles under your eyes as it is. I'm not an M.D., Sharon, but I recommend you get a night's sleep before you go tearing off on a trip like that."

Sharon drank black coffee herself, and scratched the edge of Sheila's kitchen table with a manicured nail. "No time. I can't go into it all, but we need to act fast to force the state's hand on Dycus Wilt's plea-bargain offer. If they stonewall us any longer, we're going to need Raymond Burnside to be available for some press interviews, which he won't be able to give from Huntsville."

"God, you're not driving, are you?" Sheila said. "It's a couple of hundred miles."

"I'm flying into Houston Intercontinental and renting a car."

"You-all are using newspaper publicity to try and win your case? That's prosecution strategy."

"I'm not crazy about it myself, and I'm having to hog-tie Russ to get him to stand still for it. Hey, Sheila, I know this is putting a lot on you two nights in a row. Scout's honor, when this is over I'll keep Trish for a week if you want to kick up your heels."

Sheila waved a hand as if batting mosquitoes. "Not the problem, kid. I'm worried about you going around like a zombie. You must have made quite a night of it."

Sharon lowered her gaze to her cup. "Well, let's just say it was fun. I'll give you the gory details later, okay?"

Melanie said stiffly, "I need to get home, Mom. My friends will think I've died." She folded her arms on Sheila's front porch, and leaned against the doorjamb.

Sharon stood a step below her daughter with blistering hot concrete cooking her feet through her shoes. At five o'clock in the evening, the sun was still a good thirty degrees above the horizon. "Look, sweetie," Sharon said, "I owe you one. I don't like leaving you over here two nights in a row myself, but it's important or I wouldn't be doing it. You'll have to trust me."

Melanie's lips twisted in an adolescent pout. She watched her feet.

God, I don't have time for this, Sharon thought. She said, "You behave for Mrs. Winston, Melanie," kissed her daughter's cheek, and clicked away down the sidewalk toward the Volvo.

Melanie called out, "Mom?"

Sharon turned.

Melanie was suddenly in tears. "It's just that I miss you, Mom. I hate for you to go away because I love you."

A grapefruit lodged itself firmly in Sharon's throat. Moments like this would be rare during the teenage years, but would make the end of adolescence well worth the wait. She double-timed back up on the porch and hugged Melanie to her. The girl's body shook with sobs.

"Me, too, precious," Sharon whispered. "Love you more than life. And beginning tomorrow we'll do some things together, okay?"

Sharon changed into tasteful black slacks and an oversize cotton knit pullover, and inventoried her briefcase. The habeas writ was there, along with the list of questions she wanted to ask Raymond Burnside. She snapped the catches, set her briefcase alongside her shoulder bag on the bed, and gave her room a final once-over. Her gaze fell on the bedside phone.

She hesitated, uncertain. Would she be pushing things? Finally she dug in her purse for a small white card, read some handwriting on the back, sat on the side of the bed, picked up the receiver, and punched in a number. After three rings there was a click, and then Richard Branson's pleasant recorded baritone told her that he was out, but that he'd get back to her if she'd leave a message after the beep.

Sharon started to hang up. She looked at the receiver as if hypnotized. Finally she said into the phone, "It's the lady of the night. I was just wondering about you." Then she put the receiver in its cradle and hugged herself. *Am I obvious or what?* Sharon thought. *God, I'm going to scare the guy off with that kind of crap.* Feeling foolish, muttering under her breath, Sharon Hays snatched up her belongings and hauled ass for the airport. It was all she could do to keep from sneaking by Branson's apartment, breaking in, and erasing her silly message from his machine.

8

―――♦―――

Sharon pulled into the prison's western parking lot, stopped in between a Hyundai and a Suzuki Sidekick, and leaned her forehead against the steering wheel. The flight to Houston Intercontinental had taken an hour; the irritating wait for Avis to produce her Chevy Lumina four-door plus the fifty-mile drive up I-45, two hours more. Her body ached from lack of sleep. She killed the engine; the AC quit blowing and left the air inside the Lumina still and cool. Lugging her briefcase, her shoulder bag bumping her hip, she crossed the asphalt and approached the entry guard tower. It was near eight-thirty, the sunset blending into purple warm dusk. A brisk hot breeze rumpled Sharon's bangs. Coils of razor wire topped the ten-foot fences that separated the grounds from the highway access. Gray-green cotton fields stretched in the distance on all sides, and molded with the dusk into nothingness. A single-engine Piper buzzed overhead.

The guard tower was a story-and-a-half column supporting a four-sided crow's nest with lights in the windows. Sharon walked up underneath and tilted her chin to look upward. A window slid in the crow's nest, and a pale face peered down at her. She called out, "Sharon Hays, a lawyer from Dallas. I called ahead." Her brief pay-phone conversation at DFW Airport had been with the warden's assistant. Sharon placed the odds of the headman's receiving her message at about fifty-fifty, but at least she'd adhered to protocol.

The guard backed away into the interior of the

crow's nest, then reappeared holding a clipboard. He yelled down, "Warden's waitin' for you. You must be somebody important." Sharon hoped that the gathering darkness masked her surprise. Twin mesh doors whined inward. Sharon went in under sharpened razor wire. The dull redbrick prison wall loomed nearby.

In seconds a door at the foot of the tower groaned open, and the guard approached. He wore a gray short-sleeve uniform, exhibited more of a paunch than a man in his twenties should have, and walked with a limp. After searching her shoulder bag, checking her ID, and glancing inside her briefcase, he took her on a fifty-foot walk to the prison entry. He rapped twice on a metal door; a porthole opened, and a face peered out. The door slid sideways on rollers, which needed oiling. Sharon glanced over her shoulder at rolling cotton fields, drew a breath, and followed the guard down a steel-walled corridor.

A trusty ushered Sharon into the warden's office, backed out, and closed the door. On her left was a bookcase with sliding-glass covers, exhibiting the Texas Penal Code, justice system manuals, and a copy of *Up the Organization* by Robert Townsend. The furniture was bare bones, wooden chairs with slatted backs, a gray metal desk with its top covered in thin rubber. The man behind the desk fit the decorum well, rail thin with a long neck, wearing a shirt with the collar open. He was bald with a fringe, and said brusquely, "Miss Hays. Seems we got a problem come up since you called."

It nettled Sharon that he hadn't shown the courtesy of standing up or introducing himself. She helped herself to a seat across from him and said, "Oh?"

"A fax come in." He pointed at a fax machine that sat on his credenza.

"Excuse me, but your name was . . . ?"

"Herb Tunney. Pardon the slight. Just seein' inmates most of the time, I forget the graces." He smiled without looking particularly friendly, showing crooked teeth. His cheeks were sunken. There was a lone photo on the wall, Warden Tunney with hair, twenty years younger, astride a swaybacked horse with a rifle slung across the saddle horn. In the picture he wore a guard's uniform, and the pose was intended to show that Tunney had experience riding herd over field-hand inmates. If Wynne Unit followed the norm, the warden would have cousins, in-laws, aunts, and uncles on the payroll; good-old-boy nepotism was rampant within the Texas prison system and had been for a century or more. When Tunney was ready to hang 'em up and retire, the next warden would likely be a relative.

Sharon nodded and said professionally, "Warden Tunney. I have a writ." She opened her briefcase.

"Maybe you should read the fax. Seems I can't let you see this old thing till we get this straight." Tunney produced a letter-size sheet of paper. "Old thing" was guard jargon for "inmate," the term having originated in the dim long-ago past, and having been passed down through generations of prison personnel. "Old things" were scum, which their keepers constantly reminded them.

Sharon accepted the fax and read it over. The message was under the letterhead of Hagood T. Malone, Attorney, and issued terse instructions that no one was to speak with Raymond Burnside without his lawyer present. When Sharon had examined the Burnside case file in Judge Sandy Griffin's court, she'd noted that the last paper which Motions Malone had filed on his client's behalf was six months old. She mentally winced. Malone's sudden interest in his client's welfare could only mean that Milton Breyer or Kathleen Fraterno had been busy on the phone. *Why in God's name are they so intent on killing this guy?* Sharon thought.

"Course, you don't have to see the prisoner to serve your writ on me," the warden said. "And I'd comply.

If you brought funds with you, I'd have him transferred to Dallas on the first thing smokin' tomorrow mornin'. 'S all I could do, ma'am."

Sharon tried. "I don't want to see Mr. Burnside about his appeal. He's a potential witness for me, and I'm entitled to interview him."

Tunney gave a hands-up shrug. "S'pect you need to see his lawyer about that."

Diplomacy wasn't going to work. Sharon slowly exhaled. "I'm tired, Mr. Tunney, and I'll bet you've got supper waiting. I don't suppose you got a phone call in addition to the fax, did you?"

Tunney's look was suddenly guarded. "I might've gotten a call. Seems like somebody . . ."

"Someone like Milton Breyer? You know him, don't you?"

Tunney plucked a nail file from his pocket and examined his fingers. "Never met the man."

"But you've talked to him. Or his cohort, Kathleen Fraterno."

"The fax is from Burnside's lawyer."

"I know that. I'm asking who called."

Tunney leaned back and clasped his hands behind his head. Directly behind him was a window covered in wire mesh. Darkness had fallen outside, and the guard's lighted crow's nest hovered like a UFO.

Sharon placed her writ on Tunney's desk, positioned so that the warden could read. "This permits me access to the prisoner, Mr. Tunney. It's by order of the court."

"I've seen writs before, ma'am. The fax instructs me otherwise."

Mother of God, Sharon thought. "All right then, sir," she said. "We have a few choices. I can sit here until Hagood Malone arrives from Dallas and the two of us lawyers can go in hand in hand to visit Mr. Burnside. That would comply with the writ *and* the fax. If we could get Mr. Malone on the telephone, it should take about five hours for him to arrive. But I'll warn you that I know him, and I doubt he'll take any calls at night. Which means you and I could sit here until tomorrow morning."

"I couldn't do that, ma'am," Tunney said.

"Another option is," Sharon said, "I could go into Hunstville and rent a motel. Then tomorrow morning I could roust a local district judge and ask for an injunction, ordering you to comply with the writ. You'd have a herd of state lawyers fight the injunction, of course, but at the very least you'd have to come downtown and make a court appearance. Interrupt your busy schedule a bit."

"I got to confess," Tunney said, "that'd be a pain."

"It'd be a pain for me, too, sir, but that's what they pay me for. So I propose an alternative to all that, that'll satisfy us both."

Tunney rubbed his eyes. "I'm always open to ideas. And you were right, I got supper waitin'."

"I'll write the prisoner a note. You can read it. In it I'll tell him precisely the situation, including the instructions in his lawyer's fax. If he doesn't want to see me and he'll put that in writing, I'll leave. You can transport him up to Dallas tomorrow, and I'll argue with the sheriff of Dallas County over whether I'm entitled to talk to him."

Tunney thoughtfully picked his teeth with a thumbnail. He opened his drawer and produced a pad and ballpoint, which he placed in front of Sharon. "Some o' these old things don't read too good, Miss Hays. On second thought, this Burnside's been to college. S'pect he'll understand anything you write down. I never went to college, though. So keep it simple. I don't want to be trottin' out any dictionaries, if it's all the same to you."

Raymond Burnside barely resembled his mug shots, and Sharon wasn't surprised. Six years on death row would have changed a stone sculpture. At the time of his trial, Burnside had been a young-looking guy with a smooth, puffy face. The man who faced Sharon through stout wire mesh was gaunt, with sharp cheekbones. His neck and shoulders were ridged with muscle, nervous cell-bound energy transformed into constant exercise. His eyes were clear and straightforward. He showed her a polite, somewhat embarrassed smile. Sharon returned the smile and added her most encouraging, "Good evening."

He rubbed the red marks on his wrists, where he'd been handcuffed; the guard had removed the bracelets as Burnside had entered the visiting booth. The chain between his ankle irons was long enough so that he could cross his legs. He wore white pants and a white short-sleeve shirt. His head was recently shaved, and his hair stuck out in quarter-inch quills. "Sorry I can't offer you coffee or something," he said. "I've given the maid the day off." His voice was a mild tenor, and he spoke so softly that Sharon had to strain to hear him. His laugh was forced.

Sharon hoped that her own chuckle didn't sound forced as well. "Good to see you're keeping your spirits up."

His expression sobered. "It's about all I have left." He had a narrow forehead and was, Sharon thought, just a shade short of handsome. He looked at her with guarded interest. "You don't seem surprised that I've agreed to see you," he said.

"Your note said just, 'Come on in,'" she said. "I haven't wondered about your reasons."

"You should."

"Why?"

"People have tried to see me before. A whole lot of them when I first came here, just recently some reporters from *Hard Copy*. Other attorneys barge in here waving their bar cards and want to talk about representing me for book rights. Sometimes I think my own lawyer's the only attorney who *hasn't* contacted me. I understand he's a very old man." Burnside's face was in shadow, the overhead light illuminating his torso from the neck down.

"Hagood Malone? He's retired. He's far from young," Sharon said, "though I guess old is a state of mind. You've never met your lawyer?"

"Not this lawyer. I met the joke who represented me at my trial, of course. Once my mother's money ran out he lost interest. I wanted to drop the appeal, but my mother wouldn't hear of it. The court appointed Mr. Malone, and other than in his letters I've never met him. He's known as Motions, isn't he?"

Sharon watched the prisoner. The visiting area was a long narrow bull pen, divided into cubicles with heavy wire mesh in between the inmate and his lawyer. Her adrenaline had been pumping during the meeting with the warden, so much so that the shock of entering the death house hadn't hit her until the guard had escorted her to the small table at which she now sat. A deep gloom touched her heart. She forced herself to keep smiling. "You know your lawyer's nickname, but you've never met him."

"We know a lot in here; it's like jungle drums. Until I got your message an hour ago, I'd never heard of you. Now I know more about you than you'd ever guess." He uncrossed and recrossed his legs. "I'll tell you why I agreed to see you, if you'd like. If you don't want to hear it, it's all the same to me."

Sharon felt as if she were walking on eggs with this guy. There was a strange ferocity about Raymond Burnside, an air that said he might be capable of murder. Her tremor of fear was tempered with pity; the man had been locked up a long time. In his shoes I might be thinking of mayhem myself, Sharon thought. "Sure I'd like to hear," she said.

"Because the warden didn't want me to."

"How could you possibly know that?"

"If Tunney had wanted me to see you, he'd have come to me in person instead of sending a flunky. That's the way he operates. He tried for an hour to get me to talk to the *Hard Copy* people, just so he'd get to be on television. About the only thing left to me is defiance. Defying that bastard gives me some satisfaction, so that's what I do."

"I've had clients in prison. According to them, upsetting the warden isn't the best policy."

Burnside leaned forward until his face was in the light. There was a scar of recent origin on his cheek. "Is this your first trip to death row, Miss Hays?"

"I've seen an execution downtown at the Walls, when I was a prosecutor. But yes, my first time to this unit."

"You ought to take a tour. Just another cell block, but with beefed-up security. Everyone's got a private cell here, as opposed to the poor cons elsewhere jammed three and four men to a five-by-nine. We don't have to march to chow. The guards wait on us. Justice is pretty strange. Convicted murderers get better treatment than the nonviolent folks.

"Most of us here," Burnside said, "have accepted the fact that we're going to die. We live with it. Some of the newer men have hope, but you learn that hope is a cancer eating away at your insides. A death penalty eliminates all carrots, Miss Hays. There's nothing anyone can dangle in front of me to induce me to do anything I don't want to do. You ask why it doesn't bother me to upset the warden. If I don't please him, what's he going to do? Kill me twice?"

Sharon hoisted up her briefcase and produced her notes. "I have a client who claims to know something about your wife's murder."

"In other cell blocks," Burnside said as if he hadn't heard her, "there are men who would stick a knife in someone just to get to talk to a woman as attractive as you. Not here. I know I'll never be able to touch you. So you're like a picture, a pleasant image the same as if I was seeing you on television."

Sharon flushed, irritated with herself that she felt

flattered. "If what my client says is true, then you're not guilty."

Burnside leaned back, his features once more in shadow. "If you make me angry, I'll call the guard and go back to my cell."

Sharon's lips parted in surprise. "How could what I'm saying possibly make you mad?"

"Because you're selling hope. I'm not in the market for hope."

"Did you know your wife was raped, Mr. Burnside?"

"No hope. No . . . hope. I swear I'll terminate this if you keep on."

"Aren't you hearing me? God."

"My first lawyer, all the lawyers in between. They poked straws at me, and I grabbed at them. No more grasping at straws."

"I said your wife was raped, Mr. Burnside. Doesn't that mean anything to you?"

He reached a clenched fist behind him, as if to knock for the guard.

"I can't stop you," Sharon said. "But I do have a writ served on the warden. You're going back to Dallas in the morning."

He lowered his hand. "And if I talk to you, will you let me stay here?"

"Why would you want to, when we might—"

"Because I've already been through all that, the public spectacle. Put my mother through it. Can't I even die in peace?"

Sharon felt a tightness between her eyes. "Don't you care that someone raped your wife?"

"I know Delores was raped. It doesn't matter anymore."

Sharon's chin tilted. "You know . . . ?"

"Of course I know. In the days right after the murder, it's all the police talked about. They asked for hair samples, semen samples. I was so wide-eyed innocent, I didn't even retain a lawyer, and I gave them everything they asked for. A lot of good it did."

Sharon licked her lips. "The samples didn't match?"

"How would I know? Once I gave them the samples, it was the last I heard of it. The last I heard that she was raped, too. By the time I came to trial, the prosecution's story was that I killed her to inherit her money."

"Your lawyer didn't delve into the rape business at all?"

Burnside snorted. "What lawyer? If we could have afforded someone like you, things might have been different. What's done is done. Let me live with it, for the time I've got left."

"Someone like me? I was a fledgling prosecutor myself, back then."

"Or Russell Black, your cohort."

"Sounds like you've bene doing your homework, Mr. Burnside."

"I told you, jungle drums. Don't you remember Peter Weems?"

Sharon's mouth twisted. "I'd forgotten."

"Pete lives next door to me," Burnside said. "And he sends his apologies, for spitting on you at his sentencing. Says he thought you were out to get him, but he's mellowed over the years."

"Peter Weems made two convenience store clerks lie down and then shot them in the back of the head. He's far from innocent."

Burnside waved a hand. "We don't discuss one another's crimes. We all have the same bond here, and who's guilty and who isn't no longer matters. We share information. You're Sharon Hays, and you were a tough prosecutor, one of the best. Now you're working for Russell Black, and the two of you make prosecutors think twice, as opposed to most defense lawyers who take people's money and then buddy up to the D.A. Since I don't like prosecutors, I have sort of a bond with you as well. You have a daughter by Rob

Stanley, the TV actor. Would you like to know more about yourself?"

Sharon permitted herself a smile. "I know myself pretty well already."

"I expect you do. For what we could afford at the time, we got just what we paid for. There were times when I felt my lawyer should have been sitting with the prosecution, for all the good he did."

"To give him his due," Sharon said, "murder charges are hard for anyone to defend. Especially circumstantial cases like yours. Barring an alibi . . ."

Burnside blinked in shadow. "I had an alibi."

Sharon watched him.

"The night Delores died," Burnside said, "I was doing what a lot of newly single guys do. Barhopping. Do you know TGI Friday's, on Greenville Avenue?"

Friday's was one of the better singles-in-search-of hangouts in Dallas. Hunks on display, most of them with one eye on the back-bar mirror, striking poses. "I've been there," Sharon said.

"Then you know. That's where I was, and I met three women, roommates. Went to their apartment and partied. I spent the night with one of them. When I heard about Delores the next day, I had such feelings of guilt that I threw up."

Sharon was speechless. She managed, "But if you knew these women's names . . ."

"Names, addresses, and phone numbers, Miss Hays. They were all set to testify for me."

"If that's true, and if your lawyer didn't call them at trial, then he should be disbarred."

"A lot of good that would do me now. But the women not appearing, that's one thing I can't blame him for. They were on his witness list, and he'd been in contact with them. The prosecution had a copy of the list. When it came time for them to take the stand, they simply weren't anywhere in the courthouse. We couldn't find them, and the judge wouldn't give us any time to try."

"Ralph Toner had their names?" Sharon said.

Burnside's eyes flashed fire. "You know that bastard, too, I suppose. A fine governor he's going to make. He and my ex-father-in-law have gotten quite close since my trial, haven't they?"

"Senator Bright is one of Toner's main supporters."

"So I hear," Burnside said. "Wouldn't it be ironic if they put off my execution until after Toner's elected, and he became the only avenue left for me to apply for clemency? That would be the final insult, Miss Hays. I'd go to my grave in stitches."

Sharon turned a page in her notebook and readied a ballpoint. "If you still have these women's names . . ."

"I have them. Why, are you applying to be my lawyer?"

The question threw her. This guy's not your client, old girl, Sharon thought. She said, "No, but my client has a common goal with you. If I can get the state to accept his plea bargain based on what he knows, it would have to mean your release."

"Don't even talk to me about releases. My ex-father-in-law would find a way to stop it no matter what you did."

Sharon put down her pen, curious. "What was the problem between you and Senator Bright, anyway?"

Burnside slumped and expelled a sigh. "It wasn't a problem just with him, it was a problem with my wife's kind. Delores and me, that was a marriage that shouldn't have happened. Poor boy marries rich girl, and they live happily ever after, that's a myth. I don't have any experience with interracial marriages, but I suspect they work better than mine. Ever heard of Whitewright, Texas, Miss Hays?"

"Seems I have," Sharon said. "A small town east of Dallas, isn't it?"

"A wide place in the road halfway to nowhere is a better description. We had a Dairy Queen and a town square, all that. Mother taught third, fourth, and fifth grades, all in one classroom. Daddy worked at the plant over in Mount Pleasant, along with half of the other men in town. My graduating class had thirty-one. Two of us went to college. The other one flunked out of Tyler JC in one semester. Most of the home folks still think I'm an oddball for going to Princeton. That's unheard of in my neck of the woods. I was a National Merit Scholar, the worst thing that's ever happened to me."

"Sounds pretty commendable from where I sit," Sharon said.

Burnside chuckled. "Where you sit is on the other side of the bars. But you and Mother should get together; she feels the same as you. But if I'd never won the scholarship, I never would've met Delores, and I wouldn't be talking to you from inside this cage.

"Joe Bright did everything he could to stop the wedding," Burnside said. "Had some political hack's son picked out for her, and I got in the way. Then, after we married, he tried his damnedest to remake me in his own image. Bought us that big house. Insisted we attend the so-right functions, all that. When I walked out, I wasn't really walking away from her. I was walking away from him, and he knew it."

"My memory of the case is strictly what I read in the newspapers," Sharon said. "The scuttlebutt was that she kicked you out, and that you killed her because you couldn't stand the idea of not being rich anymore."

"I know what the newspapers said. All orchestrated by dear old Daddy-in-law. I walked out, Miss Hays. After all was said and done, there was so much in the way that I just couldn't love Delores any longer. I don't think she cared for me by then, either. Joe Bright wouldn't even permit our divorce to go amicably. Kept interfering . . ."

"I think you need to hear my client's story," Sharon said.

Burnside folded his arms. His angry look returned. "I don't think I care to."

"I'm not hearing this. Excuse me, but this just beats . . ."

"I'm being rude. It's intentional. One of the perks of the condemned, Miss Hays. I'm sure you're all full of good intentions and whatnot. But I've learned to face facts, and the fact is that I'm going to die. I've read up on lethal injection, and while no one who's experienced it can talk about it, I'm relatively sure it's painless. Trying to fight it anymore *won't* be painless; it's that simple."

"My God, Mr. Burnside. "If we can put your story together with my client's, you won't die at all."

Burnside snapped his head around to look at the exit, then peered at Sharon through the mesh. "Oh, yes I will. If I don't die, it will hurt Ralph Toner politically, which in turn will hurt my ex-father-in-law. Since it's politic for me to die, I'm going to die. Please get that through your head. I have. Nice seeing you." He stood and rapped on the door.

Sharon felt a surge of anger. She closed her briefcase with an abrupt click of the latches. "You'll see me again, sir, in Dallas. My writ for you stands as issued by the court."

The door clanged open. Burnside's guard held out handcuffs. He extended his wrists, looking at Sharon over his shoulder. "Don't bother. Please. Thanks, but no thanks."

Sharon yanked on her shoulder strap and hefted her briefcase. "No way. I'm going to save your life even if it kills you, Mr. Burnside. You have a nice ride up to Dallas, you hear?"

9

It was almost eleven when Sharon emerged from the prison. If she was going to catch the red-eye from Houston Intercontinental into Dallas, she was going to have to step on it. The gates whined closed behind her; she gulped free warm air as she hustled across the asphalt. Stars shone through the smogless country atmosphere like tiny white pinpoints. In the underbrush skirting the parking lot, crickets whirred. As she drove onto the two-lane blacktop leading to the interstate, she averted her gaze from the razor-wire-topped fences.

The rented Lumina was a rocket compared to Sharon's Volvo, and sudden acceleration popped her neck as she climbed the ramp onto I-45, headed south. She set the AC blower on low, the cruise control on seventy-five, and fiddled with the radio's tuner until she located a C & W station out of Conroe. Ronnie Millsap belted out, "There Ain't No Gettin' Over Me," accompanied by crackling static. Sharon drummed rhythm on the steering wheel and hummed along.

She had the freeway practically to herself; lonesome beams swept across the median as a forty-footer lumbered north, and tall southeast Texas pines lined the shoulders on both sides. Car-generated wind whistled by outside the windows. She passed a lighted billboard showing a skyscraper under the caption "CULLEN FROST BANK LENDER HOT LINE," with an eight-hundred number. The billboards would grow more numerous as she neared Houston, and just north of the airport they would blot out the horizon. She yawned and rubbed her eyes, and absentmindedly glanced in the rearview. Twin headlights rushed her from behind like bats out of hell.

Oh, God, Sharon thought. The burgs between Huntsville and Houston were all notorious speed traps, the local economies feeding like piranhas on traffic fines, and there was a trooper behind every other pine tree. An I'm-caught sigh whistled between her lips as she kicked off the cruise control, slowed to fifty-five without touching the brake pedal, and moved into the right-hand lane. *Just little old innocent me, officer.*

The trailing vehicle slowed as well and swerved in behind her, tailgating. The headlights rode scant yards from her bumper.

So much for fooling the law, Sharon thought. She reached for her shoulder bag, dug inside for her wallet, and felt for her driver's license. At any second the roof lights would come on, and she mentally prepared to pull onto the shoulder. Be courteous but professional, she thought. Sheila Winston had gotten friendly with a traffic cop in hopes he wouldn't ticket her, and it had been a month before the guy had stopped hassling her for a date. Sharon let up on the gas and hovered her foot over the brake pedal. As she did, the car behind her moved into the center lane and pulled up alongside.

She felt a surge of relief. No cop car this; the hood ornament and grille belonged to a Lincoln, a sleek dark Town Car, first the hood and then the passenger window drawing up even with Sharon as it passed. So lucky me, she thought, I'm not getting a ticket after all. She thumbed the RESUME button on the cruise control and, as the Lumina speeded up, gave a final look sideways. God, she thought, the Lincoln's window is sliding down. Please don't tell me it's some guy wanting to get friendly, not out here in the middle of freaking *nowhere*. She pointedly ignored the other car and watched the road. Seen in the periphery of her vision, a pistol extended from the Lincoln's window and pointed in her direction.

Later Sharon would wonder why she hadn't panicked, and would decide that she simply hadn't had the time. She reacted. Her foot came off the gas as if moving on its own, and stomped down on the brake. A flash like a column of fireflies erupted as the Lincoln shot past. Her windshield shattered in a spiderweb pattern with a sound like crunching ice cubes. Sharon stared in puzzlement at a small round hole through the inspection sticker, and was vaguely aware of rushing wind as her passenger window exploded. Then the Lincoln's brake lights flashed, and it dawned on her that the sleek car had no license plate. She drew abreast as the Lincoln slowed. The pistol pointed at her head.

She stomped the brake for all she was worth, ducking down and to her right, at the same time spinning the wheel hard to the left. The bullet crashed through the splintered windshield and whined past her temple to embed in the seat back with a thud. All at once she was directly behind the Lincoln. Its brake lights flashed, and she threw her arms up to shield her face.

She rear-ended the Lincoln with a grind of metal and a crunch of glass. She slammed into the steering wheel, stunning herself, numbing her arms. The Lincoln lurched forward with the impact. Sharon gritted her teeth, tasting blood, whipped the steering wheel farther to the left, and floored the accelerator. The Lumina's engine coughed, almost died, then roared back to life. She passed on the left with a squeal of rubber. Median posts rushed past like runway markers.

She fought the wheel as the Lumina fishtailed, then straightened out, and looked in the rearview. The Lincoln fishtailed as well, chasing her. Another flash emitted from the passenger side, and a bullet smashed through the rear window and demolished the right-hand sun visor. Sharon peered up the highway as a sob escaped her throat. There was an Exxon station up ahead on her right, a sign glowing on a fifty-foot pole, gas pumps glistening through the darkness like an oasis. She'd already passed the freeway exit leading to the station; between her and the access road was a hundred-foot, down-and-up expanse of mowed grass. She glanced at the rearview. The Lincoln rushed on her as if she were standing still.

Sharon sucked in breath and held it, her lungs aching as she left the pavement and took to the grass, the Lumina bucking, dipping dangerously, bashing its fender on hard dirt as it reached the bottom of the dip, its rear wheels churning sod as it climbed the bank, gas station lights and starlit sky spinning before her eyes in a crazy quilt of color. Her bumper scraped asphalt as she crossed the access road, leaped the curb, and thundered onto the station drive. Lighted pumps rushed her at breakneck speed. No way could she stop in time.

She tried the brakes anyway, tires squealing, the pump's Exxon Supreme sign looming closer, the Lumina's bumper rattling as it jumped the gas island, smashed into the pump, recoiled, and finally halted in the driveway. Sharon looked dumbly at the pump, now tilted on the island at a forty-five degree angle, gazed out on the freeway as the Lincoln's taillights receded in the distance, then watched the man in blue coveralls as he sprinted from the station's interior. She shouldered the door open and stood in the drive.

The station attendant was huge and bald. He called out, "You all right? You hurt?"

Sharon grinned at him. "Me? No, I'm okay, what makes you think I . . . ?" Her knees buckled. Her vision blurred. She sagged against the fender, her throat constricting as she passed out cold.

10

Sharon didn't like the color scheme at all, her forearms swollen in alternate shades of purple and green. She pressed on a bruise, wincing in agony as Russell Black said to her, "What time'd all this happen?"

"I left the prison around eleven. Not over a quarter hour later."

"You recognize anybody?"

"God, boss, you sound like that Barney Fife character, with the highway patrol. Same thing he asked me. I might recognize the hand holding the gun if I saw it again, seems as though the trigger finger was pretty long." She pulled her sleeves down to cover her bruises. She vividly recalled the pain as her forearms slammed the steering wheel, but couldn't remember hurting her leg. Her left knee was every bit as sore as her arms, likely from hitting the dash as she pell-melled into the service station.

Black looked out the window as a Dallas Area Rapid Transit bus stopped at the back of the George Allen Courts Building. "Crazies roamin' the highways, no tellin' what we'll be comin' to next." The bus took on several passengers and lumbered on.

"This wasn't any random act," Sharon said. "Drive-by shooters don't go around in stolen Lincolns."

Black stroked his chin. "The highway department verify that the car was hot?"

"They will if they ever locate the owner. They found it four miles down the road on the shoulder. Plates stripped. Vehicle ID number filed. Not exactly the handiwork of the boys in the 'hood.''

"How come you didn' call me?"

Sharon used both hands to hoist up her injured knee and gingerly cross her legs. Hopefully her limp wasn't permanent. Look on the bright side, she thought, maybe I can qualify for handicapped parking. "I didn't see any point in getting you in an uproar," she said. "Once I got over the shock of being alive, spending the night in a motel in Conroe was sort of relaxing."

"Nothing broken?"

"They X-rayed everything with the possible exception of my fanny, which might be next. Other than a contusion or two, and the fact that I'll probably get the screaming mimis every time a car pulls up beside me on the freeway for a while, I'm okay. The gas station guy was worse off than I was, until he found out that Avis carries liability insurance."

Black leaned intensely over his desk. "Gives us something to think about. Whether assisting somebody like Dycus Wilt's worth gettin' killed over."

"Dycus isn't worth two cents. Raymond Burnside very well may be."

"Burnside idn your client, Sharon."

Sharon studied the older lawyer's concerned expression, and was touched. "What is it you know that I don't, boss?"

"Goin' up against the state of Texas is one thing, hell, we do that every day. This Mr. Jack Torturro and his Morgan Hill Corp., that's another story. I've been askin' around. It's a front for some people we're better off not knowin'. Back-east gang people, the kind we're not used to seein' in Texas.

"All they have to do," Black said, "is hint at legalized gambling and in those people come. They controlled Las Vegas for decades, but in the past fifteen years or so they've lost their toehold in Nevada to the so-called legitimate corporations. Bally, MGM, those guys. Most gamblers liked the mob better; in the old days in Vegas rooms were cheap, topflight entertainment free, everything a come-on to losin' money at the tables. Since big business took over Vegas, a room at the MGM Grand costs as much as one in the middle of Manhattan.

"But this recession the country's been havin'," Black said, "has panicked a few have-not states into votin' in casinos, and that's where Mr. Torturro and his kind thrive. Mississippi, Louisiana, Missouri . . . every state that's voted in riverboat gambling in the past five years, these people have got their finger in the pie. All our surroundin' states thrive on Texas money; if it wadn't for Texans drivin' across the border to gamble, Hot Springs, Arkansas, Shreveport, they'd all go broke. But now we've got horse racin' and the lottery in Texas, and the legislature's talkin' casinos. Mr. Torturro's folks have got a ton invested in land around here, and you can believe they've been greasin' the right palms. As far as New York people are concerned, gamblin' in Texas is a done deal, and once they get Ralph Toner in the governor's office, they're in Fat City. They've sown enough seeds so that old Ralph's a shoo-in, and all that can stop 'em is something like the public learnin' that Toner intentionally convicted the wrong man in the Burnside murder. Mr. Torturro's group has eliminated folks over a whole lot less."

"So we're supposed to stand by and watch them execute a man who isn't guilty," Sharon said.

"I didn' say we were going to do anything of the kind. I just want to make sure you understand what we're up against, and that what happened to you last night was just a wake-up call. I asked some questions. Talked to Senator Joe Bright for an hour last night."

"Don't tell me he's in on it, Russ."

"Not per se, but he's not above takin' donations from wherever they come. Joe's an uppity son of a gun, but he is dead certain his son-in-law killed his daughter. *Wanted* Raymond Burnside to be guilty so bad that Toner didn' have any trouble convincin' him. And Toner's no dummy, either. He saw early on in that case that a conviction would get him all the political clout Joe Bright could muster in this state, which is considerable, and so far it's worked.

"But the second thing about Joe Bright, an' this is what's kept me friends with the man all these years, he's honest. Rare as hen's teeth when you're talkin' politicians. He inherited millions an' he's not for sale. Furthermore, he's dead set against gambling in this state. I picked his brain some without lettin' the cat out of the bag, an' he knows nothing about this Morgan Hill Corp. or Mr. Jack Torturro other than that they're donatin' to his and Ralph Toner's campaigns. What that means is, Ralph Toner's figurin' to ride Joe Bright's coattails into the governor's mansion, but once he gets in he's used old Joe to the maximum. That's when Toner's colors are gonna show, and that's when it's time for him to give Torturro and company their payback. It'll be too late for Joe Bright to stop him then."

Sharon sat forward too quickly; a bolt of pain shot from her knee up into her thigh. "This is all making me dizzy."

"Makes me a little heady myself. Where I'm comin' from is, I'm ready to go all out on this. It's likely to put you and me both in some danger. You need to know that goin' in."

Sharon felt a strange surge of hilarity. "They've abused my body, Russ. What's a girl got left?"

Black looked down, then back up. "Her daughter, for one thing."

A heavy lump of ice settled in the pit of Sharon's stomach.

"It's an advantage that we're not dealing with crazy people here," Black said. "Until they're beat they're apt to do about anything. But they're not vengeful. Once they're whipped, these kind of people just say, win a few, lose a few, and go on with their rat-killin' someplace else. But their modus operandi includes family, Sharon. If they can't scare you, they figure threats to family might work. If it doesn't, they'll try somethin' else." He paused for that to sink in, then said, "Dycus Wilt's got a hearin' in the morning. When's the state supposed to deliver Raymond Burnside to Dallas County?"

"Sometime today," Sharon said.

"Okay. Your newspaper buddy Andy Wade gave a little mention of that in the early edition. That's good. You need to be sure he's kept notified of every happening in the Dycus Wilt case. Not even Torturro's likely to fool with newspaper folk. You been home yet?"

Sharon was suddenly so tired that her body was limp. "No, I haven't. I came straight to the office from the airport. And I promised Melanie I'd spend some time with her today. School begins next week."

"I recommend you spend it with her," Black said, "because beginnin' tomorrow, we're likely to be tied up some evenings. You be on your way, Sharon. I've got a guy, a guard at the jail that's gonna call me the second they check Raymond Burnside in. What I'd like to get done, tomorrow after Dycus Wilt's hearing, I'd like to see if Burnside'll give Andy Wade an interview. The more we can get the papers to play it up, the better chance somebody's going to take notice."

Sharon used her hands to hoist herself into a standing position, keeping pressure off her knee, the result being that her forearms burned as if on fire. She limped toward the door, then paused. "All we're ever going to realize out of this is a county court appointment fee. You know that, don't you? Why on earth are we doing this?"

Black studied the ceiling. "Hell's bells, I got no answer for that one. Maybe when it's all over, we can do a duet of 'Texas Our Texas.' Couple of patriots, girl, is all we're turnin' out to be."

11

~~~

Sharon took Sheila, Trish, and Melanie to dinner at Houlihan's Old Place in Northpark East, and to a movie at the UA Cinema 6 less than a hundred yards from the restaurant. Both women had quiche, while the preteens ordered salads with lo-cal dressing and pretended to like them. Their table was near the opening between the restaurant and the pretty-people hangout of a bar. Once during the meal a guy with razored hair posed his way in from the bar, and asked if he could buy Sharon a drink. She gave him the cold shoulder while Trish and Melanie showered the man with adolescent sultry glances.

There was the usual donnybrook at the movie box office. Melanie and Trish wailed that they *weren't children*, insisting that they were plenty old enough for either Quentin Tarantino's *Pulp Fiction* or *Disclosure* with Michael Douglas and Demi Moore, and went into snits when Sharon conferred with Sheila, then bought tickets for *IQ*, starring Walter Matthau, Meg Ryan, and Timothy Robbins. In spite of her protests, Melanie broke into tears during one of the tenderer scenes between Robbins and Ryan, and clutched her mother's bruised forearm. Sharon's jaws clenched, but she grinned through the pain and gave Melanie a comforting hug.

Sharon dropped the Winstons off and chugged into her driveway at a quarter to ten. A stretch of brown grass showed in the glow from the porch light. Sharon wrinkled her nose at the wilted stuff, and vowed that

Saturday, without fail, she'd haul out the hose and sprinkler. Once they'd ascended onto the porch and Sharon had unlocked the door, Melanie flounced into the living room and demanded to watch Tuesday night's *Minions of Justice,* which Sharon had taped two days ago. Sharon stood firm because she hadn't had time to edit the program, and sent her daughter to bed under protest. As a bribe she promised that *Minions of Justice,* minus all nudity, would be ship-shape for viewing by morning.

With Melanie tucked away for the night, Sharon hauled her tired and bruised carcass over to the TV, pressed the REWIND button on the VCR, and stood by feeling sorry for herself until the tape clicked smartly to a halt. Then she let Commander in from the yard. The shepherd reared up on his haunches to lick Sharon's face, sniffed his way around the living room, then stretched out in front of the television and cocked his head expectantly. Sharon retreated to the sofa with the EDIT button in hand, and let the show begin.

Though it pained her to admit it, the program was pretty good. Rob (damn him to hell) was more than passable as Detective Jack Ragan, the veteran who kept the youngsters in line around the precinct, and who screwed half the secretaries, female rookies, and widows of murder victims on the side. This episode was especially poignant, about Ragan having to arrest his own partner for sniffing cocaine on the job. There was only one R-rated scene, wherein a demure brunette detective climbed buck-naked into the shower behind Ragan and groped his privates—which Sharon had to watch three times to be certain it wasn't suitable for Melanie, and during which she thought, God, I don't remember Rob's buns being *that* fantastic, surely they're using a body double. When the brunette stripped down to her bikini briefs, Commander's tail beat a tattoo on the rug. Males, Sharon thought. She was about to make use of the CUT button when the telephone rang.

She paused the tape and double-time limped into the kitchen, determined to cut the ringing off before Melanie appeared. If some little boy is calling this late, Sharon thought, he's about to get an earful from one pissed-off mom. She reached the wall phone, lifted the receiver, and said rather testily, "Hello?"

An elderly female voice said, "Sharon? Pauline Breedlove."

Sharon's tone was instantly friendly. "Mrs. Breedlove. There's nothing wrong with Mr. Breedlove, is there?"

"No, he's still chomping at the bit to get out of the hospital. But you got company out front."

Mrs. Breedlove spent a large part of her waking hours looking out the window, and would be having a hard time sleeping with her husband gone. "Who might that be?" Sharon said.

"Don't know if it's the same young man that came the other night. But he's been out there watching your house."

Sharon was suddenly chilly. The young man from the other night, it had turned out, was Jack Torturro the gangster guy. She said, "How long has he—?"

"He's comin' up your sidewalk, Sharon. Right now, he's going up on the porch and . . ."

Sharon's doorbell *bong-bong*-ed. Commander leaped up and thundered through the living room.

Sharon looked in panic toward the front of the house, and noted that the chain lock was firmly in place. "Mrs. Breedlove?" Sharon said. Commander barked loudly and hurled himself against the door.

"He's ringing your doorbell."

"I hear it, ma'am. You watch. I'm going to check who it is, and if I scream, please call the police."

"I'm watching," Mrs. Breedlove said.

"Thanks ever so much." Sharon put the receiver down, went through the den, grabbed Commander's collar and yanked the shepherd back, and placed her ear against the front door panel. The bell sounded again. Commander whimpered. Sharon called, "Who is it?"

A strong male voice said loudly, "I thought I'd return your call in person."

Sharon frowned. "Return my . . . ?"

"You are the lady of the night, aren't you?" the male voice said. Then there was a hearty chuckle, followed by, "It's Richard Branson, Sharon. I've been missing you on the phone."

Sharon's eyes widened. She pictured Branson, his member deep within her, the animal noises they'd made as they came in unison. And the silly "lady of the night" message she'd left as she'd headed for the airport. She glanced at her own answering machine and noted for the first time the three quick flashes of the message light. She called out, "Just a minute, okay?" Then she hauled Commander to the back, pushed the shepherd onto the porch and locked him out, limped quickly to the kitchen, and snatched up the phone. "It's all right, Mrs. Breedlove. Please don't call the cops, whatever you do. I don't want anything scaring this one away."

Richard Branson's looks had knocked Sharon's lights out when she'd first met him; the dimples, the deep-set brown eyes, the athletic body, the total *manliness* of the guy. Physical lust it had been, no getting around it. Now it's time to assess his inner qualities, she thought, then thought with a surge of irritation at herself, God, Sharon, *who the hell cares*?

He sat at ease on her Spanish-style sofa, his ankle resting on his knee. He wore comfortable-looking khaki shorts and an oversize knit golf shirt that fit tightly around his biceps. The hair pattern on his legs was unusual, his calves sporting a wiry light brown growth, his thighs smooth as baby skin. He had a moderate tennis tan. Sharon had fixed him a light Scotch and water with ice, which now he sipped. "Those are nasty-looking bruises," he said.

She'd pushed up her sleeves while editing *Minions of Justice,* and now pulled them down to cover her forearms. "Makes for hurtful hugs," she said. The navy slacks she'd worn to the movies showed a few wrinkles. She wondered if she could gracefully cross her legs without screaming in pain, then left both feet on the floor.

"What happened?" he said.

"Just a little accident."

"What kind of accident?"

She had a drink of rum and Coke while she considered her response. Finally she said, "Car wreck." Commander scratched insistently at the back door. Go 'way, dog, Sharon thought.

His mouth tightened in concern. "You bust up your Volvo much? How about the other car?"

"I was driving a rental. Nobody else was hurt, as far as I know." She hoped that the bastards in the Lincoln had the world's worse case of whiplash.

"Why were you renting a car?" Branson said.

"Because I was out of town."

"Oh? No wonder you weren't home when I returned your call last night."

"I was on business."

"A case?"

"Yes."

"Oh? What were you up to?" He sat forward, rested his forearms on his thighs, and watched her over his shoulder.

She felt slightly uncomfortable. "Look, Richard."

"What is it? Hey, I'm not prying." He showed her a look of apology.

She inwardly sighed. "I've got a personal policy. The old business and pleasure routine."

He carefully placed his drink on a coaster. Moisture dripped from the glass and instantly disappeared into the porous surface. He said, "Fine, if this is just pleasure. I need to know if it is. Games have different rules."

Sharon practically squirmed. "What rules are those?"

"Well, if we're just going to be bed buddies, so be it. I can do that. If we're going to develop something, hey, meaningful, then I want to know something about your business. About your habits. Everything about you is part of it."

Sharon felt a strange sense of irony. Only moments ago she'd been thinking of assessing his "inner qualities." Now that he was turning the tables, she wasn't sure whether she liked the way the conversation was going. She said, "Everything?"

"Everything. You're hurt. I want to know how it happened, because I'm concerned for you. If you don't want me to care, just say so and I'll try not to. *Pretend* not to anyway, how's that?"

So how do I handle *this* hot potato? Sharon thought. She said, "I want you to care. I *think* I want you to care. I'm confused, Richard. This is all happening . . ."

"So fast?"

She looked down. "That's about the size of it."

"Everything has a beginning." He raised her sleeve and gently touched her forearm. "So what happened?"

She hesitated for a couple of seconds. "I don't want to ruin things," she finally said.

"You won't."

"I'm not even sure about a lot of it. You may think I'm going off the deep end."

He winked at her. "Try me."

She watched him. Relationships had to begin somewhere. Shoving misgivings aside, she told him. She left nothing out, including her disgust with her client and her compassion for the guy in prison. As she talked about the highway attack, her pulse raced and perspiration broke out on her forehead. He listened as if mesmerized, his expression showing concern. When she'd finished, she felt a sense of relief. Getting things off her chest to Sheila Winston was one thing; confiding in this understanding man was downright exhilarating. She couldn't remember opening up to a member of the opposite sex since New York, when she'd lived with Rob, God, twelve years ago.

He said soberly, "Taking that kind of chance over something like this . . . people like that will kill you. If what happened last night doesn't prove it to you, nothing will."

"They've made a believer out of me," she said.

"And how do you feel about that?"

"I'm not really sure. Mad as hell. Scared, too. I was scared to death last night, but today . . . I think I may be too damned mad to be scared."

"Jesus, Sharon. Think. All that for the kind of client you've got."

"My client doesn't count. The guy they're going to execute does. Pretty selfless coming from a lawyer, huh?"

Branson leaned back in a thoughtful posture. "If it was me, I'd have to bow out."

She chewed her lower lip. He was right, of course, but to hell with practicality. Sharon wanted to feel really daring and brave, one woman against the odds.

"That's not what you want to hear, is it?" he said. He hooked an elbow over the back of the sofa and drew up one leg. "What does Russell Black have to say about it?"

She shrugged. "That we're jumping into it with both feet."

"Damn the torpedoes."

"Yep."

"You're determined."

"Absolutely."

He laughed dryly. "Far be it from me to knock the old swashbuckling attitude. Since you're going ahead come hell or high water, what's next?"

"Dycus has a hearing in the morning. Officially it's to contest the state's search and seizure, but we're going to try and use the hearing to get the real stuff out in the open. Raymond Burnside's been transferred to Dallas County. I'm going to put my client's story about the Burnside murder on the record, in open court."

"Wow."

"They'll bring Dycus over from the jail around six-thirty. I plan to be there early, to brief him on what's going on. He's beginning to enjoy the hell out of being a snitch, so it should make him happy."

"Putting all that stuff in the record, you're sticking your neck out a thousand miles."

She lowered her lashes. "Maybe we are."

His expression softened. "So be it, huh?"

She nodded firmly. "So be it, is right."

He reached out and tenderly stroked her. "I've told you what I think. If you're determined to push ahead, then I'm behind you."

She laid her cheek on his hand. "Thanks."

"If I want to be with you, I guess I've got no choice." His breath quickened. He lowered his caress and touched her nipple with his thumb, through her sweater.

She gasped and closed her eyes. "Richard . . ."

He didn't speak, just covered her breast with his palm and gently squeezed.

She permitted his touch for a moment, then tenderly pushed his hand away. "Richard, I can't."

He leaned closer to her. "Jesus, why not?"

She forced herself to look away from the bulge at the front of his shorts. "I have to say no. I don't want to, believe me."

"Then why say it?"

She tried some levity. "I'm sore as hell, for one thing."

He touched her insistently. "We can be careful."

She had a strong gulp of rum and Coke. "There's more."

He removed his hand. "Oh?"

"My little girl's sleeping right in there." She indicated the hall leading to Melanie's bedroom. "She's almost thirteen. When daughter's home, Mommy abstains."

"She's a light sleeper?"

"No more than the next preadolescent." Sharon lowered her gaze to her lap. "You'd have to have kids."

He showed a smile of understanding as he moved away from her on the sofa. "Hey, so be it. I'm going along with everything. If nothing else, I'm proving my intentions."

She blinked. God, but she wanted him, right freaking now. She said without much conviction, "It's late."

He finished off his drink and stood. "So it is. Dinner tomorrow night?"

God, she thought, here comes the old career, screwing things up as usual. "Russ says, beginning tomorrow, we'll be working late."

His dimples shallowed in disappointment.

She said quickly, "But if you can wait till later . . ."

"I can wait as long as it takes." He reached for her hands and drew her into a standing position. "So it's good night, then." He kissed her.

She returned the kiss and moved against him, squirming. His member throbbed against her abdomen.

"Oh, Jesus," he murmured.

She was wet. She firmed her resolve. "You can't stay, Richard."

He said nothing. He nodded, then threw back his head and closed his eyes.

"You simply can't," she said, and gently pushed him away from her. He exited with a look of frustration on his face, and Sharon stood with her forehead pressed to the door frame for a full ten minutes after he'd gone. Then she went to bed and tossed through the night, kicking her covers into twisted piles.

12

There was an extra man assigned to the detail that brought prisoners from jail to court on Thursday morning. Dallas County Deputy Sheriff Nolan Blaine, a veteran with five years in the trenches as a TDC guard, was to ride herd solo on Dycus Wilt while the two regular first-year deputies handled the other inmates.

At seven-fifteen the rookies—a female officer whose uniform pants were too tight, and a carrot-topped youngster with a mole on his chin—herded six men in jumpsuits out of Lew Sterrett Justice Center's basement holding cell, and instructed the prisoners to line up. The prisoners—two blacks, three Hispanics, and one shaggy-haired white guy—sagged against the stone block corridor wall and scratched their behinds. The deputies rolled out the handcuffs and started down the row, cuffing each man to the inmate in front of him with a series of raspy, clanking noises. Dycus Wilt lounged on a bench inside the holding cell, his mouth slack, his gold inlay reflecting light from overhead.

Deputy Blaine, a husky red-faced, fortyish man who had a daughter the same age as the girl whom Dycus Wilt had raped and murdered, stepped to the door of the holding cell and crooked his finger. "C'm'ere, old thing," Blaine said.

Wilt showed a vacant grin as he shuffled out and took his place beside the chain gang. His jumpsuit was freshly ironed.

Blaine eyed Wilt head to toe. "So you're the one needs special handlin'."

Wilt yawned. "Reckon I am, boss man."

"You special 'cause they say you dangerous. You a bad ass, old thing?"

"Ain't gonna mess around none, boss man."

"All the same to me if you do." Blaine shackled Wilt's feet and cuffed his hands to a waist chain, then stood back and adjusted his service pistol inside its Sam Browne holster. Wilt yawned again and rattled his hardware. The rookie officers now had the chain gang ready for the trip through the tunnel into the Crowley Courts Building. Blaine stepped up and stood nose to nose with Dycus Wilt.

"Less you an' me get somethin' straight, diddlefuck," Blaine said. "I'm here to see you get your day in court, you heah? We're goin' to haul yo' rotten ass back and forth from jail to court many times as it takes to give yo' sorry carcass the death penalty on account of what you done to that girl. You don't got no worry about no beatin's or nothin', long as you behave yo'self. But iffen you so much as wiggle wrong, I'm goin' to take you in one of them private rooms, just you an' me. Tell you the truth, I'm hopin' you *do* start some shit." He nodded to the junior officers. "Less move these fine young gentlemen out now, folks. The judge is waitin' for 'em."

The group then shuffled down the corridor, the rookie cops fore and aft and casting wary glances in all directions, Blaine staying two paces behind Dycus Wilt, Wilt's feet moving in shackle-resisted baby steps. Once inside the courthouse basement, the officers summoned the special prisoners' elevator. They had the inmates move to the back of the car and face the rear, took the elevator nonstop to the sixth level, then herded the prisoners down the hall to the courtroom holding cell. The corridor was deserted save for two inmate trusties who swept with push brooms. When the chain gang reached the anteroom outside the holding cell, Blaine kept Dycus Wilt off to one side. The rookies lined the other prisoners up and removed their handcuffs. The inmates went into the cell, rubbing their wrists and peering around.

Blaine curled his lip, went down on his haunches, and unlocked Wilt's ankle irons. He then raised up and fumbled with the lock to the prisoner's waist chain. As he did, there was a tugging sensation at his hip. It was a fraction of a second before it dawned on Blaine that the prisoner's hands were free.

Before the deputy could react, Wilt had Blaine's service pistol free of its holster. Blaine's eyes widened in fear. The rookie officers reached for their own revolvers. Wilt said loudly, "Blow this mothafuckah away," at the same time jamming the barrel of the gun against Deputy Blaine's forehead. The rookies froze and stared at each other. Slowly they relaxed and let their hands hang at their sides. A trickle of blood oozed from a cut over Blaine's eye where the pistol had gouged him.

A string of saliva hung from Wilt's gold tooth. He disarmed the rookies and tossed their pistols into the corner, then gestured for both to get inside the cell. The female deputy had short black hair. Her mouth twisted as she moved in among the prisoners. Wilt grinned. "Got you men some pussy in there," he said. The two Hispanic inmates grinned as well. Wilt locked the cell, dropped the key with a clatter, and turned to Blaine. "Ain't no diddlefuck," Wilt said, then shot the veteran officer in the face. Blaine slammed into the wall and went down in a lifeless heap. Wilt then sprinted out the door and back down the corridor, toward the elevators. His slipper-clad feet pounded on tile. The inmate trusties looked up, watched Wilt disappear around the corner, then lowered their heads and continued to sweep the floor.

Three misdemeanor prosecutors got off of the sixth-floor elevator just as Dycus Wilt arrived in the lobby.

Wilt was breathing hard, and waved Deputy Nolan Blaine's service pistol. He yelled, "Down on the flo'," and pointed the gun. The A.D.A.'s were young men in dark suits. They assumed the prone position and covered their heads in terror. Wilt leaped into the car, pressed a button, and the twin doors rumbled closed. As the DOWN light dinged on overhead, one of the A.D.A.'s risked a squint-eyed peek between his fingers. The corridor was now deserted. The prosecutor leaped to his feet, charged down the hall, and pulled the handle on the fire alarm. Bells pealed throughout the Crowley Building.

Two deputies were on the third floor, inside the elevator lobby snack room, when the alarm sounded. Both men held plastic cups of coffee while one spun quarters into a vending machine. The other officer, a rail-thin man with a scar on his cheek, turned toward the lobby with his cup to his lips. Seen through the glass-paneled door, Dycus Wilt emerged from the elevator and walked quickly toward the escalators at the front of the building. The deputy pulled the door open and yelled out, "Hey. What's the alarm all about?" Wilt glanced back over his shoulder, then broke into a run.

The second deputy, even thinner than the first and with a big bent honker of a nose, raised up holding a package of powdered-sugar doughnuts. He looked beyond his partner at Wilt's retreating backside. Just as Wilt boarded the moving staircase headed down, the second deputy shouted, "Son of a bitch is *escaping*," dropped coffee and doughnuts on the floor, and drew his revolver. The first deputy cleared leather as well, and the two sprinted through the elevator lobby to the head of the escalator.

Wilt was already halfway to the second floor, running full tilt, taking the steps two at a time as the escalator moved downward. The moving staircases were suspended inside an open area that extended from the basement to the third level. Fifty-foot arched windows fronted the building. Visible through the windows was the elevated portion of Stemmons Freeway as it blended into the Austin Interchange.

The lead deputy dropped to one knee, steadied his pistol over the rail, and yelled, "Hold it right there." Wilt fired off a shot that whined over the deputies' heads. The officer returned fire. His bullet struck the second level, ricocheted, and made a spiderweb hole in the window. Wilt dashed across the second-floor landing and boarded the escalator headed for the building exit.

Sharon Hays came through the ground-floor Crowley Building entry at a quarter to eight, cleared the metal detectors, and mounted the escalator going up. She wore a gray pleated skirt and white starched blouse. Her shoulder bag rested on her hip and her briefcase dangled from her fingers. Her thoughts were centered on Richard Branson. She was only vaguely aware of the black man who charged across the landing above her, and barely noticed him as he sprinted onto the down escalator wearing a jail-issue jumpsuit. They'd already passed each other going in opposite directions, in fact, before she zeroed in on him. Criminy, she thought, it's my client. She said loudly, "Dycus, what the hell are you—"

Two deputy sheriffs came onto the second-floor landing at a dead run. The lead man shouted down to the metal-detector guards, "Stop that man."

Sharon turned around and hustled downward, gaining two steps to each one she lost as the stairs conveyored toward the second level. Below and to her left, Dycus Wilt thundered onto the ground floor. The metal-detector guards blocked his path, pistols drawn. Wilt looked wildly about, started to go back up, then halted in his tracks as the two deputies headed down toward him. Wilt looked straight at Sharon, his mouth open, his gold tooth exposed, his eyes bugged out.

Then he turned and aimed his revolver up the escalator at the charging officers. Both deputies opened fire at once, and the metal-detector guards shot volleys from behind. Bullets ripped into Wilt's spine and thudded into his chest and stomach. Blood flew. He dropped his pistol, fell down on his face, and pitched over onto his back.

Sharon reached Wilt's side an instant before the lead deputy pulled up, followed closely by his partner. The prisoner's breathing was hollow and a gurgling sound came up from his throat. He looked at Sharon one final time, shuddered, relaxed, and was still. A final long sigh came from his lungs. His head sagged until his cheek rested on the floor. A chain was still locked around his waist.

One of the deputies murmured, "Sumbitch tried to run off." The metal-detector guards approached and stood with Sharon and the deputies in a circle around the dead man. Dycus Wilt's tongue protruded and hung downward.

A glint of metal caught Sharon's attention. She stooped, picked something up from the floor, looked at it, then stared incredulously at the officers. Sudden tears blurred her vision as uniformed officers and civilian clerks poured from all levels toward the lobby. "It's the key to his handcuffs," Sharon said. "Who in the name of God gave him this key?"

13

Major Thomas Boles, the highest-ranking sheriff's deputy in Dallas County, didn't seem to get the point. "I don't understand," he said. "I've got a dead officer, a female deputy raped inside a holding cell, and you're worried about the guy that caused it all. Pardon me if I don't break down in tears or offer to be a pall-bearer." He dropped a pencil on his desk and folded his arms. Visible through his office door were rows of desks and the waiting counter on the ground floor of the Lew Sterrett Justice Center. Beyond the counter a gang of newspeople stood, men and women with pads held ready, Minicams hoisted on shoulders and pointed into the office. "Those people out there aren't going to wait much longer, Miss Hays," the major said. "If you'll excuse me . . ."

"It's a terrible tragedy, Major Boles," Sharon solemnly said. "And I can't say the world isn't better off without my client. But the fact remains that he didn't do this on his own. Somebody slipped him that key, and that somebody is just as much to blame as Dycus. He was what he was. Helping him escape, you may as well turn loose a rabid dog."

Boles' gaze softened in sorrow. "Damn. Sergeant Blaine was one of the best. If a guy like that can let a prisoner get the upper hand, it could happen to any of us." He had a military white-sidewall haircut, sturdy shoulders, and muscular arms. Sharon pictured Raymond Burnside as he'd appeared in prison the other night. Sheriff's deputies and inmates had a lot in common when it came to being physical fitness nuts.

"Major . . ." Sharon wet her lips. She was treading on thin ice and knew it. Boles' grief was one part genuine, nine parts ham, most of it for the benefit of the media outside. The major's job was a political plum. Boles had risked his own firing by campaigning for his boss's opponent in the last election, then had reaped the benefits when the opponent had won. Sharon would bet that Boles had barely known the dead officer if he'd known him at all. The poor girl whom Dycus Wilt had locked in the cell with that gang of savages had been nine miles down the totem pole, and Boles wouldn't be able to pick her picture out of a lineup in a million years. "I found the key," Sharon finally said.

"Oh? Where is it?" Boles' forehead wrinkled in interest.

"I think I gave it to one of the deputies." Sharon crossed her toes; the key was inside her compact, the compact resting in the outside pocket of her shoulder bag. "Has the policy within the jail changed in the last couple of years?"

"Not that I know of." Boles visibly winced; he'd answered without thinking. Gotcha there, Sharon thought.

"When I was a prosecutor, the policy was that one key remained with the deputy transporting the prisoner. Two duplicates were kept in the jail office outside the inmate area, where nobody unauthorized could get their hands on them. Is that still the system,?"

He cocked his head suspiciously. "Why do you ask?"

"It just occurs to me," Sharon said, "that Dycus couldn't have gotten his hands free without inside help."

Boles folded his arms. "Not from within *this* department."

That's what I was afraid of, Sharon thought. There'd be a lot of questions asked within the sheriff's' office, okay, but they'd cover it up from the public until the cows came home. Sharon stood. "I suppose you're right, Major. Listen, I've got a hearing scheduled upstairs. My client's not going to be there, of course, he's sort of dead, but I do have to show up to tell the judge what's going on." She walked to the door, glanced at the newspeople beyond the counter, then turned back to Boles. "If you need me as a witness, sir," Sharon said, "I'm certainly at your service. Your men downstairs didn't use an ounce more of deadly force than necessary, and I'll back the department on that till my dying day."

Sharon passed through the swinging gate and moved along the counter as the newspeople surged forward and Boles emerged from his office. Boles wore a press-agent look of concern. Andy Wade was near the back of the crowd, standing on tiptoes, steno pad and pen held ready. He wore a blue short-sleeve shirt, tie, and Docker slacks. A rind of fat pouched out over the back of his belt. As Sharon passed, she yanked on Andy's shirt.

The reporter turned and blinked through thick lenses. "Hi, Miss Hays. You like my story about the Burnside thing?"

"Shh," Sharon hissed. She stepped up closer and whispered, "The pay phone down the hall. I've got the number right in here." She tapped her shoulder bag.

Wade grinned. "You need to call your bookie?"

"No bets, the way things have been going," Sharon said. "But wander down the hall in about ten minutes. That phone may ring."

Wade glanced toward the exit, then looked at Sharon questioningly.

She winked at him. "Deep Throat itches, Andy. You're the only one with anything long enough to scratch the itch, big boy. Take advantage while you can."

"The sheriff's personnel files are public records, Andy," Sharon said. "Just go to the county computers. They'll tell you who-all works where, what their pay grade is, length of employment, any reprimands or commendations in their file. Most important, their home addresses and phone numbers." She stood in the sixth-floor snack bar, talking on the pay phone. She backed away the length of the cord and looked through the glass into the elevator lobby. A lawyer in a snazzy suit exited a car and rounded the corner headed for court, his attaché case bumping his tailored pants leg. "What's Boles have to say?" Sharon said.

"Usual b.s. Dycus Wilt was one dangerous guy. They're investigating; they'll have a statement once they're finished. The dead guy, Blaine, was the greatest cop since Sergeant Preston of the Yukon." Andy Wade's voice on the phone sounded as if he was developing a cold. There was a hubbub of corridor voices in the background. Sharon pictured the reporter ducking his head as other newspeople milled around outside the sheriff's department.

"What you'll be looking for," Sharon said, "is someone in debt. It's been common knowledge forever that county jail prisoners with money on the outside can get about anything they want in lockup, if they can find the right deputy. They bring the prisoners down the ramp just outside the jail office, on their way to the holding cells. It wouldn't be any trick at all for somebody to step out in the corridor and wait for dear old Dycus to pass. With a little creative snooping you can find the leak. The sheriff's department won't be trying to find this person very hard, that you can count on. When you find out who did it, contact them. You can agree to keep their name out of the paper in return for information. What you want to know is who paid them."

"Sounds easy for the sheriff to cover up," Wade said. "That key will never be seen again."

Sharon chuckled. "Oh, yes, it will."

"How so?"

"Because *I've* got it."

"*You've* got it?"

"Check the sheriff's roster, Andy. I've got to go be the only lawyer in the history of criminal justice to try and hold a hearing to benefit a dead man. Oh. One thing."

There was a pause, after which Wade said, "What's that?"

"Whatever you find out, call my office first. Us Deep Throats have got to hang together, okay?"

Sharon recognized Milton Breyer from fifty feet down the hall, Breyer standing in his coal-black suit, gesturing with his hands as he spoke to two people who were seated on a bench. One of the two was Kathleen Fraterno, her long dark hair tied back, her hands folded in her lap. Sharon had passed the bench before she got a good look at the third member of the trio. Ralph Toner himself. What's he doing here? Sharon thought. Toner hadn't spent much time at the courthouse while he was the district attorney, and as a gubernatorial candidate he shouldn't have any business here at all. Sharon nodded and started to go through the double doors into the courtroom.

"Oh, Sharon," Breyer said.

Sharon paused, turned around, and went over. She forced her tone to be friendly, and it was a job. "Hi, Milt," she said. "Kathleen. Mr. Toner."

Kathleen remained seated and showed a plastic smile. Toner stood and said curtly, "Miss Hays." The benches up and down the hallway were about half occupied, defendants with their lawyers mostly, a few nervous-looking people who were probably witnesses.

"Quite a mess downstairs," Breyer said.

Sharon relaxed her sore knee and put all of her weight on her good leg. "Did you see it?"

"It's all anyone's talked about. Be something they'll remember in this courthouse twenty years from now."

"Really historical," Sharon said.

"I understand you were down there when they shot your man," Breyer said, posing, folding his hands over his lapels. "Must have been scary."

"Saved you getting ready for trial," Sharon said.

"We didn't expect to see you up here. Which would be all right, of course. We can handle the dismissal with the judge. Just a formality, a form order."

Sharon shifted her briefcase from one hand to the other and adjusted her shoulder bag. "I'm not quite ready for that, Milt. There are a couple of things I want to put on the record."

Breyer and Toner exchanged a look. "Come on," Breyer said. "With the guy dead?"

Sharon smiled. "He'd want us to carry on, don't you think?"

Toner now butted in. "This business about Raymond Burnside, Miss Hays."

"Yes, sir?" Sharon said. "What about him?"

"Bringing back all those memories, that's hard on Senator Bright and his family."

Sharon tightened her mouth in an inquisitive look. "There's something I'm missing here, Mr. Toner. Are you back representing the state in that matter?"

Toner looked from Breyer to Fraterno, and ran his finger across his lip where his mustache once grew. Sharon thought the ex-D.A. had looked better with more meat on his bones; the man before her seemed emaciated. Television made people appear heavier than they were, which would be what Toner was thinking, losing all that weight for his run at the governor's mansion. Toner said, "I'm not practicing law, with the campaign. The state is consulting with me, with the execution approaching."

Fraterno chimed in from her sitting position. "He

was Burnside's prosecutor, Sharon. It's done all the time."

Which was true, Sharon had to admit. Sharon herself still got calls from the D.A.'s office, about cases she'd had hanging fire when she'd kneed old Milt and walked off the job. "I've got nothing to do with Burnside's execution, sir," she said to Toner. "Just as his case pertains to my client, that's all."

"I've seen the file on your client," Toner said. "What a South Dallas savage could have to do with the Burnside case ..."

"I've been wondering," Sharon said, "why nothing was ever said in the trial, that Delores Burnside was raped." She watched all three of them for a reaction. Fraterno's eyebrow arched quickly, showing surprise. Breyer looked surprised as well, his lips parting as he looked to Toner for the answer.

Toner said, with little confidence, "That wasn't an issue."

"Not an issue?" Sharon squeezed her own bruised forearm. "I think it probably should become an issue. Raymond Burnside's not my client, though."

"Right," Toner said. "And since your client is no longer with us, nothing about Burnside should be your problem."

Sharon hesitated, then decided to go ahead. "I get very interested in things when people begin shooting at me on interstate highways."

The remark drew a total blank, all three exchanging puzzled glances. Sharon hadn't really expected Breyer and Fraterno to be aware of the incident near the prison; Kathleen was merely working on the case from a legal standpoint, and Milton Breyer was too dumb for the bad guys to clue in. She'd halfway expected Toner to show a guarded look, that he knew what she was talking about, but the ex-D.A. was every bit as much in the dark as Fraterno and Breyer. Sharon now tried, "Do you know a guy named Jack Torturro, Mr. Toner?"

Now Toner showed the look that Sharon had expected, a slight wavering in his gaze as he said, "Why do you ask?"

"A better question might be," Sharon said, raising her voice, "whether *Senator Bright* knows that you know Jack Torturro, since your main concern is the effect all this will have on the senator and his family."

Toner unbuttoned his suit coat and placed his hands on his waist. "I don't think you understand what you're getting into, young woman." His blue tie hung down over a white monogrammed shirt.

Sharon's grip on her briefcase handle tightened, shooting little razors of agony up her forearm. "Three days ago I would've agreed with you, Mr. Toner. I didn't understand. Now I do. And if you'll excuse me, I've got a judge to see." She stepped toward the courtroom.

Breyer exchanged a look with Toner, then followed after her. "The case is *dismissed,* Sharon. Your client's dead."

Sharon paused with the door partway open. "Have you filed your dismissal yet?"

"Just a formality."

"Well, as long as we're being formal," Sharon said, "I've got a formality to go through myself. Such as getting some things on the record. Come on, Milton. I think you'll be interested in what I've got to say."

Judge Shiver wound his pocket watch with a faint clicking noise. It's an antique timepiece, Sharon thought, and might even be as old as Shiver himself. He showed a wizened look, his snow-white hair wild as if he'd spent the night in a washing machine. We're about to hear how he's been on the bench since before God, Sharon thought. Milton Breyer stood on her right in solemn, suck-up-to-the-judge posture.

"I been servin' this county," Shiver finally said, "nigh goin' on forty years. Nobody's ever wanted to have a hearin' after a prisoner's dead."

"Out of line," Breyer said. "Totally out of the question, Your Honor."

Sharon looked to her left, to be certain that the court reporter was taking everything down. "I can't disagree with the court that it's unusual," Sharon said. "But the case is still open, and the hearing is still scheduled. I want the record to reflect what my client would have had to say if he'd been here."

Shiver peered into his file. "This wouldn' have anything to do with havin' Raymond Burnside hauled up here from the penitentiary would it, Miss Hays?"

"That's exactly what it's about, Judge. My client's desire was to clear his conscience and save an innocent man." If Dycus Wilt could hear that one, Sharon thought, he'd grind the gears into reverse and stop his journey into hell.

"Unrelated cases, Your Honor," Breyer said, shaking his head. "No connection whatsoever."

"If the court please," Sharon said, "I think we're entitled to show that they *are* related, and how." She glanced over her shoulder. Kathleen Fraterno sat alone at the defense table, and Ralph Toner had taken a pew at the back of the spectator section. Otherwise the courtroom was empty, Shiver having dispensed with the day-to-day matters, and having sent the other lawyers and defendants on their way prior to calling Sharon and Breyer up before the bench.

"Well, if this *does* pertain to the Burnside case," Shiver said, "I got another motion before me. Where is Mr. Burnside, Miss Hays?"

"We served a writ on the warden at Wynne Unit night before last," Sharon said. "It's my understanding that they transported the prisoner to Dallas yesterday, though I haven't seen him."

"That mighta been premature," Shiver said.

"Premature, Judge," Breyer said. "Premature as it can be."

Shiver scowled at Breyer. "I'm capable o' runnin' this courtroom, Mr. Breyer, thanks anyway." He pulled some legal-size stapled sheets from the file and turned them around for Sharon to read. "You seen this?" Shiver said.

Sharon bent nearer the bench, as did Milton Breyer. Shiver was holding a motion, bearing today's date, and signed by Hagood T. Malone as Burnside's attorney. The motion requested that the court void the writ of habeas corpus that Sharon had served on the prison, on the grounds that Raymond Burnside had no knowledge of Dycus Wilt's case, and that the writ was therefore frivolous. Since Motions Malone had only filed the papers that morning, Sharon's copy hadn't had time to work its way over to her office through the mail.

"Problem I got here, Miss Hays," Shiver said, "is that your writ's already been served and acted upon. The prisoner's already under our jurisdiction. If I was hearin' this motion beforehand, I'd be inclined to grant it unless you could show me what evidence it is that you need to get from Mr. Burnside. To my way of thinkin', the fact that your client's gone on to his reward in the hereafter voids your writ anyhow. It's all a dead issue. So I'm goin' to grant Mr. Malone's motion here, and return the prisoner to where he oughtta be in the first place."

Milton Breyer sucked air in through his nose and strutted in place. "Just as it should be, Judge. My office will prepare the dismissal on the Dycus Wilt case, and we can all be done with it."

Sharon's shoulders drooped in defeat. Legally the judge was right and (dammit, Sharon thought) so was Milton Breyer. Sharon had no legitimate grounds for even being present in this courtroom with her client dead, and knew it. Raymond Burnside's fate now lay in the palsied hands of Motions Malone. Sharon straightened her posture. "I would at least think we've got a right to argue against Mr. Malone's motion, Judge," she said.

Shiver rattled the pages in irritation. "What's legal

and what's practical's two different things. I'm grantin' this motion." He lifted his robe, put his watch away in his vest pocket, and reached for a pen.

Sharon turned partway toward the court reporter, "On the record, I'm making a formal request for a hearing on this matter."

Shiver bent his head to sign his name. "Request denied, Miss Hays."

"Very well then, Your Honor," Sharon said. "I'm giving verbal notice of appeal. I'll follow the verbal notice with a written notice this afternoon."

Shiver looked up and cocked his head. "You're appealin' me on this?"

"I think it's our privilege, Your Honor." Visible in the corner of Sharon's eye, Milton Breyer stared at her as if she'd just grown a second head.

Shiver's lips twisted in anger. "It's your privilege to appeal. But I'm tellin' you, young woman, it oughtta be your privilege to get your bottom paddled for upsettin' this court with a bunch o' nonsense."

"Nonetheless, Your Honor, my request for a hearing stands."

Shiver seemed on the verge of a stroke. His face reddened. He opened his mouth to say something, then peered beyond Sharon out into the courtroom. The judge said loudly, "Am I glad to see you. How 'bout talkin' some sense into this young lady 'fore she drives us all into the insane asylum?"

Sharon turned. Russell Black stood in the spectator section, his weather-beaten features wrinkled in curiosity. There was a man with him, a medium-size guy in pale blue coveralls. The stranger had slicked-back hair and sideburns that were a tad too long, fifties style.

Black grinned. "I wouldn' want you any crazier'n what you already are, Arnie. Lemme confer with my associate out here in the hall for a minute. I think maybe we can put your worries to bed."

* * *

The man in the coveralls had specks of grease under his nails, as if he'd hurried through cleaning his hands, and his name was stitched inside a white oval of cloth over his pocket. His name, according to the patch, was William. He was smooth-cheeked and smelled of aftershave, and had an earnest, concerned look about him. Sharon felt as though she'd seen him somewhere before.

"Sharon Hays," Russell Black said, "meet Bill Burnside, Raymond's brother. He come by the office lookin' for you."

So that's why he looks familiar, Sharon thought, the slim nose and narrow forehead, same straightforward expression in the eyes as she'd seen in the prison visiting room. "Glad to know you," Sharon said, extending her hand.

His grip was firm. "Sorry I'm dressed this way. I had to leave the shop with just one man working, and I need to get back as soon as I can."

"Don't give it a second thought." Sharon sat down on the corridor bench, with Russell Black in between her and William Burnside.

Black had his long leg up, ankle resting on the knee, shin at a tilted angle. "Mr. Burnside's got an auto repair shop out in East Dallas, not too far from you."

Sharon pictured her own mechanic, and what he'd said about the air-conditioning in her Volvo. "I'll certainly keep that in mind," she said.

"Raymond called my mother from the Dallas County Jail last night," Burnside said. "I went down there this morning and talked to him myself. This has been a terrible ordeal for us, Miss Hays."

"I know it has. I wish I could offer more than my sympathy, but it looks like I've done about all I can." Sharon glanced at Black, who sat impassive.

"Lawyers . . . everything we ever had's about gone. Raymond's the only one of us that made it to college, and he's the best little brother . . . even when he was married to that rich woman, he never forgot his mother, the rest of us. He never killed anybody, Miss Hays. It's not in him to.''

Sharon lowered her gaze to her lap. She didn't know what to say.

"Trouble is," Burnside said, "that Raymond's given up. He's telling us to leave him alone."

"I got that the other night, when I talked to him," Sharon said.

"This last-straw lawyer, Malone," Burnside said, "is just going through the motions. We can't get him on the phone, can't even find out what he's doing."

Sharon looked at Black. Russ had a policy against knocking other lawyers' work, and if he hadn't been sitting there Sharon would have agreed with Burnside. She started to, anyway.

Black saved her the trouble. "When they're court-appointed, son," Black said, "they usually don't do much. Him takin' the trouble to file that motion in there, plus faxin' that letter to the prison the other night, that tells me somethin's afoot. Motions Malone wouldn' undertake to do all that on his own."

Burnside's forehead tightened. "Exactly what are you saying?"

"I'm not really sayin' anything, without knowin' more o' the facts. Just that it's unusual."

"I can't tell you what it's like, not being able to help my baby brother. Even Raymond, he said on the phone, if he could afford somebody like you . . ."

Black winked at Sharon, then said, "What makes you think you can't?"

Burnside sat anxiously forward. "Raymond and I inherited a little house. That's gone. Our dad left Mother a little money. That's gone, too. She's got her teacher retirement. All I could do, and I'd promise this, any work on your car you need for life, you've got it."

Black chuckled. "Tune-ups? Hell, I can't ever remember when I need one."

"I'd put you in my book, call you when it's time," Burnside said.

Black seemed thoughtful. "Anybody got power of attorney for your brother, since he's in prison?"

"Me," Burnside said. "I sold the house. Carry a copy of his power of attorney in my wallet." He bent forward and reached for his hip.

Black put a hand on Burnside's arm. "Hold it," Black said. "Let's don't be jumpin' the gun here. I got to have a retainer."

Sharon blinked. After more than a year of working with Russ, she still never knew what to expect from him. Burnside sagged on the bench, lines of disappointment showing in his face.

"Tell you what," Black said to Burnside. "You got a dollar?"

Burnside looked at the older lawyer.

Black extended a hand, palm up. "Gimme a dollar."

Burnside fished into his pocket, produced three or four crumpled bills, and handed over a one. There were wrinkles across George Washington's face, and one corner was torn.

"We got the standard employment contract, Bill," Black said. "Just happen to have one." He reached in his inside coat pocket and produced a sheet of paper folded over like a letter. "Gimme your John Henry on the bottom," Black said. "We can copy the power of attorney later, over in my office."

As Burnside signed on the dotted line, Black held the dollar out in Sharon's direction. "You want to split this, Miss Hays? Looks like there ought to be some way to handle it so the IRS don't come down on our heads."

Sharon sat at the defense table watching Kathleen Fraterno from the corner of her eye, and let Russ handle the proceedings before Judge Shiver. It had been Sharon's idea for Black to go in front of the bench; Shiver would be in less of an uproar with his old fishing buddy doing the honors.

Black unfolded his employment contract and dangled it in front of the judge. "I don't think Malone's motion is valid anymore, Judge. Me an' Miss Hays are representin' the prisoner now." Milton Breyer stood by with a resigned expression on his face. Kathleen Fraterno frowned in interest, and made a couple of notes.

Shiver put on his glasses, then took them off and read the contract with his nose about two inches from the paper. "Assumin' you do represent Raymond Burnside now, what's the point? You're tryin' to put in an appearance in a case where the defendant's dead. An' you representin' Dycus Wilt *and* Raymond Burnside, 'pears to me that's a conflict."

"I'm not worried about the Wilt case," Black said. "All I want is for you to hold off on returnin' the prisoner to Huntsville till I can put in an appearance on Burnside's behalf in Sandy Griffin's court." He turned around and looked at Sharon. "That is the court where Burnside went down, idn it, Miss Hays?" Sharon nodded.

"You're tellin' me," Shiver said, "that if I'll void this order to return the prisoner to Huntsville, you'll take your circus act and move it outta my courtroom?"

"I think that's fair to say, Arnie," Black said.

Shiver grabbed up a pen and wrote like mad. "If I can get all this rigmarole away from me," he said, "I'll sign about anything."

Raymond Burnside's perspective hadn't changed. He stoically regarded his visitors through county jail bars and said, "I told Miss Hays in prison that I didn't want to pursue this, but you've dragged me up here anyway. I can't stop you from doing that. I can only refuse to help you."

William Burnside leaned over the counter nearer

the bars inside the attorney's visiting booth. Sharon thought the brothers' resemblance was remarkable. The profiles were practically identical. William, in fact, was a dead ringer for Raymond's pretrial mug shots, before the prisoner had lost weight and bulked up his muscles.

"I talked to Mother," William said. "If you quit fighting, it may kill her." Both Burnsides spoke with woodsy East Texas accents, though Raymond's grammar was nearly perfect and William's was pretty good. Sharon recalled that the mother was a schoolteacher in Whitewright, a wide place in the road sixty miles from Dallas. She pictured family suppers with Mrs. Burnside telling her sons, "Don't say 'ain't,' " or, "It isn't 'me and Raymond,' it's 'Raymond and I.' "

"She'll be in an early grave over this, William," Raymond said, "regardless of what happens in the future. We have to get this over with, so both you and Mother can get on with whatever lives you've got left. The quickest way is to go on with the execution." He stuck out his chin in determination.

"Can I interject somethin' here?" Black said.

Both brothers looked at Black. Sharon adjusted her position in her chair.

"I been doin' this a lot of years," Black said. "And Raymond's right, tryin' to get a conviction reversed is damn near impossible regardless o' the facts. The county's going to fight us tooth and nail, more so in this instance 'cause there's politics involved. But there's some things about this case that make it more likely to get overturned. Some items in the court record, if the newspapers get ahold of 'em, now you got the public involved. Publicity's the only thing I've ever seen on a man wrongfully convicted, that'll make the system sit up an' take notice. We got that here."

"Publicity's just what I *don't* want, Mr. Black," Raymond said. "I've had plenty of that, thank you."

"I 'spect you have. If we got any chance at all,

you're in for more of it. Man wants to die, I can't stop him."

Raymond's lips tightened. "I'm not a lunatic, Mr. Black, even though everybody on death row is just a bit crazy. I don't want to die. I just know that's what's going to happen, so I've got a mind-set over it."

Russ leaned back and stretched, extending his arms over his head. He looked at Sharon, then said to Raymond Burnside, "Make you a deal."

William Burnside chipped in, "Listen to him, little brother."

"One motion," Black raised a finger. "I don't think any kind of appellate tomfoolery is goin' to help at this point. Appeals courts get to the point, after they've seen a case come up to 'em over and over, they don't want to listen to anything. I want you to let us file one motion, in the court that convicted you, for a new trial based on new evidence. We got new evidence. I think that's our best shot. If it dudn work, I'll leave you alone."

Raymond Burnside leaned up and gripped the bars. His knuckles whitened. He let go an exasperated sigh. "Just for my brother and my mother, Mr. Black. On one condition. I don't want my mother driving up here to Dallas with her hopes up, so not a word about this to her until the court's ruled on your motion. That's my terms. I think this is a waste of time, but as long as you don't build up false hope in my mother I'll go through it. If I later learn that my mother knew about it beforehand, I'll come back from that execution chamber and haunt you to your grave."

One side of Black's mouth curved up in a lopsided grin. "Instillin' confidence in my clients is what I do best, Raymond," he said.

14

"So what we got, Mr. Gear," Russell Black said, "is a case the state dudn want us to win for political reasons. Not to mention some people a lot more dangerous than Ralph Toner, who've already showed their leanings by shootin' at Miss Hays. For all that we're gettin' a dollar, out of which we got to bankroll our own expenses. So, you want a portion of our fee, or you goin' to hold us up for an hourly rate?"

Anthony Gear was middle fifties, a man who hadn't lost his suspicious FBI squint even though he'd retired from the bureau a few years ago. He wore his usual outlandish combo, a plaid sports coat, yellow shirt, and bright red tie. He had sagging jowls and deep lines in his face, and Sharon thought he'd lost weight since working with the defense on the Midge Rathermore case. Black had told Sharon many times that Gear wasn't any more of a goof-off than any other private eye. Given Russ's opinion of retired law enforcement people in general, his assessment of Anthony Gear was the highest praise.

"I think I'd stick with my usual fee," Gear said.

"Which is what I'd expect you to say," Black said, "assumin' we were willin' to pay it. Which we're not. Fifty dollars an hour is highway robbery. I'm offerin' forty, take it or leave it."

"You're asking me to compromise my professionalism," Gear said.

"Which you already compromised by gettin' on the government payroll to begin with, way back yonder.

The deal is this. Normally you charge fifty, work four hours, and then bill for eight. I won't holler about your time sheets, but I'm payin' forty."

Gear shifted in his chair and touched his fingertips together. "You drive a hard bargain."

Sharon wished these two would go ahead and get it over with. Gear was going to accept the offer. Russ Black would act pained every time Gear's bill came in, but wouldn't hire a different investigator at half the price. Gear was good at what he did, and Sharon suspected that the detective liked Black just as much as Black liked him, which was a whole lot more than either would let on.

"I *intend* to drive a hard bargain," Black said. "Keep you people in line."

"Consider me in line, then," Gear said. "Forty dollars an hour. What do you want me to do?"

Black rocked back and crossed his ankles on his desk in self-satisfaction. Gear looked pleased with himself as well, each man thinking he'd made a good deal. One of Russ's gray hand-tooled lizard boots had a speck of mud on the toe. "You study that file I sent over?" he said.

Sharon was surprised, though she shouldn't have been. So Russ had expected to represent Raymond Burnside all along, and the detective had been studying up even before Dycus Wilt's escape attempt. You've been sneaking around, old boss, Sharon thought. Shame on you.

"Looked it over," Gear said. "And seems to me there were a lot of holes in the state's case to begin with. I think you've got a good shot here."

"Not near as much of a shot as it looks to a layman." Black grandly waved a hand. "Sharon, fill our good detective in on what we're lookin' at in a motion for new trial."

Sharon winced as she lifted her injured leg and crossed it over the good one. It seemed as if the pain was subsiding some. "Pretty simple, Mr. Gear,"

Sharon said. "We have to come up with brand-new evidence."

Both older men gave Sharon their undivided attention. It was a high for Sharon, expounding on the law to an attorney of Russell Black's stature, even though she'd learned in a year and a half that Russ was much more showman than lawyer. He hated the books with a passion, and left all research up to her. Sharon put on her best law school professor's face and went on.

"Everything we really want before the court," Sharon said, "was in the defense's file at Raymond Burnside's first trial, though his lawyer either couldn't or didn't get any of it into evidence. There are three women Raymond picked up at Friday's on the night his wife was killed, and spent the night with one of them. All three were on his witness list, but none showed up to testify. We have their names and addresses from six years ago, and tracking them down will take legwork. There's the fact that the victim was raped, another little tidbit that the defense didn't see fit to bring up. But none of that's going to help us win a new trial. If we try to use any of it in our motion, they'll throw us out of court. The state will merely say that all that evidence was known, or should have been known, to the defense at the first trial, and they'll be right. It's not fair or just, but that's the law. Only newly discovered evidence can we use. If our motion's granted, we can bring out whatever we want to in a second trial, but the real hurdle is getting the new trial to begin with."

Gear said, "That doesn't sound too tough, with this . . . Dycus Wilt, right? Dycus Wilt's statement that he and his buddy did it."

"Hearsay," Black said. "Pure hearsay."

Gear looked first at Black, then at Sharon.

"Old boss is right," Sharon said, "because little Dycus has left us. The only one he said anything to is me. If I tried to testify to what Dycus told me, even Milton Breyer would make morons out of us. He'd yell hearsay, and the court would give us the hook before you could say squat. The hearsay rule is, since Dycus won't be in court for them to cross-examine, we can't bring up anything he told me. Normally hearsay works in the defendant's favor, when the dead victim's not around to testify, but here we've got the tables turned. We can use what we know about Dycus to try and dig up other evidence, but any direct statement from him will be thrown out. Period."

"So what new evidence do you think you've got?"

"If I knew that," Black said, "I wouldn' be hirin' a detective. Here I've lied to our client, tellin' him we got all kinds of new stuff and that everything's hunky-dory."

"How long have we got to come up with some?" Gear rested his ankle on his knee and clutched his shin.

"Tomorrow mornin' might be soon enough, if you can't do it tonight."

"We've got to concentrate on the guy we know actually killed her," Sharon said. "Woodrow Lee. And speaking of him, I know where we just might come up with something new."

"Best thing I do," Black said, "next to instillin' confidence in clients, is surroundin' myself with good people, Sharon."

Sharon pictured Dycus Wilt as he'd looked the first time she'd seen him in court. The image still gave her goose bumps. "Dycus told me Woodrow Lee stole a clock from the Burnside home that night. An animated clock, sort of like a cuckoo only with little people coming out. Said he'd seen the clock at Woodrow's house within the past month. If we can come up with that, that the clock's over there, that can be the entire basis for our motion.

"Part of the state's case in the first trial," Sharon said, "was that nothing was stolen from the house, therefore it wasn't a robbery, leaving Raymond Burnside as the only one with the motive to kill her without stealing anything. If we can show something was missing, and that that something is now at Lee's place, I think the court would have to go along with us. Shows new evidence that someone else might have done it."

"Where's this Woodrow Lee live?" Gear took a pad and pen from his inside breast pocket.

Sharon hunched her shoulders. "I don't know."

Gear frowned. "Can you find out?"

Black snorted. "A detective we got here."

Sharon ignored the older lawyer. "I might. Woodrow Lee was the state's snitch against Dycus Wilt. Neither Kathleen Fraterno nor Milt Breyer is going to help us voluntarily. But I might still have friends in the D.A.'s office that'll take a peek in the file."

"Well, let's get after it, then," Gear said. "Get the address, and we can call on Mr. Lee tonight."

"Forty dollars an hour," Black said. "You ought to be splittin' it with Miss Hays, Mr. Gear. Thus far she's the only one I've seen doing any detectin'."

Sharon left Russ and Anthony Gear chewing the fat, and retreated into the reception area. There was a message on the machine from Richard Branson, which caused her to blush slightly as she copied it down, and one from Andy Wade as well. She folded the call slip containing Branson's number and snuggled it into her shoulder bag, then went into her office and called Andy Wade's number at the *Dallas Morning News*. Wade answered on the third ring, still sounding as if he was developing a cold.

"Deep Throat, Andy," Sharon said. "You ready for some relief, big boy?"

There was a rustling sound over the line, after which Wade said, "Elaine Dimmit. D-I-M-M-I-T."

Sharon grabbed a pen and wrote the name on the corner of a yellow legal pad. "Who is . . . ?"

"Worked five years for the sheriff, last duty in the jail office. Husband was a city cop, fired last year for soliciting a bribe from a motorist he stopped for a traffic ticket. Guy down at the city says the Dimmits are in debt up to here."

"She'd have access to the handcuff keys," Sharon said.

"Not anymore. Because this morning she walked off the job. Quit cold, no notice."

"What time was this?"

"According to the county she left sometime after nine."

"Which means she was on duty when they paraded the prisoners down the corridor to the holding cells."

"Right on, Miss Hays. You've still got that key, right?"

"Wild horses couldn't drag it away from me," Sharon said. "You have her address?"

Wade gave the address, in a run-down neighborhood just east of downtown, and Sharon copied the street and number down. Wade said, "I'm going to drop by and see if I can chat with the lady."

"Have you asked the county about her?"

"Inquired in personnel, and they said they'd have to call me back. Typical stonewall. About fifteen minutes later, Major Boles called. He asked me what I wanted to know about Mrs. Dimmit, and who leaked her name to me. I hung up on the guy."

"Which means they know, and want to know how much *you* know."

"Sounds like it."

Sharon's gaze drifted to her flower boxes. The impatiens needed watering in the worst way, the petals beginning to droop. "You be careful, Andy," she said. "There are bad people involved in this. If you need any evidence of that, I'll let you examine my sore knee." She thought that one over, then laughed softly. "Strictly for professional purposes, of course. You can look at the knee if you'll whitewash the fence, okay?"

15

Vernon Denopoulis leaned back on the cement bank, and let his legs float underwater like strips of pale seaweed. Jack Torturro squatted down wearing slacks and a knit golf shirt, and jerked his thumb over his shoulder. "Guy I want you to meet here, Mr. D., Ralph Toner."

Denopoulis assessed the newcomer through mirrored shades. The guy, Toner, stood behind Torturro. Was a little on the skinny side, though he might beef up when seen on television. Toner wore a dark blue suit, classy but not too expensive, a businesslike-but-not-extravagant-looking guy, probably would make the right impression on the voters. Denopoulis extended a hand from which chlorinated water dripped. "The candidate, right? Glad to knowya."

Toner bent from the waist and lightly gripped the hand. "Greek. It's a pleasure to finally meet you in person."

Denopoulis' face froze. "I look like a fucking Greek to you?"

Torturro raised up from his haunches and quickly said to Toner, "Vernon don't like people calling him—"

"You want a fucking Greek," Denopoulis said, "take the boat to Athens." He jabbed a finger toward a table shaded by an umbrella, surrounded by cedar plank chairs. "You two sit over there. I'll be along."

The two men retreated, Torturro talking a mile a minute and waving his hands, and sat on opposite sides of the poolside table. Denopoulis took his time hoisting himself out of the water. He snatched a towel from a chaise longue and stood, then dried himself off as he took in the scene. Couple of droopy broads from, let's see, South Dakota, Denopoulis seemed to remember, stretched out on lounges down the way, their skins turning lobster red as they overdid the sun-bathing at Loew's Anatole Hotel's rooftop pool. The poolside bar was under a bamboo roof. Seated on a stool was a brunette with tight legs and ass, hunched over a hurricane punch while a bartender tried to get friendly. Denopoulis mumbled to himself, "The fuck's she doing?" Then he pulled on a white terry cloth robe and slipped his feet into clogs, holding up one finger in a just-a-minute gesture to the guys waiting at the table. He strolled down under the bamboo and leaned on the bar alongside the brunette. "The fuck you doing?" Denopoulis said.

The bartender looked slowly up, his grin fading. He wore his blond hair in a skater cut. His white safari jacket had the Loew's emblem stitched above the pocket.

The brunette wiggled testily on her stool. "Getting a drink. You said we'd relax a couple of days."

"Yeah? Well, I think you need your hair fixed." Denopoulis fished inside his robe and dropped a hundred-dollar bill on the bar.

"I might want to swim." The brunette had a button nose, which wrinkled as she spoke.

Denopoulis stroked her smooth brown arm. "You got plenty sun already. You want to look nice, we go out to dinner." He slapped her bottom. "Go on now, I got business with them guys over there."

The brunette smirked, grabbed up a towel and the hundred, and wiggled away toward the dressing room. Denopoulis watched her go. He held the tip of his finger over the straw in her hurricane, raised the straw, and dribbled rum punch on his tongue. He said to the bartender, "Nice ass, huh?"

The bartender turned his gaze from the brunette and looked at Denopoulis, a squatty man in his forties with thinning, frizzed-out hair. The part in his robe showed thick dark chest hair. "She's . . . yeah, pretty nice," the bartender said.

Denopoulis produced another hundred. He wadded the bill and stuffed it inside the bartender's breast pocket. "That ass is strictly for looking purposes, sonny. You remember that, huh?"

"No problem, sir." The bartender snatched the bill from his pocket and looked it over.

Denopoulis pointed a finger. "You remember, you hear?" He left the bar and strolled to the poolside table, two men waiting in hundred-degree heat. A trickle of sweat ran down Denopoulis' forehead. He sat down and hunched forward, leaning his elbows on the table. "Got to watch these young guys. Got a hard-on alla time."

Torturro showed strong white teeth in a grin. "How was the trip?"

"Shitty. Got to ride one of them puddle jumper Howard Hughes planes outta San Jose, transfer to LAX, took half a fucking day. Texas is too fucking hot; I don't understand why all these people are living around here. I don't like to make these trips. Guys don't fuck up, I don't have to." Denopoulis looked at Toner. "Why you want to be governor of *this* fucking state, Ralphie?"

Beads of sweat had popped out on Toner's forehead. "Look, I apologize for the faux pas over there, the nickname. I didn't know."

Denopoulis frowned. "What's that faw pass shit you're talking?"

"He means he fucked up, Vernon," Torturro said.

"Yeah? Well, now that you mention it, he did." Denopoulis reached inside his robe and scratched his armpit. "I'll get that out of the way, Ralphie. That Vernon the Greek shit was okay when I lived in Brooklyn younger days. Everybody had a nickname

back then, guys making book on the street corners.
Little Augie was one guy I remember; we had this
Puerto Rican they called Spanish Raymond. But, hey,
you grow up. Bet you had a nickname when you was
a kid. What was it?"

Toner grinned sheepishly. "Mine was Puppy."

"Well ain't that cute?" Denopoulis said. "So now
you're a big shot candidate and all, you want guys
coming up calling you Puppy? Shit no, you don't. So
I'm Vernon. That ought to be simple for a college guy
like you."

"Sure, Vernon, no problem."

"Now I wouldn't exactly say, no problem. Sounds
to me like we got problems out the ass down here.
So Jack Torturro tells me you're wanting to talk. So
we're talking."

"I wanted to take a meeting with Morgan Hill
Corp.," Toner said. He looked uncomfortable in his
suit, perspiration on his forehead. He bent up under
the umbrella shade.

"Which is me," Denopoulis said.

"You're what, the president?"

"President. Chairman of the fucking board, you
name it. I live in Morgan Hill, California, got my own
mountain as a matter of fact, golf course right across
my back fence, seventy degrees alla time. Pretty original, calling my outfit Morgan Hill Corp."

"So you've got the authority," Toner said, "and I'll
get down to brass tacks. I think we should terminate
our financial arrangement."

Denopoulis removed his sunglasses and folded the
earpieces. He had pale white skin around blue eyes.
"You want to call it off? Sure, Ralphie, all you got to
do is come up with about seven million dollars, which
is what we spent so far, TV commercials showing you
and your old lady, the kids, everybody grinning and
saying they love Texas and shit. Lawyer fees, paying
for all this land that ain't going to be worth shit unless

we can get gambling in down here. You want to write me a check, or what?"

"I didn't agree to be part of any murder attempts." Toner stuck his jaw out, the guy getting tough and showing he wasn't here to take shit from anybody.

"Yeah?" Denopoulis said. "That was handled bad, that I'll grant you, which is something I'm taking up with Mr. Torturro here." He slapped Torturro on the back, Torturro looking away, watching the women from South Dakota roll over onto their bellies.

"But while we're on the subject," Denopoulis said, "I didn't make no deal to bankroll a guy goes around building a frame around people. You talking about us trying to off somebody, what about you? The guy down there, what do you call it when they put him in, what is it in Texas? Gas chamber, huh?"

"Lethal injection," Torturro said. "Painless."

"Yeah? I knew a couple guys wouldda liked that, sitting in the hot seat up in New York state. Like putting a dog to sleep, right?" Denopoulis put his shades back on, ready now to get down to business with Ralph Toner. When Denopoulis had been in the federal joint in Lompoc, California, the hacks had taken his sunglasses away, said the shades made the convict look too sinister. Not long after that the hacks themselves had taken to wearing mirrored sunglasses, intimidating the prisoners as they shook down cells for contraband. Denopoulis flattened his palm on the table and said to Ralph Toner, "You don't call that murder, framing a guy which ain't done shit?"

"I don't know that he hasn't," Toner said. "Likely it was him."

"Bullshit, Ralphie. I check guys out, you know? That poor old senator lost his daughter; all you're trying to do is make a sucker out of the guy. Tell him, I can't bring her back, sir, but we can give this guy what he's got coming, right? Gives you political clout for life. You didn't have clue one who done that girl, so you figured to get the guy the senator don't like to begin with. Six years later this nigger shows up, the guy that done her, now we got to get your nuts off the block or we blow our whole operation down here. Say what you want about us guys, we come straight at you. You fucking politicians do the same thing we do, only grinning at the people while it's going on. So tell me, Ralphie. Which is better, your way or our way?"

Toner gazed into the distance, his eyes misting. "Christ, I never should have . . ."

"Never should have what?" Denopoulis said. "Come off the bullshit, okay? You thought it'd help you get elected, you'd get on a stump and fuck a cow on national television with your pants down around your ankles. So don't come on innocent with me, you prick. You called us, Ralphie, we didn't call you."

"I was merely looking for backers." Toner looked about to cry.

Denopoulis leaned back, sadly shaking his head. "Guys like you I seen all my life. Beginning in Brooklyn. I'm about fifteen years old, guys in business suits coming down to borrow money from my old man, he's selling fruit off a cart. Promised vig you wouldn't believe, fifteen percent a week some of 'em, then took the train back over to Manhattan and pretended not to know us no more. I was a young guy, I used to go up to Midtown and break some of those guys' fucking legs."

Toner rested his forehead on his palm. "I had no idea . . ."

"Bullshit you didn't. Nobody comes to us that don't get referred. You talked to a guy in Mississippi, we just put a riverboat operation in down there after helping this guy get elected, right? So what'd he tell you, we were people interested in the liberal philosophy or some shit? I don't know if you're liberal, conservative, or got a fucking cob up your ass, and don't give a shit. You told Jack Torturro first time you talked to him, you thought Texas was ripe for casino gambling. That right, or isn't it?"

Toner choked out, "Christ."

"So here's the way it is," Denopoulis said. "Like it or not, we're all one big happy family here, the golden rule being, my way or the highway. I won't insult us all by thinking you might have seven mil to bail yourself out, so here we go. Our side ain't lily-white itself, my good friend Jack Torturro here trying to have this lady shot in the middle of a superhighway. So talk to me, Jackie, what's that shit all about?" The Greek snapped his fingers, then made a beckoning motion.

Torturro brushed his center-parted hair back with his hand. "I gave her an opportunity to make some money."

"That's a real brilliant maneuver on your part. Lady's a criminal lawyer, you offer her a job doing real estate closings. Jesus Christ, why don't you just offer her a bribe? A problem we got here is assuming people are stupid. All you done so far is make her more determined to spring this guy. I hope we got enough sense that the shooters are out of sight."

"No chance anybody's going to come up with those guys." Torturro spread his hands in an umpire's "safe" signal. "Car was clean as a whistle, and she didn't see nobody good."

"For now we got to assume we're okay on that," Denopoulis said, "which ain't in no way due to your brains. So what about the nigger in jail we talked about?"

"No more," Torturro said. "Gone. Sheriff's people shot him making a break."

"So that's one plus, which is going to put a cramp in the lady's style with no testimony from the nigger. What about the other guy, the nigger's buddy? He still walking around?"

"Won't be, if we can come up with him."

"How you handle the nigger's escape?"

"We handled it. Broad works in the sheriff's office."

Toner half stood. "I can't be a party to listening to this."

Denopoulis pointed. "Sit your ass down. What, you're going to go back and file charges against us or something? Jesus Christ, Ralphie, when you going to learn you don't just ask for favors and then play like you don't know nothing about the way these favors get done? It comes down to it somebody gets busted, ain't anybody going to snitch on you, but that works both ways. Now put your ass in that fucking chair before I have Mr. Torturro put you there."

Toner sank back down and looked at his folded hands.

"That's better. Now, all you had to tell me was, you wanted out?"

Toner sighed. "That was my sole purpose."

"And I made it clear you can't get out, right?"

"I suppose. Christ . . ."

"We couldda saved me a trip, 'cause I couldda told you this over the phone. You're in. Now, you want to leave, you ask to be excused."

Toner looked up, licking his lips.

"You repeat after me, Ralphie," Denopoulis said. "Mr. Denopoulis, sir, is it all right for me to leave?"

Toner shifted his gaze back and forth from Denopoulis to Torturro. Denopoulis fished in the pocket of his robe, came up with a diamond ring, and slipped the ring on his pinky, left hand. Toner said, "Mr. Denopoulis . . ."

"Jesus, it ain't that hard. You want me to repeat it?"

Toner inhaled a deep breath. "Mr. Denopoulis, sir . . ."

"I'm not sure this guy's been to college, Jackie," Denopoulis said.

". . . Is it all right for me to leave?" Toner finished.

Denopoulis spread his hands, palms up. "So what's so fucking hard? Permission granted. We'll be in touch, okay?"

Toner stood, took a couple of steps toward the hotel entry, stopped, started to turn around, then took off at a fast clip, skirting the pool.

Denopoulis watched the candidate go, the Greek's face impassive as he said to Torturro, "All these guys fold in time, but this asshole's jumping out the window before we even get started. Wasn't so many gamblers in this state, I'd cut this off, but we're into it. Just remember, Jackie. Heat comes down on this, it's all the fucking candidate's problem. We need to keep that in mind; everything we do from now on, somebody can tie it in to Ralph fucking Toner. Guy like that, I ain't willing to take the chance of spending a day in jail, you got that?"

16

Andy Wade never went anywhere without his inhaler since he'd first developed asthma at the age of nine. The attacks came when he was excited; all of a sudden—*bam*—a tightening in his chest accompanied by a stifling sensation when he tried to breathe. He rated the attacks on a scale of three, a number one being the worst, and what he felt now was likely a two. He dropped his five-speed lever into second gear, eased out on the clutch, and let his Suzuki Sidekick drift over to the curb on East Side Drive. His right front tire scraped concrete. Wade applied the brakes, dug his inhaler from his pants pocket, shoved the cylinder into his mouth, and pumped like mad as he inhaled the vapors into his lungs. A burn filled his chest. His desperate gasping slowed, then dissipated entirely as his breathing returned to normal. He removed the inhaler and sucked in air as he looked around.

The neighborhood had been upper-middle-class before World War II; during the past three decades affluent Dallas had migrated to the north and left the poor to tough it out on East Side Drive. The two-story stucco homes, which stood behind raised yards and tall old elms and sycamores, were badly in need of repair. Most of the homes were split into duplexes or quads, some of them sharing common gas and electricity connections. Boys and girls in hand-me-down clothing played in the streets and rolled worn-out tire casings over bald, trash-strewn lawns.

Locating Elaine Dimmit's residence had been a tall

order, Wade driving at a snail's pace and squinting to read the faded-out addresses on the curbs. He put his inhaler away, climbed out onto tar-veined asphalt, and crossed the yard in sweltering afternoon heat. The house was dark redbrick, with paint flaking from yellowed eaves. As he ascended the steps onto a cracked cement porch, a tin can clanked and rolled. He reached in his pocket and switched his recorder on.

He found no doorbell button, so rapped loudly on a wooden screen door. He waited a couple of minutes, got no response, then knocked again. Footsteps within the house creaked on linoleum. The door opened the width of a chain. A hoarse female voice said, "Yes?"

Wade reached for one of his business cards. "Mrs. Dimmit?" Window shades darkened the interior of the house. From somewhere inside came the whir of an electric fan. Wade squinted into the dimness, made out a long nose, a mouth with crooked teeth, and what looked to be a flowered housecoat. "Elaine Dimmit?" he said.

"Who's looking for her?" Hesitant, suspicion in the tone.

"Andy Wade, *Dallas Morning News*. Can I speak to you a moment?"

"What about?"

Wade decided to lie; if the woman had done what he suspected, the truth wouldn't get him anywhere. "I'm doing a story," he finally said, "about working conditions in the sheriff's department."

The door closed. A chain rattled. Hinges groaned as the door opened again, wider this time, and a light-skinned black woman moved up to stand behind the screen. She was around thirty-five with square shoulders and big round eyes. "Who gave you my name?" she said.

"Didn't you just quit this morning?"

The eyes narrowed. "Why you interested in that?"

Wade shuffled his feet and put on his most disarming grin. "Look, can I come in a minute?" He was

counting on her curiosity; when the newspapers came
calling, people just had to know the reason.

The woman reached up and dropped a hook
through an eyebolt. "No, you can't. Why you want to
talk to me?"

"I told you, general employment conditions. Wasn't
your husband a policeman?"

"He don't live here anymore," she said.

"You are Elaine Dimmit, aren't you?"

"I s'pose I am."

"Five years on the job," Wade said, "and this morning you walk off with no notice. I'm just wondering
why. Sheriff not treating you right?"

"Job was okay. I want something different."

Wade pitched his curveball. "Did your leaving have
anything to do with the escape attempt this morning?"
He carefully watched her reaction.

Her mouth gaped open. "Why you ask that?"

"I thought maybe the danger, you didn't think you
were being protected."

"You work at the jail, shit happens."

"You were in the office, weren't you? Where they
bring the prisoners through going to court?"

She folded her arms. "What difference it make
where I worked?"

"Were you there when they brought Dycus Wilt
down?"

Her chin tilted. "You ain't here about no working
conditions."

"Can you remember him coming by?"

"Somebody at the sheriff's asking questions about
me?" Her tone was belligerent.

Wade tightened his mouth, took his glasses off, and
cleaned them on the front of his shirt. "They would
have been keeping him separate from the other prisoners. He'd have had his legs shackled and—"

"I don't know nothing about all that."

"In all due respect, Mrs. Dimmit, you'd have to
know that. It's part of the procedure you learn."

Elaine Dimmit's mouth twisted in anger. "I got nothing more to say to you. Go away." She backed inside and slammed the door.

Wade put his glasses on. He placed his ear to the screen and knocked. There was hushed breathing on the other side of the door. He said loudly, "Mrs. Dimmit?"

"You got trouble if you don't go away." The door muffled her words. Her tone showed fear.

Wade slid one of his business cards in the crack between the screen and door frame. "Suit yourself, ma'am. If the county comes calling, they won't be so friendly. I'm leaving my card. If you change your mind, give me a call."

"Won't be changing no mind."

"I'll be in touch, Mrs. Dimmit." Wade left the porch and crossed the yard with his pulse racing, the lead-in to his story already forming in his mind. He wondered how much his editor would let him get by with. Dycus Wilt had had the key to his handcuffs. Elaine Dimmit had access to the keys, had plenty of chance to slip a key to Wilt, and had quit her job within minutes after the escape attempt. Two plus two, dear readers, Wade thought. He whistled softly as he descended the slope onto the sidewalk, then stopped in his tracks. He said uncertainly, "Can I help you?"

The two men who blocked his path looked as out of place in the neighborhood as Andy Wade felt. One was blond with a thick neck, and towered close to seven feet. The other was about Wade's height, five-ten, and was dressed in a dark sport coat and light tan slacks. He was rangy, like an athlete. Beyond the two men a coal-black Mercury Cougar was parked behind Wade's yellow Suzuki Sidekick, the off-road vehicle with its tire touching the curb.

Wade said, "You guys lost or something?"

The rangy man took a step forward and drove his fist into the reporter's midsection. Air whooshed from Wade's lungs as he doubled over in pain. His glasses clattered to the sidewalk. The second man clasped his hands together and swung them like a mallet against the back of Wade's neck. His vision blurred. He went down on his knees, then fell forward on his face. A hard-toed shoe kicked him in the ribs. Wade yelled in anguish. Hands went inside his back pockets and took his wallet. Wade lay still. A gruff voice said, "Newspaper asshole."

Wade turned his head and said from the side of his mouth, "My editor knows where I am." Tightness built suddenly in his chest. He wheezed for breath. The shoe thudded into his ribs a second time. Bone popped as paralyzing agony shot up his side and into his neck. He tried to scream, but all that came out was a soft croak.

The hands dug in his side pocket. His recorder came out. A knobby fist held the recorder in front of Wade's eyes, then dropped it on the sidewalk. A large brown shoe stomped the recorder to bits. The hand grabbed up the cassette and shredded the tape. The empty cassette dropped inches from Wade's nose. Wade tried to inhale, fighting for breath.

Lips moved close to his ear. A hoarse, northern-accented voice said, "You forget all this shit, newsboy. You hear me?" Strong fingers twisted his ear. "I said, 'You hear me?' "

Wade shut his eyes and nodded.

"You forget what I said, we'll see you again." Footsteps retreated up the walk. Doors slammed. A starter chugged, then an engine caught and raced. The Mercury pulled from the curb and drove leisurely away.

Wade gasped and grabbed at his throat. He reached in his pocket, found his inhaler, poked the cylinder between his lips, and pumped, sucking vapor into his lungs. Finally he could breathe.

Excruciating pain shooting through his ribs, he crawled across the sidewalk and opened the Sidekick's passenger door. He groped inside for his cellular, squinted without glasses to read the numbers, and punched in 911. Then he dropped the phone on the floorboard, sat on the sidewalk, and reached for his fallen lenses. The pain was too intense for him to bend forward, so he let the glasses lie. Exhausted from the effort, Andy Wade leaned back, shut his eyes, and prayed for the agony to cease.

17

Sharon thought that Anthony Gear drove the freeways more like a squad car cop than a retired FBI agent, both hands on the wheel, the speedometer needle never inching above forty miles per hour as he stayed in the center lane and ignored the honks of annoyance from other cars. Sharon was mortified. She wanted to scootch down in the seat to hide her face from passing motorists. The detective's white Land Rover had grime on its hood and mud on its tires. Looks like the *same mud,* Sharon thought, which was on the tires back when Gear worked on the Rathermore case, a year ago, and she wondered if the detective had washed his car in all this time. She doubted it. There were candy wrappers and credit card receipts wadded and strewn at random on the floorboards, and the Land Rover's interior smelled of cigarettes. Sharon had never seen the detective smoke, but the ashtray overflowed with butts. The butts had white lipstick-stained filters, and Sharon decided that Anthony Gear's wife was just as much of a slob as Antony Gear. A match made in heaven, Sharon thought. She looked out the window and reminded herself that Gear was a good detective.

As he left I-35 South at the Illinois exit, headed into west Oak Cliff, Gear said, "Something bothering me about all this. Okay, these two guys do the crime and steal the clock. But six years later, one of 'em's still got it? A robbery like that, I'd think they'd keep it just long enough to get to the hockshop and trade it in for dope money." Dusk was fading into darkness. Gear switched his headlights on.

Sharon watched two overweight black women waddle from a 7-Eleven, carrying paper sacks, and climb into a car with dented fenders. "I just know what Dycus told me," she said. "And as far as new evidence, it's the best shot we've got if we can . . . might be, the clock was too distinctive for them to pawn."

"I think you give these guys too much credit, Miss Hays. People like that wouldn't think twice about pawning the *Mona Lisa* for fifty bucks if they thought they could get high. Where do we turn?" The Land Rover rolled east on Illinois Avenue with weatherbeaten houses on both sides. Black men and women strolled the sidewalks, in no particular hurry to reach no particular destination.

Sharon snatched the Mapsco from the floorboard. She flipped to the page she'd marked with a three-by-five index card, the detailed map showing Illinois Avenue as it wound through Oak Cliff. "Two more lights, it should be," Sharon said. "Then you take a left, a little street running close to a golf course."

"Cedar Crest Golf Course," Gear said. "My dad used to play it when I was a kid. Was a plush layout, they had the PGA there in the thirties. Now they say you're lucky to get through eighteen holes without somebody coming out of the bushes and robbing you. This neighborhood went all black in what, the sixties? Ought to have a sign at the Oak Cliff boundary saying, 'White Man, Don't Let the Sun Set on Your Head.' "

Sharon closed the Mapsco in her lap, and didn't say anything.

"See, just look at these people," Gear said. "They can say what they want about equality, they haven't changed since the Dred Scott decision. After Hoover died, the bureau had to hire a bunch of 'em. Lazy bunch of guys, could never get them to do anything."

Sharon folded her arms as anger built within.

"Don't get me wrong," Gear said, changing lanes

as the car behind flashed its bright lights. "I mean, I *liked* some of them, some of those guys knew their place and we got along. But as a general rule, anything that required intelligence . . . you probably never spent much time around these people, Miss Hays."

Sharon blinked in the darkness. "My best friend. Sheila Winston."

There were ten seconds of silence, after which Gear said, "Oh. You mean the lady that testified in the Rathermore case, the psychologist."

"She's a psychiatrist," Sharon said. "An M.D. Was a Phi Beta Kappa."

"Psychiatrist, yeah. She seemed like a nice enough lady. Hey, I didn't mean . . ."

"I think you have to turn up there, Mr. Gear."

Gear spun the wheel, and Sharon's weight shifted to her right as the Land Rover entered a twisty black-top street, rickety wooden houses, old cars and pick-ups in the driveways. "I mean, there's *exceptions*," Gear said. "But as a general rule . . ."

"Slow down, please," Sharon said. Gear braked to five miles an hour. Sharon lowered her window and shone a flashlight on a porch to read the address. She clicked off the light, and as the window hummed upward said, "Should be on the other side of the street, about third house down."

Gear steered to the other side and snugged up to the curb. "I think this is it. Typical . . ."

Sharon peered up the sidewalk toward a home with shutters hanging from broken hinges. On the tiny lawn stalks of Johnson grass waved above unmowed weeds. A tricycle with one wheel missing sat near a sagging wood porch. Sharon couldn't resist saying, "Typical nigger's house, Mr. Gear?"

Gear killed the engine and opened his door. "I wasn't trying to . . ."

Sharon stood out in the street, then leaned inside the car. "I'll bet you," she said, "that Sheila's house would put yours to shame. Come on, Mr. Gear, let's go calling. And, don't worry, I'll stay between you and these *people*. We wouldn't want anything to rub off now, would we?"

Surprisingly enough the doorbell worked, chiming three notes inside the house as Sharon pressed the button, then folded her arms to wait. She'd changed into new jeans, Nikes, and a blue cotton pullover before Gear had picked her up at home. The detective's wardrobe seemed to consist of one outfit, the noisy plaid sport coat and slacks. His brown shirt collar was unbuttoned and his yellow tie pulled down. Gear seemed nervous, his gaze roaming up and down the street as if he expected the natives to surround him at any moment. Sharon drummed her fingers on her upper arms and looked down at her feet.

The woman who opened the door was a human wreck. Her hair hung down in ratty strings, and her body odor seeped onto the porch like sewage. Grayish gum showed in the gap where one of her front teeth should have been, and her right eyelid was sewn shut. Her one good eye shifted left and right. "I done told you, I won't have no money till nex' week."

"Is this where Woodrow Lee lives?" Sharon said.

"Ain't no Woody here." She spit a wad of paper into her hand. "You see his sorry ass, you tell him he owes for dis television. Ain't non o' mine." She wore a grimy white T-shirt and no bra, tired breasts sagging onto a big round belly. Sharon thought the woman might be pregnant. Kid's got a lot to look forward to if she is, Sharon thought.

"Sorry to bother you, ma'am, but I'm Sharon Hays, a lawyer, and this is Mr. Anthony Gear. Sorry we didn't call first."

The woman's expression was vacant, devoid of all hope, all emotion. "I done told that other lady, I ain't seen no Woody in fo', five days. Told dem mens, too."

Sharon bit the inside of her cheek. "You mean Kathleen Fraterno, the lady with the county?"

" 'At sumbitch took all my money, lef' me wid nothin'."

"A slender lady, a little shorter than I am? Her hair has these really springy curls."

"Sho'. I tole Woody not to be truckin' wid no county people. Now he got Dycus Wilt tellin' on his ass an' them men lookin' to do somethin' to him."

Sharon was pretty good at masking surprise, but couldn't help letting her jaw drop. "How did he know Dycus Wilt was saying anything?"

"Sumbitch call Woody outta the jail. Tole him Woody go aroun' droppin' a dime, he gonna drop a dime on Woody's sorry ass." The woman's eyes narrowed in suspicion. "You ain't wid no county."

Sharon looked beyond the woman into the house. There was a single light glowing somewhere in back, but the room nearest the front was in darkness. "I want to help Woody," Sharon said. "Did you say some men had been looking for him?" Boards creaked on her right as Anthony Gear shifted his weight.

"Big white men. Talked funny, they ain't from 'round here."

"Did they give you their names?"

"No, ma'am. Say, you wantin' to help Woody, you got some money fo' his sorry ass?"

Sharon opened her mouth to say no, but Gear cut in and said, "We might. If he's got what we're looking for, we might buy it from you."

"Say they shuttin' my 'lectricity off. Phone already shut off, las' week."

Gear took a step nearer the door. "We're looking for a funny clock. When it strikes the hour, little people come out."

The woman's look was suddenly guarded. "How much you pay?"

Sharon took her cue. "That depends. Did Woody have a clock like that?"

"I done tol' 'at sorry sumbitch that clock worth

somethin'. He jus' want to sit aroun' an' watch them little people."

Sharon's adrenaline pumped. "Ma'am, if you have the clock, we can see that your power stays on. You'd have to testify in court about it."

The woman's lip curled. "Ain't droppin' no dime. That why Woody in all this shit, talkin' to no county."

"You wouldn't be dropping a dime. I'd just want you to say, the truth, that the clock came from your house, and that it was Woody's clock, as far as you know." Sharon dipped in her shoulder bag and produced several twenty-dollar bills. "By the way, ma'am, what's your name?"

The woman looked at the money. "Gloria. Gloria Bone." Her one good eye bugged out. She raised her voice and moaned pitifully, "Oh, Lord."

Sharon stood back. "Is something wrong?" She tried to keep from looking at the woman's sutured eyelid, but couldn't help it. Gloria Bone. Perfect name for the perfect face.

"Oh, Lordy Lord," Gloria Bone said.

Sharon squeezed the bills in her hand. "Look, if this isn't enough maybe we could . . ."

"I knowed nothin' good was going to happen."

"Maybe we could kick in a few nights in a motel. Nice air-conditioning."

Gloria looked as though a friend had just died. "That clock in here broke. Woody kep' lookin' at it, layin' aroun', finally I throwed it at his sorry ass. Them little people hangin' by springs in here."

Sharon and Gear exchanged a look. Then Sharon said, "Don't worry about what condition it's in. That clock's so valuable, we'd even pay to have it fixed. I think we could fit that in our budget. Don't you, Mr. Gear?"

18

Andy Wade is in a lot more pain than he's letting on, Sharon thought. The reporter put up a pretty good front, but occasionally the kid-like grin would freeze as if Andy was about to scream.

"I wonder if they followed you," Sharon said, "or were just watching her house to see who was snooping around. Gee, Andy, I hurt for you." Her gaze softened and she looked away.

Wade reached inside his hospital gown and touched the tape plastered to his midsection. "That's like saying, was it the cornerback or the safety that lowered the boom on you? What difference does it make?"

"Big difference. If they were only keeping an eye on her, they might've attacked anyone who came around. If they were following you, you were the target. Which means they reacted to your article, and that they're more desperate than we'd thought. We didn't think they'd go against newspaper people."

Wade's bed was cranked halfway up. His retractable tray held half-eaten toast wedges and scrambled eggs. He sipped orange juice through a straw. "One guy pulled my wallet out and checked my ID. That was after the first time they kicked me. The second kick was harder. Guess they don't like reporters too much."

"I think something's out of control with the bad guys," Sharon said. "Toner's not behind it, he's only the stooge. The gambling guys are used to people lying down for them."

"They've got my attention." Wade held his ribs and tightly closed his yes.

"Mine, too," Sharon said. She walked to the window, looked out over hospital grounds, white-uniformed nurses pushing patients in wheelchairs. "Ever since I got your message, that you were laid up, I've been wondering if this is worth it."

"Whenever I see Toner on television loving Texas to death," Wade said, "I get these chill bumps. If I'm looking out for old number one, I'll forget the whole thing and do a series on the plight of the homeless."

"And *I'd* be better off," Sharon said, "if I concentrated on a few cases that are going to produce some income. So would Russ."

The reporter winced as he pushed his tray aside and drew his legs up. "Well, are you?"

Sharon turned from the window. "Am I what?"

"Going to forget all this and concentrate on something else."

"It would make life easier."

"Sure would, Miss Hays."

"But I guess I'm taking the hard way," Sharon said. "My motion for new trial is with the typing pool even as we speak. I think I'll be filing it around two o'clock this afternoon."

"You're determined."

"Yep. Hey, Andy, I feel awful about getting you mixed up in this. Laying off is the smartest route you can take."

"Probably is," Wade said, "but no one's accused me of being brilliant. I'm having my laptop brought down here, and tomorrow morning's story will be about what happened to me. You'll keep me up to date?"

"If you'd like. If you'd *still* like."

"I'd like." Wade patted his bedside phone. "I'll always be in at this number, Miss Hays. If you should call and I don't answer, ring the nurse's station and have them check on me, okay? If I don't answer my phone, I'm probably dead."

Procedure required that Sharon send the district attorney a copy of her motion, and she did so by messenger. She handed the D.A.'s copy to the runner, a quick-looking little guy in jeans and Nike wing tips, as she left her office to file the original in Judge Sandy Griffin's court. The messenger drove a white van, and rounded the corner headed for the Crowley Building as Sharon crossed the street to pick up her Volvo from the converted gas station. Traffic was heavy for mid-afternoon, and by the time she arrived at the courthouse, the messenger had already made his delivery. He flashed her a circle with his thumb and forefinger as he climbed into his van to leave. Sharon grinned and showed him a thumbs-up sign as she drove by. She parked in the multilevel lot, hustled over to the courts building, rode the elevator to the sixth floor, and made her way down the corridor to the courtroom. Kathleen Fraterno was waiting for her in the middle of the hall. Kathleen waved the D.A.'s copy of the motion and indicated a corridor bench. "Can we talk about this?"

Sharon sat on the bench alongside Fraterno. "That's a world's record, Kathleen. The messenger just brought it to you."

Fraterno was slightly breathless, as if she'd been running. "If you really have this clock you're talking about, we're entitled to see it."

"Of course you are," Sharon said. "Once I present it into evidence and it's in the court's custody, you can gaze at it to your heart's content."

"No, I mean," Fraterno said, "we could circumvent all this. If you'd drop the clock by our office and we could verify that it's authentic, we might join you in your motion for new trial. Wouldn't have the hearing at all, since you'd be uncontested."

Sharon looked at her.

"The victim's family," Fraterno said, "would probably recognize the clock. If we could have a few days to get them together . . ."

"You want me to turn our evidence over to you," Sharon said.

"Even if we couldn't verify that the clock's legitimate," Fraterno said, "you could always ask for a hearing then. Then it would be up to the court to decide whether or not the clock belonged to the victim."

Sharon crossed her legs and tugged at the hem of her skirt. "Sure. If there *is* a clock by then. If it doesn't get lost or something."

Fraterno's lip stuck out. "Why do we always have to go through this dealing with you? The district attorney's office resents any implication that we wouldn't handle the evidence properly. I resent it personally, too, Sharon."

"I suspect my client resents being on death row," Sharon said. "I suspect that he resents certain witnesses not showing up at his first trial, and that his appellate lawyer Motions Malone has been acting as the state's stooge. You're not getting your hands on the clock until it's properly registered with the court. Then you can do whatever the judge permits you to do. The family members can view the clock in the evidence room just as easily as they can in your office. One of them is going to see it at the hearing."

Fraterno showed surprise. "You're going to subpoena testimony from someone in Delores Burnside's family?"

Sharon tugged her shoulder bag up from the bench and into her lap. "That's all I have to say right now."

Fraterno sighed in exasperation. "It's procedure like this that clogs up the system. When you were a prosecutor, you'd have thrown a fit if someone pulled this on you."

"Oh, Kathleen. You don't have a clue what's going

on here. When I was a prosecutor, I didn't go around trumping up convictions, hiding witnesses . . ."

"One of these days," Fraterno said, "we may talk to the bar association about you. Your resentment for Milton Breyer is spilling over into your professional conduct."

Sharon was livid. "Oh, stuff it." The corner of her mouth tugged to one side. "I don't blame you for this because you didn't have anything to do with prosecuting Raymond Burnside to begin with. Neither did Milton Breyer. Milt's just trying to score enough brownie points to enlist Ralph Toner's support in the judge's race. Even though Toner's resigned as D.A., he's pulling all the strings and you're the puppet. That much I understand. Toner framed this poor guy six years ago, Kathleen, and now he'd trying to cover it up to save his fanny in the election. And the guys that're pulling *Toner's* strings are running around shooting at people on the freeways and beating up newspaper reporters. Well, don't worry, I'll live. My screams of pain when I touch my knee have subsided to whimpers. And I'm not turning any evidence over to you."

Fraterno stiffened. "I think your imagination's turning cartwheels, Sharon. And Raymond Burnside butchered his wife. If you want to waste a lot of the system's time, I can't stop you."

Sharon stood. "That's what the courtroom's for, wasting time. You go back and tell Milt that I've been totally unreasonable, and that I'm going to continue being unreasonable. And while you're at it, tell Mr. Toner he should cut down on his spending for TV commercials. He may need the money to get out of town."

Sharon filed her motion in the court clerk's office, and asked the clerk to find the soonest date on the judge's calendar for a hearing. The clerk thumbed through the legal-size pages, murmured, "Old Raymond Burnside, huh?" And then set the motion aside on the counter. "Judge wants to talk to you, Miss Hays."

"To me in particular? Or just to anyone taking action on Raymond Burnside's behalf?"

"I think one goes with the other," the clerk said. "Everybody in the courthouse knows that you and Mr. Black are Burnside's lawyers now. Judge Griffin told me, when they ask for a new trial, I want to see them. 'Them' means you, since you're alone."

Sharon hadn't talked to Judge Griffin since Midge Rathermore's trial. She stood in the judge's open office doorway and knocked softly on the jamb. "You wanted to see me?"

Sandy Griffin looked up from a file. She had wavy blond hair, a pointed chin, and wore no makeup. "Not you in particular, unless you're filing a motion for new trial in the Burnside case." Her tone was businesslike and impersonal.

"I am," Sharon said.

Griffin closed the file. "I do want to see you, then, Miss Hays. Please sit down."

Sharon crossed the room, sat in a visitor's chair, and lowered her shoulder bag to the floor. Sandy Griffin had left the D.A.'s office to run for the bench during Sharon's first year as a prosecutor. As a meticulous lawyer who'd never been to court unprepared in her life, Griffin expected both defense and prosecution to toe the mark in her courtroom. Sharon thought it a point in Griffin's favor that she didn't put up with any bullshit, but the judge's demeanor wasn't going to win her any popularity contests, either. Sharon said pleasantly, "What is it, Your Honor?"

"I haven't seen your motion for new trial," Griffin said, "and until I do, and unless the D.A.'s also present, it wouldn't be proper for me to discuss the merits of the case. But there are some general ground rules that you and Mr. Black should be aware of."

"Oh?" Sharon said. "Procedural things, or . . . ?"

"Since we're entirely off the record," Griffin said, "I'm going to try and discourage you from going forward with this. Officially I'm saying, it's your right to do anything you want. Unofficially I'm saying, this is a case I want to go away. I'm quite weary of the whole thing."

Sharon did her best to hide her shock. She never would have expected such a statement from any judge, least of all Sandy Griffin. Normally Griffin bent over backward to give defendants an even break. "I'm sorry, Your Honor," Sharon said, "but we've got a man's life at stake."

"Every month or so," Griffin said, "I hear from the dead woman's family, wanting to know what's holding the execution up. I have to explain the appellate process to them over and over. It was my understanding that it was about over, but here we are with the case rearing its ugly head again."

Sharon recalled that Griffin had been on the bench less than a year at the first Burnside trial, and that the trial was Griffin's first capital case as a judge. Sharon decided to try a little buttering up. "Apparently none of the appeals have worked," Sharon said, "which means the trial must have been error-free."

"I won't say it was perfect," Griffin said. "The point is, these cases, how long can we keep kicking a dead horse?"

Now Sharon felt a surge of anger. She forced her tone to remain calm. "We have new evidence, Judge," she said. "If you want it out of the way, it's fine. Our client wants it all out of the way as well. I've asked for the earliest possible hearing date."

Griffin looked resigned. "You're going ahead, I suppose," she said, "in spite of hell, high water, or whatever comes."

Sharon lifted her shoulders in a little shrug. "We'd be neglectful if we didn't, Judge."

Griffin moved her desk calendar nearer to her and thumbed through the pages. "All right, Miss Hays, you'll have your wish as to the time of the hearing. Friday morning, three days from now. I don't think the state will object to that. And I'll warn you, Miss Hays. For the court to consider granting a new trial on Burnside, whatever evidence you claim to have had darn sure better be good."

Sharon paced back and forth in front of Russell Black's desk. "Now it's even the judge, of all people."

"That carpet's twenty dollars a yard," Black said. "You're wearin' a hole in it."

She plopped down on the sofa. "As fair as she was in the Rathermore case," she said, "I guess I was expecting too much."

"I think you're expectin' too much out of yourself," Black said. "Sandy Griffin's as good as the defense can expect to get, in most matters. But she covers her political skirts same as anybody else. Joe Bright has a lot of say-so about Griffin gettin' reelected. Upsettin' Joseph Bright idn't good politics in this fair county. Or anyplace in the state, for that matter."

Sharon concentrated on the picture of Black at the Terlingua Chili Cook-off. It certainly was a pleasant scene. "Russ, I'm scared to death," she finally said. "I'm afraid of the gangsters. I'm afraid of the politicians. And now I'm afraid of the judge. Criminy, if she's going to rule against us no matter what evidence we show, then why are we wasting our time?"

"Oh, I don't think she'll do that," Black said. "It's just that, if she has to grant the new trial, she might sound sort of sick to her stomach when she gives the decision."

"Well, after I left the judge," Sharon said, "I stopped off at the jail and had a talk with our client. I'm afraid I'm going to have to upset the politicians even further."

Black intertwined his fingers behind his head. "How's that?"

"Getting the clock admitted into evidence is going

to require two things. Woodrow Lee's concubine or whatever, she'll testify that the clock was at her house and that Lee's the one who brought it there. But to establish that the clock belonged to Delores Burnside, that's going to require a subpoena laid on someone who knows the clock by sight."

Black watched her, his eyes twinkling.

"The senator himself," Sharon said. "According to Raymond, the clock was a gift from him to his daughter. That's who we're going to have to subpoena. Joseph Bright."

Black massaged his cheeks. He took the lid from a jar and pulled out a peppermint. He grinned. "It's a good thing you're not runnin' for office, Sharon. 'Fraid you'd be outta luck if you were."

19

Richard Branson said to Sharon over the phone, "How's the knee?"

Sharon carefully adjusted her position on the bed, and reached down to test the towel that was wrapped around her leg. Nothing had soaked through as yet. "Cold," she said.

"You've got it in ice?"

"Yep. Hour a day, the doctor says. Where are you?" The digital clock/radio on Sharon's dresser showed 5:42. Visible through her window the sun beat down on drooping cannas in her flower bed. Must water, Sharon thought. *Must.* Commander loped into her line of vision, raised his leg, and wet the fence.

"I'm catching up on a few things at the office," Branson said. "Late dinner?"

A black-jacketed *Vernon's Annotated Texas Statutes* lay on the mattress, near Sharon's elbow. She'd used a copy of Raymond Burnside's motion for new trial as a bookmark. "I don't see how I can," she said.

"I thought we talked last night, and agreed that when you got through . . ." His tone was petulant.

Sharon had a surge of irritation. She absolutely *could not stand* confining relationships, where everyone had to report to everyone else. She said evenly, "Best-laid plans, and all that. The judge threw us a big old dipsy-doodle curve in the Burnside case. We have three whole days to get witnesses together, do briefs, issue subpoenas. It's going to be a mess for a while. Russ is burning the midnight oil, and so am I."

"Midnight's okay. I eat late anyhow."

" 'Midnight oil' was a figure of speech," Sharon said. "Actually it's more like two or three in the morning. As soon as my knee's sufficiently numb, I've got to haul ass over to the S.M.U. Law Library and get my ducks in a row on new evidence. Anything we try to introduce, the state's going to say is *old* evidence. I want four tons of case law to back me up in the event Sandy Griffin sides with the other guys. Which I'm afraid she will."

"Well, how long will your briefing take?" Branson said.

Sharon closed her eyes. This was really starting to press on her. She felt her knee. The towel was now damp, and she adjusted her position to be certain that the rolled-up beach towel under her leg would catch any drops of moisture. "Golly, Richard," she said, "you're a lawyer. A brief takes as long as it does. Depends on what I run into. The law library closes at eleven. Could be sooner, could be later."

"You'll be finished *at least* by eleven, then."

"After which," Sharon said quickly, "I've got to drive by the office, go in, and write up my brief. The typing pool has a night depository, and I need to get this paper to them so it'll be ready by noon tomorrow. That's so I can reserve my morning for consulting with our detective and running a couple of witnesses down. And on top of all that, my daughter's staying with a friend, and I want to bring her home tonight."

"Having a child is confining. Couldn't you just let her spend the night, and then I could come over?"

Sharon's irritation now boiled into a seething anger. "Melanie's not confining, Richard. And she's *been* spending practically every night. I want her home."

"Well, what about me?"

God, Sharon thought, what about him? She'd been with him two whole times, and had no intention of becoming anyone's property. Lust has shafted me again, Sharon thought. "You'll just have to wait," she said. "Look, after this hearing. If you're still interested next week, give me a call. If you're not, then *don't* give me a call. It's all I can say right now, Richard. Just stop pushing, okay?"

She hung up, stared at the phone, lifted the receiver to call him back, then hung up once more. You're a hothead, Sharon Jenifer Hays, she thought. The guy's obviously beginning to care for you, and you feel the same way about him. And now that you've bawled him out and likely pushed him away for good, you're having feelings of remorse. Which you should, you dumb bunny. Why must you always ruin everything? You'll be lucky if he ever speaks to you again.

She rolled painfully out of bed and limped into the bathroom, washed her face, and brushed her hair. Once the brush caught up in a tangle, and she yanked so hard on the handle she feared a clump might come out by the roots. Serve you right if it did, Sharon thought.

Sharon arrived across Hillcrest Avenue from the S.M.U. campus at about seven o'clock in the evening. School had just entered the fall term; male and female students sauntered across the grounds, or exhibited lean muscular legs as they jogged along the sidewalks. Sharon selected a two-hour parking slot in front of the Varsity Bookstore, dragged her briefcase and Walkman from the backseat, locked up the Volvo, and crossed the street at the light. She was dressed in gray warm-up pants and a pale blue Dallas Cowboys T-shirt. Her knee was stiff, but not nearly as sore as yesterday, and she could now touch her forearms without yelping in pain.

The university's law library was in a building the size of the Pentagon, a four-story structure fronting a city block at the northwestern edge of the campus. Sharon cleared the building lobby, rode the single elevator to the third level, went through the turnstile, and approached the sign-in desk. The young male student on duty was a carrottop, and was watching a

Roseanne rerun on a seven-inch Sony television with the volume low. As Sharon bent to sign in, a commercial came on and she glanced at Rob on the screen. To the accompaniment of heavy drumbeats, old Rob foiled a liquor store heist by gunning down three black youths in the doorway. What a guy, Sharon thought. The announcer said something to the effect that if one missed *Minions of Justice* this coming Tuesday night, one was certifiable. There immediately followed a political ad showing Ralph Toner, his faithful wife, June, and their two strapping teenage sons in front of the capitol with the theme from *Giant* playing in the background. One of the teenagers, Sharon knew, had suffered a cocaine bust within the past six months, and Toner had pulled a few strings to sweep the incident under the carpet. She resisted the urge to shoot the television screen the bird.

After signing in, she carried her briefcase and Walkman over to a table and made a beeline for the stacks. She returned in minutes lugging a *Code of Criminal Procedure* and two volumes of the *Federal Reporter, 2d Edition*. She plugged her earphones into her ears and fiddled with the tuner dial. Then, with her foot jiggling in rhythm to Waylon Jennings doing "I Don't Think Hank Done It This Way," Sharon went to work. A couple of students—a black girl with big round glasses and an Oriental guy in Bermuda shorts—shot curious glances in her direction. Sharon ignored the kids and concentrated on the research at hand

Three-and-a-half hours and two ten-dollar copy cards later, Sharon had armed herself with a six-inch stack of Xeroxes. Their differences aside, Kathleen Fraterno was a bang-up lawyer, and Sharon would bet a week's income that Kathleen was at the county law library right now, doing exactly the same research that Sharon was doing. She was sure she'd covered all the arguments that Fraterno would use to try and have the motion for new trial thrown out, and was just as certain she could defeat the state on a level playing field. With the attitude Judge Griffin had displayed that afternoon, however, Sharon just didn't know.

The question hinged on the newness of the evidence, the clock in this instance, and whether or not the defense had known—or should have known— about the missing clock at Burnside's original trial. Nothing else mattered. Kathleen would argue that the defense *should* have been aware of the clock even if they weren't, and would have a lot of ammunition to bolster her position. The record was clear that the defense had conducted a walk-through of the crime scene six years ago—with Raymond Burnside along in handcuffs, escorted by sheriff's deputies—and Kathleen would argue that Burnside of all people should have noted that the clock was gone. Without case law to the contrary, Sandy Griffin would quickly—and gleefully, Sharon thought—rule in Fraterno's favor, and the hearing on the motion for new trial would never get off the ground. Sharon had gone up several blind alleys in her research, following up on court decisions that really didn't deal with the issue, but in a secluded section of the library had finally located just the decision she was looking for. Supreme Court case law, precedent and all-encompassing.

The Supreme Court's decision in *Waylon* v. *Massachussetts* was direct and to the point, and absolutely tickled Sharon to death in its clarity. Where an indictment charged burglary as an integral offense—which Raymond Burnside's definitely did, and the burglary had been the deciding point in charging him with capital murder—it was incumbent on the state to conduct an inventory to determine whether anything in fact had been stolen, even though the mere breaking and entering constituted burglary even if no theft occurred. Prosecutor Toner had been so hell-bent-for-leather to hustle poor Raymond off to the death house that they'd done no such inventory. Therefore, the Supreme Court had ruled in the Massachussetts case—

and Sharon had murmured, "Therefore," several
times in a state of excitement while reading the decision—there was no duty for the defense to show that
nothing was missing where the state didn't allege that
anything was. If old Raymond had walked through
that house and the joint was stripped down to four
walls and a ceiling, he wasn't required to take notice.
He was defending himself in a burglary/murder, not a
robbery. Ergo, the clock was new evidence. Sharon
stuffed the copies into her briefcase, put her books
away, and left the library. The carrottopped youngster
was now enjoying David Letterman. As Sharon went
by, she winked confidently at the kid.

Sharon's briefcase now weighed a ton, loaded down
with Xeroxes, and its bulk tugged on her bruised forearm as she crossed the street. The campus was deserted and dark, tall elm and pecan trees standing like
sentinels. Street lamps shone at intervals along Hillcrest Avenue. The air was warm and still. As Sharon
neared the bookstore where the Volvo sat, a lone city
bus bounced through an intersection and chugged
away.

The street lamp in front of the bookstore was out,
and the Volvo was in darkness. Sharon lugged her
burden up alongside her car, and did a balancing act
with the briefcase on her thigh as she dug in her shoulder bag for her keys. The keys jingled somewhere inside, but she couldn't locate them with her fingers. She
touched her compact, her wallet, two Snickers bars,
which she kept for hunger-pang emergencies, but no
keys. Her briefcase tilted dangerously on her thigh
and started to fall. Sharon murmured, "Criminy,"
clutched the briefcase, and set it on the pavement, and
shifted her shoulder bag around in front of her body
for a better look. The street lamp being out didn't
help; she couldn't see a thing inside the bag. She
sighed in frustration and tugged on the car door
handle.

There was a faint *click,* and the door swung easily open. The interior lights came on.

A tremor of dread climbed the back of Sharon's neck. She searched her memory bank. She'd locked the car, no doubt about it. She raised up taller and peered into the backseat. A rubber duck, one of Commander's chew toys, was on the seat all by its lonesome. She tested the rear door. Locked. She peered up and down the street, at Culwell & Sons Varsity Shop, the Shell station across University Boulevard. No one on the sidewalks, no ghouls lurking in the shadows among the buildings. I must have left the car unlocked, she decided. My memory is playing tricks on me. She tossed her briefcase on the passenger seat and climbed in behind the steering wheel. She tilted her shoulder bag so that the dome light shone inside, and looked for her keys. There the little devils were, at the bottom of the bag alongside two used tickets to a matinee performance of *After Magritte* at the Dallas Theater Center. Sharon had taken Melanie to the play, and had thought the performance dreadful. She slid the key into the slot and turned on the ignition. She wasn't comfortable in the driver's seat. Something was wrong.

The seat was too far back. She wasn't imagining things; no one ever drove the Volvo except Sharon, and she kept the driver's seat adjusted halfway between front and rear. Now her feet barely touched the pedals. Dammit, she thought, somebody's been fooling around with my car.

She turned off the key and dug in the glove compartment for her flashlight, then got out and looked around. All four tires were inflated. There didn't seem to be any scratches in the paint—any *new* scratches at any rate, though more scars on the Volvo's battered hide might simply blend in with the scenery—and the hubcaps were in place. She got down on her haunches and shone the light underneath. The beam illuminated a dusty frame, brake lines, the differential and axles,

an occasional grease fitting. All apparently A-OK. She
got back in the car, adjusted the seat to her normal
driving position, and turned the key. Red lights
gleamed on the dash. As an afterthought, she pulled
the hood release. The hood thunked upward.

Sharon dug her trusty pink shop rag from the glove
box, and carried the rag and the flashlight up to the
front of the car. Then, using the coarse cloth to protect
her hand, she felt under the lip for the latch and raised
the hood. Sudden exertion sent a bolt of pain through
her forearms. She located the rod and propped up the
hood, and shone the light on the engine. The air
cleaner and battery cables seemed fine. She moved
around to the side and looked down toward the oil
pan.

She sucked in breath and bent over for a closer
look. Twin wires ran from the starter to a bundle of
dull red cylinders, which rested on top of the alterna-
tor. The cylinders, Sharon supposed, were sticks of
dynamite.

Russell Black's features were ghostly red in the
glow from the revolving beacon. He jammed his hands
in his pockets and looked at his shoes. "Beats all," he
said. "Just beats all."

Sharon's hands refused to stop shaking. "It was an
afterthought that I looked under the hood at all. I
already had the ignition on."

The two stood behind a barrier of crime scene tape,
a half block from where the bomb squad worked on
the Volvo. Two men in flak jackets stood near the car
while a third bent over the engine. The revolving beacon flashed on the roof of a DPD tow truck that had
backed up behind the Volvo. The tow truck operator
stood beside his winch, hands on hips. It seemed that
half the S.M.U. campus was now awake, students in
shorts, T-shirts, or lightweight jogging suits lining the
sidewalks, gawking on tiptoes. Four detectives moved

among the crowd asking questions. At last report, no one remembered seeing anything out of line.

A uniformed patrolman approached the tape from the other side and tipped his hat. He carried a clipboard. "Are you Miss Hays?"

Sharon stepped hesitantly forward. "Yes, that's me."

The policeman offered the clipboard along with a pen. "We'll need a release, ma'am, to tow your car down to the police lab."

The bomb squad guy now backed away from the Volvo carrying the dynamite, and gave a thumbs-up sign. The tow truck man knelt down and prepared to hook onto the Volvo's bumper.

The cop held a flashlight while Sharon looked over the release form. Dammit, the tremors in her fingers wouldn't cease. Part fear, part relief, and part just plain anger. Sharon said, "It's my only transportation. How long will this take?"

"The car's going to be at the Southwest Institute of Forensic Sciences, on Harry Hines Boulevard. They'll go over it with a fine-tooth comb, prints, odd fiber samples, any residue they find on the engine . . . I can't tell you how long before they're through with it. I can give you a guy's number to call."

Sharon sighed, bit her lower lip, and signed her name. Her signature was shaky. "I suppose I can rent something," she said.

Black removed his hands from his pockets and folded his arms. He wore a denim shirt and baggy worn jeans. "I'm parked across the street," he said, "an' I'll run you home. Any rented car you can charge to me as a business expense."

Sharon handed the clipboard back to the policeman. "Not home, Russ. To the office. I couldn't sleep at home anyway. And besides. I've got a brief to write, remember? If I didn't have all the incentive I needed before, I've certainly got it now."

20

Edward Teeter had a round face and pointed nose, an overhanging belly and pipe-stem legs. His office was on the eleventh floor of the Crowley Building, across and down the hall from Kathleen Fraterno's. He touched his fingertips together and said to Sharon Hays and Russell Black, "I can't get mixed up in the Dycus Wilt case, or the Raymond Burnside case. Those belong to Fraterno and Breyer. Besides, Wilt's dead. Why would anybody want to stir his bones up to begin with?"

"It's your duty to stir 'em up," Black said. "You're a chief felony prosecutor."

Teeter seemed to think that one over. He'd won his promotion to chief felony by turning up a snitch in the murder of a lawyer named Howard Saw. The snitch had been a cretin murderer, Bradford Brie, who'd subsequently been released to the street because of Edward Teeter's foul-up. During his brief period of freedom, Brie had very nearly killed Sharon Hays. She could have easily stopped Teeter's promotion had she reported the incident, but she hadn't. The bottom line was that Teeter owed her big-time. Tit for tat, a way of life in the justice system.

"That I am," Teeter finally said. "But Milton Breyer's also a chief felony prosecutor, with a lot more tenure and stroke, and Fraterno's his number one . . . whatever. No way can I butt in on their case."

"You're not butting in on anybody's case, Mr. Teeter," Sharon said. "You'd be working on a completely different murder. Sheriff's Deputy Nolan Blaine."

Teeter reached behind him and shuffled some papers on his credenza. "That's the sheriff's department's case. If I begin snooping around on something they're digging into, now I'm butting in on *their* deal."

"They're not diggin' into it," Black said. "They're buryin' the damned thing."

Teeter spread his hands, palms up. "What's to bury? The Dycus Wilt guy shoots the deputy on the way to the holding cell. Cut and dried."

Sharon straightened in her chair, in a posture of urgency. "What's to bury is how Dycus Wilt got his handcuff key. Someone slipped it to him on the way out of the jail."

Teeter picked up an envelope, moistened the gummed edge with a roller, sealed and tossed the envelope into his out-basket. "What key? I've heard nothing about it."

"The key I've got locked up in safekeeping," Sharon said, "which I swiped off of Dycus Wilt's body, downstairs in the lobby."

Teeter scowled. "That'd be serious tampering, Miss Hays."

Sharon smirked. "It sure would. And Andy Wade has a photo of the key, sheriff's imprint and all, in his hospital room. That's probably tampering as well."

Teeter put his hands on his armrests. "Andy Wade? The newspaper guy?"

"None other. He's awfully upset, Mr. Teeter. Seems being kicked around and having two broken ribs doesn't make him particularly comfortable." Sharon reached down beside her chair, pulled out and unfolded a morning paper. She turned the Metro page around so that Teeter could see the headline, "DEPUTY'S KILLER HAD OUTSIDE HELP IN ESCAPE ATTEMPT," over Andy Wade's byline. "You mean you haven't read this?" Sharon said. "I'd think it would be a requirement among the D.A.'s staff."

Teeter nervously twisted his fingers. "What's it say?"

"Just a description of his beating over on East Side Drive," Sharon said. "What really should be of concern to the county is what it's *going* to say. This is the beginning of a series."

"Oh? Lot of muckraking going on, these newspaper guys."

Now Black sat forward. "Problem for the D.A.'s office is, whose muck is gonna get raked. What's about to come out in the paper will put a black eye on your department, Ed. Now, you-all can try and ignore the stories and look like a bunch of fools to the public, or you can get on some kind of investigation an' reduce the damage to a minimum. Some prosecutors are gonna look awful bad down here. If a guy was to take up the cause right now, he might look pretty good."

"Hold on. That deputy killing's got nothing to do with us. So far it's all the sheriff's department." Teeter was doing his best to sound indignant, but his forcefulness was obviously strained.

"It's the sheriff's department's business," Sharon said, "until it comes out that Dycus Wilt and a friend of his were responsible for Delores Burnside's murder, six years ago. And that the Dallas County District Attorney's office swept evidence under the rug in convicting the wrong man." She rattled the pages of the newspaper. "This is going to be a mesmerizing series of articles, Mr. Teeter. The entire city will be on edge to see what happens next."

Teeter pinched his chin. "Burnside?"

Sharon and Russ looked at each other.

"That was Ralph Toner's case," Teeter said thoughtfully.

Black grinned and settled back in his best folksy posture. "This can o' worms is already open, Ed; there's nothing your department can do about that. Question is, when it's public knowledge that Toner built a frame around this poor man, how's the D.A.'s office going to look? Here's the situation right now. Toner's resigned to run for governor, so as of this minute there *is* no district attorney and won't be until after the election. It's about to be public knowledge, two things." Black held up his index and middle fingers. "Toner knew he was after the wrong man in the Burnside case and did what he did to get Joseph Bright's backing politically. Not only that, now Toner's solicited funds from some out-of-state gambling people that are buyin' up land in wholesale lots in anticipation of Toner's gettin' elected."

"Jesus Christ," Teeter said. "Do you have documentation for any of this?"

"Oh, *we* don't," Sharon said. "We're just lawyers. But the rumor is, Andy Wade does, and he's about to use it in this series of articles. Other than trying to have our client's conviction thrown out, we're not involved." She showed her best neutral smile.

" 'Pears to me," Black said, "that is the district attorney's office ignores this, it's going to tar the whole staff with the same brush that's about to get Ralph Toner. But if there was an individual inside this department that instituted an investigation *before* it all gets out, then that individual would look . . . Well, no tellin' how far that individual might go in the future."

Now Teeter's expression was cunning. "You think you could come up with some evidence to aid such an investigation?"

"No, Mr. Teeter," Sharon said, "*we* couldn't. If I was trying to find out something, though, I'd go to the hospital and have a talk with Andy Wade."

Teeter yanked out a legal pad and wrote something down. "It's an idea. Maybe I should follow up on this."

Sharon and Russ looked at each other. Sharon laughed. "I owe you a lunch, boss. That's exactly what you told me he'd say."

*   *   *

They left the Crowley Building in Russ's Buick. Sharon's eyelids felt as if they weighed a hundred pounds apiece, God, as though she hadn't slept in weeks. Black gave Sharon a sideways glance and said, "Don't imagine you got much shut-eye."

She curled her legs up underneath her and leaned against the passenger door. "Not a blooming wink. Once I got my brief finished, I was wired like two gallons of coffee, but now I'm sinking. I should be scared to death, but all I really feel is like a zombie."

"Police call you?"

"Yes. There was a message for me when I got in the office. A couple of detectives are supposed to drop by about the bomb. They'll ask a few questions and open a file, and then that will be that."

Black steered into the center lane, ready to turn north onto Industrial Boulevard. "Not like we don't know who's responsible."

"What evidence do we have?" Sharon pointed to the south. "The office is that way, boss."

Black drove across two lanes of traffic onto Industrial. "We don't have any evidence. That's the way these people do things."

"You're going in the wrong direction," Sharon said.

"Just keep in mind what I was sayin' earlier. They're not loonies. If we can win at the courthouse, these people will fade into the sunset."

"Russ, we're going the opposite direction from the office."

Black kept the speedometer on twenty-five, and stayed behind a Merchants' Motor Freight bobtail. "That's 'cause we're not goin' to the office."

Normally Sharon would have grilled Russ as to their destination, but at the moment she was too dog-tired to care. Her knee throbbed. Her shoulders ached. If a herd of gangsters were to gather on the sidewalk and open fire with machine guns, Sharon couldn't have lifted a finger to protect herself. She snuggled against the door and laid her cheek against the seat back.

"I'm too beat to be curious, boss," she said. "Just wake me when it's over, okay?"

When Black shook her gently out of a deep slumber, Sharon blinked and looked around to get her bearings. They were parked in a strip shopping center on Preston Road, in far North Dallas. The Buick was nose-on to the curb in front of a huge Barnes & Noble Bookstore displaying copies of *The Chamber,* by John Grisham, in its windows. A Land Rover with mud on its tires was in the next space. Sharon yawned and said, "Is that our detective's car?"

Black killed the engine, pocketed his keys, and opened the door. "Yep. That it is."

"Mr. Gear doesn't seem like the bookstore type," Sharon said. "Must be reading up on race relations."

"You'll see," Black said. He got out and started around the nose of the car.

Sharon tensed, then relaxed. Russell Black loved to be mysterious and full of surprises, even though his surprises were seldom particularly stunning. The fact that her boss was sort of a kook was one of the things which made him endearing. She'd learned never to open her own doors when in his company; Black was from the old school and treated all women with respect. Sharon didn't mind at all; that he deferred to her gender was a high for her. She waited for him to open the passenger side, stepped out into hundred-degree heat, and fell into step with him. They climbed up on the curb and entered the bookstore. Sudden coolness raised goose bumps on her arms.

The store was the size of a vast auditorium, with ceiling-high stacks extending the length and breadth of the place. The Barnes & Noble chain had invaded the Dallas area within the past couple of years, and already there had been repercussions for the little people. Sharon was aware of two independent dealers who'd given up the ghost within months of the New York–based superstore's grand opening, and there were rumors of many smaller bookshops to follow. As one who bought her novels in a nook-and-cranny bookery near her home—whose owner knew her reading habits and kept her up to date on titles in which she might be interested—Sharon thought the situation sad.

One end of the store was partitioned off into a coffee bar with tables and booths, a glassed-in counter displaying pastries, and an odor of fresh cappuccino and cocoa beans. Black steered Sharon in among the tables. Anthony Gear was in the corner, seated in a booth across from a woman whom Sharon didn't recognize. Black waved at the detective, fished in his pocket, and handed Sharon a ten-dollar bill. "I want coffee," Black said. "None o' that funny-tastin' stuff. Coffee. You get whatever you want." He left her, walked over, and slid into the booth alongside Gear. Sharon shrugged in puzzlement, approached the counter, ordered a coffee for Russ and a café mocha for herself, and drummed her fingers while she waited. Both Black and Gear talked a mile a minute to the woman, who twisted her fingers and remained silent.

The attendant served up two mugs, one containing straight black American coffee and the other with a mountain of whipped cream floating on top. Sharon paid, then picked up the cups, and approached the booth. She watched the woman.

The woman wore jeans and a man's white shirt with the tail out, and seemed nervous. She was thin to the point of frailty, and had auburn hair stylishly layered. Thirty to thirty-five, Sharon thought, somewhere in there, with big moist blue eyes behind small reading glasses. Every few seconds the woman would glance anxiously over her shoulder. Two paperback books lay near her elbow. Sharon slid into the booth beside the lady, set Russ's coffee in front of him, sipped whipped cream along with café mocha, and licked her lips.

Russ was saying, "I don't want anybody sayin' this

is pressure, because it idn't. At the same time I got a client."

"And at the same time I've got a family." The woman had a cultured Texas accent, and was practically in tears. "Two children. My husband, I . . ."

Black gestured toward Sharon. "This here's my associate, Miss Hays. Sharon, meet Alice Glass."

The name meant nothing. Sharon said, "Hello."

The woman picked up one of her books and squeezed the cover like a pacifier. A historical romance, Sharon noted, complete with shirtless hunk and damsel on the cover. There was a sparkler on her left hand that Sharon mentally appraised at two carats, minimum. The woman said to Sharon, "I'd like to say it's nice to meet you, but it isn't. I want this all to go away."

Sharon used her straw to stir the whipped cream, lightening the color of the café mocha. She felt like kicking Russ in the shin for not briefing her.

Now Anthony Gear leaned forward. He wore his standard-issue sport coat and slacks, and was drinking black coffee like Russ. "We're not going to ask you to recite the gory details, Mrs. Glass," Gear said. "Just to verify what Mr. Burnside says."

Mrs. Glass sniffled. "I was engaged at the time. Don't you understand?"

Sharon got it. "Are you Alice Williams? Your maiden name."

The woman said tearfully, "Yes."

Sure, Sharon thought. The woman Burnside claimed to have stayed with, the night of the murder. For all of Anthony Gear's personal shortcomings, he continued to amaze her. The former FBI agent could turn up the dead.

"Mrs. Glass is bein' kind enough to give us some of her time," Black said.

The woman straightened haughtily. "I agreed to come after your detective threatened me with a subpoena. And I'm sorry, but I don't feel particularly kind."

"Raymond Burnside dudn feel particularly kind about his situation, either," Black said. "We'll make it as painless as possible, Mrs. Glass, but we intend to get some information from you."

"Even if it ruins my marriage?"

"Look, lady," Gear said, "we're going to have you on the witness stand one way or the other. It'll be easier on you if you'll get used to the idea."

Is that tact, or what? Sharon thought. She said, "You're scaring her to death, guys." She shifted her attention back and forth between the two men.

Gear's mouth hung open. Black looked down. If he resented a dressing-down from his associate, he didn't let on.

Sharon turned to the woman and said gently, "Excuse these fellas, Mrs. Glass. Look, would you like a cup of coffee or something?"

The woman shook her head and hugged her book to her chest. "For six years I've been dreading something like this. Now that it's here, I . . ."

Sharon gestured toward Black and Gear. "Obviously I don't have to fill you in that we're trying to overturn Raymond Burnside's conviction. But I'm not sure it's been made clear exactly why we need you."

Alice's voice was slightly hoarse. "Understand this. I feel terrible about Mr. Burnside. I feel terrible about getting involved with him to begin with. Put yourself in my place. If my husband finds out, six years after the fact, that four days before our wedding I went to bed with another man, it will kill my marriage. My kids are five and three, Miss Hays."

Sharon sympathized, perhaps even more than she should. "Mrs. Glass, nobody wants to destroy your marriage. I won't lie to you, if we can win a new trial for Raymond, and if the state still wants to prosecute him after we do, we'll be calling on you to testify as to everything that happened that night. But for right now, you might not have to tell any of it."

Alice relaxed some and laid the book on the table. Black said softly, "Careful, Sharon."

"I'm being careful, boss. And what I'm telling her is true. For us to win a new trial for Raymond, she may not have to say that he spent the night with her at all."

"I only saw him that one time in my life," Alice said. "After all these years I might not even recognize the man."

"To win a new trial," Sharon said, "we have to produce new evidence crucial to Raymond's defense. We think we already have that, a clock, but for reasons I won't bore you with, we're concerned about the state's attempts to have the clock thrown out of court at our motion hearing. But your testimony could force the court to give Raymond a new trial even if the clock *doesn't* pass muster as evidence."

Anthony Gear looked confused, but Black watched Sharon with sudden respect. "Why didn't I think of that?" Black said.

"It's what you pay me for, boss."

Alice wrung her hands. "All I could tell is what happened. We were drinking. We were *all* drinking. I suspect Mr. Burnside felt just as cheap the next morning as I did."

Sharon watched her cup. The whipped cream was melting. "What I'd have to ask you at our motion hearing," Sharon said, "would be delicate."

"More delicate than my spending the night with a total stranger? Miss Hays, I'm not a slut. Just one time . . ."

"I won't lie to you," Sharon said. "In ways, what I'd ask you could be even touchier than the details of that night." She looked at Alice head-on, and had the impression that if this woman gained some weight she would be quite pretty. "Your name was on the defense witness list at the first trial," Sharon said. "We'd want to know why you didn't testify."

Alice vacantly watched her hands. "Oh."

Sharon looked away. There was a mural over the glassed-in counter, long-dead writers exchanging ideas over coffee. Sharon watched the image of William Faulkner as she said, "If you ducked out merely because you were afraid of your husband's reaction to your testimony, that wouldn't help us. If you had other reasons . . ."

"My husband's a geologist. Travels a lot to oil drilling sites. That's where he was the night it happened. My roommates were giving me kind of a pre-marital party, and that's when we met Mr. Burnside."

Sharon wondered if Alice and Raymond had spent the night together without ever being on a first-name basis. *Which do you prefer, Mr. Burnside? Bottom, top, or the doggy position?* "That doesn't exactly answer my question, Mrs. Glass," Sharon said. "Does it?"

Alice sighed. "I don't suppose it does. I certainly didn't relish the idea of Charles knowing what I'd done. That was part of the reason I didn't testify."

"But wasn't all of it?" Sharon said. Black was looking at her. Sharon concentrated on Alice Glass.

"No," Alice said. "Not entirely."

"What was your reason, then?" Sharon said. "Entirely."

"A phone call."

"You received a call?" Sharon now assumed cross-examination posture, at the same time keeping her tone as gentle as possible.

"Listen, I could get in trouble," Alice said.

"For telling about the phone call?"

"Well, not just the call. My roommates got the same call, and that's why they didn't testify, either."

"While we're on that subject," Sharon said, "do you know the other women's current whereabouts?"

Alice turned her face away and watched the wall.

"I'm going to accept that as a 'yes,' " Sharon said, "unless you tell me differently. We may need them as well, Mrs. Glass. As an incentive to your telling us how to contact them, I'm going to offer you a proposition."

Alice looked at her. The despair on the woman's face touched Sharon deeply, but then so did the image of Raymond Burnside in prison.

"If the court allows our clock as evidence," Sharon said, "we won't use your testimony at the motion hearing at all. In return for that promise, we want to know how to contact your old roomies. We won't use them, either, unless it's necessary, but we'll need all three of you standing in the wings." Black gave Sharon a sharp look. Sharon held up a hand, palm out, in his direction. "Let me run with this, boss. I think I'm on to something."

Alice said, "Nikki and Syl are even more afraid than I am."

"I'll tell you your odds," Sharon said. "The odds are, if the court allows our clock into evidence, we're going to get our new trial without your testimony. When the trial comes about—*if* it comes about; there's always the chance the state won't prosecute Raymond a second time—then we'll have to use all three of you. But it will give you several months to prepare yourself. That would include your figuring out a way to iron things out with your husband."

"What happens if I refuse to help you at all?" Alice said.

Sharon looked at Black, then at Gear.

"Then, I suppose you'd subpoena me," Alice said.

Sharon ran her thumb down the side of her cup. "I hate to threaten. But we'd have no choice."

Alice fidgeted with one of her books. "I know their addresses. Nikki's married. Syl married and then divorced since all this happened."

"Mr. Gear will need that information," Sharon said. "Now, what about the phone call? Was it from the prosecutor?"

"That was Mr. Toner. He's now running for governor."

"How well we know," Sharon said. "Did he call you?"

"No. Mr. Green, his assistant."

Sharon grabbed her cup and sipped to hide her shock. Stan Green wasn't an assistant prosecutor, of course. To someone as unfamiliar with the system as Alice, all members of the state's team would be players wearing the same uniform. Stan Green was actually a Dallas Police Department homicide detective, and just the hatchet man the D.A. would use to silence a few defense witnesses. During a brief void in her life while she was a prosecutor, Sharon had taken Green as a lover, and that fact didn't make her completely comfortable with the situation. Green had been on the other side in the Midge Rathermore case, however, and that trial had turned out pretty well for the home team. Sharon said urgently, "What leverage did they have on you, Mrs. Glass?"

Alice blinked. "Leverage?"

"They had something to use against you if you testified on Raymond's behalf. I used to work for the D.A., and I know a few of the tricks of the trade."

Alice gave a resigned sigh. "Nothing on me, per se. I was married four days after I . . . met Mr. Burnside. In fact, I was pregnant when he went on trial. But sometime before the trial, the police raided Nikki and Syl's apartment where I used to live. They found some drugs. Cocaine, I think."

Black cut in. "They suddenly raided the place, with no reason?"

"Not according to Syl and Nikki," Alice said. "They were watching television, and there was a knock on the door."

Black murmured, "Christ." Then he said more loudly, "Was it really the women's drugs, or did Dallas' finest plant it?"

"It was Nikki's. She was the only one of us who was a recreational user. I've never touched drugs."

Sharon slowly shook her head. "I think I know the

rest, Mrs. Glass. If the three of you disappeared and didn't testify, the drug charges would fade into the sunset. Am I right?"

Alice gave a brief sad nod. "I went through a lot of soul-searching. There were no charges against me, since I wasn't living in the apartment at the time, but Mr. Green said that if I wasn't included in the arrangement, there was no leniency for Nikki and Syl. Both of them called me in tears and begged me." She lowered her gaze. "I confess that since I was afraid Charles would find out what happened that night, I wasn't that hard to convince."

"So they sent you on a vacation," Sharon said.

"Just a little trip. We were in Austin when it was time for us to make a court appearance."

Sharon felt a touch of revulsion. As a prosecutor, she'd bent over backward to give defendants a break, and had never prosecuted a case in her life where she wasn't convinced of the defendant's guilt. The shenanigans she'd seen pulled by certain A.D.A.'s in order to get a conviction, a notch on the gun, absolutely turned her stomach. Ralph Toner had been playing for high political stakes, backing from Senator Bright. The higher the stakes, the greater the temptation.

Sharon looked at Russ. "I'll have to amend our pleadings, boss, to include the fact we may call Mrs. Glass and her roomies to testify at the motion hearing. I'll time it so the D.A.'s office gets their copy the night before. That won't give them much time to react."

"They might ask for a continuance," Black said. "Claim they need more time to get ready."

Sharon nodded. "They might ask. But I don't think the court will give it to them. Judge Griffin wants this over and done with. So do I. So will everyone who learns the truth behind this deal."

Vernon Denopoulis adjusted his sunglasses, leaned forward, and peered around Jack Torturro toward the front of the bookstore. "See how bad you scared that broad, Jackie? So bad it took her less than twelve hours to get back on the case. Pretty thing, huh? I'll say this, the lady's got some cods." He reached up and adjusted the AC vent so that frigid air blew directly on his face. Visible through the windshield, the blue Caddy's hood vibrated in rhythm with the throbbing engine. Denopoulis turned to the backseat and removed his mirrored shades. "Ralphie, you sure that's the same woman?"

Ralph Toner wore a hat pulled low. Over on the sidewalk in front of the Barnes & Noble, Sharon Hays, Russell Black, and Anthony Gear said their good-byes to Alice Glass. Alice held two paperbacks and nervously twisted their covers. "Christ," Toner said, "where did they come up with her? Look, a lot of people know me around here."

"You don't do something about that," Denopoulis said, pointing across the way, "they're going to know you pretty good in the joint. We ain't playing here. Jesus Christ, whose brilliant idea was the dynamite? Jackie, I don't teach you no better?"

"They left her seat pushed back," Torturro said. "Not my fault, Vernon."

"What's lucky is that it didn't blow her up. You think that other old lawyer's going to give up, you off the broad? At least this way we're not looking at any homicide beef."

"We're not stopping this shit, either," Torturro said. "Every day this goes on, our man Ralph is a little bit farther from the mansion, huh?"

Toner scooted down in the seat, folded his arms, and watched the ceiling.

"Okay," Denopoulis said, "let's assume, scaring this Sharon Hays away is farting in the wind. That stuff on the highway the other night, that should have convinced you. This is one solid woman you're talking here. The skinny broad, though, believe we can work on her."

Torturro watched Alice Glass leave the group and walk quickly to her car.

"Shouldn't be too hard," Denopoulis said. "Hell, Ralphie scared her off pretty easy, back when he was framing that guy."

"I still think Burnside did it," Toner said. "People in the throes of a divorce . . ."

"Go blow that smoke someplace else, Ralphie." Denopoulis replaced his sunglasses on his nose. "Get us out of here before we get a double parking ticket, Jackie. I want to see where Mrs. Glass lives." He chuckled. "Man, that Sharon Hays. Got to be a way to get to that woman. If she ain't scared for herself, maybe we can find somebody she worries about more. There's people like that, you know? Family or something, you think?"

21

Sharon rested her head on Sheila Winston's sofa cushion. So tired. So freaking tired.

"Do you dream about the bomb?" Sheila said, her tone even, her manner soothing.

"I can't answer that. I haven't been to sleep since it happened."

"About the shooting, then."

"On the highway?"

"Yes."

"I have nightmares. The night after it happened, I woke up several times in a cold sweat. As time passes things get better. Sometimes I dream that a car's rolling over me. Crushing me underneath."

"How do these dreams make you feel?"

"Scared out of my wits. Mad as hell."

"Which are you the most often, frightened or angry?"

Sheila's professionalism brought a smile to Sharon's lips. She did her best friend's legal work at no charge. Once she'd incorporated Sheila's practice; last year there'd been an amendment to Trish's custody order, changing her father's visitation privileges. In return for a free lawyer, Sheila provided gratis psychiatric services. Up to now she'd only given advice about Melanie's problems in dealing with her father's absence, and this was the first time Sharon had asked for help in getting her own head straight. She wasn't sure if the session was doing the job, but just talking things over with Sheila made her feel better and always had.

"More angry, I think," Sharon said. "At first I was more frightened, but as time goes by . . ."

"You stop being frightened?"

"Not altogether. I think fear's like anything else that keeps beating you over the head. You get numb eventually." Sharon closed her eyes as Sheila wrote something on a pad. Threw you a curve, Madame Psychiatrist, Sharon thought. A spicy odor drifted in from the kitchen, the remnants of the bitchin' lasagna they'd had earlier. Sheila's Italian could send a Mafia summit meeting into drooling fits.

Sheila's pen stopped its scratching. "Do you feel the same way about anger?"

"That it's numbing?"

"Yes."

"No. With me, anger's something that starts fresh every day. I'll get mad at Melanie, and that's over in a minute, but this is different. I feel it growing in the morning, about the time I brush my teeth."

"Every day?"

"Every day, Sheila, since all this started. Every day," Sharon lifted her head and opened her eyes. "What time is it, anyway?"

Sheila wore jeans and a tank top. She looked at her watch. "We have a few minutes. Wet 'n' Wild closes at eleven, and it's a thirty-minute drive."

"What about the kid who's having the birthday party? Are his parents . . .?"

"The invitation said, until the park closes."

"The parents will be there, then."

"They're responsible people," Sheila said. "They wouldn't leave any kids wandering around out there."

"I'll take your word for it. Some parents don't seem to give a damn. I can't decide whether I'm glad this is summer's last hurrah. School starting in August, I can't believe it."

"Trish has been moaning all week. You're wasting some of your session time, kid."

Sharon relaxed and closed her eyes. "Angry. I stay angry."

"At whom is your anger directed?"

"Ralph Toner, the phony . . . Milton Breyer, though I've been mad at him since the day I quit the D.A.'s office. Milt's just too dumb to be anything except a pawn. Kathleen Fraterno, though I feel more sorry for her."

"What about the people who shot at you and rigged the bomb? Aren't you mad at them?"

"Not really. Those guys are part of the environment, like roaches and stinging scorpions. If people like Toner didn't exist, they'd have nothing to feed on and they'd die away."

"Have you ever thought of dropping the whole thing?"

"Raymond Burnside's case? Not a chance. I never wanted Dycus Wilt for a client to begin with. Oh, speaking of that."

"Of Dycus Wilt?"

"And of fear. The only time I feel really scared is when I think of the look on his face, just before those deputies shot him."

"How did he look?"

"Wild. Really wild."

"What was it that frightened you so? The gunshots, seeing a man killed . . ."

"None of that. Just before they shot him, he looked straight at me. Like he knew he was going to die and didn't care."

"Like he felt his own life was cheap? A lot of guys like that—"

"Not that it was cheap. Not that it was important, either. As if his own life simply didn't matter one way or the other. You know what, Sheil? I think caring about life has everything to do with families. If I didn't have Melanie, I don't know that my own life would matter that much. Under certain circumstances, I'm not sure old Dycus and I wouldn't have been kindred souls."

"Jesus Christ, Sharon, you feel that way?"

"Not really. But sometimes. Dycus was a cold-blooded killer. I certainly don't put myself in the same category with him, but some of the people involved in this . . . Jack Torturro, Ralph Toner, people like that. I think I could kill them without batting an eye, and that's what frightens me about myself." Sharon raised her head and forced a grin. "What's the diagnosis, Frau Doctor?"

Sheila didn't return the smile. Her pretty chocolate-colored features were set in worry. She wrote something down, then looked up. "You need to get all this over with, Sharon, and I mean right now, as soon as possible. If someone came in off the street and said those things, I'd say I had a patient on the verge of being disturbed. You're putting up a front, a damned good one. But watch it, kid, that spring wound up inside you could break at any time. If it does, you could find yourself having to see me for real."

The Black Hole slide towered over Wet 'n' Wild as kids in soaked bathing suits lined up outside the exit, their eyes bloodshot from chlorine, their lashes stuck together in rows of dark wet points. The water park's floodlights dimmed, then brightened, signaling closing time. Sharon kept the Volvo's speed down to a crawl as she peered up and down the sidewalk in search of Melanie and Trish. There was a tightening in the pit of her stomach. Ever since Melanie had been old enough to go to movies or amusement parks without Mommy to chaperon, Sharon had experienced periodic touches of dread. In four short years Melanie would have her driver's license, and Mom's anxiety would grow by leaps and bounds. Being a mother sure has its moments, Sharon thought. Sheila twisted in the passenger seat and pointed. "There they are." Sharon stopped at the curb as relief flooded over her.

Melanie and Trish sauntered up, self-conscious and posing, glancing back over their shoulders to see who might be watching them. Both girls wore one-piece suits, Melanie's pink, Trish's electric blue. Trish had a mature full figure while Melanie was still on the spindly coltish side. Their water-soaked hair had drying frizzy ends, and each girl carried a mesh drawstring bag. They started to climb in the Volvo's backseat. Sharon said with some irritation, "Towels, kids. Towels." Melanie and Trish exchanged looks of exasperation as they spread towels over the seats before sitting down. Sharon pulled from the curb and into the line of traffic leaving the park.

"How was the party?" Sheila said.

"Cool." The voice from the backseat could have been either girl; Sharon was concentrating on the road ahead and wasn't sure. It never failed to shock her how old-sounding the twelve-year-olds had become. She pictured the stuffed animals stored in her utility closet at home, and reminded herself for the thousandth time that she needed to get a box of toys ready for delivery to Goodwill.

Sheila hooked an arm over the seat and faced the back. "Did you remember to tell the Stoners you had a nice time?"

Stoner. Sure, Sharon thought, Stoner, the kid having the party. The name had slipped her mind.

"*Mah*-um." The voice was definitely Trish's this time, wailing in protest. "That's kid stuff."

"It's kid stuff to thank your hosts?" Sheila said. "I don't think so. You can prepare yourself to march right back in there and—"

"I told them," Melanie cut in. "I did."

Sharon cocked an ear. Just a year earlier she could tell at the drop of a hat whether Melanie was fibbing; as teenage wile crept in, Melanie's own mother wasn't certain anymore. "You'd better have, young lady," Sharon said.

"I did, Mom," Melanie said. There was a rustling

of paper in the backseat, after which Melanie said, "Pretty sexy, Trish."

Sharon and Sheila exchanged looks of oh-my-God. The Jeep 4x4 ahead braked prior to entering the freeway access road. Sharon stopped as well and listened to the vibrations from the Volvo's engine. Headlights whizzed back and forth on I-30 in a series of blurs. Across the freeway were the floodlights above the ballpark in Arlington, where the Rangers closed out yet another dismal season.

There was more rattling in the back, and Trish squealed in delight. "Well, that's just the way I look. At least I'm not *trying* to look sexy. Look at you."

Sharon tilted an ear in curiosity. "Hey. Who's trying to look sexy?"

There was a flash of guilty silence. Melanie offered timidly, "Oh, nothing."

Sheila got into the act, extending a palm-up hand toward the girls. "Let me see those."

Trish said testily, "A man just let us take each other's picture, that's all. It wasn't any big deal."

Sharon expelled air through her nose, whipped over to the curb, and set the parking brake. She turned on the dome light as Sheila snatched some Polaroids from the backseat. As Sheila thumbed through the pictures, Sharon said, "You've been told not to talk to strangers, both of you."

Melanie screwed her features into a pout. "This wasn't any creepy guy. He was nice."

"My God, Melanie," Sharon said. "Creeps don't look like creeps, and you've been told that over and over. You're in trouble, young lady."

"He was alone and had a camera, up by the river rapids," Trish said. "He said if we'd take his picture, then we could take each other's. Awesome camera, too." She smirked. "He didn't offer us candy or anything, Sharon. We're smarter than that."

"*Miss Hays,* Trish." Sheila offered the pictures to

Sharon. "I have to confess they look harmless enough." She sounded uncertain.

A column of autos moved past them and onto the freeway as Sharon looked the pictures over. The first was Trish seated on a low cement wall, hugging her knees, with laughing men and women riding the rapids in inner tubes behind her. The second photo was Melanie standing in front of the same wall, one hip stuck out in a preadolescent version of a saucy come-on pose. Quite the little thespian, Sharon thought.

The man in the third photo was leaning against the wall, the rapids in the background, and he showed a wholesome smile. He wore boxer trunks and a yellow waist-length terry cloth jacket, had the chest and shoulders of a retired football jock, and a nose that appeared to have been broken at sometime. One hand was raised in a friendly wave. The man was Jack Torturro.

The pictures fluttered from Sharon's fingers onto the floorboard. She leaned back and hugged herself. Her throat constricted. Sheila frowned in worry. "What is it?" Sheila said.

Sharon forced her tone to remain calm. "I want you to drive, Sheila." Her hands shook so badly that she doubted if she could hold the steering wheel.

"What's wrong?" Sheila said.

Sharon glanced pointedly into the backseat, where both girls were suddenly rigid in alarm. Sharon forced a smile. "Just drive, will you? I don't feel really well. Tell you about it later, okay?"

"Stop in Austin and take them on a tour of the capitol," Sharon said. "Ride the river rapids in New Braunfels. San Antonio, there's the Alamo. If you call me here and I don't answer in person, don't leave any messages on the answering machine. In here"—she handed Sheila a sealed envelope—"is the phone number for the pay station outside Judge Griffin's court. Call it tomorrow, twelve-thirty on the dot. I'll be over there getting the judge's signature on our subpoenas for the hearing. If anyone besides me picks up the phone, hang up, wait five minutes, and call back. Try three times. If I haven't answered by the third try, forget it. If everything else fails, call Andy Wade's hospital room and leave a message for Helen Reed. Here's his number." She scribbled on a message pad.

Sheila sat on the bed. "For who?"

"Helen Reed. It's a character I played, off-Broadway once. A real ditz. She was always . . . Helen Reed, Sheila, that's all you need to know. I'll call Andy and fill him in. The main thing is, don't leave any messages with anyone giving your whereabouts." Sharon dropped four pairs of panties into Melanie's suitcase, checked the contents, closed the luggage, and snapped the catches. "My Visa's in that envelope, too. The trip's on me."

Sheila went to the doorway and peered down the hall. Trish and Melanie were in the living room watching television. When first told they were going on an impromptu vacation, the girls had been excited, but Sharon had noticed a cloud of doubt in Melanie's expression. Sharon didn't know how much she could tell Melanie without sending the child into orbit. Nearly thirteen years as a mother, and often she felt as helpless as the day Melanie was born. You're a klutz, Sharon Jenifer Hays, she thought.

Sheila turned around and said, "What about school?"

"Oh, Christ, it begins on Monday, doesn't it? I'll call them and say the girls will be registering late."

Sheila folded her arms. "And you're sure we couldn't just ask for some kind of police protection?"

"I've already got police protection, Sheila. And here's what it's worth. Two detectives came by this afternoon and asked me questions about the bomb in my car. They wanted to know if I recognized anyone. God, they didn't even know the story and I had to go over it step by step. I gave them this Torturro's name, and they said they'd keep an eye on him. You see any policemen around him in that picture? They said they'd have a squad car check my house. Periodically, whatever that means. Have you seen any police cars driving by lately? Picking up the Volvo from the police lab was really an eye-opener. They tried to charge me storage on the car, like some heap they'd towed in from in front of a fireplug, and I had to talk to six different people before I found someone who even knew why my car was down there. So, up their police protection. If we don't protect ourselves, no one's going to."

"I can't say I'm going to have a really jolly time on this trip," Sheila said.

Sharon's expression softened. "That I can't help you with. I can only apologize for getting you mixed up in this, Sheil. And I mean it from the bottom of whatever heart I've got left."

"Oh, Sharon." Sheila went back and sat on the bed. "Look. When we get to my house, I'm going to write you a prescription. They're tranquilizers. You know I'm not into chemical dependency, but you have to have something. I'm not kidding, Sharon. If you knew how close you are to blowing a cork, you might drive to the nearest sanitarium and check yourself in."

They went down to Sheila's house. Sharon helped Trish pack her things while Sheila tossed a few of her own belongings into a suitcase; then both women helped the girls load the luggage into the rear of Sheila's station wagon. By the time they'd finished, it was nearing one in the morning. Sheila had called ahead for reservations in an Austin motel, three-and-a-half hours to the south, and Sharon figured the travelers would get to bed around four. That was good; the girls would sleep until noon tomorrow. By the time Sharon had her subpoenas signed and ready for serving, Sheila and the girls would be touring the capitol a safe two hundred miles away. With Trish in the backseat,

Sheila said good-bye in the driveway. She then climbed into the station wagon and started the engine. Sharon stood by the passenger door and hugged Melanie tightly.

Melanie stepped back from her mother and said, "You won't tell me what's wrong?"

"It has to do with a case I'm handling," Sharon said. "You have a good time, sweetheart."

"I can't unless you're along, Mom. I'll be so worried . . ."

Sharon winked and firmed her mouth. "Nothing to worry about, Melanie. It's just, I have a lot of work. It'll be easier to handle if you go on this trip. I'm going to be so busy, we couldn't spend much time together anyway."

A tear ran down Melanie's cheek. "Are you sure, Mom? Are you sure?"

Sharon embraced Melanie once more and kissed her. "I'm sure, darling. You don't think Mom would put you on now, do you?"

Sheila drove a prearranged circuitous route to the freeway, taking several intentional wrong turns and then doubling back, while Sharon followed a block behind in her Volvo. Once the women were certain that no one was trailing them, Sheila proceeded down Monticello Avenue to Central Expressway. Sharon parked alongside the freeway access road as the station wagon steamed through the entry ramp, gathering speed. She didn't move until Sheila's taillights had disappeared over a rise. Then she drove a couple of blocks down the access road, located a turnaround, and headed for home. She didn't think she'd ever felt so lonely.

Once at her house, Sharon let Commander in from the yard. With the shepherd trotting along beside her, whining and sniffing, she bolted the doors and locked the windows. Then she patrolled every nook and cranny of the kitchen and living room, got down on her knees, and looked under the bed. She owned one gun, a .44 Bulldog that she'd bought during the Rathermore trial, and that she kept hidden in the back of her closet. Now she dug out and loaded the weapon, and carefully engaged the safety catch. She was terrified of guns and was a lousy shot as well. In fact, she'd planned to sell the Bulldog, but she'd never gotten around to looking for a buyer.

She laid the weapon on her bedside table and let Commander spend the night in her room for the first time since he'd been a puppy, and didn't object when the dog bounded up on the bed and snuggled beside her. She tossed and turned and finally dozed, and woke up after daylight with Commander's snout a foot from her nose. She scratched him behind the ears, and began to cry. Commander licked her face and wagged his tail.

22

Alice Glass watched her husband leave the next morning, his snow-white Lexus backing smoothly out of the drive, jerking almost imperceptibly as he braked and threw the lever into the DRIVE position, then pulling away and disappearing behind the wall of the two-story Colonial brick home at the entrance to the subdivision. She wrung her hands, pacing the kitchen, checking the clock, fighting an inner battle with herself, actually picking up the phone with the idea of canceling her appointment before slamming the receiver down in frustration. She had no choice. She had to go.

She went upstairs into the bedroom and changed into shopping clothes, a navy blue pleated dress with white medium-heeled shoes, looking over the rumpled bedcovers as she did. Sometime during the night her husband had groped her feverishly, and she'd consented to sex with him. Consent was all it was anymore with her, and she sometimes wondered if it had ever been anything *other* than consent. She'd read an article in *Woman's Day* that told her that excess drinking over a period of time destroyed all sexual urges. She drank three martinis before dinner every night, and vowed to give up the habit.

Alice loaded her three- and five-year-old into side-by-side car seats in the rear of her Aerostar minivan and drove them to the day-care center. She indicated on the sign-in register that she'd return by three, and lingered a moment in the lobby to watch her kids join the other children in play out in the yard. Her children's lack of reluctance to stay at the center surprised her; Alice did her best to be a good mother and never left her children unless absolutely necessary. Today was a necessary day. As she drove away she experienced feelings of guilt and vowed that tomorrow she'd take the children to the movies.

Her dashboard clock showed 10:35 as she left LBJ Freeway at the Tollway exit and steered into the multilevel parking garage at Galleria Shopping Mall. She wound around and around, moving ever upward, the signs of the upscale stores in Galleria—Lord & Taylor, Saks Fifth Avenue, New York Ltd—visible occasionally through the window. On the sixth level she located a space in between a Land Rover and a Buick Park Avenue, cut the engine, and sat for a moment to firm her resolve. She got out, thunked the lock-plungers into place, slammed the door, and crossed the pavement toward the elevators with her shoes scraping rapidly on concrete. A navy beaded purse hung from a strap over her forearm. She reached the bank of elevators, pressed the button, stood back, and self-consciously smoothed her collar. Footsteps approached from behind. She half-turned in that direction.

A strong gloved hand clamped over her mouth and an arm encircled her waist. Hands grabbed her ankles, lifted her legs, two men, both of them powerful. She *mmmph*-ed futilely against the hand over her mouth, trying to kick her feet, struggling, panic gripping her, her throat constricting in fear. Over to the low wall they carried her. Her eyes rolled in her head, vainly searching the parking garage for help, finding none among the rows of silent cars. The men lifted her high, and threw her over the side.

She was conscious of wind rushing past her ears, her hair tossing wildly, her arms flailing, her purse falling from her arm and dropping like a stone. Far below cars sped back and forth on the freeway like toys. The hands on her ankles tightened their grip and held her dangling there, six stories above the street. Her cheek scraped the concrete wall, but she scarcely noticed. Her skirt billowed and came over her head. She hung there, legs and pantyhose exposed to her waist, and wanted to scream. Wanted to beg. Was terrified of dying, and told the men so.

From somewhere above a gruff voice floated down to her. "You forget Burnside. You don't talk to no more lawyers. You say a word in court, you're dead. Are you hearing me?"

She waved her arms about, sobbing out of control.

The hands released one ankle, and one of her legs flopped around. "I said, 'Are you hearing me?' lady."

"Yes," she yelled. "Oh, my sweet Jesus, yes, just please ..."

Two hands now gripped her ankle and hoisted her up, back over the wall, and deposited her once more on concrete. A third hand found her jaw, forced her chin around so that she was looking out over the freeway. The voice told her, "Don't fucking look at us, you understand?"

She stood rigid and said remotely, "I understand, I ..."

"Don't you forget, and don't you turn around until we're gone." Two pair of footsteps retreated and faded away.

Alice looked out over the freeway for a full ten minutes before she dared to turn around. When she did, the parking garage was once again deserted. She walked to the elevators once more, pressed the button, and again smoothed her collar. The bell dinged, the doors opened and she entered the car. Oddly she was very calm.

The two women seated in La Madeleine's by the Galleria's basement ice rink looked up as Alice came in. They showed stoic recognition. She walked quickly to the back and sat across from them.

The women exchanged a look, then the one on Alice's right said to her. "We've been talking, and we agree with you. We can't just stand by and let them . . ."

"There's been a," Alice said, then cleared her throat and said, "there's been a change. Nikki. Syl. I'm afraid we need a lawyer. Have either of you got one in mind?" She was suddenly embarrassed. "Oh, I seem to have lost my purse. Could one of you . . . ? I'll pay you back. I promise. Is it all right?"

23

<hr/>

"We want 'em to be obvious," Russell Black said. "Anybody that might be followin', we want 'em to know what they're up against." He stood beside Sharon at his office window, his coat off, his hands jammed into his back pockets. A dark blue Ford Taurus was parked at the curb outside, carrying two men. A few minutes earlier Sharon had nearly dropped her briefcase in the middle of the street when she'd seen the men, and had given the Taurus a wide berth with her heart pounding against her breastbone as she'd entered the building.

"Anthony Gear come up with 'em," Black said. "They're retired FBI, just like him, both of them armed. I've hired eight of these guys, four of 'em assigned to you, four to me. They'll split time in twelve-hour shifts, and they'll never be more'n a hundred yards away from you. They'll follow you into the courthouse an' check their weapons at the metal detectors. They'll be visible. They'll stay visible. Nights they'll be sittin' in front of your house."

"I feel like the President, boss," Sharon said.

"That's the way I want you to feel. Good and safe." Black retreated to his desk, picked up the photo of Jack Torturro at the water park, and tossed it contemptuously aside. "For what it's worth," he said, "that's nothin' but a mind game. No way are these people goin' to harm a child."

Sharon sat down in a visitor's chair. "You couldn't have proved it by me. Not last night."

"The bomb in your car was kind of a game, too. They're experts at all this. Done it a thousand times. If you don't get killed, the idea is to scare you off, and they don't care one way or the other. Absolutely not one shred of evidence for anybody to tie to this Morgan Hill Corp. As for last night, tell me how anybody's goin' to arrest our friend Mr. Torturro just for bein' in a water park."

Sharon lifted, then dropped her shoulders. "They can't."

"Right. So we hire our own protection. Dallas County's sure not goin' to give us any." Black sat down and hunched over his desk, serious. "And with all this, I'm makin' it your choice. If you think we're bitin' off more than we can chew, just say so. We'll give it up."

Sharon managed a bitter laugh. "No way, boss. I'm in. If I wasn't a hundred percent before last night, I certainly am now."

"So that's out of the way. You're gettin' your subpoenas ready?"

"Picking them up this morning from the typists. By the end of the day they'll be signed, sealed, and delivered."

Black picked up and unfolded the *Dallas Morning News.* "We're makin' some progress in the newspapers. You seen this?" He tossed the paper onto the front of his desk.

Sharon normally read the paper first thing every morning, but today she'd been in too much of a hurry. The *News* had been folded in her driveway as she'd left the house, and she'd tossed it up on the porch before backing out into the street. She turned the paper around so that she could read it. A large headline topped the front page. "BURNSIDE MURDER LINKED TO SLAIN ESCAPEE." Andy Wade had been busy.

"Does he mention us?" Sharon said.

"Only that you were Dycus Wilt's lawyer, and that

we're now representin' Raymond Burnside. Nothin' about anybody shootin' at you on the highway or about the bomb in your car. Tells about the woman that quit the sheriff's department. The source he's quotin' for that information is Edward Teeter. Evidently Ed took us at our word and paid your newsman a visit in the hospital."

"Which means," Sharon said, "that Teeter will take all the credit, which is what we want. I imagine there are some sparks flying at the D.A.'s. I wouldn't want to be present when Teeter runs into Milton Breyer around the watercooler." She spread out the newspaper and rattled the pages. "Anything about the fact that Ralph Toner might not have been straight arrow in prosecuting Raymond?"

"Not yet," Black said. "But your friend Wade's leadin' up to it. Mentions three or four times that Toner was Raymond's prosecutor, an' leaves it at that. S'pect once we have this hearin', there'll be a spread in the paper about what evidence the prosecution knew about at the original trial but didn' own up to. If the paper handles it right, nobody's ever goin' to know we were the source." He added, almost reluctantly, "Wade's doin' a good job."

Sharon flashed an impish grin. "I hate to say I told you so. But I did."

Sharon led her entourage into the Crowley Courts Building just at noon, the bodyguards keeping five paces to the rear, casting glances in all directions. Neither man was much of a talker. Black had handled the introductions on the steps outside the office—"Mr. Tanner and Mr. Davis, meet Miss Hays" was as far as Russ had gone—and the ex-federal agents had returned Sharon's greeting with a series of grunts. They were big men in suits with all-business attitudes, and showed their credentials to the metal-detector guards before checking their weapons and following Sharon to the elevator. On the ride up to Judge Griffin's court, they stood across from her with grim faces and folded arms. Sharon indicated a bench outside the courtroom, and both men sat down to wait for her. She pushed through the double doors and went off in search of the judge. Under different circumstances, this could be sort of fun.

Judge Griffin didn't like the pile of subpoenas, and didn't make any bones about it. As she read over and signed each in turn, she clucked her tongue and uttered a series of exasperated sighs. When she came to the next-to-last document in the stack, she laid her pen aside and scowled. "I have to approve your subpoena, Miss Hays. The law requires me to. But I'd think that common decency would protect Senator Bright from all this. Hasn't he suffered enough grief without . . .?"

Sharon sat on a plain cloth sofa and studied the judge. Sandy Griffin's office was a no-frills affair—simple wood desk, nothing on the walls save for her framed bachelor's and law degrees—and pretty well reflected its occupant. Griffin was a plain woman who wore no makeup. She had no social life that any of the courthouse gossips had been able to uncover, and outside of the law seemed to have no interests whatsoever. During the national media coverage of the Rathermore trial, she'd tried gussying up a bit, but that attempt had been a clownish disaster. There were times when Sharon felt sorry for Sandy Griffin. But she also thought that Griffin was the fairest criminal judge in the county, and her open hostility to anyone stirring up the Burnside case was completely out of character. Sharon wet her lips. "Your Honor, can I speak candidly?"

Griffin testily signed Joseph Bright's subpoena and laid it aside. "By all means."

"I was a rookie prosecutor when you tried this case the first time. It was your first year on the bench, wasn't it?"

Griffin's eyes narrowed. "Get to your point, Counselor."

This is really out in left field, Sharon thought. Outside the courtroom Griffin was generally informal and friendly. What kind of nerve am I touching? Sharon thought. She said, "In all due respect, Your Honor, there were a lot of politics involved in Burnside's conviction. I want to ask you, personally, if we can put politics aside this time."

"Miss Hays, are you by any chance insinuating this man didn't get a fair trial? If you are . . ."

Sharon spoke quickly for fear she'd lose her nerve. "Not that he didn't get a fair trial. But face it. Joseph Bright is as respected around here as anyone, and well he should be. The D.A.'s office was hell-bent for a conviction just to please him. My point is, there are certain things we believe were overlooked to get Raymond out of the way and the whole case off of everyone's conscience."

Griffin's face turned red. "You are a thousand miles out of line, Miss Hays."

Sharon stood. "I may be. I might be sick and tired of being shot at and having bombs set under the hood of my car."

Griffin's chin moved to one side. "Now I'm not following at all."

Sharon raised a finger. "One time, one fair hearing, that's all we're asking for. Please, Judge. As one lawyer to another, I'm asking you to listen to us with an open mind. Not to favor us. Not to favor anyone. But if we can't get you to give us equal consideration, we're wasting our time."

Griffin expelled air between her lips. She signed the last of the subpoenas and tossed it on the stack. "I can't say you're lacking in nerve, Miss Hays. And you'll get your hearing. I'll do my best to forget this confrontation. At this point, that's the most I can do for you."

*   *   *

Sharon sent Davis, the biggest and burliest of her bodyguards, to serve the subpoenas. Normally she would have hired one of the courier services, but there wasn't a witness on her list who wouldn't be appearing under protest. Should any of those under subpoena fail to appear—and Sharon anticipated there would be one or more of those—she'd put Davis on the stand to testify that he'd served the papers. Then Judge Griffin would have her hands tied; with the entire proceeding on the record, the jurist would be forced to issue bench warrants, have the witness arrested and escorted to court under guard. Sharon handed the stack of papers to Davis along with a list of the witnesses' addresses, and her bodyguard-turned-process-server was off with a noncommittal grunt. That accomplished, Sharon left her other protector, Tanner, seated on a corridor bench while she waited by the pay phone. At twelve-thirty on the dot the phone jangled. Sharon put the receiver to her ear and said, "Sheila?"

"These kids're driving me crazy," Sheila said. "Absolutely stark raving bananas. How's it going?"

Sharon relaxed and leaned against the corridor wall. "Better. I'm in the company of two men."

"Well, hey, if that's what it takes, how about letting the bad guys chase *me* for a while?"

Sharon laughed. Sheila could take her from the depths to the heights in nothing flat. That's what's known as having a real true friend, Sharon supposed. "You-all are touring the capitol today, right?" she said.

"If I don't kill them first."

Sharon's mood sobered. "This morning things are a hundred percent upbeat, Sheil, and a lot of it has to do with you. But no matter how nice the weather is, and no matter what a good time everybody's having, do me one favor. Don't let Melanie out of your sight. Not for a minute, Sheila, okay?"

*   *   *

Raymond Burnside was down in the dumps and had some fan mail. He said without expression, "It's starting over, Miss Hays. This is one reason I didn't want to carry through on this to begin with." He poked a stack of letters through the bars in the attorneys' visiting booth, and sat with his head down while Sharon opened a few and read them over. "All this publicity in the newspapers . . ." Burnside coughed into his cupped hand.

The hate in some of the correspondence was almost physical. A woman in East Dallas suggested that Raymond give it up and go quietly to the execution chamber, that continuing to fight made him all the more despicable. A man in Garland said he hoped Raymond and his sleazy lawyers would burn in hell. The gutter language in a couple of the letters caused Sharon to set them aside. She said softly to Burnside, "It's to be expected."

"It wasn't to be expected, until those articles. My mother reads the *Dallas Morning News*. I told Mr. Black, and I'm telling you. If she shows up, I'll stand up in the courtroom and withdraw my request for a hearing."

"Golly, how could you do that? We're getting close to—"

"I could do it without thinking twice. A week ago I was . . . not happy, but serene. I had my thoughts to keep me company and I'd accepted death. You've forced me to hope. Now you're making me a public spectacle again." Burnside's forehead wrinkled in anger.

Sharon was suddenly mad as hell. "All right, Raymond. Once and for all, and to blazes with your feelings and your solitude. If you don't want anybody in your corner, it's your business. But publicity is the only thing that's going to give you a chance. Andy Wade took a beating on your behalf, and he's in the hospital. I've been shot at, bombed at, and I've had my child threatened. Russell Black's in danger, too, and he's gone out of his pocket to give everyone who's trying to help you a pack of bodyguards. If I was in your place, I'd want my mother by my side. If she was alive, which *my* mother isn't. Yours is. So you pout and mope and hang your head, but we're still going into court and try to save you. If you don't appreciate any of that, Mr. Burnside, you can pack your bags and take the first train straight to hell." She stood, spun on her heel, and started to leave.

A sniffle came from behind her, followed by a sob. She turned. Burnside wiped his nose on his sleeve and firmed up his expression. "Good-bye, Miss Hays," he said. "Go on, what are you waiting for?"

Sharon returned to sit across from him. On closer inspection, his eyes were puffy and red. Well knock me over, Sharon thought, it's nothing but a front. She grasped a bar, leaned as close as she could to the prisoner, and smiled at him. "Gee, Raymond," she said. "I don't guess any of us are as tough as we're pretending to be. Are we now?"

24

Woodrow Lee, smack coursing through his veins and cocaine stuffed up his nose, wondered if his woman had any money. As he came down from his high, panic set in. The past four days were patched together in his memory like a crazy quilt. He'd shared a needle with two dusky teenage hookers, lying on their sofa and knotting a stocking around his upper arm, but he couldn't remember having sex with either. He'd parted with his last hundred bucks, that recollection was clear as a bell, and he had a razor-sharp image of one hooker's ass as she'd bent over to stuff the money in a jar. Everything which had happened after that was lost in haze.

He woke up alone in the hookers' shotgun house, in a bed with cotton stuffing poking out of the mattress. Groggy from sleep and drugs, fixing his cool-dude New York Yankees baseball cap so that the bill pointed to the rear, he stumbled out to his car and sat there in a fog. If he wanted to stay high he needed bread. His woman collected from federal disability on the first of the month, and stood in the unemployment line every Thursday. Did the eagle fly for his woman today? He didn't know if it was Wednesday or Thursday. Could have been Sunday for all Lee knew. If his woman had money, though, he was fixing to get it. If she held out on him, he'd knock her around, which was the main reason a cool dude like Woodrow Lee needed a steady woman at all.

He tooled his white 1973 Chevy Monte Carlo down

Illinois Avenue with convenience stores and fast-food chicken restaurants on either side made the turn-around near the golf course, whipped up a narrow street, and bumped to a halt in front of his woman's house with one front tire over the curb. He craned his neck and looked around for the man. Ever since he'd dropped a dime on Dycus Wilt, and then Wilt in turn had snitched on him, Lee had expected the man to come calling. Dycus Wilt, Lee thought, mothafuckah dropped a dime.

Lee creaked the door open and jive-stepped up the sidewalk in hundred-degree heat, a light-skinned black man of twenty-nine, drug-popper thin with a tiny mustache and big round eyes. In addition to his cap he wore filthy jeans and a black Snoop Doggy Dog T-shirt, one cool dude with his mind on staying high. As he stepped up on the porch, he kicked an empty tomato can. The can clanked and rolled.

He entered the house without knocking and looked around the living room. The sofa and chairs were covered with sheets. No woman in sight. Bitch must be in back, Lee thought. He went down the short hall into the bedroom.

No woman there, either. The unmade bed had newspapers piled on top, and there was an odor of cheap perfume. He looked inside the bathroom, at a grimy porcelain tub and a toilet with a ring around the waterline. Still no fuckin' woman. Where dat bitch at? Lee thought groggily.

He returned to the bedroom and looked in the closet. The outfit he wore for night-crawling in Deep Ellum was there on a hanger, the cool-dude vest and leather pants, but the woman's clothes were gone. Woman taken a hike, Lee thought.

He craved drugs so badly that his arms and legs trembled. He dug in panic through the dresser drawers, finding nothing but underwear. No money, not a dime. He remembered his pistol, the .38 Police Special he'd lifted when the hockshop owner wasn't watching, went out into the kitchen, and looked in the cupboard. The gun was there, wrapped in chamois. He looked dully at the pistol, removing his cap and scratching his head. He had the gun, but no fucking bullets. If he'd had ammunition he would have pulled a robbery, but guessed he'd have to settle for selling the gun. He knew a dude in north Oak Cliff who'd been looking for a piece, and wondered where the dude might be this time of day. He jammed the gun into his hip pocket and went through the front door onto the porch, headed for his car. He wondered briefly where the woman had gone. Next time he saw her he'd smack her around, teach her a lesson for fucking with him. He reached the bottom porch step and paused.

A coal-black Mercury Cougar was parked behind his Chevy. As Lee watched, two white men got out of the Cougar and started up the sidewalk.

Ain't no *po-lice,* Lee thought, must be the repo man after the television; honkies traveling in pairs in the neighborhood were generally looking for the money or the merchandise. Repo men collected in cash. Woodrow Lee was desperate for cash. He decided right then and there to rob the men, fuck the honky bastards, scare the shit out of them with an empty pistol. As he reached for his hip pocket, it dawned on him that there was something peculiar about these dudes.

Both wore dark clothing and stocking masks, their noses mashed to one side in tight-fitting nylon. Lee had a fleeting thought that practically made him giggle, something about two dudes dressing like robbers when in fact they were fixing to get robbed themselves, when the lead man dropped to one knee and produced a gun of his own. A *big* fucking gun, an automatic, which he steadied with both hands in classic shooter's pose, the barrel aimed at Woodrow Lee's forehead. *Shee-it,* Lee thought, these dudes ain't playing.

A dozen years earlier, before he'd quit eleventh

grade, Woodrow Lee had been an all-star running back, and likely he would have led the South Oak Cliff Golden Bears to the city championship if he'd ever passed enough courses to be eligible. The sight of the large-bore automatic pointed at his face erased those dozen years in a flash, cleared his drug-fogged brain, and made him forget everything except that in seconds he was going to be dead. Lee reacted. He did a sidestep that would have faked an NFL corner into the bleacher seats, dived to his right, and hit the ground rolling. The gun went off with an earsplitting *boom*. The bullet whined inches from his ear and splintered the bottom step on the porch. The man steadied the pistol and aimed again. Woodrow Lee had seen enough, thank you. He leaped to his feet, turned tail, and ran.

He charged around the side of the house as the gun went off a second time, went over the rotten fence like an Olympic hurdler and sprinted through the weedy backyard. There was a snarl on his right, the woman's mongrel wolfhound coming to life. The dog strained at his rope and snapped as Lee went by, but Woodrow Lee barely noticed. Over the back fence into the alley he flew, lickety-split, as the men in stocking masks reached the entrance to the yard and aimed once more, both now toting pistols. Lee's lungs practically burst from exertion as he ran down the alley, his feet scraping gravel, expecting more gunfire at any second. No more gunshots came. He reached the end of the alley, went into the street, and slowed to a rapid walk, gasping for breath.

Who were those dudes? Lee thought. Weren't no *po*-lice. Things might be better for Woodrow Lee if he got the fuck out of town.

25

Thunderstorms blasted into the Dallas–Ft. Worth area on Friday morning, breaking the August heat spell and turning the streets into rivers. So dense was the curtain of rain that Sharon lost sight of her bodyguards in her rearview mirror. The midnight-to-noon-shift duo were named Wilson and Keegan. The two hulks parked outside her house had given Sharon a sense of security, but hadn't helped her sleep particularly well. Around three a.m., as lightning flashed and thunder rolled, she'd gone out on the porch in her robe and invited her keepers inside. She'd fixed them hot chocolate, and they'd spent the rest of the night in her living room like a pair of matching wooden Indians. Around six o'clock she'd whipped up a skillet of scrambled eggs.

She pulled the Volvo into the Crowley Building's multilevel lot at a few minutes after eight, braked tentatively thirty feet inside the entrance, and breathed relief when the bodyguards' Buick Century followed her in. Jack Torturro and his merry men could have been following her, and in the thunderstorm Sharon wouldn't have known the difference. She drove up three levels, located side-by-side vacant spaces, and pulled in and cut the Volvo's engine as Wilson and Keegan parked alongside. She buttoned her tan raincoat up to her throat, snatched her umbrella and briefcase, gave her bodyguards a come-on wave, then hustled down the steps and over the crosswalk to the courthouse. She lost sight of Wilson and Keegan once again as she dodged puddles and held her umbrella handle in a death grip, then stood aside beyond the metal detectors until the former federal agents checked their weapons, rode the escalator up behind her, and accompanied her to the sixth floor in the elevator.

It was nearly an hour before the hearing was to begin, and the corridor was practically deserted. As Sharon's bodyguards followed her through the double doors headed for the courtroom, her heart came up in her mouth. Jack Torturro was seated on a hallway bench in the company of another man.

It was the first time she'd seen Torturro since the day he'd tried to bribe her in Russ's office. He was dressed in a gray suit, Mr. Conservative Business Guy. The man sitting beside him was around fifty, with one side of his mouth turned down in a permanent droop. He had short sparse blond hair, and his suit was brown. His face was tanned, with fish-belly white skin around pale blue eyes. Mirrored sunglasses hung from his breast pocket by an earpiece.

Sharon looked straight ahead as she swept past with Wilson and Keegan on her heels. God, she was scared to death, bodyguards and all. She kept a steady pace for ten steps or so, then thought, to hell with it, spun on her heel, went back, and faced Torturro. Wilson and Keegan stopped in the center of the hall. The man beside Torturro looked at Sharon as if seeing through her. Torturro chewed vigorously on a wad of gum.

Sharon forced a smile. "Morning, Mr. Torturro. Are you here for a real estate closing?"

Torturro glanced nervously up and down the hall.

"Quite a coincidence you decided to go swimming the other night," Sharon said sweetly. "You must have known it was going to rain today. Did you get your fun in before the weather changed?"

Torturro continued to look away. His buddy nudged him with his elbow. "Lady's talkin' to you, Jack."

Sharon stepped sideways and stood before the stranger. "And this is . . .?"

Torturro cleared his throat. The man said deadpan, "Vernon Denopoulis. Glad to know you."

"Oh, you don't know me, but I'm Sharon Hays. You must be one of Mr. Torturro's land investors."

Torturro opened, then closed his mouth. Denopoulis folded his arms and leaned back on the bench. "Yeah, Jackie and me got a few things going."

"I imagine you do," Sharon said. She returned her attention to Torturro. "I guess this is supposed to be the silent scare, you sitting here glaring and everybody's supposed to faint dead away. Well, I'm not fainting. Andy Wade's not fainting, either, and Russell Black certainly isn't. By the time this hearing's over and Andy gets through with his series of articles, I imagine everyone in town will know who you are and what you're doing in Texas. And Mr. Toner may have trouble showing his face, much less getting elected governor. So you just sit there and glare all you want, gentlemen. I'll check with you at lunch break. If you've scared anyone by then, I'll be very surprised."

Torturro glanced at Denopoulis. "I don't know what you're talking about," Torturro finally said.

"Oh, of course you don't," Sharon said. "Just a couple of land speculators, right? Well, gentlemen, you have a nice day." She turned around and headed for court. Her bodyguards started to follow. Sharon made it halfway down the hall, paused, then turned around and approached Torturro once more.

Torturro and Denopoulis looked at her without expression.

Sharon showed them a frigid smile. "Oh. And one more thing. If you ever go within a hundred yards of my daughter again, I'll kill you, sir." She turned her grin on Denopoulis. "That's something you and Mr. Torturro should understand. If you don't, maybe I should say it a little louder. More volume might do the trick, don't you think?"

*   *   *

Two hours later Sharon found herself in a quandary, stalling for time, with no one in her corner except for Russell Black. All of her witnesses had showed up under subpoena save one, but the missing witness was the most important. The ones who'd showed now occupied benches in the corridor, waiting to be called. Judge Griffin called the hearing to order. Raymond Burnside sat glumly in his chair at the defense table beside Sharon, wearing jail clothes.

Sharon fidgeted in place, then held up one finger to the bench. "I need just a minute, Your Honor."

Sandy Griffin glared. "Please hurry, Miss Hays. There is other business before the court besides yours."

"I understand that, Judge. One second, please." Sharon bent sideways and whispered to Russell Black, "I'm going to ask her to issue a bench warrant."

Black's pinstriped suit was freshly pressed for a change. "Warrant for who?"

"Senator Bright, who else? He's the only witness who didn't show."

Black scratched his nose and scowled. "We can't go around half-cocked, askin' for warrants for United States senators. I doubt Sandy Griffin would give us one anyhow."

"If he doesn't come voluntarily, we have to. He's the only one that can identify the clock as belonging to Delores Burnside. Without his testimony we can put on witnesses from here to sundown, and it'll all be a waste of time."

Black turned and looked to the rear of the courtroom, then hunkered nearer to Sharon. "I can't argue about that," he said. "But give him more time. Hell's bells, if he thumbs his nose at a subpoena we'll have to try and bring him in, senator or no. Call the rest of your witnesses, and I'll get Anthony Gear and go out to Joe Bright's place and try to find him. You're sure he got served?"

"According to the guy delivering the papers the senator himself got them, at his front door."

"Okay, then. Go to town, girl. I'll check with you after lunch." Black got up and exited the courtroom.

Sharon felt suddenly very lonesome. She offered Raymond Burnside what she hoped was an encouraging smile, then stood and faced the bench. "We're ready, Your Honor."

"Nice to hear it." Sandy Griffin leaned back and pursed her lips. "Call your first witness. You've got us all on pins and needles, Miss Hays. Let's hope the wait has been worth it."

Dr. Willem Foster looked the part. He'd come to court in a white bloodstained smock, as if he'd interrupted an autopsy to testify. His brown hair was disheveled, mad-scientist style, and his faint German accent recalled images of World War II A-bomb research. Foster was a pro at turning defense attorneys around, but in this hearing the M.E. had no bone to pick. Since she wasn't questioning Foster's autopsy methods, only the prosecution's use of the information he'd provided, Sharon didn't expect the usual medical examiner's gymnastics in dodging the issues. She led him through his career—twenty-three years with the County of Dallas, ten before that as an assistant M.E. down in Houston—and intentionally took more time than necessary. When she was ready to get to the meat of the issue, Judge Griffin was practically yawning from boredom. Foster had testified so often in her court that Griffin likely could have recited the M.E.'s credentials in her sleep.

Sharon dug in her file and came up with a copy of Delores Burnside's autopsy. She'd taken a few seconds to have Griffin's clerk certify the copy, so there would be no question that it was the real McCoy. Sharon winked at Raymond Burnside, carried the autopsy report over, and showed it to Kathleen Fraterno. Fraterno was representing the state on her own this morning; likely Milton Breyer was too busy hustling votes for the judge's election to attend the hearing. Fraterno looked at the certification stamp on the autopsy and made no objection. Sharon went through the rigmarole of having the judge look the document over, thus admitting it into evidence, then approached the witness stand and laid the paper on the rail in front of Foster. "Doctor," Sharon said, "I show you this piece of admitted evidence and ask if you can identify it."

Foster went over the report like a man considering his future. "It appears to be," he finally said, "a copy of an autopsy I performed in 1988. I've done so many since then, I can't specifically remember this one."

So much for Foster not feinting and dodging, Sharon thought. She suspected that the M.E. had met with Kathleen Fraterno earlier, and that Foster would balk in saying that fat meat was greasy. Sharon gave a thinly disguised, exasperated sigh. "Well, if you can't remember it, sir, would you please read the title of the report into the record."

Foster squinted at the page. "Apparently the deceased was one Delores Burnside."

"And if you would, Doctor," Sharon said, "please look over the signature on the report and tell the court if it's yours."

Foster turned to the back page and said almost triumphantly, "It's a copy. I couldn't swear to that."

Oh, Jesus, Sharon thought. "Is it a *certified* copy, sir?"

More frowning and squinting. "It seems to be marked as certified," Foster said.

Sharon hooked an elbow over her chair back and nudged Raymond Burnside as if to say, Watch this. She said to the witness, "Well then, Dr. Foster, could you please tell us whether that is a *copy* of your signature?"

Foster fiddled with the papers. "I can't . . ."

"Your Honor," Sharon said, "we ask that the court instruct the witness to answer."

Sharon wasn't sure how Sandy Griffin would react, inasmuch as the judge had already picked out her favorite team in this hearing, but was dead certain she had the right to request the judge's assistance. We're just asking if he signed the damned thing, Sharon thought. She turned her gaze on the bench.

Judge Griffin seemed unsure of herself. Finally she leaned over and said to the court reporter, "Let's go off the record here." The court reporter sat back from her machine. Griffin said to Dr. Foster, "Bill, we want to get this over with before sundown. Nobody in the M.E.'s office does any autopsies without signing them. Are you saying that Miss Hays has somehow counterfeited your signature?"

Foster uncrossed his legs and rested his forearms on his knees. "No, Sandy, I'm not."

"Okay," Griffin said testily. "Then it's your signature, and you're to own up to it. I don't want any more delays in this hearing, and I'm instructing you, and you can pass the word to the rest of the county witnesses she has under subpoena, no more fooling around. Answer questions when they're asked. Is that clear?"

Foster looked at his lap. "Yes'm."

Sharon felt a surge of elation. No matter how Griffin felt personally, she was going to make certain the hearing went according to Hoyle. Small victory unless we can come up with Senator Bright, Sharon thought. She risked a glance to the rear of the courtroom. No Russ, no Anthony Gear.

"Back on the record," Griffin said. "Repeat your question, Miss Hays."

"Dr. Foster, is that your signature on the autopsy report?" Sharon said.

This time, Foster didn't even look at the report. "Yes, it is."

"Great," Sharon said, then after a sharp look from

Griffin said, "Thank you. Now, if you would, Doctor, please read . . ." She checked her copy of the report. "Please read aloud, lines three, four, and five of the third paragraph of your report."

Foster looked at the page and read without hesitation, " 'Vaginal bruising noted. More bruises on the insides of the thighs and in the area of the buttocks.' " He looked up, deadpan.

"Thank you. Now, Doctor, in your experience, what would vaginal bruising indicate to you? In addition to the other bruising which you described in your autopsy."

"Well . . ." Now Foster looked to Kathleen Fraterno. Kathleen had yet to voice an objection, which had surprised Sharon. The prosecutor continued to stay mum. Foster said, "It could indicate a number of things."

Oh, give it up, Sharon thought. She considered calling on Griffin again, then changed her mind. She had just the medicine for this act. She said, "Doctor, do you recall a case, *State of Texas* v. *John Barry Wilton*?"

Every ninny in the county recalled the Wilton case, which involved the rape-murder of three little girls on a school bus. John Barry Wilton, the lovely soul, had been the bus driver. Foster said, "Yes, I do."

"And do you recall that I was the prosecutor in that case?"

"Yes."

"And you testified for me under direct examination, didn't you?"

Fraterno opened her mouth as if to object then relaxed.

"Yes," Foster said.

"Okay. And in that case, didn't you state under oath that, in your experience, vaginal bruising accompanied by bruising of the thighs and buttocks indicated that the victim had been raped?"

Foster sighed. "I believe I said, 'violated.' "

"All right, 'violated,' then. Does that still hold true, or has forensic science changed?"

Now Fraterno did object, and Griffin sustained. The judge's tone of voice had mellowed, indicating that while she was sustaining the objection she did want to hear about the rape. We're gaining ground, Sharon thought. She tossed her head and changed gears.

"Doctor, let's switch for a moment to page three of the report, the second paragraph. I ask that you please read the first sentence into the record."

Foster hemmed and hawed. He looked openly at Fraterno, who seemed to be concentrating on something within her file. Kathleen's not wasting time with objections, Sharon thought, because she knows this evidence was available to the defense at Raymond's first trial and isn't new. Finally Foster read, "Contents of vaginal tract shows presence of semen."

"Thank you," Sharon said. "Doctor, in view of what you've just read, doesn't the autopsy on Delores Burnside indicate that the victim had been violated?"

Foster apparently decided that Fraterno wasn't going to pull him out of the fire, and gave it up. "Yes, it would seem so."

Sharon practically sagged in relief. "Thank you. Finally." She turned to the judge. "I have no further questions of this witness, Your Honor. I apologize to the court for the length of this hearing, but I do feel I should serve notice to the court. If I continue to have to pull teeth to get replies from these witnesses, we may all be here throughout the summer."

Sharon called Ralph Toner. Her bodyguard-turned-process-server had delivered the papers at Toner's campaign headquarters, and Sharon would love to have seen the candidate's face when Davis had laid the subpoena on him as he filmed a TV commercial. Toner's appearance in court hadn't escaped the media's attention. As the bailiff stumped into the hallway in search of the witness, Sharon let her gaze roam the reporters' section. There were seven or eight young men and women in everything from coats and ties to jeans and pullovers, all intensely taking notes. Sharon recognized two of the newspeople, one from the *News* and the other from the *Observer*, and smiled briefly at each one in turn. There was movement in the corner of her eye as the rear courtroom door opened. She looked in that direction as Andy Wade came in. Sharon blinked in surprise.

Andy wasn't getting around really well. He walked stooped over, and halfway down the aisle he gingerly touched his ribs. He grinned painfully in Sharon's direction and threw her a thumbs-up sign. Sharon supposed that Wade had come directly from his hospital bed. Seeing Andy reminded her of her own injuries, which had practically healed. Her forearms were barely sore, and she had to twist her knee around intentionally for it to hurt at all. She leaned over and whispered to Raymond Burnside, "The young guy with the glasses that looks in pain, Raymond. That's Andy Wade."

Raymond showed about the same reaction to Wade as he had to the rest of the proceedings so far. Exactly none. He dully watched Andy until the reporter had taken a seat, then said merely, "Oh."

"He's the one that's been doing the articles," Sharon said.

Burnside faced the front without interest and folded his hands. "I know who he is."

Sharon felt a touch of despair. Burnside had retreated into his shell, and none of her attempts seemed to shake him out of the doldrums. She opened her mouth to say more to him when the rear door opened once more. The bailiff came in, followed by Ralph Toner and another man.

The stranger was slim and assured, middle forties, with brown hair receding halfway, and his dark blue pinstripe suit was a thousand bucks off the rack if it was a dime. He wore a slim gold watch—looks like a

Piaget, Sharon thought—and his black thin-soled shoes were polished like mirrors. Ralph Toner wore a black suit with a pale blue pinstripe. He hung back behind the rail and let the stranger come through the gate alone. The stranger carried a thin leather attaché case, which he opened on the defense table. He said condescendingly, "Miss Hays?" Sharon nodded. "Your copy," the stranger said, then dropped a stapled sheath of legal-size papers in front of her. He hefted another stack of identical pages, walked to the bench, and laid them in front of Sandy Griffin. "For the court, Your Honor," he said.

Sharon picked up her copy and read. The document was entitled "Motion to Quash," and, in perfectly typed, eloquent prose, stated that Sharon's subpoena was all a bunch of b.s., and that sterling citizen Ralph B. Toner shouldn't have to testify at this hearing, no way. Sharon thumbed through four pages and looked for the signature on the motion. Apparently the eloquent stranger was Benjamin R. Spacer, an associate in the firm of Bowles & Hackney. Bowles & Hackney was the same firm that represented Morgan Hill Corp. and its distinguished representative, Jack Torturro. She looked over her shoulder to glare beyond the rail at Toner. Toner folded his hands and looked at the floor. My God, Sharon thought, now the lawyers have lawyers. She faced the front as Judge Griffin finished examining the motion and raised her eyebrows expectantly.

Benjamin Spacer strutted in place. "Our position is threefold, Your Honor. Number One"—he raised a manicured finger—"is that our client Mr. Toner has no information whatsoever, personally, that is relevant to the case at hand. He was a county employee at the time of Raymond Burnside's original prosecution—a position he no longer holds—and knows nothing that isn't available to Mr. Burnside's attorneys through public record county documents." Spacer's voice was mellow and carried well, his tone and bearing straight from Harvard, Princeton, and points east.

"The second matter we wish to argue," Spacer said, "is that Mr. Toner didn't have sufficient notice in which to refresh his memory. The subpoena was served yesterday afternoon. Mr. Toner is six years removed from this case, and doesn't claim to possess total recall. My client acknowledges that this matter is sensitive to him, inasmuch as Miss Hays' request for new trial hinges in part on an allegation of impropriety on the part of the prosecution. It is public knowledge that Mr. Toner is currently engaged in an intense political campaign which occupies all of his time. In view of this, it's our position that if the court decides he *does* have to testify, his testimony should be delayed until his campaign is completed, so he will have time to prepare."

Pompous, Sharon thought, but a long way from dumb. If they could delay Toner's testimony until after the election, old Ralph could be in the governor's mansion for four years no matter what his stint on the witness stand revealed. Let's hear it for the gamblers, Sharon thought. She pushed her chair back and stood, conscious of Raymond Burnside's questioning gaze on her.

"And finally," Spacer went on, "if the court rules that my client has to testify, we submit he's entitled to privilege. Any knowledge he might have, he gained as a lawyer with the county as his client. As I'm sure Your Honor will agree, the attorney-client relationship is sacred. He has to state nothing under oath which he learned as a result of that relationship."

Which absolutely takes the freaking cake, Sharon thought. Criminal lawyers hid behind attorney-client privilege all the time, when asked if they knew whether their man was guilty, but she'd never heard of the *state's* lawyer ducking behind the privilege rule. She came around the table and approached the bench to stand alongside Spacer. Kathleen Fraterno kept her

seat; since the witness was challenging Sharon's subpoena, the state wasn't involved in this. Spacer
smelled of expensive cologne.

Judge Griffin lifted the motion from the bench. "Do
you have a response to this, Miss Hays?"

Sharon was entitled to ask for a recess to research
what the law had to say, and knew it, but decided
against making such a request. The result would be
delay piled on delay. "Their motion to quash our subpoena is threefold, Your Honor," Sharon said, "so if
the court please, I'll deal with one point at a time."

Griffin didn't try to mask her surprise. She'd probably been planning her shopping spree during the recess she expected to grant at Sharon's request. She
said, "You mean, you're ready to proceed right now?"

"Yes, Your Honor."

Griffin resignedly rested her chin on her intertwined
fingers. "Enlighten us, Miss Hays. Please."

"Their first point," Sharon said, "that Mr. Toner
has no information that isn't a public record, is invalid
as a matter of law. If he in fact knows nothing, that
will develop during his testimony. Allowing him to
refuse to testify would only permit him to shield what
he *does* know."

Griffin's expression remained stoic. Spacer inhaled
through his nose. Sharon cleared her throat. She'd
been sure of her grounds on that point. The rest of
the way she'd be flying by the seat of her pants.

"As for the argument that Mr. Toner didn't have
sufficient notice," Sharon said, "that is preposterous,
Your Honor. We acknowledge he's conducting a campaign, but my client's conducting one as well, which
is a whole lot more vital to him than an election. To
delay Mr. Toner's testimony would lengthen Mr.
Burnside's period of anxiety as well as his incarcera-
tion. We're not asking for anything which requires research on Mr. Toner's part, only for information
contained in his memory.

"And as for Mr. Toner's knowledge of this case

being privileged, well . . ." Sharon really felt out in left field on this one. Think on your feet, Sharon Jenifer, she told herself, "If the court wishes, we're certainly willing to have our questions monitored. Only information gleaned from Mr. Toner's client is privileged. What he observed and what he did on his own without conferring with his client is not. If any of our questions tread on ground, we'll certainly withdraw them at the court's instruction."

Which dumped the whole thing in Griffin's lap, a position in which not one judge in ten liked to find himself. Sandy Griffin, though, was the one in ten, and loved to make decisions normally reserved for the lawyers in her court. I'm counting on your ego, Sandy, Sharon thought. "We move that the witness's motion be set aside," Sharon said, "and that he be instructed to testify."

Spacer now took his cue. "Our motion to quash stands as raised, Your Honor," he said.

Griffin rubbed her hands together and assumed her best judgelike look of concern. Sharon wondered if Griffin would call a recess herself, in order to bone up on the law. A delay would give Toner more time to rehearse what he was going to say, but also would give Russ and Gear more of a chance to come up with the senator. Sharon had mixed emotions.

Griffin reached inside her robe, pulled out a St. Christopher medal on a chain, and played with it. She cleared her throat. "Mr. Spacer," she said, "I'm not going to let your client off the hook. Not entirely. Miss Hays' first point is valid. If Mr. Toner knows nothing, he can show that in his testimony.

"As for your second objection, you have a point. But Miss Hays has a point as well. I'm going to let her question him about what he recalls. If she asks him anything that requires him to look at his notes, I'll disregard any answer until he has time to prepare."

Uh-oh, Sharon thought. Not good. Now Toner will claim he has to see a file about every freaking thing.

"And as for the privilege question," Griffin said, "I'll tell Miss Hays to proceed with caution. Mr. Toner's a lawyer. Anything he thinks is privileged, he can so state. I'll make those rulings on a question-by-question basis." She looked from Sharon to Spacer, and back again. "Is that clear to everyone?" Griffin said.

Sharon nodded. Spacer looked down and said, "It is, Your Honor."

"Very well. You may proceed, Miss Hays. As quickly as possible, please. I have a trial beginning in a week or two. Let's try to have this hearing over by then, shall we?"

26

Woodrow Lee spent the night under a bridge along with four old homeless dudes. The homeless dudes were safe from him because they didn't have any money. Lee in turn was safe from them because he had a pistol, unloaded though it was. He slept with his back to the concrete wall, his cap shading his eyes, and the gun in full view between his knees. The homeless dudes huddled against the opposite wall with a trickle of water in the trough between. Lee woke with a start at dawn to the drumbeat of rain. The homeless dudes were gone. The trickle had grown to a rushing torrent, drenching his feet to the ankles.

Lee drew up his knees to escape the flood, and groped for his pistol. Gun in hand, he staggered to his feet and cringed against the wall. Curtains of rain covered the bridge's open ends, and the water was rising fast. Stiff and miserable, his shoes making a squishing noise, he crept along the wall to the end of the bridge. Rivulets cascaded down the weed-infested creek bank. So heavy was the downpour that the street above was invisible to him. His hands trembled, and his innards cried out for drugs.

Within seconds the water had risen to the soles of his shoes, so Lee made a run for it. Up the muddy bank he scrambled, his brain fogged, his clothes drenched. He slipped and fell to his knees, and made it up to the sidewalk along the culvert bank with mud covering his pants legs. A narrow street ran beside the culvert, and across the street were vacant storefronts with an awning overhead. Lee charged blindly for the protection of the awning. Brakes squealed and a horn honked in anger. Lee ran out of the rain and sagged against a storefront as a pickup drove away, giving one last honk for good measure.

He waited for his breathing to slow, and had a few seconds in which to think. Where in the fuck was he? The image came back, the memory, two white dudes shooting at him. Lee didn't know why they wanted to kill him, but also knew he couldn't return to the house to pick up his car. He wondered if the dudes were friends of Dycus Wilt's, jailhouse homeboys, wanting to kill Woodrow Lee for dropping a dime. Well, Dycus Wilt had snitched as well, the rotten mothafuckah, that was something Lee could tell the two dudes. His legs quivered, and there was an awful empty feeling in the pit of his stomach. He had to get high. The rain slacked off to a steady drizzle. Head down, his cap shading his eyes, his Snoop Doggy Dog T-shirt soaked and clinging to his skin, Lee left the protection of the awning and shuffled down the street.

Three blocks down was a four-lane thoroughfare, and on the opposite corner of the street was a convenience store, a 7-Eleven, open twenty-four hours. Lee thought it to be around seven o'clock, just after summertime dawn, but with the thick cloud cover he wasn't sure. There was a rusty old Ford in front of the store by the gas pumps. As Lee crossed the street and stood in the driveway, a young black woman came out of the store, cast a fearful glance in his direction, hopped in the Ford, and drove away. Lee ducked inside the store and stood before the newspaper rack, pretending to read the headlines, fucking around. One headline read, "CANDIDATE TONER SUBPOENAED IN BURNSIDE HEARING." The air-conditioning chilled his wet clothes. He sneezed and wiped his nose with the back of his hand.

The clerk was Oriental, a young man in his twenties with coal-black hair swept over his forehead. He wore a white jacket with the 7-Eleven emblem on the pocket, and was by the coffee machine filling a cup. He carried his cup behind the counter and regarded Lee with one upraised eyebrow. "Something for you?" the clerk said. He had a faint Far East accent.

"Milk," Lee mumbled. "Wants milk." He went down an aisle between loaves of bread and packages of doughnuts and sweet rolls to the coolers, slid the glass door aside, and fiddled with a carton of milk. There were no other customers. The clerk unfolded a newspaper on the counter and slurped coffee as he read a magazine.

Lee made up his mind in a flash. He dug in his hip pocket, came out with his .38, walked quickly back up the aisle, and stood before the counter. He extended the gun in both hands. His voice quaking, he said, "Blow yo' ass off, mothafuckah."

The clerk looked slowly up. His eyes widened. He froze.

Lee gestured with the gun toward the cash register. "Gimme yo' money. Wants all yo' fuckin' money."

The clerk backed away from the counter, his hands spread, palms down. "Now, don't get nervous. Here. Sure, the money, no problem." His tone was strangely calm, his manner confident. He stepped to the register, put his finger on a key. "Here," he said. "Sure thing." He pressed the key, and the cash drawer dinged open.

Lee stepped to the counter and put the gun in the clerk's face. "All yo' fuckin' money."

The clerk dug in the register and came up with a few bills, dropped them on the counter. "I'm giving you no trouble. Just take it and go."

Lee's hands trembled; he held the pistol in his right and reached with his left, the barrel wavering. He scooped the money toward him. As he did, his trigger finger involuntarily tightened.

The hammer fell on an empty chamber with a hollow *click*.

The clerk winced and tightly shut his eyes, then

opened them. His lips spread in a grin as realization dawned.

Lee backed toward the door. "Don't move, mothafuckah." He stuffed the money in his pocket.

"Don't move?" the clerk said. "I'll show you, don't move, you filthy . . ." He stooped beneath the counter and came up holding a pistol of his own.

Lee squeezed the trigger and fired off two more hollow clicks, his expression puzzled. The clerk pointed his own weapon and called out, "Hold it. Right there."

Lee pushed the door open and ran. The rain had strengthened into a downpour. Drops like falling lead pounded his shoulders and the crown of his hat. His sneakers splashed in puddles. He looked back as the clerk raced onto the driveway in hot pursuit.

Woodrow Lee had time to think, Mothafuckah's comin' after me, and had time for one instant of total panic before the clerk's pistol went off. The noise was like a clap of thunder. The bullet smashed through sinew and shoulder bone. Lee screamed and fell on his side near the pumps. The clerk approached and stood over him. Lee's head flopped to one side. Blood poured from his shoulder and mixed with falling rain. His body shook in a spasm. Then there was blackness, a strange peaceful feeling as the pain disappeared.

He came groggily to and was conscious of a rocking motion. A coarse sheet covered him, and there was a pillow beneath his head. His shoulder ached. Somewhere on his right was a faint creaking noise.

He opened one eye. He lay on a gurney inside an ambulance. The creaking noise was a suspended bottle swinging back and forth, back and forth. A tube ran from the bottle to a needle inserted in his arm. His shoulder felt tight. He was shirtless, and reached for his shoulder to touch adhesive tape. There was a drug in his veins, blessed painkiller. He relaxed and grinned.

A white-coated paramedic stood near the bottle, adjusting something. A uniformed policeman sat on a stool by the gurney, the stool rocking with the motion of the ambulance. Outside, a muffled siren wailed.

The policeman returned Lee's grin. "Feelin' better?" the cop said. "You ain't going to die, old thing. Which to my way of thinkin', is too fuckin' bad."

27

Sharon wondered how Sandy Griffin felt, having Ralph Toner as a witness in her courtroom. Griffin and Toner had worked closely on a number of cases as assistant district attorneys, and Toner had been elected D.A. within a year after Griffin had taken the judge's bench. All during Sharon's tenure as a prosecutor, Toner and Griffin had served together on numerous committees. If Griffin had any plans to protect the witness from attack, it wasn't evident in her manner. She sat attentively on the bench as Sharon posed her initial question.

"For the record, Mr. Toner," Sharon said, "you resisted testifying today, didn't you?" It was a leading question. Kathleen Fraterno shifted in her chair as if to object, then relaxed. Sharon had gotten the court's permission to treat Toner as a hostile witness, so there would be no holds barred in this examination. Let's see you answer that one, Mr. Candidate, Sharon thought.

Since there was no jury on which he cold hone in, Toner directed his response toward the media section. "I felt I had nothing to add, and felt that time spent away from my campaign would be unfair to the voters." As a lawyer, Toner understood the hostile witness rule quite well. Sharon had leeway, but so did he. As a friendly witness he would have been restricted to yes and no answers, but as a hostile witness he could wander, change the subject, and say about what he damn well pleased. Under subpoena, facing allegation

that he railroaded this poor man into the death house,
Sharon thought, the pompous ass is still hustling votes.
It was going to be a long day.

"But you did resist giving testimony, and had your
attorney appear, is that right?"

"For the good of everyone concerned." Toner
stroked his smooth upper lip as if he'd forgotten he'd
shaved his mustache for the campaign. Come to think
about it, Sharon thought, some villain's facial hair
would be right in character.

"So now that we're clear on that," Sharon said,
"please tell us whether you were the prosecutor in the
case in which Raymond Burnside received the death
penalty, six years ago."

"I was representing the people's interest in that
matter. Yes."

"Yes, sir, the people's interest. Are you currently a
candidate for governor, Mr. Toner?"

"It's my wish to serve."

"Well, as long as you're wanting to *serve*, Mr.
Toner . . . no, strike that." Sharon stopped herself
just as Kathleen Fraterno drew breath to object, an
objection which Griffin would have properly sustained.
You can't openly attack the witness, Sharon Jenifer
Dodo, she told herself. Keep your cool and give him
enough rope. She poured a goblet of water from a
chrome carafe on the defense table and had a sip. "In
your campaign, sir," she finally said, "do you have
the support of Senator Joseph Bright, our Washington
representative?"

"Objection." Fraterno sat bolt upright. "His political ties have no bearing on this hearing, Your Honor."
Kathleen wore a slim gray suit, and now stretched out
her legs and crossed her ankles.

Judge Griffin seemed in deliberation with herself.
She knew quite well the connection between Senator
Bright and the Burnside case, but as a political animal
wouldn't want the senator sullied in her courtroom.

Sharon said quickly, before Griffin cold sustain,

"We will show that the witness's motives in this case go directly to his relationship to the senator, Your Honor. We ask that the court remember that this witness is hostile."

Griffin pursed her lips. Sharon had her there, and knew it, and was pretty sure an appeals court would see it her way. Griffin apparently decided that saving Toner's political ass wasn't worth a reversal. "Objection overruled," she finally said. Fraterno testily rattled papers at the prosecution table.

"Do you need the question repeated, Mr. Toner?" Sharon said.

"No, I don't. I've been proud to have Joe Bright as a mentor during the past years. A finer teacher you couldn't—"

"Where did you first meet Senator Bright, Mr. Toner?"

"—Ever want to . . ." Toner trailed off, his gaze vacant as he looked to the media section. Sharon risked a glance over her shoulder. The reporters were scribbling like mad except for Andy Wade, who watched the witness with an open look of contempt. Toner regained his posture to say, "Excuse me? Where did I . . .?"

Sharon snapped her head around, eyes front. "My question was, Where did you first meet Senator Joseph Bright?"

"He had a severe personal tragedy."

"Because his daughter was the victim of a homicide?"

Toner looked sadly at his lap. "Tragic . . . yes."

Sharon would have to give Toner his due; he was playing it for all it was worth. Even Sandy Griffin looked sympathetic. Sharon glanced at Raymond Burnside, Burnside's jaws now clenched in anger. All wrong, Raymond, Sharon thought. Her client looked as if he'd gotten rid of one victim and would like to have Toner as his second helping. Sharon said,

"Wasn't she the victim in the case at hand, Mr. Toner? Delores Burnside?"

Toner picked just that moment to meet Burnside's gaze head-on. The ex-D.A. put on his best protector-of-the-people scowl. "Yes, she was. That man's victim."

Sharon was conscious of movement among the reporters. Toner's last answer was bound to make headlines. "So it was after the conviction in this case that Senator Bright lent you his political support, wasn't it?"

"He did. And I'm everlastingly grateful to him."

Kathleen Fraterno half rose. "Objection, Your Honor. This is *so* out of line."

This time, Griffin didn't hesitate. "I'm going to sustain. You've made your point, Miss Hays. It's time to go on."

Sharon pretended to study her notes, in order to give herself time to think. On her right, Burnside inhaled air in large gulps. Sharon leaned over and whispered, "You have to cool it, Raymond. It's hard, but you have to." Now her client glared at her, then zeroed in on Toner once more.

Sharon had to get the court's attention away from the fact that her client was acting every bit the killer he was supposed to be. She grabbed her copy of the autopsy report and rattled pages. Griffin's attention went from Raymond Burnside to the papers in Sharon's hands. Sharon said, "Your Honor, may I approach the witness?"

Griffin seemed curious. "You may."

Sharon left her copy on the table, retrieved the original document from the clerk, walked up, and dropped the autopsy in front of Toner. "Mr. Toner, I show you what's been marked, Petitioner's Exhibit Number One, and ask if you can identify it."

Toner barely glanced at the report. "It's the autopsy."

Sharon couldn't resist smirking at the witness. Toner

hadn't been too busy with the old campaign to drop
by Kathleen Fraterno's for a rehearsal on how to handle the autopsy report. Sharon said, "Are you familiar
with its contents?"

Toner raised I'm-so-innocent eyebrows. "It's been
six years."

Yeah, Sharon thought, or one day, since you and
Fraterno went over this autopsy with a fine-tooth
comb. Sharon folded her arms. "I direct your attention, Mr. Toner, to the third paragraph, lines two,
three, and four, and to the second paragraph on
page three. Please read them over. I'll tell you
they've already been read into the record by a previous witness, so it's not necessary for you to read
aloud."

Sharon stood by and brushed imaginary lint from
her skirt while Toner glanced at the first page, flipped
the pages, and glanced at the third. World's fastest
speed reader, Sharon thought. She looked pointedly
at Fraterno, who was suddenly busy with a button on
her blouse. Toner laid down the report and said,
"Yes?"

"You've completed your . . . *examination* of that
document?"

"I have, the parts you pointed out."

"Mr. Toner, in your ten years as a prosecutor with
this county, how many murder cases did you try?"

Toner showered the media with a beatific gaze. "It
would be difficult to estimate the number of criminals
I prosecuted."

"Murder cases only, sir."

"I'm . . . sorry. I simply don't recall."

Sharon walked pointedly to the defense table and
dug in her satchel, and came up with a printout six
inches thick. The printout was a list of all felony trials
during Toner's tenure as an A.D.A., and Sharon had
ignored the protests of the people waiting in line as
she'd printed out the list downstairs in the county
clerk's office. Toner knew what the document con-

tained and so did Kathleen Fraterno. More importantly, Sandy Griffin knew as well. No point in hedging, guys, Sharon thought, I've got the goods right here.

Sharon walked halfway to the witness. "Mr. Toner, would it surprise you to know that you participated in eighty-three felony trials as a prosecutor?"

Toner showed a modest smile. "That many? My, that's quite a few. I didn't realize—"

"And would it surprise you, sir," Sharon said, "to know that forty-seven of those were murder cases?"

Toner slowly shook his head. "My. Forty-seven . . ."

"And that thirty-one of those murder cases included felony rape, the portion of the indictment naming a collateral offense to support a death sentence?"

Toner's thin jaw protruded slightly. "I am a strong supporter of the death penalty, Miss Hays. With the crime rate rampant in our state—"

"Which gives you a great deal of experience in prosecuting rape cases, doesn't it?" Jesus Christ, Sharon thought, the man's a walking campaign billboard.

"And I've never taken such prosecutions lightly."

"I'm sure you haven't, sir. I'll ask you now, did you review the autopsy report on Delores Burnside as a part of your preparation of the county's case against Raymond Burnside?" Sharon extended a hand toward Raymond, palm up. Raymond had calmed down, and now regarded the witness stoically. Not perfect, Sharon thought, but better than snorting like a wild bull.

Toner leaned back in the witness chair. "I have no recollection of that. It's been six years."

Sure, Sharon thought, and you have no recollection of your first time in the old sackeroo, which has been a damn sight longer than six years ago. She laid the printout on the defense table in plain view and walked up by the witness box. "Well, then, sir, wouldn't you say it's procedure to review the autopsy report when you're prosecuting a murder?" Judge Griffin now watched the witness with an incredulous look on her face. If Toner tried to say the autopsy wasn't a required prosecutorial tool, the judge was likely to switch teams. Sharon waited for Toner's answer.

Toner seemed to feel the judge's gaze on him. He said rather nervously, "Oh, most certainly. It's just that, I have no independent recollection of that particular case."

Because there were so many other cases that put your political career on track, right? Sharon thought. "In preparing to try a murder case," she said, "isn't it standard procedure to meet with investigators? Policemen, forensics people, and whatnot?"

"Oh, most certainly," Toner said.

"And didn't you meet with those people in this case?"

"I'm sure that I did."

"Mmm, hmm. Mr. Toner, did those investigators tell you that they'd collected semen and hair samples from Raymond Burnside as part of their investigation?"

Toner seemed lost in thought. He looked down, then slowly back up, and locked gazes with Kathleen Fraterno. Finally Toner said merely, "That would be a privileged conversation."

Oh, my God, Sharon thought, the privilege barrier rears its ugly head. Toner was going to claim attorney-client privilege on every damned thing he'd discussed with the police, if he could get away with it. Sharon looked to the bench. "We ask that the court direct the witness to answer, Your Honor."

Griffin spread her hands apologetically. "It's a conversation between lawyer and client, Miss Hays. In this case, those investigators were representatives of Mr. Toner's client, Dallas County. I can't ask the witness to violate privilege." She sat back and looked at Toner.

Sharon strolled around for a moment, thinking. Privilege, privilege, privilege. Only covers what he discussed, not what he did. She stopped pacing. "But you did meet with those people, right?"

"That I did," Toner said.

"And after that meeting, did you then review any materials they might have given you?"

Toner shrugged. "If they gave me materials, I did."

"Yes, sir. And didn't those materials include results of testing of hair and semen samples from Raymond Burnside?"

"I suppose they might've."

Sharon looked at Raymond, then whirled around to face the witness. "But you didn't use any of those results in prosecuting the case, did you?"

Now Toner looked helpless, and gazed at Fraterno as if begging her to jump in with an objection. Kathleen's not about to object, Sharon thought, because she knows I'm blowing a lot of smoke here. If Toner admitted to shelving the tests because they didn't match Raymond Burnside, it mattered not to the state because the samples were available to the defense at Raymond's original trial. Fraterno's trying to uphold a conviction, Sharon thought, not save the witness's political ass. Sharon said firmly, "Did you use any of the results, Mr. Toner?"

Toner sighed. "I'm afraid I don't recall."

Now Sharon dug in her belongings and came up with a file so thick it had to be held together with four rubber bands. She thumped the file onto the defense table. "Would it refresh your memory to review the case file?"

He looked at the folder, speechless for once.

"Isn't it a fact," Sharon said, "that nowhere in the trial did the prosecution even *mention* that Delores Burnside had been raped?"

"I think . . ." Toner licked his lips, then virtually beamed at the media section. "It's my recollection that we wanted to spare the victims."

Sharon's jaw dropped. "Spare the . . . ?"

"Yes," Toner said, the assured politician once more.

"We felt we could secure a conviction without having the family go through the pain, the brutality . . ."

Sharon would give her eyeteeth to have Senator Joseph Bright in the courtroom, to hear this in person. If he could listen to this baloney, Sharon thought the senator would likely jump on the bandwagon to free Raymond. Sharon stared Toner down while saying, "To save the victims? Or did you shield the rape from the jury because the semen and hair samples didn't match my client, Raymond Burnside?"

Fraterno came to her feet as if shot from a cannon. "Objection. That's combative, Your Honor. She's badgering the witness."

Sharon said, contemptuously and without thinking, "He *needs* badgering, Judge."

Toner shifted testily in his chair. Sandy Griffin recoiled in shock. Then, as if she was having trouble believing her ears, she said, "You will approach, Miss Hays. You, too, Miss Fraterno."

Sharon was out of line and knew it. The march to stand before the bench seemed a thousand miles, and even Kathleen Fraterno gave Sharon a look of sympathy. Sharon stood before Griffin and lowered her head in saying, "Your Honor, I . . ."

Griffin sat sternly forward and said in a hushed voice, "There's no provision in the rules of procedure to make allowances for attorneys with PMS. Do you have PMS, Miss Hays?"

Sharon kept her head down. "No, ma'am."

"Because if you don't," Griffin said, "then you are totally without excuse for your behavior. I might give leeway to a twit straight out of law school, but not an experienced trial attorney."

Sharon looked up. "I'm awfully wrapped up in this."

Fraterno stood silently.

"Not only are you out of line," Griffin said, "you aren't even dealing with issues which might grant your client a new trial. There is nothing you're bringing up which even hints at evidence that wasn't available to the defense at the first trial, is there?"

Sharon began, "Prosecutorial misconduct—"

"Deals with withholding evidence," Griffin interrupted. "This evidence wasn't withheld. It's right there in the case file jacket. That Mr. Burnside's attorneys didn't deal with these matters at the first trial isn't Mr. Toner's fault. All you seem to be accomplishing here is to take potshots at Mr. Toner's electoral qualifications. Are you a member of some opposing political faction to Mr. Toner, Miss Hays?"

Now Sharon was a mite p.o.'d. She'd apologized, and didn't think she'd committed an offense severe enough to warrant such a mauling from the judge or anybody else. She firmed her posture. "We're entitled to show collateral issues, Judge, to go along with the new evidence we plan to present. It's all permissible at a hearing such as this. The case law . . ."

"I'm familiar with the case law, thank you," Griffin said. "You can only present this sort of thing *after* you've established that you have new evidence. Not before."

"Well, we may be presenting the cast out of order of appearance," Sharon said, "but there's nothing that says we can't bring up collateral issues *before* we show the new evidence." Sharon was desperate. Where were Russ Black, Anthony Gear, Woodrow Lee's one-eyed girlfriend, and the U.S. senator from Texas when she needed them?

"You're not the only one who spends time in the law library, Miss Hays," Griffin said. "And the trial court has broad discretion in these matters. I'm not going to permit you to continue to beat Mr. Toner up unless you tell me, right now, exactly what new evidence you plan to present."

"A clock."

Griffin expelled air through her nose. "A clock? Now, that would be interesting."

Now Fraterno chirped, "A clock that she won't

show the state, Your Honor, in spite of the fact that I've requested to see it."

"I'm not required to show it to them, Judge. We don't have reciprocal discovery in Texas. As far as I know that's only in California, the O. J. Simpson matter, and whatnot."

"You're not *required* to," Griffin said, "though it would speed up matters a bit. What's with this clock?"

"It was stolen from Delores Burnside's home," Sharon said. "We found it in the possession of the party whom we believe actually committed the crime." Which was a little white lie, since Woodrow Lee's girlfriend was actually in possession of the clock. Sharon resisted touching her nose, to see if it had grown.

Griffin's testiness seemed to deflate a bit. She looked interested. "And you're prepared to present this clock in evidence?"

"Yes we are, Your Honor," Sharon said. And can even prove it was Delores's, she thought, if we can get the freaking senator on the stand.

Griffin looked at her watch. "Okay, Miss Hays, here's what we're going to do. It's a quarter to twelve, and we're going to break early for lunch. I'm going to excuse Mr. Toner, and hold him in recall until after I see this new evidence you're going to present. If and when you produce this clock, you can put Mr. Toner back on the stand and flay at him to your heart's content. If you don't produce, Mr. Toner will be excused permanently and this hearing will draw to a close. No one's going to use my courtroom for political posturing for the benefit of the media. Is that clear?"

So much for filibustering to allow Russ and Anthony Gear more time, Sharon thought. We've got to have the senator, chop-chop. "I understand, Your Honor," she said.

"Fine. Return to your stations, ladies, and I'll declare the noon recess." Griffin sat back with an air of finality.

Sharon returned to the defense table feeling as if

she was walking in quicksand. Producing Senator Joseph Bright was the only chance that Raymond Burnside had left. As she took her seat, she was unable to look Raymond straight in the eye.

28

Sharon hustled into the corridor in search of Russ, Anthony Gear, or any combination thereof, and bumped into Andy Wade. She was so intent on scanning the benches along the walls that she didn't notice Andy standing there, and collided with him while she was under a pretty good head of steam. The reporter grunted in pain. Sharon put a hand on his arm and said, "Gee, Andy, I'm sorry. They release you from the hospital?"

Wade folded his arms over his ribs. "Day pass. I'm supposed to be back in at night, two or three more days."

Her face muscles relaxed in sympathy. "Please don't say, 'It only hurts when I laugh.' That one's too old."

The reporter flashed his customary grin. "How about, it only hurts when I'm sexually aroused? That'd be more like it."

Andy's sense of humor was infectuous. Sharon winked at him. "Guess you'd better not get too close to me, then, right?" She looked up and down the hallway. "Have you seen Russ?"

"Nope. Haven't been exactly looking for him, but I . . ."

Sharon's gaze was on three men near the elevator. Ralph Toner, Jack Torturro, and Vernon Denopoulis, the gruesome threesome. Toner was talking nonstop, glancing around to see who might be watching. Torturro seemed upset. Denopoulis stood stoically by, chewing on a toothpick. Toner's lawyer, Benjamin

Spacer, stood a few feet away from the men in all his Ivy League eloquence, looking away, pretending he didn't know what was going on between his client and the other two guys. A knot of reporters stood a respectful distance away. Toner noticed the reporters, smiled, and raised a just-a-minute hand in their direction. Sharon said to Wade, "You want some fodder for tomorrow's story?"

The reporter followed her gaze.

"The dude in the middle is the local representative for the fine upstanding company Morgan Hill Corp.," Sharon said. "The capo di tutti-frutti type, or whatever they call them these days, is in from California. He's Mr. Torturro's fine upstanding superior in said fine upstanding company. The fine upstanding gentlemen who beat the living crap out of you are in those gentlemen's employ, though I doubt you can prove it, and our fine upstanding candidate Mr. Toner looks to those gentlemen for financial support to help sweep him into the governor's mansion." She blinked demurely at Wade. "Sic 'em, Andy. A better Deep Throat you'll never find."

Wade muttered, "The sons of bitches," touched his ribs, and approached the men with pad and pen held ready. Sharon overheard Wade saying, "Could I talk to you guys a minute," and watched Toner and the others stare openmouthed at the reporter, before she did a right-face and marched down the corridor toward the ladies' room. She halted in mid-stride.

Anthony Gear was seated on a bench. A shoe box was on the seat beside him, and next to the box sat Gloria Bone in all her one-eyed splendor. Gear was casting furtive glances up and down the corridor. Sharon recalled her racial discussion with the detective, and very nearly giggled out loud. She went over to the bench and sank down beside Gear. "Where's Russ?" she said.

Gear pointed at the floor. "Downstairs on the phone."

Sharon reached across Gear's lap and patted the box. "Is that the clock?"

Gear nodded. "Yep. I couldn't find anybody to fix it. The little people are sticking out, bouncing around on springs."

"Better," Sharon said. "It should be in the same condition as we found it for evidence purposes, anyway." She leaned forward to peer around Gear. "How are you, Ms. Bone?"

There simply wasn't any way to dress up this poor woman. Sharon had fronted seventy-five bucks for a new dress, a shapeless print that ballooned over Gloria's pulpy midsection like a maternity outfit. She'd also had Gear take Gloria to the beauty parlor, where they'd apparently decided that a wash and dry was the best they could do with the stringy hair. There was a patch over Gloria's sutured eye, which helped some, but not much.

Gloria said, "I's tired." She looked up and down the hall with obvious fear, and Sharon suspected that the criminal courts building wasn't Gloria's favorite place in the world.

Sharon smiled sympathetically. "Motel bed too hard?"

"Too much noise." Gloria sat with her knees splayed out. "An' I'm scared of goin' to court."

"I won't have you on the stand but a few minutes," Sharon said. "Really simple questions. All you have to say is that Woody brought the clock to your house when he moved in. I doubt that the state will even cross-examine you." Which is the truth, Sharon thought, because the state won't have to say a word. So Gloria had a clock, so what? Without the senator to testify that the clock had been his daughter's, Raymond Burnside was dead in this hearing. Kathleen Fraterno would win simply by sitting on her hands.

Sharon looked to the end of the hall just as Russ Black came through the double doors. Russ was moving at a fast clip and looked worried. He sidestepped the Gruesome Threesome, said something to Ralph Toner—which from Toner's reaction wasn't very complimentary—spotted Sharon, and came toward the bench where she sat. Russ's two bodyguards trailed him by twenty steps or so. They spotted Sharon's protectors, Wilson and Keegan, seated near the courtroom door, and joined them on the bench like four peas in a pod. Sharon waggled her fingers at the former federal agents, who stoically looked away.

Russ jammed his hands into his pockets. "How're we doing so far?"

"I'm shooting threes from everywhere on the court," Sharon said, "but none of them seem to be falling. Toner brought a white-collar lawyer along to argue that he wasn't supposed to testify at all. I dodged that guy, and had our friend Mr. Toner on the run, but now the judge says we have to lay off Toner unless we put our new evidence in first. Which brings us back to square one. Gloria here can testify that the clock was in her house and belonged to Woodrow Lee, but all that means nothing unless we have the senator to confirm that it was Delores Burnside's clock."

Black's look of concern deepened. " 'Fraid we got major problems there. Joe Bright's left town."

Sharon's heart sank. "Then, I don't think we've got any choice, boss. We'll have to ask the judge to issue a bench warrant for him."

"Also I'm afraid he's gone the only place that a warrant wouldn' help us. Washington. Some kind of emergency Senate committee's in session. Nobody can touch him. I called his headquarters in D.C. S'pect Joe was there an' wouldn' take my call."

"Good God," Sharon said. "What could Raymond Burnside have done to make his father-in-law hate him enough to . . . ?"

"For whatever reason," Black said, jerking a thumb down the hall in Ralph Toner's direction, "our fine gubernatorial candidate has got Joe convinced that

Raymond did the deed. Joe Bright simply ain't goin' to testify. As a U.S. senator he's got all the shields he needs to keep from comin' to court."

Sharon looked helplessly at Gloria Bone, whose testimony was suddenly not worth the price of the dress she was wearing. Sharon felt a sudden tug of hope, and said to Russ, "There's still Alice Glass and her roommates. If they'll say Raymond was with them, and that the prosecution spirited them out of town at the first trial, we can still . . ."

Russ and Anthony Gear looked at each other. Both men regarded the floor.

Sharon sat anxiously forward. "Alice and her roommates are all under subpoena. Aren't they . . .?"

Now Gear spoke up, the detective's features sagging in defeat. "They're here. All three of 'em. Downstairs in a waiting room across from the clerk's office. Made it as far as the courthouse, subpoenas in hand. Before you put any of 'em on as witnesses, Miss Hays, I think you ought to have a talk with 'em."

Sharon looked inquiringly at Russ.

Black shrugged. "I've already visited with the young ladies. I'm invitin' you to have a go at 'em, but warnin' you not to expect much." He checked his watch. "You still got an hour before the hearing's back in session. If you think you had problems with Ralph Toner's lawyer, just wait till you see the one that these ladies have brought along."

Patricia Hampton was less than five feet tall. She'd graduated U.T. Law School a couple of years before Sharon, and Sharon considered her a bitch second to none. Patricia was the ultimate femi-Nazi. Her clients were nearly all women in the throes of divorce, and she went after soon-to-be ex-husbands like the Lord himself after the temple money changers. Sharon had no idea how Patricia would handle herself in criminal court, but would bet that the little woman would give 'em hell. Upon entering the courthouse basement anteroom to find Patricia Hampton lecturing Alice Glass and two other ladies, Sharon decided that she was in for a battle. She wasn't disappointed.

Hampton stopped pacing and turned at the sound of the door closing. She arched an eyebrow. "Hello, Hays. My clients have nothing to say to you." She had black hair done in tight little curls, and wore a severely cut deep purple suit with padded shoulders.

Patricia's clients were seated in folding chairs. Sharon smiled at Alice glass—who quickly looked away—and nodded in turn to the other women. One was a redhead with hair flipped up in back, dressed in a tight-fitting skirt and high heels. The other had brown hair in a bun and wore a pleated dress. Sharon recalled—from the meeting at Barnes & Noble Bookstore—that one of Alice's former roommates had married and divorced since Raymond had gone to prison. The redhead in the fuck-me spikes, Sharon thought, that's the divorcée, which explains how Patricia Hampton got in the act. "Nice seeing you again, Patricia," Sharon said.

"I've reviewed this matter front to back," Hampton said, "and none of these ladies have information that's going to aid your client. Sorry."

"I'm sorry, too. Mrs. Glass had a long discussion with me and Russ and our investigator, and I explained to her—"

"Without her lawyer present." Hampton marched to a mail-sorting table, leaned her fanny against the corner, and folded her arms. "Nothing she said without her lawyer present counts."

Sharon hadn't had but four or five conversations with Hampton since law school, none of which had been particularly pleasant, and she'd forgotten how quickly Patricia could grate on the nerves. She noted that the originals of her subpoenas were on the table near Hampton's hip. She pointed. "Those papers count. I'd hate to be pressed into it, but I could ask for contempt citations. I've got a client facing death."

"By all means, then," Hampton said, making an eloquent palm-up gesture, "put them on the stand. You're in the criminal arena all the time, Hays, so I'm sure you know the Fifth Amendment by heart. Or if you don't, you will by the time you're finished questioning these ladies. It's all you're going to hear from them."

"Fifth . . ." There was a second, smaller table in the room, holding an old-fashioned paper cutter mounted on a measuring grid. Sharon walked over, hoisted herself up to sit on the smaller table, let her feet dangle, and crossed her ankles. "There aren't any criminal charges pending against these women, Patricia. No one's entitled to Fifth Amendment privileges unless they're afraid of prosecution themselves."

Hampton clapped her hands lightly in mock applause. "Thank you, Laura Law-school. I've researched it, Hays. They'll take the Fifth, believe me."

"Then, you'll be facing a motion for contempt, and we'll ask the judge for the maximum punishment. Look, I'm not out to harm anyone."

"That's nice to know," Hampton said, "because you're not going to. Not *my* clients, anyway."

Sharon turned her gaze on Alice Glass, but continued to address Hampton. "I told Mrs. Glass that we'd do everything possible not to upset her marriage, and I meant it. All we need from her is that Detective Stan Green put pressure on her and her roommates not to testify in Raymond's first trial. Green was the main investigator on the case, and reported directly to Ralph Toner. That in itself is prosecutorial misconduct, which is enough to get our motion for new trial granted. I gave her my word not to ask any questions about what she and Raymond did that night." Sharon now looked at Hampton, eye to eye. "My word is good, Patricia. It always will be."

Hampton's pointed chin tilted. "Spoken like a real protector of the downtrodden, Hays. Bring me your lame and all that. But no sale. The subject of Detective Green's conversation with these women—*if* such a conversation ever occurred, and we're not prepared to say it did—is exactly what brings the Fifth Amendment into play. This alleged conversation had to do with charges of alleged drug possession on the part of my clients. Pending criminal charges allegedly dropped in return for their not testifying, which charges could crop up again. Since they could still be subject to prosecution, they don't have to swear on the witness stand to diddly. Fifth Amendment, pure and simple.''

Sharon exhaled and forced control. God, this woman was unbearable. And as for Hampton's clients . . . Sharon looked at each in turn, Alice Glass with her head down, the redhead with her legs crossed, bouncing a foot, the subdued woman in the print dress, all three nervous as cats on tin roofs. Sharon would like to have a nickel for every speech she'd heard in her life, usually from some law enforcement type, wherein citizens were beseeched in criminal matters to "do the right thing" in coming forward. "Doing the right thing," Sharon had learned, translated to, "protecting one's own ass at all costs." Without these women's testimony, and with the senator hiding behind official immunity, Raymond Burnside was almost sure to die. Sharon felt despair coming on as an idea popped into her head.

"As long as we're talking legal," Sharon said, "let's talk practical, too. In order to press the drug charges, Dallas County's going to have to admit to pulling shenanigans six years ago to keep them off the witness stand. No way will they do that. Plus, and I'll have to refresh my memory, but I think the statute of limitations on the drugs is *five* years. The state can't come after your clients at this late date, no matter what they say on the stand.''

"I'm ahead of you there," Hampton said smugly. "State statute is five years, you're right. *Federal* statutes are ten. Until all statutes of limitations expire, my clients are taking the Fifth. Now, you could change all that. All you have to do is, in the next half hour or so, bring me a letter of immunity from the federal people." She smirked.

Even as she sat on the table, Sharon towered over Hampton. Madam Midget Field Marshal, Sharon thought. She said, "That's absurd, Patricia. The feds aren't a bit interested in some six-year-old drug possession case, and you know it."

"They may not be interested, and they might be. Officially the statute is ten years, and that's what I'm relying on."

Through her anger, Sharon was also confused. The Dallas county D.A.'s office wouldn't touch a six-year-old possession case with a fifty-foot pole, even if the statute hadn't expired, and the odds of the feds stepping in to prosecute anything so trivial were something like a zillion to one. What in the name of ever-loving hell were these women afraid of? Sharon's expression softened as realization dawned.

She looked on Hampton with widened eyes. "This isn't about any drug possession case. Is it, Patricia?"

Hampton glanced at her clients, all of whom seemed occupied with their laps.

"Who's threatened them, Patricia?" Sharon said.

Alice Glass cleared her throat, *ahem*, but didn't say anything. The redhead yanked on the hem of her skirt. The woman in the pleated dress took off her glasses, and then put them back on.

"Jack Torturro," Sharon said. "Or someone working for him. Come on, Alice, that's a bluff. They wouldn't dare touch you. There are too many people around here now who know what they're up to."

On first meeting Alice Glass at the bookstore, Sharon had thought the woman quite thin. Now she seemed absolutely emaciated, nervously wringing her hands, her jaw working from side to side. Alice said, her lips trembling, "I'm terribly sorry, Miss Hays, but I—"

"Not a word." Hampton pointed a finger at Alice

and came away from the table in fighting posture. "They have nothing to say to you, Hays. Nothing now. Nothing from the witness stand. If you call them to testify, you're wasting your time."

Sharon watched them, the feisty pint-size lawyer, all three of the women in the chairs seeming to cower before Patricia Hampton. "Have it your way, Patricia. My guy didn't do this murder, and I want every one of you to know you're very likely killing him." she swung down to the floor and started to leave. "But you have your clients on benches in front of the courtroom in a half hour, Ms. Hampton. If you're five seconds late, I'm asking for bench warrants." She glared at Alice Glass. "If you ladies want to take the Fifth Amendment, it's up to you. But it's going to be before God and everybody. And if you do, I'm glad I won't be in your shoes when you have to look in the mirror again."

Anthony Gear opined as how he'd never heard of such a thing. "Can they just do that?" he said. "Take the Fifth Amendment whenever they feel like it?"

"Dudn happen very often," Russell Black said. "But the law is, if they're questionin' you on matters about which you've ever been the subject of a criminal investigation, you're entitled to plead self-incrimination unless somebody gives you a letter of immunity. If they testify that good Detective Green pressured 'em not to take the stand in Raymond's trial, they've also got to tell about the drug bust that gave him the ammunition to pressure 'em to begin with. I warn my own clients, whether it's a lawsuit, divorce pleading, whatever, they don't have to testify to anything as long as their criminal case is pendin'." He pinched his chin. "Ask me, Sharon, I think they're walkin' a fine line."

Sharon was seated on a corridor bench alongside Anthony Gear and his shoe box, with Gloria Bone on the detective's other side. At mention of the Fifth

Amendment, Gloria's one eye had lighted up as if she thought pleading the Fifth was something she should look into.

"It's worse than a fine line," Sharon said. "Patricia Hampton's relying on the federal statute of limitations, even where federal charges were never filed against those women. But, fine a line as it is, she's got a winnable argument. How Sandy Griffin will rule, as much as she likes to study points of law, that's a toss-up. If they get away with pleading self-incrimination, we're probably dead. Or Raymond is." She leaned back and looked at her knees. "I wonder what Mr. Torturro and his merry men did to harass those poor women."

The doors at the end of the corridor opened, and Torturro and Denopoulis sauntered in, speak-of-the-devil fashion. They took side-by-side seats two benches down the way and folded their arms. Sharon's bodyguards sat with Russ's two watchdogs directly across from the mobsters, and the six men engaged immediately in a staring contest.

"I'd give my right arm," Sharon said evenly, "if there was something, anything, we could hang our hats on to file charges against those two bastards."

Russ looked at Torturro and friend as well. His upper lip curled. 'They been doin' this too many years to slip up. Count on it. No matter what happens in this hearin' and the election and the legalized gamblin', bet your boots that those two will come out smellin' like roses. A whole lot smarter people than the D.A. of this fair county have had shots at those guys. Bet the feds have a file on 'em a foot thick. If there was any way to prosecute 'em, it wouldda been done long before now." He watched Sharon, his weather-beaten features wrinkled in sympathy. "Your hearin', Miss Hays. Your call. What do we do?"

Sharon uttered a sigh that was near defeat, but not quite. "We need more time," she said.

Black kicked an imaginary pebble and studied the

floor. "We got no time. We asked for a hearin', and the judge scheduled it. The burden's on us to produce witnesses to back up what we're pleadin'. If we can't, the court's entitled to deny our motion for new trial, and there's not an appellate court in the land that'll do anything about it. If we show up with one witness that'll identify a clock, but nobody to testify the clock has anything to do with the Burnside killin' . . . then we produce three more witnesses that'll get up there and plead the Fifth Amendment, Sandy Griffin will give us the hook quicker'n you can go from here to Fort Worth."

"She can give us a continuance till Monday," Sharon said.

"Yeah, but she won't."

Sharon looked down the corridor as the double doors parted and Patricia Hampton came in, followed by Alice glass, the redhead, and her former roommate. Hampton smirked in Sharon's direction and marched toward a corridor bench. She nodded at Torturro as she passed the two gangsters, then looked quickly away. The mobsters remained stoic, just a couple of men seated in a public corridor minding their own business.

Sharon firmed her mouth, got up, and said to Russ, "I'll get us more time, boss. I don't know exactly how, but I'm going to."

Try as she might, Sharon couldn't work up much anger toward Kathleen Fraterno. She sat beside Russ at the defense table and watched Fraterno, Kathleen's pretty face attentive as she studied her file. In spite of her faults, Fraterno was a damned good lawyer and was just doing her job. Her job in this case was to help the state keep Raymond Burnside convicted and on the way to the execution chamber, and Fraterno had nothing to do with the shenanigans that had gone on in the original trial. The big decisions, Sharon supposed, are made by the Jack Torturros, Vernon Denopoulises, and Ralph Toners of the world. Milton Breyer hadn't had the nerve to show his face, and had left Fraterno to carry on by herself. In certain ways, Sharon even pitied Kathleen.

The side door opened, and the bailiff brought Raymond Burnside in from the holding cell. Raymond's jailhouse jumpsuit was pressed, and he was freshly shaved. There was a quickness in his step, and the helpless acceptance he'd shown when Sharon had visited him in prison was gone. His expression now showed eager anticipation along with . . .

Hope. God, Sharon thought. He told me he didn't want any hope, but now I've gone and given it to him.

Raymond took his seat alongside her. He smelled of cheap prison commissary aftershave. Sharon turned her gaze to the front as the judge's entrance swung wide. Sandy Griffin swept grandly in, robes flying, and ascended to her throne.

Gloria Bone sat in the witness chair as if looking for an escape route. When she'd gotten a load of the reporters in the spectator section as the bailiff had escorted her in, Gloria had stopped stock-still in the aisle, and Sharon had breathed a sigh of relief when her witness hadn't bolted and run right then and there.

The clock in Sharon's hands was a pitiful-looking affair, the jolly porcelain husband and wife waving on springs like bug antennae. Gloria had said that Woodrow Lee seemed fascinated by the clock, but his fascination hadn't extended to taking care of the expensive timepiece. The edges were scarred, the paint chipped away in places. Sharon showed her evidence to Kathleen Fraterno, to give Kathleen a chance to voice an objection. Fraterno looked at the clock, wrinkled her nose, and didn't say anything.

With an evidence sticker applied to the clock's miniature roof, Sharon approached the witness. "Ms. Bone," she said, "I show you what has been marked

Petitioner's Exhibit Number Two, and ask if you can identify it."

Gloria looked at the clock with her one good eye, canting her head. "You mean, does I know what it is?"

Sandy Griffin leaned forward for a good look at the witness. The reporters beyond the rail were staring. Andy Wade had gotten up and walked hunched over to the front row for a better vantage point. Sutured eye and all, Gloria was the center of attention. "Yes, ma'am, if you could tell us," Sharon said.

"A clock."

"And have you ever seen it before?"

"Over at my house. Been there two or three years."

"If you know, how did this clock come to be at your house?"

"This man brought it."

"Woodrow Lee? The man who's been living with you?"

Gloria straightened, assuming as dignified a posture as was possible for her. "He gots his own room."

There was a twitter of laughter from the newspeople, and even Griffin smiled.

"But this clock did belong to Woodrow Lee, as far as you know," Sharon said.

"Yes'm. It 'as his."

Sharon stepped over and set the clock on the court reporter's table, for all the world to see. She paused to rehearse her next question in her mind, knowing that she was tossing a spitter and wanting to get it all out before Fraterno could stop her with an objection.

"Are you talking about the same Woodrow Lee," Sharon said, "who was going to be a state's witness in the murder of Mary Ann Blakely—"

"*Objection.*" Fraterno stood so quickly that she knocked some papers askew on the prosecution table. "That's hearsay, Your Honor."

"—Before the suspect, Dycus Wilt, was killed in an escape attempt?" Sharon finished quickly.

The reporters wrote furiously, just as Sharon had intended them to, as Sandy Griffin pretended to think it over before sustaining Kathleen's objection. Fraterno was right, of course. Since Woodrow Lee wasn't present in the courtroom, anything he'd told Gloria about his snitch role in the Dycus Wilt case was pure hearsay. So you just try and disregard what I said, Judge Sandy, Sharon thought. Better yet try and keep it out of the papers.

Before Griffin could speak, Gloria blurted out, "I tole Woody not to be no snitch for them people."

"*Ms. Bone*," Griffin practically screamed, then composed herself and said calmly, "I'm sustaining the objection. Answer will be stricken, and both question and answer will be disregarded." She looked helplessly toward the media section, where the reporters continued to take notes like mad. "Don't pull that again, Miss Hays," she said sternly.

"I apologize, Your Honor," Sharon said, without trying to sound apologetic at all. She turned back to the witness. "But Woodrow Lee did bring the clock with him when he moved in with you, is that right?"

"Yeah," Gloria said.

"And if you know, how did Woodrow Lee come to be in possession of the clock?"

"Objection," Fraterno called out.

Griffin regarded Fraterno with a puzzled frown. "On what grounds, Miss Fraterno?"

"Same as before," Kathleen said. "Any answer would be hearsay. If they have this Woodrow Lee person, let them put him on as a witness." Fraterno sounded as if she'd never heard of Woodrow Lee. Sharon nearly laughed out loud.

"All right," Griffin said. "Sustained."

"Don't know nothin' about where Woody come by that clock," Gloria said. "Probably stole it offa somebody."

Griffin drummed her fingers. "Question and answer disregarded. Ms. Bone, you're not to answer any objected-to question until the objection has been ruled on."

Gloria twisted her head around to regard the judge through her good eye, then looked back at Sharon.

"But the clock was at your house for a period of approximately two years?" Sharon said.

" 'Bout that."

"Is it in the same condition as when you first saw it?"

"No, ma'am. It got broke." Gloria stated the obvious.

"But you're certain it's the same clock."

"Yes."

"The very same?"

"Objection." Fraterno testily straightened the papers in front of her. "Asked and answered, Your Honor. If it will speed things up, the state will stipulate to the clock, that it was at Ms. Bone's house, and that a man named Woodrow Lee brought it there."

"Objection sustained," Griffin said. "Let's move this along, Miss Hays. The clock is in evidence as a clock. Unless the witness knows something personally about the clock's origin, don't question her any further about it."

Sharon thought the terseness in Griffin's instruction a bit out of order, but the judge was right. Unless Gloria had personally seen the clock at the Burnside home, she'd said all she was entitled to say. Sharon checked her watch. Gloria Bone's testimony had consumed a total of six minutes. More time, Sharon thought. God, we need more time. "Pass the witness," she said resignedly, then went to her table and sat between Russ Black and Raymond Burnside. Raymond raised his eyebrows quizzically. Sharon looked away.

Griffin mildly regarded the prosecution table. "Cross, Miss Fraterno?"

Kathleen half stood. "No questions, Judge."

Of course she doesn't have any questions, Sharon

thought. Without the senator's testimony, as far as the clock's concerned we're dead, dead, dead.

"Very well," Griffin said. "You're dismissed, Ms. Bone. Call your next witness, Miss Hays. If we continue to move quickly, the court will be pleased."

Alice Glass had come to the courthouse in a shopping dress, the everyday housewife in the flesh, complete with everything but her grocery list. She raised her hand for swearing in, then sat properly in the witness chair without ever glancing in Raymond Burnside's direction. Raymond kept his attention riveted on something at the defense table. God, Sharon thought, after six years they can't even look at each other. Must have been some burning passion between those two.

Alice answered two questions, giving her name and current address without hesitation. Then Sharon asked, "And are you acquainted with the petitioner in this matter, Raymond Burnside?"

Alice's beige dress had a waist pocket, from which she now produced a folded sheet of paper from a legal pad. She spread the paper out and read, "On advice of counsel, I claim my right under the Fifth Amendment of the Constitution of the United States, and respectfully refuse to answer on the grounds that any answer I might give could implicate me in an unresolved criminal investigation." She sounded like a recording.

Sharon uttered a sigh heard throughout the courtroom. Russell Black grumpily rested his ankle on his knee and propped his leg against the edge of the defense table. Raymond Burnside watched his folded hands. In the media section, mouths gaped open. Sharon pictured the speculation in tomorrow's newspapers: Was Alice Glass a conspirator? Did she stand by cackling in glee while Raymond Burnside hacked his estranged wife to pieces? You're not even in the ballpark, folks, Sharon thought. All this lady did was provide Raymond with a warm but limp body for the night. She looked toward the bench. Even Sandy Griffin's face was blank in puzzlement.

"Your Honor," Sharon said, "we ask that the witness be instructed to answer." She waited, alternating her gaze between Alice and the judge. The request was a lead-in to a contempt motion; Alice couldn't be held in contempt unless she violated a direct order of the court.

Griffin reached inside her robe, pulled out and fiddled with her St. Christopher's medal. Finally she said, "I'll withhold such instruction, Miss Hays, until I hear more."

In other words, Sharon thought, as long as my witnesses aren't helping Raymond Burnside, you're reluctant to hold them in contempt. In the Rathermore trial, Griffin had been as fair as any judge whom Sharon had ever stood before, but now the judge had Senator Bright's wishes to consider. When it came to covering her political skirts, Sandy Griffin was just another face in the vote-grubbing crowd, and Sharon understood in a flash how the state had gotten away with murder in Raymond's original trial. Sharon made no attempt to conceal the edge of anger in her tone. "Mrs. Glass, did you by any chance see Mr. Raymond Burnside on the night his wife was murdered?"

Paper rattled as Alice gripped her instructions. "On advice of counsel . . ."

As Alice read her Fifth Amendment declaration a second time, Sharon watched the prosecution table. Kathleen Fraterno seemed genuinely surprised. Well, Sharon thought, at least Milton Breyer's office isn't in on this. Which helps matters not one iota.

". . . In an unresolved criminal investigation," Alice finished, lowered the page to her lap, and looked around expectantly.

Sharon once again asked the judge to instruct the witness to answer.

Griffin released her St. Christopher's and fooled

with her watch. She addressed the courtroom at large. "Is the witness's counsel present?" she said.

"Here, Your Honor." Patricia Hampton marched from the spectator section through the gate, and stood midway between the defense table and the judge. She'd managed to enunciate "Your Honor" as if she were saying, "You inferior bitch," and further managed to stand so that she blocked Sharon's view of the witness. "Patricia Hampton," Hampton said, standing at attention, "representing Mrs. Glass and the other two ladies under subpoena. I think it will be better to get all three subpoenaed witnesses' arguments out of the way at once, don't you?" She carried a thick brief folder under her arm.

Judge Griffin literally bristled. Patricia Hampton treated the divorce courts as her own personal queendom, and most of the family law judges cringed at the sight of her. Sandy Griffin, however, had her own femi-Nazi tendencies, and Sharon suspected that Hampton was in for a surprise in this particular courtroom. This should be interesting, Sharon thought.

Griffin rested her elbows on the bench, lifted her hands with her palms facing her, and made identical, simultaneous, come-hither gestures. "Both sides approach. You, too, Ms. Hampton."

Sharon got up, came around the defense table, and went up to stand beside Hampton while Alice Glass relaxed in the witness box. Kathleen Fraterno walked up to stand on Hampton's other side, both Kathleen and Sharon a head taller than the midget field marshal. Sharon watched Kathleen cast an almost-fearful glance in Hampton's direction, and it was all Sharon could do to keep from snickering.

"I'd thought I was having a hard day before," Griffin said, "but it seems to be worsening. What is this all about."

Hampton tapped her file. "I have briefs, Your Honor."

"Ms. Hampton, I'd as soon not pore over any briefs

just now. I have the beginnings of a headache. What I would like is for you to explain to me why your clients shouldn't have to testify. Can we begin with that?" Griffin's tone was condescending.

Hampton wasn't fazed. "For the very reason Mrs. Glass just stated from the witness stand. Criminal charges which haven't been disposed of."

"I'm assuming," Griffin said, "that these charges don't have anything to do with this murder case. If they did, your clients would be testifying from jail, wouldn't they?"

"In a nutshell," Hampton said, "Miss Hays wants them to testify about contact with Raymond Burnside which would cause them to discuss some criminal charges filed, then dismissed, six years ago, but which still fall under the statute of limitations. My research tells me that my clients aren't required to say a word."

Griffin looked at Fraterno, who stood mute, then concentrated on Sharon. "Miss Hays, are you trying to make your clock relevant through these witnesses' testimony?"

"No, Your Honor. This has to do with additional new evidence we're pursuing."

Griffin rolled her eyes. "That's what I was afraid of. I suppose we'd better retire to the old officeroo, ladies. My chambers." She looked toward the spectator section. "You're going to have some of those newshounds straining their eardrums, if we try to discuss this here."

Judge Griffin didn't invite Russ to sit in on the conference, which surprised Sharon down to her toes. Being left out didn't seem to faze Russ in the slightest; he sat contentedly at the defense table and chewed the fat with Raymond Burnside as Sharon and the other women retired from the courtroom. Into the big meeting all by my lonesome, Sharon thought. If nothing else, I'm gaining respect around here.

A few minutes later in Griffin's no-frills chambers,

however, Sharon wished her mentor had come along. She spread her hands in frustration. "Judge Griffin, this is a smoke screen. Even if they *were* entitled to Fifth Amendment privileges, which we aren't prepared to admit that they are, their rights couldn't possibly take precedence over a condemned man's."

Patricia Hampton twisted around in her chair. "Why couldn't they? Her client's already been convicted, which the law says forfeits certain rights. My people's records are clean thus far. Clean record, more rights."

Griffin was seated behind her desk, and had opened her robe to reveal a plain white blouse. Her St. Christopher's medal dangled from a chain. Sharon and Patricia Hampton occupied visitor's seats across from the judge while Kathleen Fraterno had a backstage role, relaxing on a sofa in the corner. This argument was between Sharon and her subpoenaed witnesses, but Sharon knew which side Kathleen was rooting for. And how.

Griffin seemed thoughtful. "Weighing a condemned man's rights against a potentially accused's rights, that's an intriguing question. Can you point me to some law on that, Miss Hays?"

Sharon's enthusiasm dropped a hundred degrees, replaced by despair. Griffin knew good and well that the only one who'd done any research at this point was Patricia Hampton. "No, I can't," Sharon admitted. "This has all hit me as cold as it has you, Judge. I haven't had time to look up any cases."

"Ah, but I have." Hampton reached inside her accordion folder and brought out two thick sheaths of stapled pages. "One for Miss Hays"—she plunked a stack in Sharon's lap, then dropped another on Griffin's desk—"and one for the court. All the statutes, case law, everything, point to one thing. If you've ever been charged or even investigated for a crime, you're not required to testify about it under oath unless you have immunity. I told Miss Hays earlier, if she can bring me letters of immunity from both the state and the feds, my little girls will sing to the beat of the band." She smirked first at Sharon, then at Griffin.

"Which she knows to be impossible, Judge," Sharon said. "This *crime* Patricia's referring to was a drug bust, which barely qualifies as a felony, which the state has forgotten long ago, and which the feds wouldn't prosecute on a bet."

"And which my clients don't have to say a word about. Please read my briefs, girls," Hampton said.

Griffin's lips firmed. "The only *girls* I know are still in school, Ms. Hampton."

Hampton looked at the ceiling. "Ladies, then. Have it your way. But my clients still don't have to testify, and they're not about to."

Griffin seemed ready to explode all over Hampton, but calmed herself enough to say, "I can't consider anything discussed in chambers in my ruling on the motion for new trial, but now I have a separate decision. Miss Hays will ask for a contempt citation if they *don't* testify, and I'd as soon not have to decide whether three proper ladies go to the pokey for a while. So give me some background. What information are you trying to elicit from these women, Miss Hays?"

Sharon let her hands hang off the ends of her armrests. "They were with Mr. Burnside when the murder happened. One of them stayed all night with him."

Griffin lifted her eyebrows. "I presided over his trial, you know. I don't remember any testimony to that effect."

Sharon lifted, then dropped her shoulders. "There wasn't any."

"Three alibi witnesses, and nobody called them? That's incredible. Why weren't they on the defense's witness list?"

"They *were* on the list," Sharon said.

"Well, in that case," Griffin said, "the defense knew about them at the original trial, so I couldn't consider it as new evidence in any event. So why are we even discussing this?"

"Because there were drug charges dropped in return for their taking a powder, Your Honor," Sharon said. "Pressure from the police, at the direction of the district attorney."

Griffin's eyebrows now moved closer together. "Are you alleging misconduct on the part of the prosecution, Miss Hays?"

Sharon testily crossed her legs. "Darn right. Mr. Ralph Toner in particular."

"You want to discredit Mr. Toner. You'd likely ruin his political career, but I suspect you already know that."

"Mr. Toner's run for the governor's mansion isn't my concern," Sharon said. "My client's death sentence is."

"You're treading on dangerous ground. The Dallas County D.A.'s office has enough black eyes without you taking more potshots at them." Griffin seemed to swell under her robe.

"I'm not taking potshots, Your Honor. I'm a former prosecutor the same as you are, and the type of thing we're alleging hurts everyone involved in the justice system. Like it or not, though, my client's welfare dictates that I pursue this."

"And *my* clients' welfare," Hampton cut in, "has to do with testifying about their criminal charges. Which my research says they don't have to."

Griffin patted her desk alongside Hampton's brief. "Isn't there some way around this? You spent a lot of time having your clock admitted, Miss Hays. What's the clock got to do with it?"

"The same guys who raped and murdered Delores Burnside stole the clock from her house. At the original trial the state failed to mention the theft *or* the rape."

Griffin's tone was suddenly friendlier, and tempered with surprise. "If you can prove that, you've got a point. But what does that have to do with Ms. Hampton's clients?"

"The rape and robbery?" Sharon said. "Not a thing."

"Then, why don't you forget these three women," Griffin said, "and concentrate on establishing that your clock is stolen property? That would be grounds for a new trial in itself. Then, we could forget contempt motions and Fifth Amendment rights and all that folderol, all of which frankly make my head hurt."

Sharon filled one cheek with air, then expelled the air between her lips. "I can't go any further with the clock, Your Honor, because my witness who could verify that the clock was Delores Burnside's is no longer available to testify."

"Don't you have that witness under subpoena?"

"Yes, ma'am."

"Then, ask for a bench warrant. That I'd grant without any problem."

"Even if the witness is Senator Bright?" Sharon said.

Griffin leaned back and grabbed her St. Christopher's like a pacifier. "Oh."

"Besides," Sharon said, "he's hiding in Washington, in a committee meeting. He'd claim official immunity to a subpoena anyway."

"And would be entitled to it," Griffin said firmly. She gestured toward Hampton's briefs. "Which leaves us with this, I suppose."

"Leaves you without my clients as witnesses if you adhere to the law," Hampton said. "I invite you to shoot holes in my briefs."

Griffin showed Hampton a smile that doubtless required effort. She's known Hampton five minutes, Sharon thought, and already hates her. Who could blame Griffin? I certainly don't, Sharon thought. Griffin said to Hampton, "I think the decision as to

whether your clients testify is up to me, isn't it? Or
have you replaced me in some way?"

Hampton nodded, touché. "Of course it's up to you,
Judge. Assuming the law is on your side."

"My kingdom that it were, Ms. Hampton," Griffin
said. "My kingdom that it were." she began to button
her robe. "I'm putting us in recess until Monday
morning, at which time I want briefs, both from Miss
Hays and Miss Fraterno, on the question of these
women's Fifth Amendment rights under the circumstances. Miss Hays, if you can show me that Ms.
Hampton's argument doesn't hold water, her clients
are going to testify or I'll put them in jail. If you can't
defeat her argument, you're out of luck. Sorry to put
you to work over the weekend, but I'm going to do
some briefing as well."

Sharon blinked in surprise. "I beg your pardon?"

Her robe now fastened, Griffin rose. "Wasn't I
clear?"

"We're in recess until Monday?" Sharon said.

"I believe I said that," Griffin said. "I'd hate for
you ladies to find something to topple Ms. Hampton's
house of cards. That would disappoint me im-
mensely." Her tone said that if anyone could shoot
holes in Hampton's arguments, the judge would jump
for joy.

"I'm sure it would," Hampton said, picking up her
briefcase. "But don't count on it."

Sharon constricted her throat to keep from yelping
in elation. She no longer despised Patricia Hampton.
At that moment, in fact, Sharon *loved* the little . . .
Hampton's true purpose aside, she'd bought Raymond
Burnside the weekend. You've got the extra time you
craved, Sharon Jenifer, Sharon thought. Whether it's
enough to save Raymond remains to be seen.

29

Sharon leveled with Raymond Burnside. "This isn't what you're going to want to hear. But I'd have to say that our chances have gone from nonexistent to poor. It's not what any of us expected, and I can't tell you how sorry I am. We thought we had a wonderful shot going in, but the outlook since this morning has turned a hundred and eighty degrees because of the trouble getting all these witnesses together." She couldn't look him straight in the face, and watched the point of his chin.

Burnside gripped the bars from inside the holding cell, glanced toward the deputy lounging in a chair behind Sharon, and lowered his voice. "So all of this, more publicity, hasn't accomplished a thing, has it? You people simply wouldn't let me go in peace, would you? Had to stir it all up again."

Sharon couldn't ever remember feeling so helpless. Even back in New York, riding the subway three-months pregnant looking for an acting job. She lifted her gaze and said to Burnside, "Blame me. It's all me, my fault. I forced you into this. Understand it isn't over, Raymond. That catfight I just witnessed in the judge's office has given us more time. Maybe this weekend Russ can get in touch with Senator Bright. They're old friends. If anyone can talk some sense into him . . ."

"That's pointless, Miss Hays. Just pointless. It's politically advantageous for me to die, so I'm going to. I told you that the first time I met you, and I'm telling you now. If you'd left well enough alone, my family wouldn't be going through all this again." Burnside's eyes were misty. It seemed to Sharon that the prisoner's muscle tone had diminished during the past week; likely his county cell was too cramped for exercise. "I didn't even recognize Alice. Barely remember her name, that's how much the encounter amounted to."

"We're going to research the dickens out of the law," Sharon said. "I'm not admitting defeat until . . ."

Burnside looked at her.

Sharon dropped her chin. "I doubt we'll get the women to testify, Raymond. I doubt we'll get anybody. Fifth Amendment privileges are pretty omnipotent. I haven't hit the books yet, but experience tells me Patricia Hampton will likely win her point. Our advantage is, the judge is dying to rule against her. Anything we can hang our hats on . . ."

Burnside's features were wreathed in anger. "That hat rack doesn't exist. I'm not even a lawyer, and I know that much. Once the system makes up its mind, that's it. Stop trying to pump me up, will you? Why don't we just drop the whole thing, return me to death row, and forget about it. I'd rather do that than go through any more roller-coaster rides."

Sharon searched his face. He meant it. The irony of the situation chilled her. Cutthroats fought forever and ever, appeal after appeal. The man standing before her, the only innocent man she had ever seen on death row, this man wanted to die and get it over with. "We've got to give it this one last shot, Raymond," she finally said. "This is going to sound like a strange request, but I'm begging you. Go through it for me. Please. If we give up now and they execute you, I'm never going to be able to live with myself. So do it for me, Raymond. Just, please, okay?"

For the only time in Sharon's memory, Russell Black seemed old and tired. As they crossed the street from the covered parking to the office, Russ's shoulders slumped and there were aging lines around his eyes that she'd never noticed before.

"I'll spend the whole weekend trying to roust Joe Bright," Black said. "But don't depend on him talking to me. He's a hardhead. When his mind's made up, Joe don't listen to anybody."

They came abreast of two sedans parked at the curb, one in front of the other. Russ's bodyguards sat in the lead car, in sagging postures like stakeout cops. Tanner and Davis occupied the second car, having relieved Wilson and Keegan sometime during the day at the courthouse. Sharon nodded at the men. Tanner raised one finger in her direction, then went back to his magazine. Sharon and Russ stepped up on the curb and started to enter the office. Black spun on his heel and walked toward the two sedans.

Sharon took a step after him. "Where you going, boss?"

Black paused and turned. "To tell those guys we don't need 'em anymore."

Sharon chewed her lower lip. "Do you think that's safe?"

"For us? Sure it is. Those people got no reason to roust us any longer. They've scared your witnesses off. Figure we're beaten, and likely they're right. Havin' these men hangin' around, they'll just be in the way."

Sharon stood on the curb and watched as Russ went to dismiss their bodyguards. It seemed to her that his shoulders slumped even more.

They entered through the reception area, and had company. William Burnside sat on the sofa, wearing his mechanic's coveralls. A frail elderly woman was with him and needed no introduction. The same slim nose and narrow forehead. Sharon set her briefcase down, went over, and gripped one of the woman's hands in both of hers. "You'd be Raymond's mother," Sharon said. "He's your image, ma'am." The hand that she held was tiny and wrinkled, like a bird's claw, but held on with surprising strength.

William looked uncomfortable. He started to speak.

Mrs. Burnside stopped her son with a reproachful look. "I can speak for myself, William. No one's to blame for my coming but me." Then, to the lawyers, "He tried to talk me out of it. I wouldn't stay at home."

Sharon sat between William and his mother. "I'm Sharon Hays, Mrs. Burnside. That's Russell Black."

Russ leaned against the wall, hands in pockets. "Hidy."

"Glad to know you, Mr. Black. I'm Ethel Burnside." The old woman returned her attention to Sharon. "You'd be the young lady who visited Raymond in prison." Her voice was crackly and almost feeble, with a slight woodsy twang, but her grammar was as perfect as Sharon had known a small-town teacher's would be.

"Yes, ma'am, that was me."

"It's you we've got to thank." Ethel Burnside's hair was halfway between white and gray, with delicate loose ends waving. She wore a modest pleated schoolmarm's dress and black lace-up shoes. Her facial skin was pale and loose and the cords in her neck sagged. She had a distinct dowager's hump, and Sharon doubted if the woman weighed a hundred pounds. "Raymond won't know I'm in town until after a decision is made on his release, Miss Hays. I know my son and how headstrong he is. How did your hearing go?" She widened eyes with wrinkled lids.

Black said with forced enthusiasm, "I want to tell you, Mrs. Burnside. This young lady here put on quite a show in court today."

Sharon looked at Russ. His lower jaw worked from side to side. You're every bit as bad a liar as I am, old boss, Sharon thought.

"It's going well, then?" Ethel Burnside said.

Sharon inhaled through her nose. One corner of her

mouth tightened. "It's not going well at all, ma'am. I wish I could . . ."

Mrs. Burnside's pleasant look faded for an instant; then she smiled and patted Sharon's hand. "I'm sure you're doing everything you can."

William squeezed his mother's shoulder. "Mom . . ."

"It's all right. It's all right, son. You said to prepare for the worst, and I have." Mrs. Burnside then alternated her gaze between Sharon and Russ. "Do we have any hope at all?"

"There's always hope," Sharon said. Given the circumstances, that this woman would worry about Sharon's feelings said a lot for Mrs. Burnside and her entire family. She swallowed her emotions and forced herself to put on a businesslike air. "I'll outline our problem, and if you have any suggestions we'd appreciate it. We've got three women whom Raymond . . . met, on the night of the murder, and who can provide an alibi for him. They're using a legal loophole to get out of taking the witness stand. Trying to force them to testify is us lawyers' job, but there's something else you might help us with."

Sharon swallowed and composed herself. She'd played down Raymond's tryst on the night of the murder as much as she could. William Burnside looked at the floor in silent embarrassment. Mrs. Burnside's gaze faltered slightly; she had read between the lines and had accepted the facts. Her son wasn't perfect, but he was still her son. Sharon mentally placed a couple of marks in the plus column for Raymond's mother, then forged quickly ahead.

"You'll remember from Raymond's first trial, one thing the state used in convicting him was to show there was no robbery committed, which gave no one but Raymond a motive to kill his wife. You remember that?"

"The prosecutor went on and on about it," Mrs. Burnside said. "I thought at the time it was strange, that anyone would do that to Delores without stealing something."

"Okay," Sharon said. "The two men who we now know committed the crime, one is dead and the other is in hiding somewhere. Even if we found the second man, we probably couldn't get him to admit to anything.

"But they stole an animated clock from that house, and we have found the clock. Have it into evidence, and also produced a witness who can place our fugitive in possession of the clock. What we can't do is prove the clock was ever Delores Burnside's in the first place. Our witness for that is Delores' father, and he's left town. Specifically to keep from testifying, but he's hiding behind senatorial duties in Washington. If there's any way you can exert influence over the senator to get him to . . ." Sharon trailed off, helpless.

William lifted his head and spoke up. "That old political hack hated Raymond, Miss Hays, and treated us like poor relations. He wouldn't speak to any of us, and right now Mother and I are probably the only people in Texas who don't vote for him." His expression was suddenly hopeful. "But, hey, if the clock was in that house, Raymond could identify it. He lived there, too."

Sharon gently shook her head. "That's a last resort, and don't think we haven't considered it. The problem is, and this is legal rigmarole once again, but in a hearing without a jury it's up to the judge to be the trier of fact. Decide what is fact and what isn't. That means, she can believe who she chooses to believe. The condemned man testifying won't carry much weight, I'm afraid. The judge would probably decide he's not telling the truth and deny our motion. We couldn't even appeal her on that."

William snorted in anger. "Raymond's never told a lie in this life."

"I've gotten to know him," Sharon said, "and I believe you. But the judge doesn't know him like we do. Believe me, William. Having Raymond testify just wouldn't work." She looked at Black, who leaned in thoughtful silence against the wall, then lowered her gaze.

Ethel Burnside said, "That clock was the dickens to dust."

Black stood away from the wall. Sharon snapped her head up and said, "*You* saw it, ma'am?"

"Those little figurines," Mrs. Burnside said vacantly, "only came out on the hour. I'd have to stand there with a dust cloth and get 'em when they appeared. I stayed with Raymond a month once, when his wife was on a cruise somewhere. Had that house shipshape when I went home, I'll tell you."

Sharon blinked. "You could recognize the clock?"

"There was a button on the back to stop it from running. Spring-loaded. When the little man and woman came out to dance, I'd have to hold the button in with one finger and dust like mad with the other hand."

Sharon looked at Russ. He said, "She's his mother, Sharon."

"That she is. It's a step better than having Raymond testify."

Mrs. Burnside wrung her hands in her lap.

Sharon felt excitement fighting its way up through the despair. "It's an outside shot, ma'am. What Russ means is, the judge can consider the fact that you're his mother in deciding whether to believe you. But I'm afraid we don't have anything else. Are you certain you could identify the clock if you saw it?"

Black fidgeted, shuffling his feet. "Let's don't be gettin' anybody's hopes up."

Sharon sat upright, her face brightening. "The way I'm thinking of having her testify, the judge will have to believe her."

Black, Ethel, and William Burnside gave Sharon their undivided attention.

"First of all, Mrs. Burnside," Sharon said, "and you

already know this. If Raymond suspects what we're up to, he's likely to go bananas and not even let us go on with the hearing. So if we put you on, it'll have to be out of the blue. First Raymond knows of it is when you walk in the courtroom."

Sharon now directed her words to Black. "The first thing we'll do is have Mrs. Burnside describe the clock on the stand without first seeing it. It's in the clerk's evidence locker, so the state can't accuse us of showing it to her in secret. Once she's told how the thing looks, then we'll haul it out and have her testify, yes, that's the same clock I dusted in Raymond's house. No way can Sandy Griffin give us the hook if the evidence matches the description the witness has already given."

"It's sure a thought." He was toning down his excitement, not wanting to get the Burnsides' hopes up, but Sharon could tell that Russ was as fired-up as she was.

Sharon stood, her mind working nonstop. "Okay. Step one, Russ will take Mrs. Burnside in his office and have her write down every single detail of that clock, so much detail that a blind person could tell she knew what she was talking about. That'll take a while. Be precise, Mrs. Burnside. This is probably the most important thing you've ever tried to remember."

"I raised two boys," Ethel Burnside said. "I've got an eye for household items. Never forget what's out of place and what goes where. I can see that clock in my mind as if it was sitting right there." She pointed to a spot on the floor.

"Great," Sharon said. "Now my work is, and this is why I'm turning you over to Russ. I've got some studying to do." She picked up her satchel. "Patricia Hampton's brief, Russ. I've still got to find some law to shoot holes in it if I can. Mrs. Burnside may or may not do it for us, but if we can force those women onto the stand, we could be home free." She noted Black's glum expression, and grinned at him. "Relax, boss, you're still in charge. Those would be your orders, wouldn't they?"

Sharon started for her own office as Black led William and his mother past the law library, toward Russ's place. Sharon stopped, retraced her steps, and hugged Mrs. Burnside around the neck. "You asked if we had any hope," Sharon said. "Of course we've got hope. Miles of it, Mrs. Burnside. It just takes awhile for us to get our hopers in gear, is the only problem."

30

A half hour later Sharon leaned back at her desk, folded her arms, and blew a puff of air upward through her bangs. Criminy, how much time did Patricia Hampton spend on this thing?

Hampton's brief lay on Sharon's desk alongside a yellow legal pad. On the pad Sharon had copied thirty-one cases and points of law that Hampton had listed in her research, and she wasn't yet halfway finished. This must have taken days and days, Sharon thought. Who in hell is paying this abrasive woman's fee? Sharon pictured Torturro and Denopoulis, side by side at the courthouse like two rotten peas in a pod, and thought she knew. Those three women certainly couldn't afford to pay Hampton to . . .

Sharon's impatiens drooped. She carried her long-spouted can down to the ladies' room, filled it, doused the flowers, sat down once again, and stared at Hampton's brief. She was getting exactly nowhere. She plugged in her earphones, listened to perhaps thirty seconds of David Allen Coe's rendition of "Please Come to Boston," then dropped the earphones on her desk in disgust.

She went down her list of Hampton's citations, all from different reference sources, and pictured miles and miles of trudging through library shelves just to look up all that crap. For just an instant she longed for her days as a prosecutor. Anytime an A.D.A. felt pressed for time, all it took was a call to the briefing clerks. The clerks would then hustle to the library and come up with forty thousand points of law before you could say, Ready for trial. Well, crying over spilt milk wasn't going to help; Sharon had no clerks at her disposal and had to do what she could all by her lonesome. Working solo, she imagined at least a week's worth of research just to locate Hampton's points of law; all of which was likely a waste of time. Sharon suspected that the women's Fifth Amendment rights were unbeatable. Still, she had to try. God, she needed help. Needed help in the worst way, someone to . . .

Richard Branson, Sharon thought. Rhodes scholar, *Law Review* student. She wanted to spend more time with him anyway. God, did she ever. She'd been too busy to miss him, but now that she could possibly have him help her with this research they could go to the library together, maybe have some dinner afterward. She felt a twinge of guilt because she hadn't talked to him since . . .

Since you were so short with him over the phone the other night, dummy, she thought. Since your reaction to his wanting to see you was to tell him to go jump in the . . .

Would he now have anything to do with her? Or had Sharon the Moronic managed to blow another relationship? Only one way to find out, Sharon thought.

She dug in her purse for Richard Branson's card, checked her watch to be certain that business hours hadn't passed her by—they hadn't, it was only a few minutes after four—and punched in the number for Stratford, Field, Ruston, Howard, and Long. She cleared her throat and brought up her most seductive, please-help-me-voice as she listened to a series of rings on the line.

There was a click in her ear, after which a young woman said through her nose, "Stratford *Fee*-yield."

Sharon rolled her eyes. "Richard Branson, please."

"One moment." Another click sounded. Sharon drummed her fingers, felt guilty for having the nerve to make such a request of Branson, then pictured Raymond Burnside in his prison cell and the guilt fled in a hurry. Besides, she *wanted* to see Branson, wanted to . . .

The click sounded again, and the operator was back on the line talking through her nose. "I'm sorry. Mr. Branson is no longer *with* us. Can someone else—"

Sharon gripped the receiver hard enough to break a nail.

"—Help you?"

"Excuse me?" Sharon watched her dripping impatiens. "It's Richard Branson I'm calling for, are you . . . ?"

"No longer with us, ma'am."

"I had some . . . business with Mr. Branson recently. Can you tell me how long since he's . . . ?"

"A month. Mr. Whitlow is handling Mr. Branson's former cases, would you like me to . . . ?"

A sudden coldness spread through Sharon's chest. "I'm sorry, miss, but there must be some mistake. It's only been a couple of days since Mr. Branson and I spoke. Are you sure?"

"Certain as I can be, ma'am. If you'd like to leave your number, I can have someone call you to discuss your problem. Would you like me to?"

Sharon's pulse raced like a berserk Geiger counter. She spun around and faced the wall, reading her bachelor's and law degrees. How did such a dumb ass ever get through college? Sharon thought. "No," she said. "No thank you." She hung up quickly, picked up a pencil, and broke it in half.

Could I be mistaken? Sharon thought. No way. It was Branson who'd given her the business car, had been specific in saying he was with Stratford, Field when she'd first met him at the fund-raiser, just before they left together and he took her out and . . .

Screwed her. Probably he had the whole sexual encounter on videotape, and was at this very moment showing the tape to some of his buddies and laughing over how he'd tooled that stupid broad around. Why did guys have to be so . . .

She allowed herself to feel used and deceived for a period of about thirty seconds. The half minute of self-pity expired, she allowed herself to be mad as hell.

She fished in her bottom drawer for her bar association directory and thumbed savagely through the pages. What was that chick's name? She found it, a smiling picture posed like a college annual shot. She picked up her phone and called Stratford, Field, Howard, and Long again.

The same nasal voice chirped, "Stratford *Fee*-yield," in Sharon's ear.

Sharon lowered her voice an octave and tried her best Hispanic accent, straight from an off-Broadway production of *Manuel and Luisa,* for which she'd once auditioned. "Mees Trina Hill, pliz," she said, and then thought, God, no wonder I didn't get the part.

If the operator recognized Sharon as the person who'd just called, she didn't let on. There was a series of clicks, then a husky female voice said without much feeling, "Trina Hill."

Sharon resumed her normal tone. "Sharon Hays, Trina. Been a long time."

"Sharon?" Trina was obviously trying to sound friendly, but there was suspicion in her voice as well. The two had never been buddies. "Don't think I've talked to you since the bar exam," Trina said. "Are you a lawyer now?" The dig was intentional. Sharon's picture had been front-page during the Rathermore trial, and had appeared in the Metro section numerous times during her tenure as a prosecutor. Typical Trina Hill, the I've-been-too-busy-to-keep-up-with-you attitude. During law school years, Trina had often accompanied dates to restaurants where Sharon worked. She'd always had the guy leave a few bucks extra as a tip, and had always made Sharon feel as if Trina, personally, was throwing her a few crumbs.

"I'm . . . practicing, yes," Sharon said. "Suppose you've made partner."

"Next year, I believe. To what do I owe the pleasure of this call?"

Phony, phony, phony, Sharon thought. What would be wrong with, Glad to hear from you, something like that. "Frankly I'm checking on a man," Sharon said.

A dry humorless laugh. "Well, aren't we all."

"He was with your firm."

"Oh? Someone you're involved with, or is this a business call?"

"Little of both," Sharon said. "Richard Branson. Look, I know there are a couple of hundred lawyers in your firm, maybe you don't know . . ."

"Richard? You've got to be kidding," Trina said.

"You do know him, then. Listen, Trina, I understand he's quit."

There were five seconds of silence, tempered with even breathing. Trina said, "Why are you asking?"

Sharon looked at the ceiling. "Oh, a case I had with him," she lied.

"Richard didn't practice any criminal law."

Which caught Her Phoniness with her pantyhose down, after asking earlier whether Sharon was even practicing law. Trina did read the paper after all, though her interest was mostly in the society pages. Sharon said quickly, "I do some things that aren't criminal. Actually this was a will I was doing for a lady, and I ran into Richard at a party. I was going to refer this woman to him, but this is the only number I have. Do you have his current . . . ?"

More silence, after which Trina lowered her voice and said in a catty tone, "Is anyone else listening to this?"

Aha, Sharon thought. If it's gossip I want . . . "I'm alone in my office," Sharon said. "And confidentiality is my middle name."

"*Weh*-ell. Richard didn't exactly resign."

The coldness in Sharon's chest spread instantly

through the rest of her body, all the way to her toes. "You mean, he was asked to leave or something?"

"I'd put it a little stronger than that. I can get in trouble for carrying tales, Sharon. Stratford, Field doesn't want anyone knowing about this. Deb still works here, and it's a sticky wicket."

Sharon was confused. "Deb who?"

"Deb Branson, of course. One of our family law people is handling her divorce for free, but that's hush-hush as well."

Now the coldness gave way to a crawly feeling, like maggots wriggling on Sharon's skin. "Richard Branson is married?" He'd told her he'd just moved into his apartment from East Dallas in order to be nearer the office. What the hell, he'd told her a lot of things.

"At the moment. Not for long. Oh, you poor thing, have you been . . . ?"

Not that I'll admit to you, nosy, Sharon thought. Hopefully I'll never have to admit to anyone. "No, nothing like that," Sharon said. "What was the trouble? He wasn't pulling his load, or . . . ?"

"Financial problems, can you believe it? His wife about to make partner, between the two of them they're making a couple of hundred K. Deb's really in a fight over who owes what."

"He didn't," Sharon began, then cleared her throat to give herself time to think, then said, "He didn't have a drinking problem, did he? Didn't seem like the type."

"Just as bad. Gambling."

Sharon turned and faced the wall. Two plus two equals . . . "Gambling?" she said weakly.

"Spent every weekend in those casinos over in Mississippi. The big cheeses here got some nasty calls about Richard's tabs in those places. Rumor is, he owed over a hundred thou to some not-so-nice folks. More than enough problems for Stratford, Field not to want him as an associate any longer, but the firm put up with it for longer than you'd expect. He is a brilliant lawyer, for all the other things, but finally the last straw came and they had to fire him."

"Which was?" Sharon held her breath.

"Caught him doing some free legal work at the firm's expense, in exchange for washing out part of his gambling debt. That's a big no-no in this organization, doing anything for free."

Sharon sighed. She already knew the answer to her next question. "Was the work for an out-of-state company? Morgan Hill Corp., by any chance?"

There was a sharp intake of breath, followed by, "How did you know that?"

Oh, my God, Sharon thought. She forced herself to say calmly, "I guess I can forget about referring any clients to him, then. Thanks ever so much for the information, Trina."

"How did you know that, Sharon? Listen, you won't believe how much trouble I can . . ."

"You can depend on me not blowing your cover," Sharon said. "So nice to talk to you, Trina. Let's do lunch sometime, shall we?"

Sharon told Russ a little white lie and felt guilty about it, but was too upset to go into a lot of detail. She called him over the intercom, said she was leaving to get a head start on her research, and practically ran across the street to get her Volvo. She drove home in a fog, her hands trembling, picturing Jack Torturro saying to Richard Branson, something like, "You want off the hook? Just get us some info from the little lady. Oh, yeah, and while you're at it, hump her a good one for me, buddy."

Hump her a good one for me, buddy.

She came out of her daze parked in her own driveway without the slightest memory of the trip home, with no recollection of anything she'd seen or heard along the way. It was five o'clock, the sun high in the sky, the inside of the Volvo like a pizza oven.

Commander raised a ruckus from the backyard, raging and yelping.

Sharon killed the engine, pocketed the keys, opened the door, and just sat there for a moment. "You're a freaking moron, Sharon Jenifer," she finally said out loud.

Her throat constricted with shame, shock numbing her hands and feet, Sharon said softly over the phone to Sheila Winston, "There can't be any doubt. I met him two weeks ago. He's been gone from the firm for a month."

Sheila said firmly, "That tears it, Sharon. We're coming home."

"No need to. No need *not* to, now. Melanie's out of danger, there's no need for them to bother any of us any longer. If Raymond Burnside dies, it's going to be all my fault." She was seated on the Spanish sofa, wearing shorts, her legs curled up. Commander was stretched out beside her. Normally the sofa was off-limits to the shepherd, but Sharon had barely noticed when he'd bounded up from the floor. Now she snapped her fingers. Commander scooted down to sit on the carpet, watched her with his head cocked to one side, and wagged his tail.

"I thought you said his mother was going to testify about the clock."

"She is. It's a chance. But the judge can decide she's lying to save her son, and there won't be anything we can do about it. But running my mouth to this man I trusted for no reason other than that I had the hots, that's what got Dycus Wilt killed. The world won't miss Dycus, but Raymond Burnside certainly will. He was Raymond's best chance. God, I even told him what time they were moving Dycus out of the jail, Sheila. I might as well have drawn them a map."

"Are you sure you're not blowing this up in your mind?"

"He's also the only one who knew what time I was

going to be at the law library. If I hadn't found the dynamite when I did, I'd have only myself to blame. Stupid, stupid, stupid.''

"Have you called the police?"

"And told them what? We're dealing with professionals here. There isn't any evidence I could show them that could get Richard Branson so much as a parking ticket. I suspect some of those cute little male homicide cops I know would get a charge out of the way he tooled me around, but that's about all I'd get out of it.''

There was a rustling noise over the line, and Sharon pictured Sheila on a motel room bed, shifting her position. Sheila said, "You're sure there's no question you're out of danger?"

"Me personally? Not a chance. Why should they bother, Sheila? Russ has even dismissed our bodyguards. They've eliminated our main witnesses, built a Fifth Amendment wall that we're not going to be able to get around, and all we've got left is Raymond's mother, who the judge can choose to believe or not believe. The chances of winning Raymond a new trial are about ten percent at the moment, and the chances of upsetting Ralph Toner's political applecart are something less than that.''

Sharon paused for a moment, watching Commander, the shepherd worshipful in spite of everything. If you only knew, big guy, Sharon thought, that your idol's feet are clay. Or dog poop, that's more like it. She sniffled as she scratched Commander between the ears.

"Come on home, Sheila, will you?" Sharon finally said. "I want to see my little girl. When daughter's been bad, she can always come to Mommy, and you know what? I think it works the other way around as well.''

31

Sharon tossed and turned through the night, dozing fitfully around two, wide awake once more at three o'clock. Gray dawn found her sitting on the edge of her bed in total despair. She trudged barefoot into the bathroom, squeezed Ultra-Brite onto her toothbrush, and turned on a trickle of water. She looked mutely at her reflection in the mirror. Her bangs drooped pitifully, there were dark circles under her eyes, and there was a blotchy red spot on her chin.

Hump her a good one for me, buddy.

God, Sharon thought, why would anyone want to?

She viciously brushed her teeth, stripped out of and tossed her nightshirt into the corner, and climbed into jean cutoffs and a stained Bart Simpson T-shirt. Then she went into the garage for shears, cotton gloves, and a plastic lawn bag. The morning's first rays caught her down on her haunches in the front yard, attacking weeds with a vengeance. By nine o'clock the bag was half-filled with Johnson grass, ragweed, and uprooted dandelions. Rinds of dirt spotted the fingers of her gloves. Perspiration covered her forehead and ran down her body inside her clothes. Her sore knee throbbed a bit, so she intentionally shoved the knee against the ground in order to increase the pain. She wanted to hurt, wanted to toil until she was ready to drop. Anything to forget about . . .

Across the street Mrs. Breedlove came out to turn on her sprinklers, raised a chubby arm, and waved. Normally Sharon would have suspended her digging to go over and visit awhile, but she didn't think she could face the older woman. She returned the wave and attacked the weeds with more vigor than before.

She was finally exhausted, though in no better frame of mind, so she hauled her own hose and sprinkler out of the garage and turned the water on. The thirsty ground had sopped up yesterday's rain like a sponge, and the dirt was dry and packed. After entertaining herself for a while by watching droplets fall on parched brown Bermuda, she stalked to the curb, retrieved the newspaper, and went inside. She took a couple of oranges from a basket on the counter and cut them in half—pausing for a moment with the knife in her hand, thinking of slashing her wrists. Nah, she finally thought, suicide's too good for me. She tossed the knife into the sink with a clatter and flopped down at the table. She unfolded the paper, chomped into an orange half, and began to read.

Andy Wade was doing all he could, but Sharon suspected that Andy's editor had muzzled him. Sandy Griffin's cutting off Ralph Toner in mid-testimony had stifled Andy's daggers, and all the article said was that Sharon had questioned Toner about his conduct in Raymond Burnside's trial. So what? Defense lawyers attacked prosecutors all the time, what else was new? Andy had been able to slip in a mention of Torturro and Denopoulis at the end of the story, but all he really said about the mobsters was that they were in from California, that they'd contributed to Toner's campaign, and that they were interested in the court proceedings. Sharon pictured Andy pleading with his editor to let him say more, and supposed that Andy felt about as much frustration this morning as she did. Beneath Wade's article was a headline reading, "WOMAN FILES SUIT; CLAIMS SHE WAS MISLED INTO HAVING SEX." Sharon angrily rattled the paper and turned the page. She was halfway into an article alleging that Kato Kaelin had had something going with Nicole Simpson, when the phone rang. She laid the paper aside, reached for the wall phone, and said drearily into the receiver, "Hello?"

"Miss Hays?" said a tenor male voice that Sharon didn't immediately recognize.

Sharon swallowed tart orange pulp and spit a seed into her palm. Buddy, if you're a salesman, she thought, you're in for a real dressing-down. "Yes?" she said.

"Ed Teeter, Miss Hays. Sorry to bother you at home on a Saturday, but Russ Black's number isn't listed, and I . . ." He trailed off.

Sharon had blistered Teeter pretty hotly over his handling of Bradford Brie's release from jail during the Rathermore trial, so much so that the A.D.A. had walked on eggs with her ever since. If he's got the nerve to call me, Sharon thought, it must be something important. She got up, stretched the cord over by the sink, dropped the orange seed in the trash, and leaned on the counter. "No problem, Mr. Teeter."

Teeter's voice rhythm quickened in excitement. "Since you and Russ came by the other day, I've been looking into that stuff we talked about. Dycus Wilt's escape, remember? The deputy getting killed."

Sharon felt a tremor of interest. "Somebody needs to look into it. How are you coming along?"

"Like a turtle. The woman that quit the sheriff's department's moved out of town. I got guys looking all over for her, no soap."

"They shuffled her off someplace right after the two thugs beat up Andy Wade in front of her house. I'd be surprised if you ever do find her, Mr. Teeter. If you do find her, she won't know anything. Or she'll be dead; it's a toss-up as to which." Sharon looked at her bare toes. "I'll be surprised if anybody finds out anything about all of this. The sheriff's department is stonewalling you, I guess."

"I got to call it officially, lack of cooperation, but the fact is I'm lucky to get anybody at the jail to tell me what time it is. Tell you the truth, I was about ready to close my file as of yesterday. I got Milton Breyer and Miss Fraterno, they're not speaking to me. Makes for tension around the office, you know? Claim I'm sticking my nose in things that don't concern me."

"They would," Sharon said. "We owe you an apology, getting your motor running. This cover-up's going to be too dense for you to get to the bottom of. You're wasting your time."

"Maybe, maybe not. Yesterday afternoon I get this call. Might amount to something. We got this LNU, FNU in custody, claims to know something about how Wilt got out of jail."

Sharon crossed her ankles and folded her arms. "Last Name Unknown, First Name Unknown. Won't let you take his fingerprints?"

"Won't say anything except 'ouch.' This guy's on a totally unrelated case, tried to stick up a convenience store with an empty gun and the clerk shot him. Every LNU, FNU I ever saw is somebody with a rap sheet a mile long. These guys get a little bit savvy to the system; they think it's cute not to give their name and tell the fingerprint man to stick it up his . . . You were a prosecutor, Miss Hays, you know what I'm saying."

There were some assistant district attorneys who would have the sheriff withhold food from LNU, FNU's until they 'fessed up their identity. Sharon had never stooped to such tactics, but had considered LNU, FNU's to be the ultimate pain. She said, "So you'll have to get a court order to force him to give you his prints. Should take about a week to learn your mystery guest's true identity. You say he was shot?"

"Right on. They're holding him in the jail ward at Parkland Hospital, and this guy won't say boo to anybody about himself. But claims to know something about how Wilt escaped. Looking for a deal."

"That was all in the papers. Anybody under arrest can claim to know something, and most of them won't have information worth two cents. Haven't they appointed him a lawyer?"

"Tried to, and this is how I got in on the act. Guy wouldn't even tell his court-appointed lawyer his name, but started talking Dycus Wilt. I had feelers out, you know? Anything about Wilt's escape as it related to the deputy's murder, that's supposed to come to me. Problem is, the Wilt file's tickled to send the information to Milton Breyer, too, which is how Milt found out I'm checking on the case. Anyway, I go out to the hospital to see the guy."

Sharon sat down at the kitchen table and rubbed her sore knee. Grubbing in the yard had aggravated something; the knee was beginning to swell. "Was he anybody you recognized?" she said. "Regular county offenders you see all the time, sometimes they . . ."

"Never laid eyes on this guy," Teeter said. "Black guy, skinny, a pill head if I ever saw one. Wouldn't give me his name, either, but said if I get him the right deal he'll tell me things, help me pin down the way Wilt got out of his handcuffs. You're still hanging on to that handcuff key, aren't you?"

Sharon pictured the key in her top dresser drawer. "Wild horses couldn't drag it away from me."

"Some things make me think this guy may know what he's talking about. Such as for instance, he wants to see you."

Sharon quit rubbing her knee and switched the phone from one ear to the other. "Me?"

"That's what makes me think he knows something. Nothing in the papers ever said you were Wilt's lawyer, and I've read every story about the case. Our LNU, FNU says he wants you because you did Wilt such a good job. You do good jobs for these prisoners, Miss Hays?"

"What I can."

"I'd want you to cooperate with me where anything he knows relates to Wilt and the deputy's murder," Teeter said. "This guy's looking at big time just for trying to rob the convenience store. Like all these

LNU, FNU's, once we get him identified, I'll bet a week's pay he's into a bunch more."

Sharon rummaged in her kitchen drawer, found a pad and pen. "I couldn't promise any cooperation on his current charge, the stickup, if he retained me to represent him. But if he knows something about Dycus's escape, that could work to his advantage on a plea bargain. We're talking generalities unless I was officially his lawyer. But I'd do what I could, Mr. Teeter."

"That's all I'm wanting," Teeter said. "Hell, a stickup, we got a million LNU, FNU's doing those. Dime a dozen. If the convenience store was all we were talking about, I wouldn't even put my oar in the water."

Sharon got ready to write. "As long as we understand each other, what's his bed number in the prison ward? Maybe I should visit with Mr. FNU." She copied the number down, hung up, called Russ's private home line, and told him to meet her at the hospital. As she headed for her dressing area, she had a sudden image of Richard Branson, his hot breath on her face as he'd squirmed on top of her. The image made her sick to her stomach.

Parkland Hospital towered over the intersection of Harry Hines Boulevard and Inwood Road, just a couple of blocks off Stemmons Freeway. Directly across the street sat the mammoth bulk of an upscale private institution, St. Paul, whose grand portals opened beneath the image of the Savior on the cross, and the close proximity of the two medical facilities caused a lot of confusion. The staff at St. Paul was willing to set the misdirected straight in a hurry, however; all who entered below the master's feet were frisked for insurance polices or Medicare certificates and, found wanting for funds, dumped across the street at the county. Parkland's doors were open to all, including knifing and scalding victims from within the county jail. The inmates' ward was on the fifth floor, north wing, with uniformed sheriff's deputies acting as orderlies, and nurses going about their duties under heavy guard.

Sharon hopped off the elevator and hustled down the corridor at a few minutes after noon. She'd raced through her shower, given her hair a lick and a promise, put on khaki Docker slacks and a pale green Izod knit, and driven over in a hurry with one eye on her side view, watching for traffic patrols. Russell Black had already arrived; he stood before the steel jail ward door with his hands in the pockets of his jeans. In addition to the jeans, he wore a checkerboard cowboy shirt, and he'd dragged Anthony Gear along. Apparently the detective owned no weekend clothes; his plaid sport coat and tan slacks stood out like a uniform. Edward Teeter was there as well, his pipe stem legs and whalelike girth encased in Bermuda shorts and a golf shirt. Sharon thought the A.D.A. looked ridiculous. She stopped before the three men and said to Black, "I'm not promising a thing, boss."

Black jerked his head in Teeter's direction. "Ed was fillin' us in. Prisoner's still remainin' anonymous."

"I'm staying in the background," Teeter said, "long as we're in agreement we got a deal."

Sharon and Russ exchanged a look. After an imperceptible nod from Black, Sharon turned to Teeter and said, "That's fine, as long as we all understand the deal going in. The prisoner's asked to see me, apparently to talk about legal representation. So I'm going to interview him. If he and I strike an arrangement, and it's advantageous to my client to offer information on unrelated matters to the district attorney's office, we'll all work together like army ants. But I'm not compromising my client's position on what he's in jail for, Mr. Teeter. That understood?"

Teeter nervously shuffled his feet. "If you could just get me his name, Miss Hays."

"He'll give you his name," Sharon said, "if he *wants*

to give you his name and I think it's advisable for him to if I'm representing him. Otherwise you'll have to wait for your court order next week." She turned to Black. "Rules are in the jail ward, only one lawyer at a time. We can take an investigator in. Since the guy's asked specifically for me, I think Mr. Gear and I should be the first to visit him. If you don't think that's advisable, boss, I'll sure defer to you."

Black looked slightly irritated, then showed his standard craggy grin. "You're runnin' the show, girl. Me an' old Ed will wait on that bench over yonder and talk about the baseball scores."

"That'll work." Sharon nodded to the detective. "Mr. Gear. You and me." She stepped professionally to the door and banged on a portal. The portal opened, and a sheriff's deputy peered out. Sharon flashed her ID and gave the prisoner's bed number. The door clanked and slid, revealing a long narrow corridor with hospital beds lining the walls. Sharon started to enter, then turned to Teeter and flashed a grin. "Oh," she said. "Thanks for the referral, Ed. Us private lawyers need all the business we can get."

Inmate-patient LNU, FNU had bandages covering the upper right portion of his body and his arm was in a sling. A sheet was bunched around his waist, and he seemed to be asleep. His bed was cranked halfway into the sitting position, and a tube carried glucose from a suspended bottle to the vein in his inner left elbow. Portable partitions hid him from the other patients. There was a barred window next to his headboard. Sharon thanked the escorting deputy, who retreated to his post; then she stood beside the jacked-up portion of the bed. Anthony Gear rolled the glucose apparatus aside and moved up close to the patient as well. Sharon gently shook Mr. LNU, FNU's bare left shoulder. She lowered her voice to a whisper. "Hi, Woody. You're not dead, are you?"

Chocolate-colored lids fluttered, then opened wide.

Eyes with corneas the color of burned coal bugged out. "Don't know no Woody."

Sharon shook her head. "Won't do. You're a been-around guy, Mr. Lee. Next week they'll have a court order for your fingerprints, and the jig will be up. I'm Sharon Hays, the lawyer you asked to see."

The eyes moved in their sockets to look at Gear, then shifted back to Sharon. "Who's '*at* dude?"

"That's my investigator, Mr. Gear. You asked for a lawyer. As of right now any communication you make to me is privileged, and that goes for Mr. Gear as well. He's here in case you say something we'd need a witness to substantiate, nothing more." Sharon leaned her hip against the bed. "So, your nickel, Woodrow. What's on your mind?"

A thin mustache wiggled as Lee licked dry lips. "Thirsty. I'm thirsty."

Sharon held a glass of ice water so that the patient could sip through a straw, then set the glass on a rolling table. "That better?"

"You the lady Dycus Wilt had, right?" Lee said.

"As a lawyer. Not in the carnal sense, but yes."

Lee directed his gaze beyond Sharon, at the partition. "Mothafuckah dropped a dime on me. Been frens all 'is time."

"That sounds like a rerun of what he told me, Woody. Dycus said you dropped a dime on him."

"I'm catchin' a little case on a robbery here. Gun didn' have no bullets."

Sharon clucked her tongue, glanced at Anthony Gear, then said to the prisoner, "Still a felony. I suspect you've had three or more. How many times have you been a guest at TDC, Woody?"

"Fo'. One time don't count, 'cause that conviction diversed." Lee touched his bandages, his forearm like a sliver of ebony wood.

"You mean reversed. Third time's a charm in this state. Automatic twenty-five to life unless you can make a deal, but you already know that or you wouldn't be a LNU, FNU. One thing bothers me. How did you know I was Dycus' lawyer? That wasn't in the paper."

Lee rolled his eyes. "Shee-it. M'arm hurts. Ast that deputy, can I have some mo' drugs."

Sharon felt a surge of pity in spite of herself. Total burnout, this one. "Now, that would be just what you need," she said, "more morphine. The longer I do this, the less I understand people like you. You snitch on Dycus, he in turn snitches on you. Shouldn't make you the best of buds. But you two were still communicating, weren't you?"

Lee watched her in silence. Anthony Gear coughed nervously. Somewhere down the line, a life-support machine *whoosh-whoosh*ed.

"Of course you were," Sharon said. "He'd call you from the jail, to threaten if you didn't stop talking about him, he'd start talking about you. By the way, he'd already tried to deal information about you to the district attorney, but they weren't buying. Then he told you he had a lawyer, me. That's the only way you could know about me, Woody. It's also the only way you could know anything about his escape attempt, for him to call you from the jail."

"Naw, them telephones all monitored. I went downtown an' seen Dycus, right 'fo he break. Dude tole me a lady in the office gonna slip him a key."

Sweet hosanna, Sharon thought. Woody snitches Dycus off on the Mary Ann Blakely murder, Dycus in turn drops information about Delores Burnside. Still Woody visits him, like buddies forever. What a society, Sharon thought. "Everybody's way ahead of you there," she said. "The lady and the key are common knowledge. You're not going to buy a bit of leniency if that's all you know." Sharon moved back a step and folded her arms. "The major question is, how did Dycus know in advance that someone was going to slip him a key? Someone had to tell him."

"He say, a lawyuh come to see him. Not you, another dude."

Sharon arched an eyebrow. None of the civil lawyers working for the gambling folks would chance getting involved in an escape attempt unless the gamblers had something to use as pressure. Which left one likely candidate whom Sharon could think of. "A lawyer visited him in the jail?" she said.

"That what he say. Goddamn, woman, talk to that deputy. Hurtin' bad. Hurtin' bad."

"It's called withdrawal symptoms," Sharon said, "and for now we need your head on straight. If a lawyer came to see him, he had to show a bar card. Had to sign in at the jail. Those sign-in sheets are public records, Mr. Gear. If you check Dycus' visitors for, say, three days before the escape, that should tell us something. It will likely tell us he had a visit from a man named Richard Branson, but you should check to make it official."

Anthony Gear fiddled with the glucose stand. "I'll add it to my list," he said.

"So, Mr. Lee," Sharon said, "do you want me to represent you?"

"Sho'. On dis robbery. Plead me down to about a nickel."

"You said you wanted a lawyer, not a magician. Five years, the D.A. would go into stitches over that offer."

"I'm givin' 'em how Dycus broke out."

"There are two problems with that. Number one, other than that a lawyer visited him, you're not telling anyone anything they don't already know. Secondly, and this is the main thing, Dycus is dead, making anything he told you hearsay. I'll bet you already knew that, as many times as you've been around the block. You must be desperate, Woody."

The prisoner glumly dropped his chin. "Ain't doin' no habitual beef. Ain't doin' no twenny-five year."

One corner of Sharon's mouth bunched. Not one

lawyer in a hundred could quote the Habitual Felon Statute, but near-illiterate cons knew it by heart. "You'll do more than the minimum," Sharon said. "With your record you're looking at life, bet you a dollar."

Lee sniffled. "Don't no lawyuh evah do nothin' for a man."

Sharon smiled sweetly. "It's hard to do anything for a man who's already done so much for himself. Okay, Mr. Lee, I think I can help you."

Anthony Gear looked up, surprised. Woodrow Lee watched her with a string of saliva hanging from one front tooth.

"Now I can only make it easier on you," Sharon said. "And you make up your mind, prepare yourself to do some heavy time. To do what I'm thinking of, though, you're going to have to come up with something better than the Dycus Wilt escape. We all know you can do better, don't we?"

Lee coughed, holding his injured shoulder in pain. "Know a couple of dudes sellin' dope out South Oak Cliff. Drop a dime on them mothafuckahs, you think that help?"

Sharon gave a dry laugh. "Come on, Woody. Some dope dealers in exchange for an armed robbery? You know better than that. You'd have to talk something really heavy to do what I've got in mind. Something like . . ." She pretended to think it over. "Something like Delores Burnside, six years ago."

Lee's eyes widened, and his voice was suddenly hoarse. "I ain't talkin' bout no *deaf penalty*. You talkin' crazy, woman."

Sharon caused her expression to go blank, made her tone calm and matter-of-fact. "You stabbed her with that bone knife, Woody. Thirty-something times."

Lee watched his feet, where the sheet tented. "Shee-it, I never stabbed no woman. Dycus Wilt done that hisself, shee-it, dude tryin' to say I did."

Sharon sighed. It was exactly what she'd known he

was going to say. She'd seen the two-man act many
times as a prosecutor, he-did-it, no-he-did-it, and without any witnesses it was impossible to tell which one
was lying. Sharon had developed the attitude that it
didn't really matter, with vermin like these, all were
equally guilty no matter who did the actual killing.
"He told me you did it, Woody," she said.

"Well, he a lyin' . . ."

"If you want to say *he* did it," Sharon said, "I can't
stop you from doing that. But you're going to have to
say you were there. It's the only way I can help you."
She looked across the bed at Anthony Gear, who
seemed every bit as puzzled as the prisoner. Sharon
winked at the detective, then returned her attention
to Woodrow Lee.

"I know what you doin', woman," Lee said. "You
the lawyuh for the dude caught the deaf penalty over
that case. You tryin' to give me up, save that white
dude's ass. Dycus Wilt say you a good lawyuh. Shee-
it, you just like them other dudes, give a man up."

"I don't know what other dudes you're talking
about," Sharon said evenly, "but I'm not like them,
and I'll tell you something. I represent Raymond
Burnside, which I consider many rungs up the ladder
from representing you. Just so we're clear. But if I
take your case, I won't give you up. I'll make every
effort, and I think I can do this, to have this robbery
charge dropped. But it's going to take your giving up
the Burnside case. If you'll do that, I think I can make
it easier for you."

"Shee-it, give up a *deaf penalty* just to beat a robbery beef? Who you think you talkin' to?"

"I think I'm talking to you, Woody. And as we were
having this pleasant discussion, I got this idea. Sometimes I get them. It's a long drawn-out legal rigmarole
that you won't understand, but it has to do with putting the hurt on some people, some mob people that
you don't even know."

Sharon paused. Anthony Gear watched her as if

expecting her to fly off to never-never land. The same look Russell Black gave her sometimes, when she got these ideas. She cleared her throat and went on.

"So I ask you, Woody. If I can make the deal of the century, get you a proposition you won't even believe, are you willing to get on the stand and talk about the Burnside murder?"

Lee looked doubtful. "You mean, you going to get me reunity?"

"Immunity," Sharon said. "And I don't think so. Dealing with the state, I know I can't. I'm thinking about a different jurisdiction."

Anthony Gear's expression began to clear, showing understanding. He murmured, "Pretty slick, Miss Hays."

"Let's don't break our arms patting me on the back just yet," Sharon said. "There are a lot of loose ends to tie up here." She directed her attention to the prisoner. "My boss and I haven't reaped a great deal of financial reward out of all this, Mr. Lee. I don't suppose you've got any money, do you?"

"You think I'm going in to rob somebody with a gun I can't shoot, I got any money in my pocket. Shee-it."

"That's what I was afraid of," Sharon said. "Okay, Woody, listen up. Until we do something to hurt one another we're going steady, okay? I'm your lawyer. I'll continue to be your lawyer until I get a conflict of interest, which I won't have as long as we're working in the same direction. You're wanting a better deal than you've got. In order to get it you're going to have to help my other client, Raymond Burnside. We can accomplish what you want and what he wants at the same time, which is what deals are all about.

"First order of business," Sharon said, "is for you to do exactly nothing. You're LNU, FNU. Keep it that way, and that's important. Until I get some arrangements made, nobody in Dallas County's employ is to know your real name. No D.A.s, deputy sheriffs, no one. I don't want the same people you were dealing with when you dropped a dime on Dycus Wilt, I don't that those people down here messing with you. Understand?"

"I don't tell nobody shit," Lee said.

"I'd probably put it a little differently," Sharon said, "but yes." She dug in her shoulder bag for a business card and laid it on the bed. "That's what you wave at everybody. If anyone wants to talk to you, and I mean anybody, you just give them my number. It's going to take until probably next Thursday or Friday for them to get a court order to take your prints and identify you. By then I'll be able to do something, one way or the other. Are we in sync on this?"

"Don' tell them mothafuckahs nothin'," Lee said. "Don't tell 'em shit."

Sharon closed her bag, stepped away from the bed, and prepared to leave. "Not exactly the language of the ladies' bridge club, but right on." She demurely fluttered her eyelids. "So nice meeting you, Mr. Lee. A more pleasant chat, I swear I can't recall."

Russell Black looked scowlingly doubtful. "You got any idea what all that's gonna take?" He hooked his thumbs into his belt loops, cowhand style.

"I don't think it's going to be as hard as you think," Sharon said, "as long as we all go in the right directions and put the right feathers in the right caps. You'll need to talk to a county judge to find out about bail. The rest of it I think I can handle."

Black looked to the opposite end of the hospital corridor where Anthony Gear entertained Edward Teeter, likely with some old FBI stories. Mr. Gear's got a million of 'em, Sharon thought. Teeter stood first on one foot and then the other, looking in Sharon's direction and obviously wondering what was going on. Black jerked his head toward the A.D.A. "What are we going to tell that guy?"

Sharon shrugged with her hands. "He's going to be

ticked, but that can't be helped. I'll shoulder the blame, boss. Come on." She led the way, Black falling in step behind her as she walked down to Teeter and the detective.

Teeter raised a hand and cut Gear off in the middle of whatever story the detective was telling. "You get me a line on that guy, Miss Hays?" Teeter said. Visible through the window behind him, traffic rolled east and west on Inwood Road.

Sharon smiled vacantly. " 'Fraid not. He's still LNU, FNU."

"All that time with the guy, that's all you can tell me?"

Sharon manufactured a scowl of frustration. "Can't get a peep out of him. Be an interesting arraignment on the robbery charges, don't you think? 'Who's your client, Miss Hays?' 'I don't have the slightest idea, Your Honor.' Should make for lovely conversation down at the courthouse."

Teeter looked about to explode. "You're telling me," he said, pointing a finger, "that you talked to this guy, you're taking his case, and he won't even tell you his name, right? Come on, Miss Hays, I thought we were going to work together on this."

"I thought we were, too, Mr. Teeter," Sharon said. "But strange things happen in Wonderland. Actually it's going to be an experience, representing a client who's incognito. Might be better not knowing his name, come to think about it. Keep the relationship strictly on a nonpersonal level, you know?"

32

Sharon parted company with Russell Black in the hospital parking lot, and Black drove away in his Buick in search of a bail-setting judge willing to work on Saturday. Sharon watched her boss through the Buick's rear window as he meshed with southbound traffic on Inwood Road, Black shaking his head in consternation. He's ready to fit me for a straightjacket, Sharon thought, and I really couldn't blame him. She climbed into her Volvo and pointed its nose to the north, chugging along in hundred-degree heat with both front windows rolled down. Next week, come hell or high water, she was going to spring for a Freon charge.

Her dashboard clock showed five minutes after four as she eased off of LBJ Freeway through the Preston Road exit ramp, skirted the jam-packed parking lot outside Valley View Mall, and continued a half mile more to the north to turn left on Alpha Road. Then she crawled along Alpha, peering at cross-street signs, and almost entered three different apartment house driveways before locating the one she was looking for. She bounced over double dips and turned in between two three-story sandy brick buildings with shingled roofs.

After entering the drive, the Volvo crept slowly between rows of jazzy sports cars—restored MGs and Mustangs and even one fire-engine red Jaguar—before she spotted a metallic blue Mercedes. She set the parking brake and left the Volvo running, got out and went around to the Mercedes' passenger side, bent from the waist, and shaded her eyes to squint in through the window. Yep, she had the right car. A plaque above the glove compartment identified the Mercedes' oh-so-lucky-and-full-of-prestige owner as "R. Branson." Sharon gritted her teeth, picturing herself yanking the lug wrench from the Volvo's trunk and—her eyes glowing insanely, screaming like a banshee with drool running down her chin—breaking every window in the Mercedes, bashing in the headlights, and reducing the luxury vehicle to a mass of twisted metal. The fantasy will have to do, old girl, she thought. She climbed back into the Volvo and motored down the way, finally pulling into a slot between a BMW and a Lexus and killing the engine. She locked her shoulder bag in the trunk for safekeeping, then made her way across sun-baked asphalt to mount the stairway leading up to Branson's apartment. Her nerves were Dead Sea calm. Her pulse beat time like a metronome.

The stairway led to a landing, then a walkway extended to a balcony overlooking the apartment house's interior courtyard. The courtyard contained patches of green mowed St. Augustine grass and a network of bleached sidewalk. As Sharon moved along the balcony, touching the metal handrail at intervals along her way, the sound of male and female voices reached her ears accompanied by splashing noises. She rounded a bend, and the complex pool came into view. A volleyball game was in progress, suntanned bodies leaping in chlorine-blue water, delighted shouts splitting the air as the ball flew back and forth across the net. Sharon passed the pillar where, on the night of Ralph Toner's fund-raiser, she and Branson had stopped to feverishly grope one another on the way to the apartment. Involuntarily her upper lip curled.

She reached his door. *Knew* it was his door, could actually feel his free hand on her as he'd twisted his key in the lock in a frenzy, remembered her own wanton lust as she'd unzipped and dropped her dress on the floor just inside the foyer. She battled the resistance of her own emotions as she lifted her hand and knocked firmly, *rap-rap-rap,* three solid blows on wood. She turned her back and gazed down on the pool as she waited. Her pulse quickened. She resisted the impulse to run. Fifteen seconds passed, then thirty. As she stepped over to knock again, her gaze fell on Branson himself, one story below in the courtyard.

Gee, she thought, he's having a jolly old time by the pool. *Seemed* to be enjoying himself anyway, stretched out on a chaise longue in silken boxer swim trunks, broad tanned shoulders relaxed, long muscular legs splayed out. A small round table was by his elbow, and on the table sat a glass of iced something-or-other. Branson wore sunglasses. Two wiggly, giggly young women sat nearby on a second chaise, giving Branson their undivided attention. Their bodies were brown as walnuts. Both wore bikinis, and both looked good in them. Branson reached out and playfully stroked one of the bikini-bunnies' cheeks. She drew coquettishly back and grinned at him.

Well, isn't that just the picture of freaking health, Sharon thought. She leaned on the rail to watch.

Branson bent forward, picked up his glass, and sipped. Then he apparently told a good one, both nymphets giggling and wriggling, throwing their heads back and laughing like comedy-club customers. Branson laughed as well and had another drink, tilting his glass, raising his head as he swallowed, his gaze moving upward behind sunglasses, his expression freezing, his chin remaining slanted upward as he set the glass on the table, removed his glasses, and let them dangle from his fingers by an earpiece. Merriment reigned on all sides, the yelling and splashing continuing in the pool as Richard Branson and Sharon Hays locked gazes from thirty yards apart, him on the chaise by the pool, her standing on the balcony above.

Sharon raised a hand to shoulder level and waggled her fingers.

His expression went from puzzlement to shock in a fraction of a second. Then the mask was back in place, the pleasurable, what-me-worry guy returning his attention to the bikini-clad women for a few seconds, then excusing himself to stand and move toward the stairway up to the balcony. He held a finger up to the girls in just-a-minute fashion, and Sharon supposed they'd wait with bated breaths until hell froze over. He ascended the steps two at a time with an athlete's easy grace, then moved down the balcony walkway in her direction. His tan line showed, the skin on his upper thighs white above the hem of his trunks. The trunks were gray-green with an Izod emblem on one leg. He was twenty feet away now, the mask firmly in place as he smiled at her. "Hi. Hey, hi. The last time we talked, I thought you'd be tied up until next week." His look was confident, with just a hint of worry at the corners of his eyes.

Sharon flashed back to acting class, recalled a part she'd had in a college play, and put on her best submissive smile. "I had a few hours I hadn't counted on. Did I interrupt something?" She looked toward the pool, then back at him.

He spread his hands. "You? Hey, *you*? Interrupting, of course not. I'd *want* you to interrupt anything I was doing, Sharon." He gave her shoulder an affectionate squeeze.

Sharon's flesh crawled.

He gestured toward the pool. "Hey, I'll bet you could fit into a suit one of those ladies has stashed away. I've got influence. You want to take a swim, maybe play some volleyball?"

I'll just bet you've got influence, sweetie, Sharon thought. She retained her acting-class smile. "I thought we could visit inside," she said.

He showed a quick look of uncertainty that disappeared in a flash. "Sure. Sure, inside if you want. It's

not locked, come on and . . . hey, I haven't had time
to clean up, hope you . . ."

"Drop-ins take potluck," she said, then stepped
around him and opened the door to his apartment.
Refrigerated air blew through the doorway and cooled
her arms. She watched him over her shoulder. "Come
on, Richard," she said, then crossed the threshold. He
followed her in and closed the door behind him.

He'd added some knickknacks since her last visit,
but not many. There was a leather sofa dead center
in the room, probably used, and a couple of padded
armchairs. No pictures on the walls. She wondered
briefly whether his estranged wife had let him have
some of the household furniture, or if he'd had to buy.
"Shaping up," she said.

"Shaping. . . ? Hey, yes, I've gotten a few things."
He went over and stood beside the counter separating
the kitchen from the living room. "Something to
drink, or . . . ?"

Sharon sat in one of the armchairs. "No. We need
to talk."

The worried look appeared once again, and this
time didn't go away. He sat on the sofa and leaned
on one armrest. His pecs were solid muscle. A hunk,
Sharon thought, no doubt about it. Could pass for a
bathing suit model. He said, "I suppose you're mad
about something."

Sharon arched an eyebrow. "Oh? What would I be
mad about?"

He waved his hands. "Maybe . . . that I haven't
tried to call? You said you'd be busy." He didn't look
straight at her, concentrating instead on something in
the vicinity of her shoulder.

He knows, she thought. She was conscious of the
exit on her right, had a fleeting surge of fear that
dissipated in the flick of an eye. She folded her arms
and crossed her legs. "Oh, I have been busy. How's
your law practice, Richard?"

He scratched above his eyebrow. "The usual. Couple of closings. Did a will this week."

She looked at him.

He shifted nervously, rested his ankle on his knee, and rubbed the sole of his bare foot. "I don't have to ask about yours; you've been in the newspapers." He tried a grin that looked rather sickly. "You're getting to be quite the media star."

"That's showbiz. How are things at your office?"

He seemed puzzled.

"You know, at Stratford, Field," she said.

"It's . . . convenient," he said weakly. "The apartment's convenient to—"

"That's interesting. I was looking at the bar association roster. There are two Bransons listed with your firm. Any relation?"

He cleared his throat, leaned over, and clutched his midsection as if he was about to be sick.

She locked her gaze on him. "Ran into an old law school *compadre* of mine. Trina Hill, do you know her?" She felt a twinge of guilt, having promised Trina that she wouldn't blow her cover. The guilt was fleeting, however; the odds of Branson ever talking to anyone at Stratford, Field again were something like a million to one.

Branson put both feet on the floor, stood, and walked halfway to her. He extended his arms. "There are some things I need to tell you, Sharon. Come on, sit over here by me."

She looked at his big open hands. "First I'll tell *you* something. If you so much as touch me, even by accident, I'll kick you in the balls." She winked. "I will, too. Sit down, and stay as far from me as possible."

Air eased out of his lungs. He retreated and sat on the couch, his eyes glazed as if he was in shock.

Sharon licked her lips. She sadly shook her head. "Rhodes scholar. God, what I wouldn't give."

He tried, "Sharon, I . . ."

"Sharon you what? You *what*, Richard? You poor,

immoral gambling sicko, what is it you want to say to me?"

He looked about to cry. "I haven't been honest with you."

She looked at the ceiling. "Good Jesus Christ and all the angels."

"I wasn't faking any attraction to you," he said. "That's the ..."

"Oh, sure. *Sure,* Richard, I make you quiver like a big bowl of jelly. That's why you told those guys where my car would be parked, so they could rig the dynamite under my hood."

He clenched his jaws. "I didn't know they were going to do that. I swear to you."

"Probably you didn't," Sharon said. "They don't normally let the flunkies in on the major plans. Probably you thought they were merely going to shoot me."

He stiffened, suddenly pugnacious, his eyes narrowing. "I think you'd better leave now. This conversation isn't getting us anywhere."

She laughed in mild amusement. "Why, what happened to the bit about, you'd want me to interrupt anything you were doing? Don't you love me anymore?"

"If you have some suspicions about me," he said, "then you should offer proof."

Sharon lightly clapped her hands. "Spoken like a true member of the bar. Which you won't be for long, by the way." She dropped her hands into her lap. "I can't offer any proof."

Branson folded muscular arms. "Then, you shouldn't go around casting accusations."

"Or what, you'll turn me in to the grievance committee? We're not in court now, Richard, and I don't have to put on any witnesses. I can't get you arrested, you're right about that. I can only get you killed."

His lips formed a sneer, though his eyes shifted uncertainly.

"You think I can't?" Sharon said. "I know things I can't prove, so I'd have to take them to people who don't require any proof. Such as your buddies, Torturro and Denopoulis. What do you think they'll say when I tell them Richard's been talking about how you sent him to the jail to carry tales to Dycus Wilt? They won't say anything to me, of course. But then you'll be embraced by the light, Richard. Should make you happy. Being embraced by the light is one of life's ultimate goals, isn't it?"

He snorted incredulously. "Those people wouldn't listen to you. You might be putting yourself in danger."

"Not any longer," Sharon said. "They're through with me. Don't you even know the rules? They couldn't scare me off and bungled killing me, so they switched to other tactics such as scaring witnesses and having gambling sickos like you run little errands for them. I'm here to give you one chance to save your life, Richard. Don't you want to hear my idea?"

He squeezed his biceps, as if in love with himself. "I don't think I'm interested in anything you have to say."

Sharon leaned forward and rested her palms on her knees. "Well, you'd better be. We're no longer playing lay 'em and leave 'em here, big boy. That game's over. It's *Fatal Attraction* time.

"Personally," Sharon said, "I couldn't care less if they do turn out your lights. I think they would anyway, regardless of the outcome in the Raymond Burnside hearing, the gubernatorial election, or anything else. Do you want to know why?"

His lips parted. He scooted his rear end forward and leaned back against the cushions.

"These people keep emotion out of it," Sharon said. "Do nothing merely because they've got a mad-on. They no longer care about me or Russ because we don't have any information that can hurt them. You do. You took direct orders from Torturro, to show up at that party and meet me, and pump me for information. I don't know whether he ordered you to take me to bed or not. If he did, you were a good little soldier.

"You also were their errand boy to fill Dycus Wilt in on his escape plans," Sharon said. "You're the only one outside their organization who can hurt them. If you don't hurt them, and right now, you're going to be dead. You'll have a car wreck, or maybe someone will walk up behind you, slap you on the back, and prick you with a needle. Then you'll have a heart attack. Dirty shame, a man as young as you are."

Branson's hands trembled. He said weakly, "Jesus Christ, what can I . . . ?"

Sharon smiled, unable to resist twisting the knife blade. "Do to make it up to me? I don't think anything. But I'll ask you. Did you do enough practicing of law, in between calling your bookmaker and tripping off to exotic lands to gamble, that you know your way to the federal building?"

Branson said, his voice low and childlike, "Please, Sharon."

"Don't 'please' me. I'm only doing this for my poor dope of a client, who's been sitting on death row for six years while all you Rhodes scholars have been having such a good time. If it was strictly up to me, I'd as soon they shot you."

"The state prosecutors wouldn't be interested in what you have to say," Sharon said, "because it would help get Raymond Burnside off the hook. But the feds are a different story. People like Mr. Torturro and Mr. Denopoulis make U.S. attorneys absolutely drool. Throw in Ralph Toner and his political juggernaut, and the federal folks will foam at the mouth like rabid dogs." Sharon stood up. "I've got to be going, Richard. If I stay much longer, I'm afraid some of you will rub off on me."

She walked to the door, opened it, and stood with one hip against the jamb. Branson hadn't moved, his gaze on the ceiling, his eyes misty as if he might burst into tears.

"Monday morning, nine o'clock," Sharon said. "I'm having a long talk with the federals. Earle Cabell Federal Building, seventh floor. Love to have you. Only chance of keeping yourself alive for more than, say, a week or two, so maybe you'd better sleep on it. They've got some really nice witness-protection programs, which might include a few quarters for you to dump in the slot machines."

She stepped onto the landing and closed the door partway, then pushed it open and stuck her head inside. "Oh. And if you stand me up, I'll have to visit with Mr. Torturro and associates on my way in to Raymond Burnside's hearing. So don't turn me down without a lot of thought, Richard. I'd sleep hard on it, if I were you."

33

Russell Black went to court on Monday morning ready to stage a filibuster, but almost lost his client before the proceedings could get underway. With reporters—from San Antonio, Houston, and Austin, in addition to the regulars from the *Dallas Morning News,* the out-of-town rags having gotten wind of the hearing's potential effect on Ralph Toner's gubernatorial campaign—jamming the media section in anticipation of a continuation of Friday's donnybrook, and Judge Griffin not yet having appeared from her chambers, Black flopped into a chair alongside Raymond Burnside and said, "Sharon's gonna be a couple of hours late, takin' care of some business. Listen, there's somethin' I need to talk over with you."

Burnside was freshly shaved and wore a clean, pressed county jail jumpsuit. The bailiff had escorted him in from the holding cell just moments earlier, and now lounged against the rail with one eye on the prisoner. Burnside sat intently forward and said to Russell Black, "It's the three women, isn't it? You can't make them testify."

Black wanted to lie, but found it wasn't in him. Twenty-five years as a criminal lawyer, he'd never yet told an untruth to a client and didn't suppose he ever would. "I'm afraid that dog's not gonna hunt, Raymond," he said. "Lawyers a damn sight smarter'n me an' Sharon combined have been tryin' to shoot holes in the Fifth Amendment for a coupla centuries, an' so far nobody's been able to."

Burnside regarded his folded hands. "Which means I'm going to die, just as I've been saying all along. You lawyers have had your day in the spotlight, but the bottom line is, I'm no better off than when you started all this." His tone was even, no panic in his look, just a man with all the fight knocked out of him, ready to accept what was coming.

"Now, I didn't say it was over," Black said, "an' it's a long way from it." He gestured toward the exit. "We got a corridor full of witnesses out there, Ralph Toner an' his lawyer, the three women, everybody we got under subpoena. Anything can happen. Sandy Griffin might fool me, rule in our favor an' make those women take the stand, anything."

"And the heavens may fall," Burnside said, "and elephants may fly."

Black hunched over the table and didn't say anything.

"You've brought up two issues," Burnside said, "and I've listened to both of them. You can win with the stolen clock, or you can win with the alibi from the ladies. But now you can't prove either. My ex-father-in-law's hidden himself in Washington and the women will hide behind their right not to testify. I'm dead, Mr. Black. Please don't try to pump me up anymore." He gave Black's arm a pat of encouragement. "And don't think I blame you and Miss Hays. You were beat going in. What will be will be, I suppose."

Black had never had a client with Raymond Burnside's attitude. Most convicted men blamed their lawyers, the courts, and the prosecution—not necessarily in that order—for their predicaments, but Burnside seemed to point the finger at no one. What will be will be. "We're in business to make it, 'What will be *won't* be," Black said. "An' we're not a bunch of predestination Presbyterians. You got another way out, Raymond. That's what I'm wantin' to talk to you about."

Burnside seemed strangely amused. "Unless that bailiff is going to be kind enough to provide me with a key to the holding cell," he said, "I don't believe there is any way out. I just don't want to grab at any more straws."

"This is a whole lot stronger than any straw."

Burnside made a gesture of patience. "All right. Give it to me, then."

Black inhaled, then exhaled in resignation. "Somebody else that can put the clock in Delores' possession. We want you to put your mama on the stand."

Burnside's features twisted in anger. He looked toward the exit, swept the spectator section with his gaze, then leaned nearer his lawyer and hissed, "I made that clear at the outset. If anything's done to involve my mother in this, I'll withdraw my motion for new trial. I meant it then, and I mean it now."

"Dammit, Raymond, it's a way to save your life."

"Quit playing me for a fool. There isn't any way to save me. There's only a way to make a spectacle of my mother, and I won't have that."

"She saw the clock on your mantel when she was stayin' with you while your wife was on a trip. She can identify it, same as the senator could."

Burnside leaned back, thinking. He said in more control, "That's right, she did. I remember now." He firmly shook his head. "But that changes nothing. My mother is old and feeble, and her memory isn't what it once was. She doesn't have much time left, and all this has shortened what time she does have. Just leave her up in Whitewright where she is. I won't have her suffering anymore."

Black looked toward the exit, considering his response. What's it matter? Black thought. He's going to find out eventually. "She idn in Whitewright. She's out there in the hall, with the rest of the witnesses."

Burnside's mouth gaped in shock. His head hunched down between his shoulders. "That's betrayal, Mr. Black. After all our discussions, you've betrayed me."

"Not true. Her bein' here's none of my doin'."

"Then, why wasn't I notified before?" Burnside said.

"Because *we* wadn notified. When we got back to the office from court on Friday, she an' your brother were sittin' in our reception room."

Burnside's anger was tempered with sadness. "Oh, my sweet ..." He expelled a long sigh. "That's just like her, Mr. Black. Enough of this." He turned, raised his voice, and said over his shoulder, "Bailiff. Come here a moment, please."

The bailiff left the rail and stumped over, a uniformed sheriff's deputy in his thirties with a big brush mustache. When he was close enough, Burnside said to him, "Please deliver a message to the judge, that I'd like a word with her."

The bailiff looked quizzically at Black, then said to Burnside, "That okay with your lawyer?"

"I'm dismissing my lawyers," Burnside said. "And I want to call this hearing off."

Black said urgently, "Dammit, Raymond ..."

"I know what I'm doing." Burnside scowled at the bailiff. "Please contact the judge for me."

The bailiff gave a noncommittal shrug. He started to walk toward the entry to the judge's chambers, behind the bench.

Black stood and grabbed the bailiff's arm. "Not just yet. Mr. Burnside's havin' delusions, son. 'Fore you go talkin' to the judge, let me have one word with the boy."

The bailiff looked at Black, then at Burnside, then at Black again, and nonchalantly went over and resumed his seat at the rail.

Black sat down and hunkered near the prisoner. "Man wants to kill himself," Black said, "I'm not goin' to let him without tryin' to stop him. If we keep your mama out of it, can we go on?"

"Only if you do keep her out of it," Burnside said calmly.

"An' you know in advance that her testimony's the only thing likely to save you," Black said.

Burnside spread his hands in an umpire's "safe" signal. "I don't think her testimony would do anything except cause her more heartache. She's my mother, and the judge could choose not to believe her. I've made my decision, sir. It's final."

Black expelled air through his nose, scooted his rump forward in his chair, and propped his knee against the edge of the table. "All right, then. We'll go forward tryin' to shoot holes in the women's Fifth Amendment rights. You're killin' yourself, Raymond. Like you said, though, it's your decision. Far be it from me to keep a man from makin' up his mind."

Judge Griffin wasn't much help. She took her seat at the bench, summoned Black and Kathleen Fraterno up to stand before her, raised her eyebrows questioningly, and said, "Where's Miss Hays this morning?"

Black was like a fish out of water. His bread and butter were cross-examination and argument in front of a jury, and well he knew it. Preliminary matters, research, and hearings were all Sharon's department, so where in hell was Black's assistant anyway? All he knew was, Sharon had left a message that she'd be a couple of hours late, and that she was depending on Russ to stall things until she could get herself in gear. Black looked carefully around the courtroom, pretending to search for someone, then said to the judge, "She's held up this mornin'. Be here 'fore too long."

Griffin wasn't having any of it. She said testily, "That's unfortunate. What about the Fifth Amendment matter on which I called for briefs? Do we have any answers this morning?"

Kathleen Fraterno said mildly, "State's brief, Your Honor." She laid an inch-thick stack of papers up before the judge, then looked at Black expectantly. Fraterno wore a dark charcoal suit with a slim skirt. Her face was scrubbed, her curls springy as if she'd just come from the stylist. "It's apparent to us," Fraterno said, "that the Fifth Amendment is pretty well cut-and-dried. County records speak for themselves in that there were prior charges against these ladies, and as their attorney's brief indicates, there are still federal statutes of limitations in play. We don't believe they have to testify. Our research finds nothing to contradict this position."

"Aw, come on," Black said. "Their research didn' find anything 'cause they weren't lookin' for it."

"Which is the way law is practiced, Mr. Black," Griffin said. "The burden for defeating the Fifth Amendment argument is on your team, as you of all people very well know. What about your own research? Did you find anything to the contrary?"

Black waved a hand as if batting mosquitoes. "Sharon does all that, Sandy. You know that."

"So I do," Griffin said. "But Miss Hays isn't with us now, is she?" She reached beneath the bench and produced a stack of papers on her own. "As I said I would on Friday, I took a trip to the law library myself. And I'm afraid, with nothing from your side, Mr. Black, that I'm going to have to uphold these ladies. No one has to testify for the prosecution without immunity, and as far as I can find out, the same goes for the defense. I'm going to excuse these women, Mr. Black. So let's go forward with your other witnesses."

Black folded his hands behind him and looked at his shoes. "There's a problem with that, Judge."

Griffin snappishly drummed her fingers. "Well, there shouldn't be. You've got a witness list a mile long and have spread subpoenas all over the county. The court established this hearing at your convenience. If you're not prepared to go forward, I'm afraid we'll have to make a decision on what we have."

Black's jaw thrust forward. "We need a little more time."

"You don't *have* any more time, Mr. Black. Miss Hays has made a lot of noise here, but I'm afraid I see very little results. We have testimony that a clock was located at a house in Oak Cliff, which is far removed from the scene of this crime. We have innuendos that the defendant has an alibi not previously disclosed, but his alibi witnesses have pleaded the Fifth Amendment. If you have nothing further to present, I see no point in going forward. I'll have to deny the motion for new trial and remand the prisoner to the Texas Justice Department, so they can carry out this sentence."

Black looked at Fraterno, who stood alert in eyes-front posture, then directed his attention to the defense table. Raymond Burnside sat at ease, idly studying his copy of the motion for new trial. He's accepted all this, Black thought, likely he's wonderin' what time the train leaves to haul him back to Huntsville. Black faced the judge. "I been doin' this a lotta years, Sandy. Never had a client before that I was more sure's innocent."

Griffin's face softened in respect. "In that event I sympathize with you, Mr. Black. But without any evidence . . ." She lifted her hands, palms up.

Black indicated the back of the courtroom. "I got one more witness out in the hall I need to confer with. Just give me a little time, willya?"

Fraterno's shoes whispered on carpet as she drew herself up straighter. "The state vigorously opposes any extension, Your Honor. If we can't go forward right now, we move that the motion be summarily denied, for failure to show proof at the proper time."

Griffin shot the cuff of her robe and wound her watch. "Miss Fraterno is right, Mr. Black. *Technically* she's right, and you know it." She pursed her lips. "Out of respect for your reputation, sir, and that's the only reason I'm doing this, I'll give you a half-hour recess. If you and Miss Hays can't produce something in that period of time, I'm afraid this hearing is over.

A half hour, sir. Please show your appreciation by not stretching the court's patience any longer than that. Not one second more, Mr. Black, is that entirely clear?"

Black took the full thirty minutes, sitting on a corridor bench in between Ethel and William Burnside, checking his watch every five minutes or so, peering anxiously toward the elevators in search of Sharon Hays. Ralph Toner and his high-dollar lawyer occupied a bench midway between the courtroom and the elevator exit, with Torturro and Denopoulis across from them like wooden Indians. Farther down, Patricia Hampton hovered over Alice Glass and her two former roommates like a feisty mother hen. As Black watched, Ralph Toner rose and paced back and forth, talking to his lawyer. A reporter approached Toner, pad and pen in hand. Toner waved the newsman away. Black murmured to Ethel Burnside, "If you don't take the stand, those guys down there are going to get clean away with this."

Ethel Burnside wore a blue beltless dress that was ten or fifteen years out of style but appeared brand-new. Black supposed that there weren't that many dress-up occasions in Whitewright, Texas. Ethel's hair was tightly drawn around her head and secured in back with a rubber band. "That settles it, then," she said. "I will testify."

"Wish it was that easy," Black said. "I already told you what Raymond says."

"My son isn't thinking. I'll go have a talk with him."

Black checked his watch again. "Afraid you can't do that, Mrs. Burnside. Raymond's in custody back in the holdin' cell, and he can't have any visitors except at the jail, on certain days. He's already come within a whisker of firin' me an' callin' the hearing off, just because I said you *might* get on the stand."

Ethel assumed the same posture she'd likely used before making one of her students stand with his nose in the corner. "I am going to testify, Mr. Black. If Raymond tries to interfere, I may just box his ears."

Black studied her, the prim-and-proper elderly woman taking a determined stand. He couldn't resist a smile. "Idn Raymond a little big for that?"

There was a tug on Black's arm. He turned. William Burnside wore a plain brown suit instead of his customary overalls, and his fingernails were spotlessly clean with no telltale spots of mechanic's grease. He leaned over and whispered to Black, outside his mother's hearing, "Let her, Mr. Black. Raymond talks big, but he'd never defy Mama to her face. Neither one of us would have the nerve. And believe me, I know what I'm talking about."

Black put his misgivings aside and, without a word to his client, stood at the defense table and said, "Call Mrs. Ethel Burnside."

Raymond Burnside sucked in air with a hiss heard throughout the courtroom. He rose to his feet and said angrily, "Your Honor, I want to be heard. I *demand* to be heard."

Judge Griffin looked at the prisoner, then at Black, and back at the prisoner again. Visible in the corner of Russ's eye, Kathleen Fraterno sat at the prosecution's station with her chin tilted in curiosity.

Griffin recomposed herself. "Mr. Burnside, you are represented by counsel in this matter. All communication with the court should be through your lawyer."

"Then, I will terminate my lawyer, here and now." Burnside put hands on hips in a pugnacious attitude.

"The fact that you aren't pleased with what's going on," Griffin said, "is not an excuse to upset protocol. And I'm telling you, sir, you don't just jump up in the middle of a hearing and take charge. If you want another lawyer, the procedure is—"

"I'm not interested in the procedure," Burnside said.

Griffin closed her mouth with an audible click of

teeth. Black felt like crawling under the table. His damn fool client seemed determined to kill himself, and there wasn't anything Russ Black could do about it.

"What I'm interested in," Burnside continued, "is terminating this entire hearing. I'm sorry we've wasted your time, Your Honor, but I'd just as soon withdraw my motion for new trial from consideration."

Griffin was angry, but seemed thoughtful as well, and Black understood her dilemma. Sandy Griffin would like the hearing to be over, all right, but she had to be careful not to violate the prisoner's rights and get her decision overturned by some later appeal. Griffin opened her mouth to speak. Before she could, an elderly but authoritative female voice said from beyond the rail, "Raymond."

Griffin closed her mouth and looked out into the audience.

Raymond turned around, and Black followed suit. Ethel Burnside stood behind the gate, her shoulders stooped, her limbs frail, her features set in determination. She said calmly, "Sit down, Raymond."

Raymond sagged in place. He said, "Mama, you shouldn't—"

"*Sit down,* Raymond." Ethel stood her ground, unflinching, speaking to her son as if he'd just tracked mud on the kitchen linoleum.

There was pin-drop silence, punctuated by the frantic scratching of pen on paper in the media section. Raymond started to say something, then seemed to change his mind. He hung his head, and without another word sank down in his chair.

"Thank you, Raymond," Ethel said. She came through the rail in a rheumatic shuffling gait and stood near the defense table. "What should I do now, Mr. Black?" she said.

Sandy Griffin regarded the old woman with a look of respect. She smiled. "You should be a judge, ma'am," she said. "I never get that satisfactory of a response in my own courtroom. If all that's out of the way now, I suppose we're ready to proceed."

Russell Black was a whiz at reading juries, at telling from postures and facial expressions within the twelve-seat box whether he was getting his points across, and whether the jurors liked what they were hearing. Judge Sandy Griffin, he thought, was even easier to read than a jury. She listened to Ethel Burnside with a look near rapture on her face. The judge's infatuation was contagious; the reporters laid their pads and pens aside and listened in silence, and Black himself was caught up in the spell. Ethel Burnside was a charmer with a capital *C*.

In response to Black's request to state her occupation, Ethel said, "I've been retired, but I suppose everybody in Whitewright over fifteen and under fifty has sat in my classroom at one time or the other." Black nodded, and Griffin's smile broadened. Kathleen Fraterno wore a worried frown at the prosecution table, which was an even better sign than the grins from the judge. If the state didn't like what they were hearing, the witness was doing a bang-up job.

"Whitewright's the town where you live?"

"Two last names combined," Ethel said. "Neighbors. One wore blue and the other wore gray, in the Civil War."

Black allowed the town's founding fathers to sink in, then leaned back in his chair and hooked his thumbs under his lapels. "You were a teacher, then."

"Fourth though sixth, all in one classroom in the old schoolhouse. The new building, I had my own room. Fifth grade." Ethel sat in a tired-looking slump, which was right in keeping with the image Black wanted her to project. The weary elderly woman enduring years of pain over her son and who wouldn't tell a lie if her life depended on it.

"I remember bein' in school, ma'am," Black said.

"Don't know as I'd of liked the same teacher, three straight years."

Ethel laughed. So did Sandy Griffin, though the judge's laughter was more of a subdued chuckle.

"Fraterno half stood. "Objection. Leading."

"Leadin' where?" Black said quickly. A few giggles came from the media section.

"Sustained," Griffin said. "Please, Mr. Black." There was no irritation in her voice, and her gaze remained mildly on Ethel Burnside. Fraterno shifted testily in her chair.

Black switched gears, extending a hand palm up in his client's direction. "Do you know the petitioner in this case, Raymond Burnside?"

"I suppose I do. He's my son." The look of adulation that Ethel showered on Raymond spoke volumes. Raymond sniffled and looked down. He had acted as if he was protecting his mother by not wanting her to testify, but Black suspected that was only part of the reason. It was possible that the prisoner feared breaking down at the sight of her as well.

"He's your boy," Black said gently. "You raised him, then."

"Raised him proper. I won't take credit for his being a National Merit Scholar and winning grants-in-aid to take him through Princeton. Raymond did that through hard work and—"

"Objection." Fraterno was on her feet. "The petitioner stands convicted, Your Honor. Character references are for trials, and have no relevance in a hearing such as this."

Griffin looked at Fraterno with some irritation; the judge had obviously been enthralled. Fraterno was legally on target, however. "Sustained," Griffin said mildly.

"Since he's your son," Black said without missing a beat, "then I guess you knew him when he was married to Delores Bright."

"Delores was my favorite daughter-in-law," Ethel

said, "up until my other boy, William, got married. Then I liked both of my daughters-in-law equally." Her voice carried surprising authority, her meaning clear. Ethel Burnside played no favorites with her children.

"So you and Delores had a good relationship, wouldn' you say?"

Ethel swelled up in dignified pride. "When she married my boy, she was family. Just as my own child."

"Those of us that're parents understand that, ma'am," Black said.

Fraterno popped up once more. "Objection. Your Honor . . ."

"Sustained. Mr. Black . . ."

Black grinned. "Sorry, Judge, I'm susceptible to gettin' carried away." He said to the witness, "When Raymond an' Delores were married, did you visit 'em some?"

"Not too much while I taught. After I retired, sometimes."

"Ever go to stay with Raymond when his wife was away?"

"Her family was rich," Ethel said. "She went on cruises, trips, things like that."

"Without her husband?"

"Raymond was working. He never depended on her family to—"

"*Objection.*" Fraterno's voice was forceful, but she appeared to feel a bit guilty for butting in.

"Sustained. Please move along with this, Counsel." Griffin's look at the defense table was far from reproachful.

"Sure, Judge," Black said. "Did you stay with Raymond sometimes, while his wife was away?"

Ethel nodded pertly. "Certainly did."

"Helped him out while he was batchin' it . . ."

"Yes."

". . . Cleaned up and whatnot?"

"Just kept things straight," Ethel said. "I never

wanted my daughter-in-law to think I'd been going in behind her. Tried to keep things the same way Delores did, while she was home."

"Didn' want to be the interferin' mother-in-law?" Black said.

"Never. That sort of thing causes a lot of problems in some families."

Fraterno started to rise, then sat down. She seemed resigned.

"So in cleanin' up around there," Black said, "did you get pretty familiar with what went where?"

"Made it a point to," Ethel said. "Not to move things around."

"That true in the den area? Where the fireplace was?"

"That den was as big as my whole house. Really took some straightening up."

"Lot of knickknacks. Maybe, statuettes on the coffee table?"

"Delores was really a collector. And her father gave her a few things."

"Your Honor," Fraterno said, "we must inquire where this is going."

Griffin lifted her eyebrows. "I'm wondering the same thing, Mr. Black."

"I'm gettin' there, Your Honor," Black said, "an' I think the prosecution *knows* where it's goin'."

As snickers came from the media section, Fraterno yanked on one of her permed curls and fell silent. Judge Griffin sat back, hands folded. Raymond Burnside's attention was riveted on his mother, his gaze piercing as if he was trying to help her any way he could.

Black beamed at his witness. "Mrs. Burnside, do you remember what it was like to have to dust things on the mantel?"

"I had to drag a chair in from the kitchen," Ethel said, "to stand on."

"Anything up there you remember," Black said, "that was especially hard to keep clean?"

The judge's chin tilted in thought. Black supposed that Sandy Griffin had some hard-to-get-to corners around her own place. He looked at the witness and waited for her response.

"There was a clock," Ethel said. Griffin now leaned forward, all ears. Fraterno looked down at the state's table. Raymond's chair squeaked as he scooted forward.

Black straightened out of his slumped posture and hesitated. The country-boy act was finished. His next few questions had to be precise. He couldn't lead his witness; Fraterno would butt in at every opportunity. He cleared his throat. "Can you describe this clock, Mrs. Burnside?" he said.

Ethel showed not a second's indecision. "Really expensive piece, hand-carved. Oak, I think, with a walnut finish. Gold face, gilt pointed hands. It was animated."

"The clock was animated?"

"Yes, sir. That it was."

There was rustling in the media section as pads and pens came out. In the court reporter's cubicle there was movement as well, as the slim elegant black woman took her hands away from her keyboard, rolled her chair back, and looked at something at her feet. That's where she keeps the evidence, Black knew. The clock would be down there in all its broken elegance, out of view from the witness box.

"What kind of animation are we talkin' about, Mrs. Burnside?" Black said.

"It was so sweet. Chimed on the hour. Little doors popped open. A farmer and his wife came out and did a little dance."

"Little figurines?"

"They were hand-carved." Ethel raised frail hands spread apart in descriptive attitude. "Painted, and they sat on pedestals. The little man had a pipe in his mouth, and the woman wore a blue apron. They spun around and around while the clock chimed, and then bowed and popped back in."

Black kept his tone even, with no suggestiveness, just a man asking questions without concern for the answers. "Was this clock hard to dust, Mrs. Burnside?"

"Not the clock itself. But the figurines collected dust. You had to catch them while they were out."

"While they were out," Black said. "You mean, you swiped at 'em while they were spinnin' around?"

Ethel smiled, and Sandy Griffin looked ready to laugh out loud. "Oh, no, sir," Ethel said. "There was a button in back, so you could freeze the action. Stopped the clock from running. It was spring-loaded, and I'd have to hold the button in while I cleaned the little man and woman. You'd risk breaking the mechanism otherwise."

On Black's right, Raymond Burnside sucked in breath. Black looked at the prisoner and wondered what the trouble could be. Ethel Burnside was performing like a champ. Raymond showed Black a look of urgency. Black imperceptibly shook his head and returned his attention to the witness.

"I'll ask you, Mrs. Burnside," Black said, "how long's it been since you saw that clock?"

Ethel's forehead wrinkled in thought. "Last time I stayed there. Winter of '88, before Delores was murdered." She looked down at her lap.

"You've never seen it since?"

Ethel shook her head. "Not that I remember."

"To be sure," Black said, "I never took you over to my lockbox since I got to be Raymond's lawyer and showed you the clock, did I?"

Ethel was more firm. "No, sir."

"Or my assistant Miss Hays? Or our investigator—"

"No, sir."

"—Mr. Gear?"

"Absolutely not, sir."

"An' you're sure of that," Black said.

Ethel straightened. "I certainly am."

Black paused for the testimony to sink in. He put his hands on his armrests and started to rise. "Okay for me to approach, Your Honor?"

A couple of reporters in the second row stood up for a better look. Fraterno leaned back, pyramided her fingers, and rested her chin on the tip of the pyramid. Raymond Burnside put a hand on Black's arm and started to say something. "Not now, Raymond," Black whispered.

"You may approach, Counsel," Griffin said.

Black got up, strolled to the court reporter's cubicle, and grinned at her. "You got it, huh?" he said.

She returned his smile, bent over, and hoisted up the clock. The painted figurines dangled from springs, partially obliterating the face. Black took the clock in both hands. The oak wood added weight; the heft was surprising. He held the clock out in Fraterno's direction, then in Griffin's, then carried his burden over and set it on the rail before the witness. Ethel Burnside blinked in recognition.

"Mrs. Burnside," Black said, "I'm showin' you what's marked, Petitioner's Exhibit Two, an' I'm askin' if you can identify it."

The corners of Ethel's mouth turned down in sadness. "My, someone's abused it."

Black leaned on the rail. "Looks like they broke it, dudn it?"

"Objection," Fraterno offered weakly.

"Sustained," Griffin said, with equal lack of force. Her gaze was riveted on the clock.

"You ever seen that before, Mrs. Burnside?" Black said.

Ethel brightened. "It's the same clock."

"The one that used to sit on your son's mantel?"

"Yes, it is."

At the defense table, Raymond Burnside rested his forehead on his crossed forearms. What's wrong with that guy? Black thought. He said to Ethel, "Or, to be more specific, on your daughter-in-law, *Delores* Burnside's mantel, is that right?"

"It's the very same one," Ethel said. "I couldn't forget it, as many times as I've dusted it."

Black couldn't resist a triumphant look toward the prosecution. Fraterno's expression was stoically accepting. Black kept his gaze on Fraterno and said from the side of his mouth, to the court reporter, "For the record, the witness has identified one wooden clock with a gilt face and hands, two figurines, now damaged, but ..." He touched the small wooden man. "The male figurine's got a pipe in his mouth, and the woman ..." He laid a finger on the little lady. "The woman's wearin' a blue apron."

Raymond Burnside raised his head, his features wrinkled in concern. Black frowned at his client, but kept on.

"Mrs. Burnside," Black said to Ethel, "is that a fair description of the piece of evidence you're lookin' at?"

Ethel sat happily forward, and her smile made her appear ten years younger. "That's right," she said. "And there's a springloaded button in the back to stop the mechanism. It's right ..." She put one frail hand on the back of the clock. Her smile faded.

Black raised his coattails, jammed his hands into his back pockets, and waited.

Ethel's look was suddenly uncertain. She rubbed the back of the clock, her movements panicky now, her eyes widening. "It's right here, I ..."

Griffin frowned, her gaze darting back and forth between Black and the witness. At the state's table, Kathleen Fraterno sat up straight.

"It's right ..." Ethel said helplessly.

Raymond Burnside exploded from the defense table, "It's a *lever,* Mama. A lever, on the front of the block near the bottom. The clock with the button on back was upstairs, in the bedroom. My *God,*

Mama . . ." His voice quavered, and he seemed near tears.

Fraterno came to her feet like a woman on fire. "*Objection.* Your Honor, we ask that you silence that man."

Ethel reached around to the front of the clock, and found a small metal movable piece. "Yes, a lever. Right, Raymond, a lever."

Griffin said sternly, "Objection sustained. Mr. Burnside, you are to sit down, sir. One more word from you and I'll have you gagged, is that clear?"

Black was stunned, as if someone had punched him in the solar plexus. He'd lost. Christ, in one split second he'd lost the judge, lost the . . .

"My client's," he finally managed to say, then cleared his throat and said, "My client's upset, Judge. Sorry."

Raymond once again hid his face in his folded arms.

Black tried to recover, though he knew it was useless. "You're sure that's the same clock, Mrs. Burnside?"

"I'm sure. The very . . . same." Ethel's voice cracked, and she was once again very old. A tear rolled down her cheek.

Black glanced at the judge, then looked quickly away. "No . . . further questions," he said, and then limped to the defense table and sat beside his client. His chest constricted as if he might have a heart attack.

Griffin's lips pursed skeptically. "Cross, Miss Fraterno?"

Fraterno continued to sit erect. "Just a couple of questions, Your Honor." She looked at the witness, the elderly woman now hunched over in defeat, wringing her hands in her lap. "Mrs. Burnside," Fraterno said, "was there a second animated clock in that house, upstairs in the bedroom?" She glanced toward Raymond, then looked quickly back at his mother.

Ethel hugged herself. "Yes, but it was—"

"With a spring-loaded button in back, to interrupt the clock's functioning?"

"Yes, but that wasn't . . ." Ethel trailed off, looking helplessly at the judge.

"Wasn't what, Mrs. Burnside?" Fraterno said.

Ethel stammered. She finally managed, "I think it was . . ."

"Wasn't *what,* Mrs. Burnside?"

"Wasn't . . ."

"Mrs. Burnside," Fraterno said forcefully, "you can't identify that clock at all, can you?"

Ethel watched her lap in the silent courtroom.

"I have no further questions, Your Honor," Fraterno said, pointedly dismissing the witness with a wave of her hand.

Ethel began to cry. Her shoulders heaved.

"You're excused, Mrs. Burnside," Griffin said without emotion.

"But I . . ."

"Your testimony is finished, ma'am," Griffin said. "You may go."

Raymond leaned over near Black and hissed, "I *told* you her memory was failing. You had to drag her through this."

In all his years, Russell Black had never felt so helpless.

Ethel tried to rise, staggered, aided herself to her feet with one hand on the rail. She stepped down from the stand at a snail's pace, made it halfway to the gate. She stopped and turned, sobbing. "Oh, son, I'm so . . ."

Raymond leaped up and hurried to his mother. The bailiff sprang to his feet as well and hustled in pursuit of the prisoner. Ethel finished, "Sorry," and collapsed in Raymond's arms, sobbing into the hollow of his shoulder. The bailiff reached the edge of the table. He dug at the back of his belt for his handcuffs.

Black stood up and blocked the bailiff's path. He looked at the uniformed deputy, eye to eye. "Leave 'em be, son," Black said. "Just leave 'em the hell alone for a minute. Don't any of you people have any compassion for anybody?"

The bailiff looked uncertain. "We can't let prisoners have any outside contact, Mr. Black, and you know it."

"Yeah, but—" Black stopped in mid-sentence as a familiar form came through the railing gate and went by him in a hurry. A female scent reached his nostrils, a touch of Enigma. His jaw dropped in astonishment.

Sharon Hays rushed up to Raymond Burnside and his mother, nodded to Raymond, put her own arms around the old woman and took her away from her son. "It's all right, Mrs. Burnside, you did fine. Believe me, it's all going to be just fine." Sharon wore a beige summer-weight business dress and matching spike heels. She winked at Raymond and led his mother slowly toward the gate.

With the bailiff standing helplessly beside him, Black said to Sharon, "Where've you been?"

Judge Griffin said loudly, "Will someone please explain what's going on here?"

Sharon continued to hold Ethel Burnside close and pat her back. She said to Russ, "Got held up, old boss, it couldn't be helped." She turned to face the bench. Ethel continued to cry. "If it please the court, Your Honor," Sharon said breathlessly, "we've got some more witnesses to put on. Won't take much time, Judge. Just bear with us, okay?" She returned her attention to Russ. "In a nutshell, Russ, and listen hard. I don't think we've got but a minute or two."

34

Her thumbnail sketch to Russell Black went something like this: A quarter hour earlier, Sharon had entered the Crowley Building's multistory parking garage. She led quite a parade. An ambulance with its flashers on followed just off her bumper, with a midnight-blue four-door Plymouth bringing up the rear. She wound around and around inside the garage until she located three side-by-side vacant spaces on the fifth level, and slanted in with the Volvo's nose overlooking Industrial Boulevard. The ambulance parked alongside her. The Plymouth wheeled into the space beside the ambulance. Sharon stood behind the three vehicles with her satchel propped against her thigh, and waited.

Two paramedics emerged from the ambulance, hustled around to the back, and opened the double doors. They angled an aluminum ramp down to the pavement, then climbed up in back and rolled Woodrow Lee out in the wheelchair. Lee wore a pale blue robe and black cloth slippers, and groaned effectively as the wheelchair slanted downward and bumped onto the floor of the parking garage. His left wrist was handcuffed to the arm of the wheelchair. His robe parted to reveal his bandaged shoulder; Sharon set her satchel down, brought Lee's lapels together, and turned up his collar around his throat. "There, Woody, that's better," she said. A pair of sheriff's deputies came down the ramp and stood on either side of the prisoner.

Six men in suits emerged from the Plymouth to

form a circle around the wheelchair. One was Richard Branson, who stood nervously in between a barrel-chested, sandy-haired young man and a tall, skinny drink of water with a big bent honker of a nose. Sharon locked gazes with Branson for an instant. He looked quickly away, toward the elevators. She smirked and brushed imaginary lint from her skirt.

The other three men from the Plymouth remained in front of the wheelchair, and one seemed in charge. He was medium build with regular features, and wore thick glasses with gilt rims. He nodded to Sharon as he said, "I suppose we're ready."

Sharon said brightly, "This way, gentlemen," then led them down the slanted walkway with her light cotton skirt flapping around her calves and her satchel bumping her hip. The deputies followed pushing the wheelchair, with the suits forming a guard detail fore and aft. The men on either side of Branson put steering hands on his elbows. He followed the wheelchair with his head down. The paramedics returned the ramp to the rear compartment of the ambulance with a bang and clatter, closed the doors, and returned to sit in the cab. Sharon reached the elevator, pressed the DOWN button, and stood aside. Woodrow Lee continued to moan.

A young lady in slacks and pullover came from the other end of the parking lot and stood beside Sharon, waiting for the elevator. She said pleasantly, "Awfully hot, isn't it?"

To which Sharon replied, "It certainly is." She glanced back over her shoulder toward the group of men.

The man in the gilt-framed glasses exchanged a look with the man beside him, then stepped up as the bell dinged and the double doors slid open. He reached inside his coat, snapped open a wallet, and exhibited his ID to the lady in the slacks. "Sorry, ma'am, official business. You'll have to wait for another car."

The lady stepped back with a gasp as Sharon, the

deputies, the still-moaning Woodrow Lee, and the six men in suits boarded the elevator. The doors closed, leaving the lady alone. She murmured with exasperation, "Ex-*cuse* me, Joe Friday," thumbed the DOWN button, and stood back tapping her foot.

The posse arrived on the sixth floor of the Crowley Building with Sharon in the lead, the deputies pushing Woodrow Lee along behind her, and the cordon of men in suits moving hallway passersby aside and keeping Richard Branson firmly within their midst. Jack Torturro and Vernon Denopoulis occupied the same seats as the previous day, halfway between the lobby and the courtroom. Denopoulis watched with his mouth agape and a toothpick dangling from one corner of his mouth. Sharon went over, stood before the two, and smiled at them. "Good morning," she said cheerily.

Denopoulis closed his mouth and chewed vigorously on the toothpick. Torturro said deadpan, "Miss Hays."

"Fine, thank you," Sharon said. "But I'm afraid you guys aren't doing so well. You know that man over there? You should meet him, he's quite a stud." She pointed at Richard Branson as he walked head down between his escorts, their hands on his elbows steering him along.

Torturro and Denopoulis exchanged a look. Both folded their arms.

"He's quite a talker," Sharon said. "Oh, and the cute little guy in the wheelchair, he's the one your two hit men or whatever, he's the one they've been looking for. Their search is over, isn't that sad? Just about now, in fact, some federal marshals are out at that motel where your hit men are staying, putting them in custody. Whether they're talkers like Richard Branson, that remains to be seen. If they do choose to talk, the U.S. attorney will be hanging on their every word. Oh, yes. The guys with me yesterday were rent-a-cops.

Those men with Mr. Branson are the real thing. How's that make you feel?"

Torturro moved his eyes upward and regarded Sharon from beneath shaggy brows. "I think you'd better move along," he said. "Tend to your business, and let us tend to ours."

"Oh, I plan to," Sharon said. "I just thought you'd want to know, I've had a long chat with the federal people this morning, and you wouldn't believe how interested they are in your affairs. Have been for several years now. Especially yours, Mr. Denopoulis. Vernon the Greek, right?"

Denopoulis' head snapped around. He sourly looked Sharon over, head to toe. He began, "Ain't no . . ." Then he trailed off, and riveted his gaze on the far wall.

Sharon raised her eyebrows in mock innocence. "Ain't no fucking Greek? How charming. That's just what some of your associates have told the federals you'd say. They had you down to a tee all right, even your cute little mannerisms. Have you ever thought of an acting career? I have a few contacts in that field."

Torturro's mouth turned up in a full-blown sneer. "I'm telling you for the last time, lady. Move along."

Sharon shuffled her feet and shifted her satchel from one hand to the other. "Or you'll what, trot out your submachine gun?" Two benches down the corridor, Patricia Hampton had Alice Glass and her two ex-roommates strung out along the pew beside her. Sharon held up one finger toward Hampton, raised her voice, and said, "Be with you in a minute, Patricia," then returned her attention to the two mobsters.

"You've already tried shooting me," Sharon said. "That didn't work, but it scared me to death. The dynamite in my car put me in absolute orbit, frankly, but you should have left well enough alone. Going near my daughter at the water park made me too mad to be afraid anymore.

"I'll leave you gentlemen with one happy thought,"

Sharon said. "The U.S. attorney's convening a grand jury tomorrow, and guess who they're going to be discussing? I'll give you some advice, not that you'll take advice from a broad, but sell your Texas properties for whatever you can get and dismiss your fancy law firm. Then talk to some real down-and-dirty criminal attorneys—I'll bet you already know plenty of those—and get a hookup with a bail bondsman who's got plenty of assets. Your bonds are going to be quite high, I'll bet. You have a nice day, fellas. I'd love to chat some more, but I don't have any more time to spend with you." She left the mobsters twisting nervously on the bench, walked down the hall, and stopped before Patricia Hampton and her clients. "Hi, Patricia," Sharon said.

Hampton stood up, the tiny woman's forehead on a level with the point of Sharon's chin. Alice Glass still couldn't meet Sharon's gaze, and looked vacantly away while her ex-roommates sat with folded hands. Hampton said, "You shoot any holes in my arguments, Hays?"

"I didn't have time to try," Sharon said. "So I suppose the old Fifth Amendment guarantee is safe for now. We won't be needing your clients, Patricia. We've found a new avenue of attack. I'll withdraw my subpoenas, and you're all free to go."

Hampton's clients exchanged relieved looks, then each one in turn glanced fearfully down the hall toward the mobsters. Hampton said feistily, "You couldn't have beaten me anyway."

"That's something we'll never know, Patricia, but let me put a bug in your ear. Those men over there"—she pointed toward the dark suits surrounding the wheelchair, all of whom now clustered outside Sandy Griffin's courtroom—"are FBI. They're interested in your friends down the way, Mr. Torturro and Mr. Denopoulis. That's who's paying your fee for representing these ladies, isn't it?"

Hampton folded her arms. "That's confidential, Hays. You know that."

Sharon moved nearer Hampton in a you-and-me attitude. "Well, this is confidential, too, dearie. Your friends down there are going to federal jail, so if they owe you any money you'd better hurry up and collect. And, thinking about it, you might want to hit them up for an additional retainer. That Fifth Amendment research of yours is something they likely can use." She nodded for emphasis, turned, and started to walk to the courtroom. A long-fingered male hand fell on her arm. Sharon paused, then stopped still.

The hand belonged to Benjamin Spacer, he of the thousand-dollar pinstriped suits, he of the eloquent command of legal smoke screens. Spacer's suit of the day was black, with a dark charcoal pinstripe, straight off the "Dressing for Power" rack. His client, Ralph Toner, lurked in the background wearing a solid blue suit, perfect for the old campaign. Sharon showed Toner a look that could melt solid steel, then said to Spacer, "Hi."

Spacer glanced across the hall, to the spot where Patricia Hampton gathered her things off the bench. Spacer said, "Excuse me, Miss Hays, but I couldn't help overhearing your conversation over there."

Sharon blinked. "Oh, I'll bet you could have helped overhearing it if you'd really wanted to. But it wasn't any deep dark secret. What's on your mind?"

Spacer showed a fleeting look of irritation, then once again was cool as a legal cucumber. "I'm assuming if you're withdrawing your subpoenas for those ladies, that goes for my client as well."

Sharon's chin moved to one side. She looked around Spacer and hooked her thumb toward Toner. "For *him*?" she said.

"That's my client, Miss Hays," Spacer said. "I assume we're free to go."

Sharon laughed out loud. "Well, you assume wrong, Mr. Spacer. Please keep your client front and center.

We're going to give him another chance to shine in the public eye." She brushed around the lawyer, walked to the courtroom door, paused, and turned. She pointed toward Toner as she said to the FBI agents, "He's the cornerstone of your case, guys. If he tries to run I'd tackle him, if I were you."

With that, Sharon marched into the courtroom, and paused halfway down the aisle. Ethel Burnside sat hunched over in the witness box, holding the clock in both hands, searching frantically for the button that wasn't there. Sharon sank down in a pew and listened to the rest of the elderly woman's testimony. As Ethel climbed trembling down from the stand, then burst into tears as her son hurried toward her, Sharon cried in sympathy. Before she realized it, she was running down the aisle through the gate, brushing Raymond aside and holding Ethel in an embrace of consolation.

After Sharon finished her story, Sandy Griffin called a five-minute recess to restore order and allowed Sharon to accompany Ethel Burnside into the corridor. Ethel moved slowly, sobbing out of control, as Sharon kept her arm around the elderly woman's shoulders and said over and over, "It's all right . . . it's all right, Mrs. Burnside, you did fine. I'm telling you, you did fine."

William Burnside was seated at the rear of the courtroom. He got up and joined the two women, hugging his mother to him as they went out through the double doors. The witness waiting room was on the left. Sharon directed William and his mother to go in, sit down, and wait. "This won't take long," she said.

William paused. "Are we beaten, Miss Hays?"

Sharon firmed her posture. "Not by a long shot. Just wait in there and stay with your mom. It will all be over soon." William led his mother into the witness room and sat beside her, flashing a look of pleading in Sharon's direction. Sharon gave a smile of encouragement, turned, and reentered the courtroom.

Just before she went through the railing gate, Andy Wade stopped her. He stood bent over, holding his ribs. Visible beyond him, Russ Black and Raymond Burnside were turned around at the defense table, watching her. Sharon nodded to them and turned her attention to Andy Wade.

Wade said, "They check me out of the hospital for good tomorrow. How's this going?"

"Glad you're feeling better, Andy. It wasn't going well at all, but that's about to change."

Wade looked interested. "What's up your sleeve, Miss Hays?"

Sharon looked into the jam-packed media section, at reporters turning their heads as one in her direction. "Looks like you've got plenty of company," she said. "Your articles are stirring something up."

"Problem with fame is," Andy said, "it brings out competition. How about giving me something exclusive, Miss Hays? For old times's sake, huh?"

She shook her head. "Not now, Andy. I'm busy."

He grinned ruefully. "Hey, what happened to our Deep Throat deal?"

Sharon smiled at the reporter in genuine respect. "Nobody deserves special treatment more than you do, Andy. Stick around after the hearing and I'll give you some things for your ears only." She gave his forearm an affectionate squeeze. "Got to go now, and save this man's life. I'm deep-throated out, okay?"

Griffin resumed the hearing. Sharon called Woodrow Lee to the stand. As the deputies wheeled Lee down the aisle, the reporters stood and craned their necks for a better look. Kathleen Fraterno bounced to her feet. "This is a delicate situation, Your Honor," Fraterno said. "May we approach?"

Griffin seemed as fascinated by the witness as were the media people. She said, "By all means."

At a nod from Russ, Sharon attended the bench conference alone. She stood beside Fraterno with her hands folded. Kathleen said, "We know this witness, Your Honor. Our office has been looking for him."

"Does he have criminal charges?" Griffin asked.

"No, ma'am. He was a witness for us in another matter, having to do with the man who escaped the other day and killed one of our deputies. We think he may have information about the escape."

Griffin eyed the two deputies as they pushed the wheelchair. "Looks like to me he's already in custody, Miss Fraterno."

"That's the problem we have, we didn't know he was under arrest. Before he gives any public testimony, our office needs to interview him to be sure he's not going to jeopardize our investigation into the deputy's killing."

Sharon could take it no longer. "Oh, beans, Kathleen. What you mean is, you want a preview of what he's going to say in this hearing. Well, forget it. Not in this lifetime."

Griffin seemed relaxed, and even amused. "Decorum, Miss Hays. Decorum." She assumed a more businesslike posture. "I've got to confess, I don't see the relevance between the two matters, Miss Fraterno."

"We won't know that unless we can question him, Judge. We'd object to any testimony, particularly with all this media here, that has to do with the deputy's murder. That's all we're asking for, a recess. Since he's in our custody, that shouldn't be any problem for Miss Hays' side. She can put him on the stand as soon as we're finished. It's for the public good, Your Honor."

Sharon's mind was racing a mile a minute. By the time Fraterno and her troops were through grilling Woodrow Lee, he might change his mind about cleansing his soul. She said quickly, "I'd have to advise him against speaking with the district attorney, Your Honor."

Now Griffin seemed confused. "How could you advise him not to speak," she said, "when you've just called him to testify under oath, Miss Hays? Only his lawyer can advise him. You represent Mr. Burnside, the last time I checked."

"Well . . ." Sharon swallowed a gulp of air. "I represent Mr. Lee, too, Your Honor. On robbery charges, completely unrelated to the Burnside case *or* the deputy's murder."

The deputy parked the wheelchair in front of the witness box. Lee moaned softly and looked around for sympathy. Griffin watched the prisoner as she said, "Been a busy boy, hasn't he?"

Fraterno clicked her heels together as if to say, Aha. "If what she says is true, then Miss Hays has a conflict of interest. I'd ask for a full hearing on her conflict before he's allowed to testify here. She could be advising him against his best interests. Helping her client Mr. Burnside while hurting her client Mr. Lee."

Griffin showed an urgent frown. "She has a valid point, Miss Hays. I'd want to know there's no breach of ethics going on."

Sharon felt like throwing an elbow and knocking Fraterno for a loop. Breach of ethics, my ass, Sharon thought. "It's pretty simple," she said. "Mr. Lee's a three-time loser and subject to the habitual criminal statutes. In return for his testimony here, I've made him the cushiest deal possible, and if *that's* a breach of ethics I'll eat every book in the law library."

"No one's contacted the Dallas County District Attorney's office regarding a deal for Mr. Lee, Judge." Fraterno looked at Sharon in righteous indignation. "If she's making such a statement, I'd want the court to inquire into what deal she's made. As I said, my department didn't even know the guy was in custody."

Griffin raised her eyebrows. "Sounds reasonable to me, Miss Hays. As long as he's under Dallas County's jurisdiction, they're certainly entitled to inquire as to what plea-bargain arrangement they've made. If it exists, which Miss Fraterno is apparently going to deny."

Sharon breathed in through her nose. She looked at her feet. Finally she said, "Oh, the plea bargain exists. The reason she didn't know he was under arrest is, on the robbery charge he's a LNU, FNU. And, currently, Mr. Lee's not exactly under their jurisdiction, Your Honor."

Both Fraterno and Griffin stared at her.

Sharon lifted her chin. "The deal I've made . . . Your Honor, those gentlemen seated on the back row are FBI agents. They're pursuing a federal case involving Mr. Ralph Toner and some other people, and I've made a deal with Mr. Lee to be a federal witness. Some of Mr. Toner's associates tried to kill Mr. Lee recently, and his testimony will be crucial to the feds. For now, the feds hold Mr. Lee as a material witness. Later, he's agreed to plead guilty to some federal firearms violations, involving the gun he used to try to rob a convenience store."

"Oh, my goodness," Griffin said. "We're still pursuing Mr. Toner?"

"Right to his lair, Your Honor," Sharon said curtly.

Griffin sighed. "This all sounds complicated."

"Not that much," Sharon said. "As a three-time felon, Mr. Lee's subject to a life sentence under federal law *and* state law. The state can't impose the death penalty on him—wouldn't even know he's guilty of a terribly gruesome murder, in fact, if it wasn't for the testimony he's about to give—and after you hear what he's got to say, you'll understand what I'm talking about. In the federal pen he gets a softer bed, better pillow, a whole lot better food. Better medical care. More recreation. The deal I've made for him merely means that he can serve his life sentence in federal custody. In either prison he's not going to get out until he's too old to do anything except maybe gum somebody to death. He's satisfied with that, given his choices. After you hear his testimony, Your Honor, you'll agree that the public will be better off as well."

"All well and good," Fraterno said stiffly. "Except that he's got us to deal with first. We're holding him on the robbery charges, according to what Miss Hays herself just said."

Sharon looked at the judge, then sideways at Fraterno. "You're not exactly holding him, Kathleen. Mr. Lee's posted bond on the state robbery charges. Officially, the feds have him now."

Fraterno's jaw dropped. She stared at Woodrow Lee, then looked at the judge. "I don't believe anybody in their right mind would post bond for that guy, Your Honor. I'm sorry, but I don't."

"Doesn't sound reasonable," Griffin said.

Sharon showed them both an impish grin. "I guess Russ and I are the crazy ones, then. We put up bail for Mr. Lee on Saturday." She looked toward the parked wheelchair, where Woodrow Lee's groans had gone up a decibel. "Why?" Sharon said. "You don't think he looks like a risk to flee, do you?"

Woodrow Lee testified from his wheelchair, his voice low, barely audible beyond the rail. The newspaper sat intently forward, taking notes, straining their ears for every word. Fraterno tried a couple of objections at first, but once Lee got into his story even Kathleen sat back and listened, her jaw slack as a horror movie patron's. The state was beaten, and Kathleen well knew it. Strangely, Sharon felt no sense of triumph. She was glad that the senator didn't have to be here to listen firsthand to what had happened to his daughter, and even felt somewhat sorry for Raymond Burnside, considering that Delores had been his wife. Even the judge appeared a bit green around the gills, and as a criminal district jurist, Sandy Griffin should have heard about everything by now.

"So you stayed with Mrs. Burnside while Dycus Wilt searched the house, is that right?" Sharon said from her seat in between Russ Black and Raymond Burnside.

Lee grunted and touched his shoulder, wincing, just as he had at least a hundred times during his testimony. "Yes'm. Most o' that stuff in there, Woody done."

Sharon doodled on her legal pad. Dycus Wilt had told her just the opposite, of course, that he'd stayed with Delores while Lee ransacked the house. Sharon supposed that she'd never know the truth, and would always have doubts. It didn't really matter which one killed her, Sharon supposed. Woodrow Lee was getting a thousand percent better than he deserved, but with no witness to the crime left alive other than himself, the state couldn't have convicted him anyway. More the pity, Sharon thought. "Did both of you rape her?" she said.

Lee's eyes widened in innocence. "Oh, no, ma'am. Dycus, he done all that stuff, fucked that woman."

A gasp sounded from the media section, and Raymond Burnside lowered his head. In a pig's eye, Sharon thought, my client is lying here. It had been a joint rape, and Sharon knew it. As Woodrow Lee's lawyer, though, she was obliged to let him say what he wanted from the witness stand. Sharon felt a bit sick to her stomach. "And the killing?" she said. "Tell us about that, Mr. Lee. If you would."

"Dycus done that, too, wid dat bone knife. I tried to stop the dude, but he wouldn't listen."

Sharon's throat was dry. She poured water from a chrome carafe and had a sip. "To capsule, Mr. Lee. You and Dycus Wilt went to the home of Delores Burnside, robbed, raped, and murdered the woman, is that right?"

Lee shook his head. "Dycus. Dycus killed that lady."

Sharon didn't think she could stand another minute of looking at this piece of dung. She squeezed Raymond Burnside's arm in sympathy as she said, "But you witnessed it, didn't you?"

"Sho' nuff. I 'as standin' there."

"And you saw Mrs. Burnside with no clothes on, didn't you?"

"Yes'm."

Sharon took a second to rub her eyes before going on. This last part was necessary, and what the witness was about to say hadn't required any prompting on Sharon's part. Lee's memory of the killing was clear as a bell, and he'd recited the details that morning for the feds without missing a beat. Sharon watched the table as she said, "Do you remember anything unusual about her physically, Mr. Lee?"

"Had a butterfly tattooed on her butt."

"Besides the tattoo, is there anything else you recall about her?"

"Sho' do. Woman had this scar."

Sharon expelled a long sigh before saying dully, "Could you describe the scar for the court, Mr. Lee?"

"Run down her backside, between the cheeks of her ass."

Sharon looked up and directed her gaze to the bench, trying not to see Woodrow Lee, though his outline stood out in the periphery of her vision. God, but she hated the guy. She said to the judge, "The autopsy report is already in evidence, Your Honor, placed there during Dr. Foster's testimony. For the record, the scar and the tattoo are recorded on page three. If necessary, we can return Dr. Foster to the stand and place the scar into evidence through him." She flashed Kathleen Fraterno a look that said, Go ahead and object if you want it, sweetie, but making us recall the County M.E. will be a waste of everyone's time. Fraterno sat unmoving, her arms folded, and didn't say a word.

Griffin picked up a ballpoint and wrote something down. She regarded the prisoner with a look of open contempt.

"One final question, Mr. Lee," Sharon said. "Did you ever read any newspaper accounts of this crime?"

"Seen 'em back when they convicted this dude." He pointed waveringly at Raymond Burnside.

"In any of the accounts you saw, was there any mention of the scar or the tattoo?"

"Didn't see none."

Sharon reached into her satchel and withdrew a stack of paper. "Your Honor, I wish to offer photocopies made this morning from the archives of the *Dallas Morning News*. Their computer search indicates that these are the sum total of everything printed in the newspaper about this case. We stipulate that newspaper accounts are hearsay, and do not offer these as proof, only as evidence that what Mr. Lee has testified to did not appear in any public accounts of the crime." She looked toward Fraterno. "The state is entitled to an objection, Your Honor, and we realize that we're skipping a few steps in offering these. We have the newspaper's director of their archives standing by, and if necessary we'll go through the motions of putting him on to verify that these copies are the real thing." She gave Fraterno a look of pleading. "It's been six long years for Mr. Burnside, Kathleen. Will you stipulate to this one little thing?"

Fraterno hooked an elbow over her chair back and studied her lap. She looked up. "No objection, Your Honor."

Griffin nodded. "Under the circumstances the court would have been disappointed if you hadn't stipulated, Miss Fraterno. I'll admit the copies, Miss Hays."

Sharon carried the stack of paper up to the court reporter. She looked at Woodrow Lee, then at the floor. "I don't have any more questions of this witness, Your Honor." She felt slightly weak in the knees. She returned to the defense table and sat down. Russ Black reached out and patted her hand. Sharon dully returned the pat. Her vision was blurred. There was pin-drop silence in the courtroom.

Griffin sat forward, her shoulders hunched. "Cross, Miss Fraterno?"

Kathleen looked at Woodrow Lee. "Mr. Lee," she began, then reached up and closed her file. "For once

I'm agreeing with Sharon, Judge. The state has no questions, Your Honor. Will someone please get this guy out of here?"

As the deputies rolled Woodrow Lee up the aisle, the feds took over. Two agents relieved the county men of wheelchair duty, and took Lee out through the double doors. Sharon nudged Russ with her elbow, and as the older lawyer bent to listen, she said to Raymond Burnside, "I think we've won it, Raymond. But I want to put another witness on. "I'll leave it up to you."

Black frowned. "Who you talkin' about?"

Sharon's chin tilted at a saucy angle. "Why, our esteemed gubernatorial candidate, who else? I don't think Raymond can be fully vindicated until that happens. But up to you, Raymond. Your call." She regarded Burnside with her eyebrows raised.

Raymond wiped the sleeve of his jumpsuit across his chin. "You mean Mr. Toner, right?"

Sharon nodded. "None other. The judge made him subject to recall if we could prove up the other parts of our case, remember? You haven't gotten to enjoy anything in this entire miscarriage, Raymond, but I think you might like to hear this."

Burnside showed the first smile that Sharon had ever seen on the prisoner's face. He chuckled softly. "You know, I think I might," Raymond said. "Put him on, Miss Hays. Wouldn't miss it for the world."

Sharon called Ralph Toner, and watched over her shoulder as the audience shifted around. Three FBI agents, with Richard Branson still in their company, paraded down the aisle for ringside seats. They finally settled for the third row, directly behind the reporters. Torturro and Denopoulis had entered the courtroom sometime during Woodrow Lee's stint on the witness stand, and now came forward as well to sit across the aisle from the federal men. Denopoulis continued to chew on a toothpick.

Toner came down the aisle with his lawyer, Benjamin Spacer, two paces behind. Spacer took a seat midway down, brushing the front of his dress-for-power suit, and Toner continued on his own. The candidate kept up appearances, Sharon would have to say that much for him. As he went through the gate, Toner showed his best politician's smile to the media section. The reporters watched stone-faced. Toner nervously cleared his throat, accepted the judge's warning that he was still under oath with a nod, and climbed up on the stand like a man approaching the gallows.

Sharon began with, "Do you recall your previous testimony, sir?"

"Basically."

"Anything you don't recall that you said previously, we can have the court reporter read your testimony back to you, is that clear?"

Toner smirked as if to say, Are you kidding? "I'm familiar with courtroom procedure," he said.

"That we don't doubt, Mr. Toner." Sharon straightened her posture. "When last we spoke, I'd asked you if the reason you didn't mention Delores Burnside's rape in her husband's previous trial was that you wished to shield the rape because the forensic evidence didn't match Mr. Burnside. Do you recall that I asked that question, sir?"

"Seems that I do," Toner said.

"And your response is . . . ?"

"The same. I merely wished to protect the victim's family from the details."

Sharon thought, Oh, you righteous prick. "You were protecting the victims," she said. Sarcasm dripped from her words like sorghum.

"As is a servant of the people's duty." Toner continued to play to the media, lifting his chin in the reporters' direction.

"I'm sure that was part of your duty, sir. Well, now

that the victims aren't present to hear the gory details, let's get into that. Did the forensics evidence in that case, semen, hair samples, did they in any way connect Raymond Burnside to the crime?"

"I don't recall that. I'd have to see the report."

"You don't recall." Sharon pointedly looked over her shoulder at Andy Wade, who watched the proceedings with a happy grin on his face. She expected Toner to dodge every issue, and wanted the reporters to get all of it. That, plus something else she had in mind. She snapped her hand around and said to Toner, "Let's get into something else, sir. Were you ever aware during Mr. Burnside's trial that there were three ladies who could testify as to Mr. Burnside's whereabouts on the night of the crime?"

Toner shifted around in his chair. "Those would have been defense witnesses. Not my responsibility to call them."

"Oh? Do you know a homicide detective named Stan Green?"

The beatific expression dissolved into a look of pure hatred for an instant, then Toner was at once the politician again. "Mr. Green is well-known to everyone in the district attorney's office."

"That he is," Sharon said. "And Mr. Green was the detective investigating the Burnside case, wasn't he?"

Toner looked upward, obviously pretending to think. "It seems that he was, yes."

Kathleen Fraterno sat back, watching her former boss with a look halfway between disbelief and contempt. She's through objecting, Sharon thought, now she's just taking it all in with the rest of us.

"It seems that he was," Sharon said. "Yes, indeed." She folded her hands and glared at the witness. "Mr. Toner, did you at any time instruct Detective Green to find a way to keep those ladies from testifying?"

Toner's complexion paled. He looked to Fraterno for help. She pointedly ignored him, pretending to study something in her file. Toner finally said, "I wouldn't have done anything like . . ."

"Would it surprise you to know, Mr. Toner," Sharon said, "that these women have said that Mr. Green threatened them with charges if they *did* testify, and told them that he was working on your behalf?"

Toner showed the media section a smirk of indignity, then turned his gaze on Torturro and Denopoulis. His expression changed at once into a terrified grimace. He licked his lips compulsively. Finally he said, "Anything I said to the detective, that would be privileged. Lawyer to client."

If it's pity you want, you'd best look elsewhere, Sharon thought. She squeezed her forearm. Her bruises had practically healed, but were still tender enough to serve as reminders. She tapped impatiently on the table. "I didn't ask you what you said to the detective, sir. I asked if it would surprise you to learn that the ladies said that he told them you'd ordered him to talk to them."

Toner swallowed air.

Sharon was conscious of Russ watching on her left. She said impassively, "Your Honor, we request that the court instruct this witness to answer."

Griffin didn't hesitate. "So instructed. You are ordered to answer, Mr. Toner." The judge's lips were pursed.

Toner looked wildly about him, as if seeking the nearest escape route. He said suddenly to Fraterno, "Aren't you going to object?"

Kathleen folded her arms and jiggled her foot.

Sharon turned around. Every reporter in the house scribbled like mad. Time for the good stuff, Sharon thought. "You've been instructed to answer, Mr. Toner. In anticipation of your further reluctance to testify, I'll ask an additional question. So you'll know, we're going to request the court to hold you in contempt each time you refuse. It's up to the judge to determine punishment for contempt, but you are aware of the possible penalties, aren't you?"

Toner's mouth opened and closed.

"You are a lawyer, aren't you?" Sharon said.

"A lawyer? Yes."

"So you are familiar with contempt citations, fines, time in jail . . ."

Toner sat back and tried his best to seem assured. "I am." His self-important glare missed the mark a bit; his lips quivered.

"Good," Sharon said. "So in addition to the question regarding Mr. Burnside's alibi witnesses, I'm going to roll the clock forward a few years. Are you by any chance acquainted with Mr. Jack Torturro and Mr. Vernon Denopoulis? Those gentlemen seated . . ." She turned around and pointed at the mobsters. "Right back there," Sharon finished.

Toner gaped. Torturro and Denopoulis stared at him. Toner said, "I . . . I . . ."

"We're waiting, sir," Sharon said.

In the spectator section, someone loudly cleared his throat. Sharon and Russ turned as one while Raymond Burnside kept a white-knuckled grip on the arms of his chair and glared hatred at the witness. The noise from the spectator section had come from Benjamin Spacer, Toner's dapper lawyer, now standing in the aisle, watching his client. Spacer said forcefully, "Ralph."

Toner stared at his lawyer.

Spacer said once again, "Ralph." More warning in his tone this time, raising up on the balls of his feet.

Sharon swiveled her head around. "You've been asked a question, Mr. Toner."

Toner exhaled air like a death rattle. He nodded in the direction of his lawyer, then vacantly watched the floor and spoke in a lifeless monotone. "I claim my right under the Fifth Amendment of the Constitution of the United States, and respectfully refuse to answer on the grounds that any answer I might give could implicate me in a criminal investigation."

Sharon turned around and looked pointedly beyond the media people, to the spot in the gallery where the FBI agents all showed happy grins. Even Richard Branson had sort of a smile on his face. Toner's lawyer continued to stand in the aisle with his arms folded. Torturro and Denopoulis got up, strolled quietly to the rear, and exited the courtroom. Likely headed for the airport, Sharon thought. Doesn't matter, they won't get far. As if reading her mind, two federal agents broke rank and followed the mobsters into the corridor. Richard Branson's circle of friends was now reduced to two. The newspeople exchanged meaningful looks and wrote like mad.

Sharon zeroed in on Toner. "Mr. Toner, as a former district attorney of Dallas County and a candidate for governor of the state of Texas, is it your intent to plead the Fifth Amendment to any further questions regarding your association with Mr. Jack Torturro and Mr. Vernon Denopoulis because you fear . . . *criminal charges* of some kind?" She thought she sound properly incredulous, and wondered briefly if she should return to the stage.

Toner seemed about to choke. He continued to watch the floor. "I claim my right under the Fifth Amendment . . ."

Wonder if he's using Patricia Hampton's version, Sharon thought. She sat back and waited for Toner to finish pleading the Fifth, and for Sandy Griffin to make the move which Sharon knew was coming. Griffin didn't take long; she gave the defense and state simultaneous come-hither motions. Sharon affectionately squeezed Raymond Burnside's shoulder, then got up, went around the defense table, and stood alongside Kathleen Fraterno in front of the bench.

Sandy Griffin showed a pointed look to Ralph Toner, who continued to sit in the witness chair and stare at the floor, then said loudly enough for Toner

to hear, "I can't say I'm not enjoying this, Miss Hays.
But from a legal standpoint, aren't you wandering a
bit far afield? I've been expecting some noise from
you, Miss Fraterno."

Kathleen looked in open disgust at the witness, then
said to the judge, "I might be amiss in not making
some noise. But I think I've been enjoying it as much
as you have. Off the record, of course."

"Well, happy old us," Griffin said. "But I'm afraid
we're not here for entertainment. I've got to move
this along, Miss Hays."

Now Sharon showed Toner her own glare of dis-
dain, then faced the judge. "I'm at fault," she said,
"but in all due respect I'm not apologizing. I promised
those feds back there I'd ask those questions, and I
confess it does my heart good for the media people
to hear Mr. Toner take the Fifth Amendment. And
frankly, after what I've been through I'm entitled to
some revenge." She turned and smiled at Raymond
Burnside, winked at Russ Black, then faced the judge
once more and folded her hands. "I'm through with
this guy, Your Honor. I think our point is made. Over-
made, is more like it. After six long years, I think my
client's ready to go home."

Ethel Burnside cried tears of happiness on a corridor bench. Her son William sat beside her with his
arm around her shoulders. Sharon said from a standing position, reaching out to pat Ethel's cheek, "I've
made arrangements for you to duck those guys, Mrs.
Burnside." She indicated the cluster of reporters outside the courtroom, craning their necks toward the
bench where Ethel Burnside sat.

Ethel looked up, her wrinkled eyelids red, and blew
her nose into a Kleenex. "How can you . . . ?"

"I've got some influence with the jailers," Sharon
said. "The judge is releasing Raymond, and all that's
left is for the bailiff to go over and bring him some
civilian clothes from the jail. Once he's dressed, they'll

take him down the back elevator and out the side entrance. If you and William will have a car out there in about twenty minutes, you can whisk your son away." She smiled, and her own vision blurred. "I expect you-all have a lot to catch up on," Sharon said.

William had unbuttoned his shirt and yanked down his tie. Sharon suspected that Raymond's brother was dying to climb back into his coveralls and, wrench in hand, get underneath someone's hood, where he felt at home. Shut out the world and do what made him comfortable. William nodded toward the reporters and said to Sharon, "Won't they follow us? They act like bloodhounds."

"We've got some influence there, too," Sharon said. "The young guy in the horn-rims? That's Andy Wade, the reporter that's been doing the articles for the *News*. Just about the time they're due to take Raymond downstairs, Russ is going to call a press conference. Andy's going to lead the charge after Russ. Since the other reporters think Andy's in the know about this case, they'll follow him like sheep. While Russ is telling them all a few jokes down the hall, you and your mother can make a clean getaway." She winked. "It'll work, William. We've pulled the stunt before."

Ethel stuffed the Kleenex away inside her purse. "I insist on paying you something by the month, Miss Hays. It's the least we can do."

William nodded as if emphasizing what his mother had said.

Sharon looked down the hall, where the FBI agents were clustered around Richard Branson. Woodrow Lee, still moaning and still handcuffed to the wheelchair, was parked to the right of the lobby exit. Just moments earlier, two feds had led Torturro and Denopoulis away in cuffs. As Sharon watched, Ed Teeter came through the double doors and talked excitedly to the agents. Teeter's investigation into the deputy's killing by Dycus Wilt would be on permanent hold now, with Woodrow Lee in federal custody for life. The U.S. attorney would put Torturro and Denopoulis away for quite a spell, Sharon knew. Ralph Toner and Benjamin Spacer stood near the federal men, Toner's lawyer waiting to get a word in edgewise once Teeter had finished. Sharon imagined that Toner was more than ready to make a deal with the feds. Which was none of her business. Sharon was bushed. She wanted to go home, kick off her shoes, put Robert Earl Keen on the stereo, and visit with Melanie. Trish and Melanie had begun classes in private school that morning, and Sharon had been so wrapped up in the Burnside case that she'd had to call on Sheila to help with Melanie's last-minute shopping and to handle carpool duties. She owed Sheila big time, and made up her mind that payback started immediately. From within the knot of federal agents, Richard Branson stared pleadingly at her. A surge of guilt went through her that might not ever go away. She sneered at Branson and turned back to the Burnsides.

"Won't hear of any payment, Mrs. Burnside," she said. "We're taken care of. I'm going to mosey down that way"—jerking her head toward the end of the hall—"and hopefully lure some of those reporters out of your escape route. You-all call me next week. I want to know how Raymond is getting along." She started to walk away, then stopped and came back. "Oh," she said to William, "there is one thing."

William squeezed his mother's hand. "Just name it, Miss Hays."

"My car's sort of hot this time of year," Sharon said. "You think we could make a deal on a dose of Freon? From what my regular mechanic tells me, you could hire a herd of lawyers for what Freon costs these days."

35

Sharon cupped her hands, scooped, and dribbled chlorinated water on her thighs. The sun hovered near the treetops that blotted out the western horizon, warming her back and shoulders, and within a half hour the pool would be in shade. Beyond the Cyclone fence were the picnic tables and majestic elms that surrounded the University Park Public Swimming facility. Still further in the distance, autos rolled back and forth on Lovers Lane. In the pool's shallow end, kids floated on inner tubes, splashed, squealed, and held their noses before plunging beneath the surface. Sharon was just beyond the deep-end yellow rope, seated on the bank with her shins immersed. Twenty feet away, Melanie and Trish sat on an inflated raft as they flirted with a couple of high school boys. Melanie caught Sharon watching, pointedly ignored her mother, and turned her back. One of the boys said something that must have been hilarious. Trish and Melanie giggled.

"Isn't it nice to be wanted?" Sharon said.

Sheila had her elbows on the bank, her body underwater from the shoulders down, her legs stretched out behind her. Both women wore one-piece, conservative-mother swimsuits: Sheila's red, Sharon's green. Early in the summer Sharon had bought a French-cut bikini on sale at Lord & Taylor, had been dying to show herself off in the skimpy thing, but had never gotten up the nerve. A mommy-daughter outing at a public pool was hardly the place, Sharon thought, but longed for the bikini anyway.

Sheila twisted in the water to regard the teenage boys through slitted eyes. "How old are those kids?"

"Mmm . . . fifteen or sixteen, maybe. It's hard to tell anymore."

"My left foot," Sheila said. "I heard one of them say something about graduating next year, for God's sake." One of the boys now had his elbows up on the raft, and he and Trish were practically nose to nose. "If they get much chummier," Sheila said, "Mommy's going to horn in, welcome or not."

Sharon looked toward the pool office, where a brown-skinned lifeguard took admission fees through a wire-covered window. Two more guards sat on the towers, a boy and a girl, both sporting healthy tans. Both seemed more interested in grinning at one another than in guarding lives. "Wonder when this place closes for the fall," Sharon said.

Sheila dribbled water on her shoulder. "Public school doesn't open until next week. S'pect this week is it for the sun worshippers."

"Be our last outing, anyway. Back to the grind."

"The Burnside thing closed for good?" Sheila said.

"As far as my client's concerned. The FBI has those two shooters in custody, are pretty sure they're the same guys who rigged the dynamite. Whether I have to testify against them depends on whether they want to talk about Morgan Hill Corp. and its illustrious president."

"Meaning the gangster?" Sheila said.

"Meaning the gangster."

Sharon watched the teenagers, Melanie now hanging off the end of the raft and smiling at the larger of the two boys. Up until this summer Sharon had considered Trish far the more mature of the girls, but now wasn't sure. Melanie had budded out in places that Mommy hadn't noticed before. "Sheila?" Sharon said.

Sheila turned to her, coal-black eyes soft in concern. The women had a sort of ESP, something neither could have explained, but Sheila knew when her friend was troubled. "Sure," she said. "What is it, Hays?"

"God, don't call me that. You sound like Patricia Hampton."

Sheila didn't smile. "What is it, Sharon?"

Sharon brought her legs up on the bank, stretched her body out, and rested on her elbow. "Nothing really. Just that, I don't feel really good about myself."

"After the way you helped those people, that guy? You've got the inferiority complex to end all complexes, if that's the way you feel."

Sharon adjusted the elastic at her hip. "Not that. I feel pretty good about that. It's Sharon herself I'm not happy with."

Sheila hoisted herself up on the bank, turned around, and sat with water cascading down her body in rivulets. The concrete around her fanny was at once soaked. "Tell Mama, Sharon."

"It's just that I feel sort of . . ."

Sheila watched over her shoulder.

Sharon rolled onto her back and looked at the sky. "Like a slut, maybe?"

"Jesus Christ, Sharon." Sheila's voice came out like a soft sigh. "That's the silliest thing I ever heard."

"I can't help it. I see these women every day, have these relationships that mean something. Every time I think something's happening to me, it turns out bad."

"Look, you went to a party and met a guy. Bells rang. He took you to bed. It's happened to everybody once, or more than once, and that includes the ladies at the Junior League. I wouldn't give it a second thought."

Sharon raised up and looked at her. "Oh, yes, you would. I know you, Sheil."

"Well, let's say, I wouldn't give it *much* of a second thought. Listen, if I come over and find you sulking in the closet, you're in trouble."

Sharon tried a smile that didn't work very well. "I just feel confused. It's not that I'm looking for Mr. Goodbar or anything, it's just ... oh, hell. Why does he always turn out to be a bastard?"

"Because ninety-nine percent of the men in this world are bastards," Sheila said. "It's in the hormones. Listen, you'll be fine. If the right thing comes along someday, fine. If it doesn't, fine as well. That's the way you have to look at it."

Sharon's eyes widened. "You think?"

Sheila nodded emphatically. "I think."

"I'll get over it," Sharon said. "I know I will. Just these thoughts I'm having, that Sharon Jenifer isn't number one on my list right now." She drew up a leg, flexed her knee, and stood. "I owe you guys dinner, Sheil. Come on. If you catch me staring off into the hereafter, just throw a pie in my face, okay?"